Number one bestselling author Wendy Holden has written ten consecutive *Sunday Times* Top Ten bestsellers. A former journalist on *The Sunday Times, Tatler* and the *Mail on Sunday*, she contributes features and short stories to a range of publications and is a regular TV and radio contributor. She was a judge for the Costa 2013 Novel and Book of the Year Awards and is a *Daily Mail* book reviewer. She lives with her husband and two children in Derbyshire.

For more about Wendy Holden, visit her website at www.wendyholden.net.

Make your world a brighter place. Pick up a Wendy Holden.

The critics loved WILD AND FREE

'This hugely entertaining novel is chick lit at its best!' *Closer*

'Cue lust, sunshine, jokes and a heist – Holden is a master storyteller' *Daily Mail*

'Using her trademark wit, readers are swept into this hilarious and heart-warming romp . . . Immensely satisfying' *Sunday Express 'S' Magazine*

. . . *relished* GIFTED AND TALENTED

'Deftly combining romance with satire and expertly choreographing her cast, Wendy Holden's sure-to-be-bestseller is smart, sharp and hugely entertaining' *Daily Mail*

'Chirpy, saucy and funny, this is the perfect novel to curl up with' *Bella*

'A brilliant trademark Wendy Holden novel' *Heat*

Honeymoon Suite

WENDY HOLDEN

REVIEW

First published in 2016 by HEADLINE REVIEW
An imprint of HEADLINE PUBLISHING GROUP

First published in paperback in 2017 by HEADLINE REVIEW
An imprint of HEADLINE PUBLISHING GROUP

2

Cataloguing in Publication Data is available from the British Library

ISBN 978 0 7553 8535 5

Typeset in Adobe Garamond by Avon DataSet Ltd,
Bidford on Avon, Warwickshire

Printed and bound in Great Britain by Clays Ltd, St Ives plc

HEADLINE PUBLISHING GROUP
An Hachette UK Company
Carmelite House
50 Victoria Embankment
London EC4Y 0DZ

www.headline.co.uk
www.hachette.co.uk

To everyone at Headline for everything they have done.

PART ONE

CHAPTER 1

The Cornish hamlet of Tremadoc was giving good spring. Walls thick with yellow gorse, edged fields glossy with deep-green grass. Birds sang in bushes bursting with white elder blossom. A powerful sun shone down.

At the centre of the village, its sculptured finials lacy against the blue of the sky, rose the mediaeval granite tower of St Fennec's. Beside it squatted the pub, the Miner's Arms, its beer garden dancing with parasols.

Around that was a scattering of grey cottages whose tiled roofs were orange with lichen. Behind the village the dwellings thinned out to the cliff edge. Here the gentle green land suddenly ended. It turned abruptly downwards, changed into a sheer face of grey jagged rock and plunged into the white spume of a tossing and troubled sea.

On the very edge, almost at the point where the field became the cliff face, stood a building that had been, until recently, a ruined barn. Now the roof had been repaired and out of it poked, periscope-like, the silver funnel of an Aga chimney. Windows had been pierced in the thick stone sides and fitted with custom-made frames painted, like the stable door, a modish lavender blue.

Inside, fishing nets with glass balls hung from the ceiling and papier-mâché fish swam along the stone walls. There were lanterns of a seafaring type and a framed poster recruiting 'Fit Young Men' to a Georgian frigate bound for the Americas. Upstairs were two small bedrooms with driftwood-effect headboards and a tiny bathroom with a lifebelt-shaped mirror and a little wooden lighthouse dangling from the light-switch cord. The clear plastic loo seat was set with pearly shells.

'Bosun's Whistle' had once been an upscale holiday cottage but, failing to get the expected returns, had been put on the market. Dylan, the writer who had bought it fully furnished a year ago, was relaxed about the cheesily nautical interior. He had wanted to escape the London literary circus and have somewhere quiet to work. And apart from the boom of the waves, the howl of the wind, the scream of the gulls and the farmer yelling at the loudly complaining cattle, quiet it tended to be.

He liked the name too, obvious though it was that a bosun had never been near the place, let alone whistled in it. 'Bosun's Whistle' seemed to Dylan an amusing euphemism. It had the ring of a phrase that could be used suggestively to replace something infinitely ruder. He could imagine the Two Ronnies singing about it; he had made up a song himself, or at least the last line of one, in their style:

'*She was up all night, and so was the bosun's whist-le . . .*'

Dylan hummed now at his desk at the downstairs window whose pale blue curtains were printed with little red boats. Before him was a sea of scribbled-on papers on which a laptop was in full sail. His fingers were idle and his face turned to the sea view, eyes resting on the distant horizon.

'*It's big and it's shiny, it must be the bosun's whist-le . . .*'

He must get on with his work, not sit here composing puerile ditties. He had no excuse now; there was no longer anything

4

between him and what he was supposed to be doing.

Finally, Beatrice had gone and he could write.

Last night, she had slammed out of the cottage amid a storm of Gallic curses and the shrieking assurance that their relationship was over. It was by no means their first row, but it was certainly the worst. The décor of Bosun's Whistle had suffered irreparably; driftwood sculptures were swept off shelves and naïf paintings of lighthouses ground beneath Beatrice's stiletto heel. Even the shell-embedded loo seat was wrenched from its moorings and hurled at the shell-patterned tiles of the shower before Beatrice made a door-slamming, cottage-shuddering exit.

Would she be back? Dylan was pretty sure she would. She always was after a row.

Did he want her back? This was more difficult. It was an understatement to say that Beatrice was a handful. She was a tsunami, a whirlwind, a maelstrom, a tornado. Her rages were violent and sudden. One minute she might be passionately devouring him, the next scratching his eyes out. But there was no question he found all that exciting.

And while she was hardly a soul mate, her body more than made up for it. Beatrice was beautiful, with her waist-length black hair, thick, straight black brows and pneumatic pouting lips. She wasn't tall – in fact she was petite – but her slender limbs looked sensational clothed in tight black rubber. Dylan had met her at Fennec Cove, the local surfing beach, and had been struck by her unusual surf boots. They had 'Devil' stamped on the side in red letters and divided the big toe from the rest of the foot by means of a black plastic cloven hoof.

Despite this, Beatrice had initially made Dylan think of the village church. St Fennec's contained a black fourteenth-century pew-end on which was a mediaeval carving of a mermaid. Her tiny waist swelled out to huge hips. You could see her navel and her breasts, partly concealed by long, thick hair. Even in the sexually free-and-easy twenty-first century Dylan had felt a frisson on seeing the carving. The effect it must have had on the generations of repressed yokels who had worshipped here could only be imagined.

Men who never saw a woman naked till their wedding night, and possibly not even then, must have positively fought to get the nearest pews. So when Beatrice had emerged from the sea like a siren, to Dylan's literary fancy she had seemed the Tremadoc mermaid made flesh. She had been so goddamn sexy it had been hard for him to look, especially wearing something as revealing as a wetsuit.

Beatrice had looked, however, and had liked what she saw. She had wasted no time, told him that she wanted him, and had taken him shortly afterwards in a lay-by in the back of his car. That was how Beatrice did things.

She was twenty-one, beautiful and restless. Before coming to Cornwall she had been doing a film course in London, but it hadn't worked out for some reason. Surfing didn't seem to Dylan the natural next step, but Beatrice had heard that it was fashionable and she was obviously from the kind of wealthy family that allowed her to follow her urges. She wasn't much good on a surfboard, in fact, but she was very good at a lot of other things.

And if these didn't include conversation, empathy, or even humour, Dylan certainly wasn't complaining. He was young, healthy and twenty-four and Beatrice was a sex-crazed beauty three years his junior who talked dirty in husky Franglais. She was also fascinated by the fact that he was a writer.

'You must put me *dans ton roman*,' she would gasp through her tumbling hair from above him. '*Je voudrais être ton inspiration*.'

She wasn't his inspiration, though. Nothing was these days.

Writing suddenly seemed such a slog, when it had all been so easy before.

Perhaps too easy. *All Smiles*, Dylan's first novel, had been a smash hit. One minute he'd been writing a book in the evenings after work. The next, he'd sent it to an agent, it had been accepted and become a literary phenomenon overnight.

His second novel, *Charm Itself*, was the one he was currently writing. It was eagerly awaited by hundreds of thousands of fans. When it was published, Dylan would be an even richer man than *All Smiles* had made him. He supposed he should be excited about this.

Beatrice certainly was. She loved to swank about Tremadoc showing off about her famous boyfriend. It was not something that endeared her to the locals. There weren't many French people in Tremadoc, or even many locals, except in half term when the place was swamped with Boden-wearing families staying at National Trust cottages. But the handful of farmers, scented-candle-makers, fudge entrepreneurs and home-educators who made up what passed for the resident population certainly treated Beatrice with caution.

Even the contrarian landlord of the Miner's Arms refrained from irking Beatrice's ire. She was the only customer who he never asked for a table number after she'd ordered food. This was usually the Waterloo of everyone else, who, faced with the fact they had no idea what their number was, were forced to go outside, find it, then join the back of the queue again. It was, Dylan suspected, the landlord's twisted idea of a joke, but it blew up when he tried it with Beatrice. She had yelled at him to stuff his *numéros de table* up his arse and stormed out.

Now, Dylan knitted his brows and tried to concentrate on his keyboard. He should be able to crack this. Pull off the whole trick again.

But maybe a trick was all it had ever been. *All Smiles*, to be sure, had won a whole string of book prizes and garnered him a fortune. There had been film options left, right and centre. It was all terribly flattering. But had he deserved it, really?

Because it had all been won with so little effort it had left Dylan feeling curiously empty inside. So perhaps it made sense that he now sought physical sensation, something that made him feel real. Not just sex, but surfing too.

He had taken up surfing after he met Beatrice, and to his immense surprise, having never done it before, he'd proved a natural from the start. He loved the struggle in and out of the water, thighs pushing against the stiff, resisting swell, the struggle to keep upright amid the stinging white spray, balancing on the surge of pure power that was a wave. The freezing exhilaration of it was completely different from the heat and sweat of making love to Beatrice, but identical in its powerful release. Both activities calmed and exhausted him. Both required huge reserves of energy. Both, in their way, were a struggle, which writing never really had been.

Now, Dylan drummed his fingers on the table and tried to ignore the ocean. His mind remained on it, even so. Before he had come to Cornwall he had thought that the sea was just the sea. Big. Blue. Cold to swim in. Had fish below it and boats on the top. Sometimes, if the fish were caught and the boats sank, the other way round.

Now he knew better. The sea wasn't just blue, for a start. Its colours and textures changed all the time. Sometimes it was billowing pale blue silk, sometimes wrinkly purple leather. You got patches of liquid silver, sulky pewter and dark flint, often simultaneously.

The sea had personality. It was as moody, contradictory and capricious as any person, as Beatrice, in fact. Sometimes, like her, it was roaring; furious with an insatiable rage. Then, walls of water reared and crashed and tides pounded like fists into the rocks and cliffs. At other times it was feminine, spreading sheets of lace on the sodden sands and turning a coy, baby-doll pink in the sunset while small white waves like feather boas rolled in. Like the feather boas Beatrice wore during her marabou feather routine.

He had, with enormous difficulty, only just regained his concentration when his mobile rang.

'How's *Charm* going, dear boy?' Dylan recognised the rich, purring tones of his agent Julian. 'Eve's been asking me for updates.'

Eve was Dylan's editor. 'It's going OK,' he lied.

'Marvellous. Because I need you to take a day off. Come up to the big smoke. Various new TV offers have come in and I'd like to discuss them with you in person.'

Dylan groaned inwardly. *All Smiles* had sold all round the world and there were various international telly versions in the pipeline. He'd long got used to all of that. It was spoilt of him, he knew, and complacent; nonetheless, it was how he felt. It just wasn't exciting any more.

'Can't you deal with it?' he asked Julian.

Fond as he was of his agent, a long, hot journey to London did not appeal. Not when the surfing weather was like this. It was almost overwhelming, the urge to get up and go out to the car, where his rubber wetsuit waited, still damp from yesterday and probably full of scratchy sand.

'Not really, dear boy. Documents to sign, you know the kind of thing . . .'

Dylan pictured himself in the oak-panelled office at Copley & Co., Julian's agency, while Julian himself, with his round Bakelite spectacles, glossy wings of grey hair and the red suede shoes which were his trademark, sat opposite him on the leather-buttoned chesterfield. Despite being one of the savviest players in a hi-tech business, Julian preferred the accoutrements of patrician tradition.

'Over lunch,' the agent added.

Dylan's heart sank further. Not even the oak-panelled office; he was to be taken out and displayed in public. He would have to look smart; shave off his stubble; brush his unruly, over-long, salt-roughened mop and search in his wardrobe for something that wasn't just ancient, torn shorts and faded T-shirts.

'We'll go to Bruton Street,' Julian declared. 'Seriously, you haven't heard of it? Been in the boondocks too long. It's the new club, dear boy.'

Dylan tried his best to muster some enthusiasm. Julian was a member of every smart club going. He knew everyone and lunch with him, as Dylan knew from past experience, was a succession of famous media faces swooping in for air kisses over reductions of cauliflower and black pudding ice cream. It was exactly that kind of exposure, as well as that kind of food, that Dylan had come to the West Country to escape.

He knew he had no choice, however. The arrangements were made and Dylan clicked off his mobile with a heavy heart.

It soon lifted again, however. The door of Bosun's Whistle slammed and the familiar clack of high heels on kitchen lino could now be heard. Heels so high and sharp that they had pierced the floor tiles like bullet holes. Eyes burning, hair flying, nostrils flaring, Beatrice now appeared round the door.

'Hi, hurney,' she pouted in her heavily accented English. She was already unbuttoning her blouse. 'I'm 'ome!'

Dylan rose from his desk and went towards her. *Charm Itself* would just have to wait – again.

CHAPTER 2

It was May, and a dull Tuesday afternoon in North London. In a downstairs flat in a row of Victorian semis, a mobile buzzed.

Nell, at her bedroom mirror pulling straighteners through her hair, put them hurriedly down on the floor. The phone was spasming about the surface of her desk; the bedroom was also her office. Nell leapt to grab it. Her heart was thumping. Surely not. With only an hour to go?

The screen in her shaking hand confirmed her worst fears.

Sorry. Can't make tonight. Babysitter probs. Will reschedule. Lx

A wave of rage and helplessness swept through Nell. 'Shit!' She rumpled her just-straightened blonde mane in sheer frustration.

It was always the bloody same. Whichever one of her friends she arranged dates with – and she was always the one doing the arranging – they always got cancelled in the end.

Usually this happened the night before. But as this was the actual day she'd had high hopes of this drink with Lucy. Lucy was one of her more reliable friends and Nell's one-time business partner at Vanilla, the small PR and marketing operation which the recession had put paid to two years ago.

Nell had fought hard to keep Vanilla going. She had worked

11

every hour possible. But in the face of squeezed client budgets she had had to accept the inevitable. The business had died, but Nell believed in Fate and was sure that, in the future, she would set up again.

Even though she now worked at home she still wore a crisp white fitted shirt each day; still put on her make-up and did her hair. She still had her pride and self-respect; she was still investing in her appearance. How, otherwise, could she expect anyone to invest in her?

And now this self-belief, she had hoped, was about to pay off; the economic outlook was improving. Perhaps Vanilla could rise again, phoenix-like from the ashes. 'Phoenix PR' had a good ring, and it was about this that she had hoped to talk to Lucy tonight. But Lucy had let her down.

An acrid smell alerted her to the hair straighteners burning into the floor. Nell pounced on them and stared miserably at the smoking black line eating the gold weave of the carpet.

There was no phoenix, but there were certainly ashes. Her recently installed sisal was ruined.

Nell took in a deep breath and fought a sudden urge to cry. For goodness' sake, it was only a carpet. Albeit a very new and very expensive one.

And she was a grown-up. Almost thirty. She was educated, reasonably attractive, financially independent, she had her own flat. She had a career, even if, following the collapse of Vanilla, this was working at home writing catalogue copy.

But what she didn't have was either a partner or children. And this, Nell had discovered, made dates with you eminently cancellable.

Take tonight. Lucy's children had come first. Everyone's children came first. Children were the great enemy of the single woman.

All her friends – people she had been at university with, or had worked with – had families now and had moved to the provinces or to suburbs so remote they might as well *be* the provinces. Not that Nell would ever have dared to say so. People clung to the idea of living in London even when they were actually deep into Surrey. Or, like Lucy, practically in Brighton.

And just as the tide of friends had receded, the work colleagues one had too. Her professional interactions now took place, not in an office with real people, but online with commissioning editors she'd never met and who changed so frequently there was no chance to build up even an email friendship.

Nell wasn't quite at the stage of going to zumba classes for the social opportunities. But she was definitely getting there. The white shirt's days were numbered too; it was getting harder and harder not to shuffle to her keyboard in her onesie.

Nell now turned off her mobile, dropped a book on the scorch mark to cover it and tried to concentrate on her work.

She flexed her fingers and began to type. 'Splash some colour about in this appliqué top, made from ultra-strong hi-tec fabric.'

Hi-tec or high-tech? Or hi-tech? Or high-tec? Nell consulted the style sheet. Hi-tec.

Every catalogue had its own style sheet and for ease of reference Nell kept them in a box file tucked into a copy of the relevant publication. The box file lived on her desk and she looked at it now, counting the small volumes.

Here was *Urban Fox*, an interiors and lifestyle catalogue which offered 'tradition with a twist' to image-conscious thirty-something men. This seemed to boil down to silver shaving brushes, underpants with Latin mottoes and witty neon chess sets.

An Englishman's Castle supplied vintage coat hooks, framed destination boards from old Routemaster buses and Twenties-look gramophones that concealed state-of-the-art music systems.

Eggheads sold ironic crocheted antimacassars and other knowingly grannyish knitted goods. *Croker & Descendants* was a retro furniture catalogue specialising in corner units upholstered in PVC and other examples of 'Sixties penthouserie'.

Some of the catalogues were designed to go out with museum membership packs and acknowledged the subscriber's cultural interests. They sold headscarves printed with the rose window of Salisbury Cathedral, Charles Rennie Mackintosh cardigans and Ancient Egyptian-themed wristwatches.

Year Zero was an eco-chic catalogue offering weekend bags made of recycled Cambodian rice sacks, sustainable armchairs upholstered with vintage Welsh blankets, and underpants made from cotton produced by Indian farmers whose access to Wi-Fi the catalogue helped fund. Buy underpants, connect people, was the subliminal message.

There was *The Knitting Sheep*, an upmarket children's emporium selling miniature deckchairs, personalised ballet bags, child-sized croquet sets and hand-crafted wooden play-forts. *Buttermilk* dealt in undateably plain and floaty women's clothes in light wool and linen. Every item had a name chosen to trigger certain associations: the 'Elizabeth' coat, the 'Margaret' dress, the 'Cate' pyjamas, the 'Angelina' thong. Sometimes, as in the case of the *Morpheus* beds catalogue, Nell chose the names herself. She had worked her way through the atlas of Europe this way, with beds called after towns from Albi to Verona.

Less romantically, there were several catalogues for financial services, all featuring images of people in vaguely horticultural environments. This, Nell had guessed, suggested growth whilst euphemistically avoiding any suggestion of actual money. The models were obviously selected to represent all social types – a man with a trim white beard (older savers) smiling at an apple tree; a blond tot by some daisies (parents and grandparents); a groomed young man of vaguely Asian appearance squatting over some tomatoes (a complex catch-all including middle-youth, couples, homosexuals, career types and people of ethnic origin).

And here was *Toe Be Or Not Toe Be*, a cashmere sock catalogue which required a Shakespearean reference in every description. Nell always had to rifle the *Complete Works* for that one and enjoyed it so much it made her wonder whether a career in academia might, in other circumstances, have been a possibility.

Looking at her range of clients, Nell tried to fan her sense of pride; she had done well, after all, to launch herself as a freelance copywriter. At least she was still working with words. Even if it was describing lamps and bathmats. She was still paid for ideas.

And yet her ability to persuade people from the back bedroom of 19a Gardiner Road N1 wasn't quite the same as holding meetings in Vanilla's Soho offices and advising clients over an entire range of marketing options – brochures, posters, websites, ads. It wasn't the same at all.

'Every man's favourite casual shirt. Great price too. As easy as life should be!'

Nell paused over her keyboard and wrinkled her nose. Was that quite the right description? A price tag of £99 did not strike her as especially great. And where did the idea of life being easy come from, exactly?

Everything she had achieved had been through sheer dogged hard work. Especially Vanilla. Its collapse had been heart-breaking, but tonight, she had hoped to persuade Lucy that they could resurrect it. Oh well. If Lucy hadn't even managed to make it into town she was hardly a good bet as a business partner. Even if she'd been a good one in the past. But these days Lucy was a full-time mum and seemingly content to be so.

They probably wouldn't have talked about Vanilla at all. Lucy would have spent the whole evening – or the couple of short hours before she had to get her train back – banging on about her children or complaining about her partner Uri, who sold eco heat-pumps for a living. They were always going wrong, apparently, and poor Uri spent his life snorkelling around in people's filthy ponds trying to fix them.

Nell wouldn't have wanted Uri herself, but at least he was a partner. Even ones covered in pond slime were in short supply, especially as one grew older.

Nell had been single for over a year now, ever since things ended with Toby. He had dumped her, although not in any dramatic fashion. Nothing was ever dramatic with Toby which, actually, had been the problem. They had parted amicably but had not kept in touch; he was married now, Nell had heard through the grapevine.

Well, good for him. She hoped he would be happy. But in the middle of the night sometimes the fear gripped Nell that she had rather easily let go what might prove to be her last ever relationship. London, after all, was famously full of single ladies. Sternly she would tell herself that she was an independent woman, better off alone than with the wrong guy.

She focused on her screen again. An expensive, swingy little miniskirt needed a breezy caption. Resolutely, Nell poised her fingers over the keyboard. 'Life's a party!' she wrote. 'And you've been invited!'

CHAPTER 3

It was the afternoon of the next day. A new estate agent's board was going up outside Nell's house. The upstairs flat was for sale. It had been empty since Choon, a friendly Chinese man Nell had been fond of, had moved to Wimbledon some months ago. Having done the rounds of several local agencies, No. 19b Gardiner Road was now on the books of a smart new one, Carrington & Co. Nell had seen its gleaming offices on the main street. Would it succeed where the others had failed?

She forced herself back to work; finding a caption for a rather horrid stag-beetle-printed T-shirt ('Insectious good humour'? 'Unleash beetlemania'?). Her landline rang.

'It's Rose,' said a voice. 'I'm at St Pancras and my train's been delayed. Want to meet for a drink?'

Nell had met Rose at university. They had lived next door to each other in halls. Rose always had more success with men, despite being short, dark and hairy to Nell's tall and blonde. 'Big tits, though,' Rose always said, jiggling them smugly whilst looking at Nell's comparatively flat chest.

'I'd love to,' Nell said now. 'What about the champagne bar?'

Life was a party, after all, and she had been invited.

*

Rose looked curvier than ever, Nell saw as she strode across the concourse at St Pancras. Perhaps having four children had done it. Nell could not imagine why anyone needed so many, or why Rose had called them Alder, Wolf, Moonshine and Sid. It seemed only partly explained by the fact that Griff, Rose's husband, had become a pagan after Sid was born.

Ten minutes after sitting down at the champagne bar Nell was digesting the news that Griff was currently suspended from work, locked in a dispute with HR for wearing a phallus round his neck. 'It's an ancient fertility symbol, but can they get their heads round his value system?' Rose complained.

Rose, who had moved with her pagan brood to Kettering, had come to London for a charity board meeting. GroomRoom aimed to educate children about the dangers of online chatrooms. All Rose's children, even Moonshine, who was four, had smartphones. 'Denying access is no way to deal with the problem,' Rose pronounced when, cautiously, Nell pointed this out. 'That's head-in-the-sand territory.'

Nell was beginning to regret the champagne bar idea. They were on their second glass each and she'd bought both rounds. Rose evidently had no plans to get in the third.

They were talking about Nell's love life now. 'Non-existent,' said Nell. Like the wine; the glasses were both empty again.

She signalled, resignedly, to the barman. They should have bought a whole bloody bottle, like he suggested in the first place.

'Why don't you do internet dating?' Rose asked as she lifted her newly-full glass. 'Everyone else does.'

Nell knew this. People were always suggesting it to her. But online had never appealed. What was that phrase – the odds were good but the goods were odd? 'I've never really fancied it.'

'It's a well-known fact,' Rose announced, 'that people who meet on the internet are much happier than people who don't.'

'*Is* it?' Nell had never heard this before.

'Absolutely. There was a survey recently of Dutch couples who met online.' Rose spoke with magisterial authority as she hoovered up a second bowl of nuts. 'They shared more interests.'

A booming, incomprehensible voice echoed across the concourse. 'Ooh,' Rose exclaimed, sliding off her stool. 'That's my train. I'd better go. Good to see you.'

She swigged back the rest of the champagne, lunged at Nell in an attempt at an air kiss, and was gone. There was no suggestion she might contribute to the bill.

Perched on her bar stool, Nell lifted her glass in ironic salute to the figure, draped with lumpy bags, hurrying towards the gates. She was in no rush to leave herself. What self-consciousness she might have felt had been removed by the champagne, and besides, what was there to go back to in Gardiner Road? Especially now the waiter had once again replaced the nuts.

It was pleasant here at the bar, with the great Victorian red-brick walls behind her and the pale blue iron arches soaring overhead. After the solitude of her bedroom St Pancras was all glamorous bustle. It reminded her of the places she had taken clients for drinks and lunch during Vanilla's heyday. She felt once again plugged into the world.

The champagne bar was a glowing island in a sea of shining marble over which glided the easy rumble of suitcases and people bound for exotic destinations. Nell looked over to the golden windows of the lit-up Eurostar. People were seated within, smiling, chatting. Off to Paris, Brussels, Bruges . . .

She sipped her champagne and wished she was on the train as well, wherever it was going. She thought about the travel centre on the floor below and pictured herself in the Eurostar

19

queue, slipping a large ticket into one of the brushed-steel entry gates, seeing them spring back, being waved through by one of those smart workers in their dark blue and yellow uniforms. Her fingers twitched. Should she? Could she?

No. She reached for a macadamia instead. Running away wasn't really the answer. Wandering around Europe would solve nothing and cost a fortune. She must face up to things here, in London. Her drifting career. Her non-existent love life.

So – internet dating. She had resisted it so far, but it was true that everyone did it. Were couples that met that way – Dutch or otherwise – really happier? Might it be worth going online to find love?

Two days later, Nell had selected 'Elite Connections' from an infinite number of other possible cyber meat markets. She had done so on the entirely practical grounds that the joining fee was so steep it would preclude, if not the psychopaths, then at least the skint and the seedy.

That was the easy bit. Then she had had to compose a pithy description in twenty-five words. She should be good at it after years of writing catalogue copy to length.

London girl looking for thoughtful guy. Into reading, music, country walks . . .

Nell paused after this first attempt. Did it make her sound boring? Would it attract men in bottle-bottomed specs obsessed with Wagner? And where had the country walk bit come from anyway? It had sort of just slipped in.

She tried again. *Chic city chick seeks cool guy. I'm beautiful, clever and I like champagne.*

That was the other extreme – too brassy and boastful. Would a compromise work? *Chic city chick seeks cool guy. I'm into reading, music, country walks . . .*

Picking the right image to post online took almost as long as the personal statement. Other women on the site had a black-and-white crop of just their lips, or a come-hither, much-mascara'd lowered eyelid.

Nell scrolled through her computer photo library and found one of herself in a white shirt, her make-up minimal and her pale hair drawn back into a ponytail. It gave her the faintly clinical look of an assistant at an Estee Lauder counter, but hopefully had a bit of restrained glamour about it as well.

Having joined Elite Connections, Nell resisted the temptation to log on for the whole of the first day. Fortunately she had an excuse to be out, a client meeting of real-life people for once. It was a school furniture supplier in Kennington, but Nell threw herself into the interaction all the same. She returned clutching armfuls of product information, her mind stuffed with the details of desks and adjustable chairs.

Armed with a stiff gin and tonic, she logged on to Elite Connections and gasped. The page was black with the bold type of unopened messages; more were pinging in even as she watched. She had received over sixty replies.

Her initial feelings of nervous, flattered relief faded as she realised that many responses were generic, from men who presumably mailed all the women on the site. Having removed these, and the ones from SexBeast and TightBuns, Nell was left with around fifteen with sufficiently inoffensive online tags and personal statements to qualify them – in greater or lesser degrees – for inclusion on the possibles spectrum. She then did a further edit, deleting all replies with emoticons. What self-respecting guy used winking smiley faces in a pick-up line?

This left only one contender. OutdoorsGuy.

His picture was tiny and blurry, but he seemed to have dark hair and a broad smile. *Single, 30s, financially comfortable and bookish. Into music and walking at weekends*, went his description. There was nothing else. After pondering every syllable, Nell decided he sounded just what she was looking for. A confident personality, comfortable in his own skin.

She emailed him, and was amazed when a reply came straight back. *Hey there. Let's meet.*

Nell wasn't sure about the *Hey there*. A bit glib? On the plus side, he didn't waste time. *Great*, she replied.

How about Wednesday? immediately suggested OutdoorsGuy.

He was keen. Because he was desperate? Or because he had instantly spotted her own worth and value?

She messaged back. *OK. Where?*

Where do you suggest?

Nell pondered. Coffee was obviously safest. You could escape easily from a Costa or Starbucks if things went wrong. But wine always helped things along. Perhaps the champagne bar at St Pancras? It was where the original cyber dating idea had taken root. The spiritual home, as it were, of the whole enterprise.

She sent off the suggestion and waited. A reply came back.

How about Paddington, if you like stations? I'll be working near there on Weds. The Apples and Pears at 6?

This relative tsunami of information sent Nell into a mental tailspin. Did he think she was a trainspotter? The Apples and Pears sounded a bit pubby, oh dear. And what was OutdoorsGuy doing near Paddington? Was he a ticket clerk? A newsagent? There was a hospital there, St Mary's. Perhaps OutdoorsGuy was a doctor? Yes, that was possible. He had said he was financially comfortable.

Six it is, she replied. *How will I recognise you?* The Elite Connections picture wasn't big. Perhaps he could wear his doctor's coat, and a stethoscope.

I'll be carrying a copy of All Smiles by Dylan Eliot. Why don't you do the same?

Good idea, Nell replied. *All Smiles* was on her bookshelf, as it was on most people's. It was one of those books that everyone had read, like *One Day* a couple of years before. She'd loved it. The author's comic struggle to adapt, post-university, to life in London and launch himself as a writer had struck a chord with her, as it had with her entire generation of migrants to the metropolis.

So OutdoorsGuy was not only – almost certainly – a doctor, but a Dylan Eliot fan. He definitely sounded promising.

CHAPTER 4

Julian's new club had a lot of terrible art in it, Dylan thought. Shapeless glass sculptures were dotted throughout the dining room, and Dylan and Julian sat beneath a vast gold canvas covered in thick oil-paint smears. It wasn't clear what it represented.

On the wall opposite was a painting of a monumentally slaggish woman clad in a black PVC lace-up bodice, thigh-high, spike-heeled leather boots and dangling a whip. It reminded Dylan of Beatrice, who, at that exact moment, was stocking up on just this sort of wardrobe in Soho.

The thought filled him with fear rather than excitement. Since her latest return, Beatrice had become even more insatiable; she dominated – in every sense – his every moment during the day. Only when she was asleep was he free. And even then she contrived to have her legs draped over him, as if trying to prevent him getting away. He would lie there, trapped under the naked thighs of a stunning beauty.

All of which would have been fine, had the deadline for *Charm Itself* not been looming. And so Dylan had hit on the idea of writing at night. Having waited for her breathing to become regular – even asleep it had a rasping, rapacious quality

– he would inch out from beneath Beatrice and creep downstairs. He would switch on his laptop and pound away.

The funny thing was, writing in these conditions worked better than during the day. Being half asleep made it easier, for some reason. By the time he had fully woken up, he had several thousand words under his belt. And so he would write without pause until pink and purple ribbons twisted in the pearly dawn sky. Only then, as the sun rose, did he switch off his laptop and creep back upstairs to where Beatrice – and her libido – would be stirring.

He was, as a result, permanently exhausted, but also making rapid progress. *Charm Itself* was now almost finished and one advantage of the London trip was that, unhindered, he might be able to get the final chapters done on the night train from Penzance. Then he could hand the whole thing in to Julian when they met.

These hopes had foundered late Tuesday afternoon when Beatrice – evidently suspecting him of going to the capital to meet another woman – announced she was coming too. She had found in the sleeper cabin's space restrictions a whole new source of noisy stimulation and Dylan had emerged the next morning not only exhausted but unable to meet anyone's eye.

Beatrice had come with him in the taxi to the club's very door and Dylan had feared she might insist on coming to lunch as well. He felt he would be powerless to object if she did.

But fortunately Beatrice seemed satisfied when the girl at the front desk said Julian was waiting for him in the restaurant. She had kissed him a long, lingering goodbye (people had stopped on the street to stare); hailed a cab to Soho – about six skidded to an immediate halt – and arranged to see him later, at the station.

Now, Dylan suppressed a yawn and the urge to rub his eyes.

The wine that Julian had ordered was shutting down his systems even as he sat there.

His agent was chatting to a table-hopper of which there had been a constant stream since they had come in. Some actress, Dylan gathered, staring down at his *amuse-gueules* so as not to be drawn in to the conversation.

Bruton Street was the type of place where lots of little bits and pieces preceded the actual meal. So far Dylan had had a parsnip crisp anointed with three dots of cauliflower foam and now he was biting into a tiny ice-cream cone filled with foie gras mousse. It was delicious, but odd. He would have been just as happy with a plate of spaghetti. But Julian would not have been seen dead in a mere bog-standard Italian.

The actress had gone but someone else was at their table now. 'I *loved All Smiles*,' a deep-cleavaged television blonde was gushing. 'When's the next book out?'

'All in hand, my dear,' Julian assured her from behind his glass of Puligny-Montrachet. He'd said the same to someone from Radio Four who'd gasped and said they'd like to put a marker down for *Book of the Week*.

The blonde sashayed off and Julian poked his teaspoon into his reduction of eel risotto. 'You know, dear boy, you really should let me see the first three chapters of *Charm Itself*.'

Dylan shook his head. He was reluctant to reveal anything he wasn't happy with. When the book was finished – and the time was imminent – Julian could see all the chapters then.

'Yes, but you don't want to lose it all at this stage,' Julian warned. 'Hit the wrong button or leave it all on the top of a bus. Authors do, you know. Emailing it to me is quite a good way of keeping it safe.'

But Dylan wasn't going to fall for such an obvious ruse. 'Sorry.'

'Well if you insist. Just make sure you keep saving it on a USB stick.'

'Of course I will,' Dylan assured him. 'Relax, Julian. It's almost there, OK?'

Later, Dylan sat in the taxi on his way back to the station. Lunch had gone on for longer than he had expected. There had been various contracts to sign and even more interruptions from the media great and good. Then, after the coffee, his agent had produced a new cover for *All Smiles*. 'Eve's decided to re-jacket it to keep sales up,' he explained. 'Just in case you don't deliver *Charm* on time, although I've reassured her it's all in hand.'

The traffic outside the taxi window was not moving. They had hit some major roadworks, which was a bore rather than a worry. The night train didn't leave until ten. Dylan cursed himself for suggesting to Beatrice that they meet back at the station. He hadn't been thinking. If they met at six thirty, as arranged, they would have three hours to kill before they could board. Had they met in the West End, they could at least have gone to the first half of a show. Or seen a movie. Still, he could always go and sit somewhere and read the news on his Smartphone.

The other side of the glass screen, the taxi driver was muttering into his hands-free. The radio was on; two blokes talking, as they always were in London taxis, about Arsenal. Dylan had no interest in football; something he had explored at length in *All Smiles*, which was, in its way, the anti-*Fever Pitch*, describing the author's efforts to avoid going to the Emirates on Saturdays with his Gunners-obsessed friends. He had imagined this would doom the book from the start but it seemed to have struck a chord.

The green-lit figures on the fare display were the only thing moving in the stationary car. The enormous amount would have given him a heart attack once, Dylan knew. He would have got out and walked, and wondered now if he should do so. But it was hot outside and the pavement was a maze of barriers, rubble and people trying to pick their way around it all.

From inside the taxi Dylan watched and wondered how he had ever lived in this city. Everyone looked so grim and exhausted; everything was so dusty and bright, with the sun blazing pitilessly off the same hard surfaces that amplified the drills and clangs of the endless construction works. London, Dylan felt, was never finished. But he had definitely finished with London.

He pulled the re-jacketed book out of his bag to look at it again. The new cover had been slipped over the old one to give an idea, but Dylan wasn't sure he liked it. The original *All Smiles* jacket had featured a large, Rolling Stones-type grinning mouth which had stood out a mile in the bookshops. The new version was bold orange and white stripes, which was evidently expected to do the same job, although it was, Dylan felt, less specific.

He looked at the photograph of himself on the rear flap. Eve was still using the old one, the one with the beard. He'd shaved it off after moving to Cornwall; beards and surfboards hadn't really gone together. It wasn't just the aerodynamics; salt water had turned his chin into a mass of dry frizz that no amount of fashionable beard oil could tackle.

Now, looking at the unflattering great bush beneath his lips in the photograph, Dylan wondered what on earth had possessed him. Peer pressure, he supposed. Every young man in the capital had sported a beard at the time and there were fashion imperatives that even a literary iconoclast was not capable of resisting. But he'd managed to throw it off now. Shave it off, too. When a man was tired of London, he was tired of excessive facial hair.

In the back of the taxi Dylan rubbed his chin, on which the five o'clock stubble was coming through right on cue. Life without a beard was much easier. He wouldn't be growing one again. *Charm Itself* would need a new, updated author portrait.

Dylan yawned. It was warm in the taxi and he was so, so tired. His lack of sleep overwhelmed him and he slipped into blessed unconsciousness. The next thing he knew, a Cockney voice was cutting into his dreams. 'We're 'ere, guv. Paddin'ton.'

He scrambled to collect himself, grabbing, just as he left the taxi, the copy of *All Smiles* that had slipped on to the floor. He paid and entered the station, clamping his book under his arm. Only once the taxi had driven away did Dylan realise that he had left the book's new jacket in there.

CHAPTER 5

It was so easy if you were a bloke, Nell thought, standing before the mirror on her wardrobe door. You just chucked on a T-shirt, jeans, trainers, ran your fingers through your hair and off you went. She had tried so many combinations that the floor of her bedroom was a sea of scattered clothes. In the end, the only thing that felt right was what she had been wearing in the first place, the white shirt and jeans she sported to her bedroom 'office' every day.

The tube was crammed with tourists and commuters and was hotter even than usual. The train kept grinding to a halt. Hanging on to a sticky pole by the door, Nell felt her heart thump in her ears. She couldn't be late!

Finally at Paddington, it took her a while to spot the old-fashioned station pub tucked unobtrusively at the back of the concourse. She walked towards it slowly, trying to persuade herself that the dirty decorative ironwork of its exterior had some sort of particular London character. But in reality she was wondering who on earth would arrange to meet here on a first date. Unless, of course, it was some sort of test.

Yes, that was it. OutdoorsGuy, being, most probably, a doctor, would be an altruistic type. If she was the kind of woman who cared only about expensive treats and outward show, a place like the Apples and Pears would soon reveal it. Well, Nell thought, pushing open the pub's battered saloon doors, she would surprise him.

Dylan had chosen the tiny, dingy pub at the back of the station because he had at least three hours to kill before the train and it was the place most likely to be free of noisy people. He wanted to read the BBC news website in peace and quiet.

He liked the Apples and Pears. For one thing, it was a world away from the concourse coffee shops with their flat whites and extra shots. For another, it had definite atmosphere. It was a pocket-sized Victorian drinking hole, a piece of history which Dylan guessed had been built at the same time as the station for railway workers to refresh themselves in. The brass plates on the entrance doors had the soft, worn look of a century's polishing, although no one seemed to have polished them recently.

Inside, dust motes danced in the soft light of the opaque windows. A padded bench of burgundy leather ran round the painted wooden wall. At the little bar, a drooping landlord was serving pints of lager to a row of skinny barflies on high stools. Dylan looked at the beer pumps and rejoiced at the lack of craft ales with witty names. That the Apples and Pears was a style-free zone was a relief after the Bruton Street club.

The barflies were friendly enough. They acknowledged him with unsteady gazes and slurred salutations. They might have been any age from twenty to sixty and, like the pub itself, seemed to have been left behind by the rest of the world. Dylan sensed that it would not be long before the Apples and Pears was swept away, refurbished to within an inch of its life and turned into an oyster bar or maybe another café full of baristas and laptops. He felt that would be a pity.

Having got his half-pint, Dylan went to the corner and sat down behind a small round table supported by a heavy wrought-iron stand. He placed on it the copy of *All Smiles* that he had been holding since emerging from the taxi. Then he got out his phone and sent a message to Beatrice, telling her where he was. Then he logged on to BBC News.

As the saloon bar doors swung shut behind her, Nell took in the brass rails and old-fashioned paintwork. Three drinkers at the bar were fixing unsteady, reddened gazes on her. She pushed aside the initial, ghastly possibility that one of them was OutdoorsGuy.

There was someone else, in the corner. Someone dark-haired looking intently into a Smartphone. With, yes, a copy of *All Smiles* beside him on the table.

OutdoorsGuy! She felt a rush of pure fear, mingled with pure excitement.

He was much better-looking than his picture on the Elite Connections website. His dark head was bent but his face, from here, seemed all cheekbones. He was wide-shouldered, evidently tall, and had well-defined muscles. His white T-shirt contrasted with his deep, healthy tan; he looked as if he spent a lot of time in the sun. Could there be any doubt that this was OutdoorsGuy?

She took a deep breath, pulled her own copy of *All Smiles* out of her bag, and went over.

Dylan's first thought was that Beatrice wasn't normally early. Far from it, she prided herself on being late. But now he saw that the woman standing before him wasn't Beatrice. In fact, she was about as far from Beatrice as could be imagined.

Where Beatrice was short, dark and curvy with black hair, this woman was slim and tall with hair so pale it was almost silver. It touched her very straight shoulders and framed her long white neck. Instead of Beatrice's Venus flytrap eyelashes and painted pillow pout, a pair of wide blue eyes looked down at him from a clear, fresh face with spots of colour glowing in the cheeks.

'Hello,' Nell said. Her eyes gathered the details of the face tipped up to her. Long dark brows, straight nose, full lips. The dark eyes had bags beneath, which was not only unexpectedly sexy but fitted with the doctor theory. Long, long hours saving people's lives.

'Hello,' Dylan answered, matching her tone of cautious friendliness. He wasn't exactly sure what was going on here. But this girl was definitely a knockout.

'You must be OutdoorsGuy,' Nell went on.

'You must be an outdoors guy,' was how Dylan heard this sentence. It was an unexpected remark, and he still didn't know why she was talking to him. Of course, there were reasons why a single woman might approach a single man in a big London station. But she didn't look that sort. Far from it; her silvery fairness had something pure about it.

'Yeah,' he said. Sure, he was an outdoors guy. He surfed, did he not?

This brought forth from her a smile that dazzled him. He watched, spellbound, as she glanced down at the copy of *All Smiles* on the table. She then produced her own out of her bag.

And with that, all was clear. She was a fan, Dylan realised, disappointed. Despite the fact he no longer had a beard, she had worked out who he was. She liked his novel, that was all. No doubt she just wanted her book signed.

He was just rummaging for his pen in his bag when he heard her speak again, saying something so odd that Dylan stopped his search and looked back up at her.

'What was that?' he asked.

'I think Dylan Eliot's a great writer and I can't wait for his next book,' Nell repeated obligingly.

Dylan narrowed his eyes at her. Was this some strange third-person manner of addressing him? 'I've heard it's on its way,' he said, watching her reaction.

Nell's face lit up. 'Great. I really enjoyed *All Smiles*. Didn't you?' she asked him.

Dylan was confused once more. So she didn't think he was Dylan Eliot after all. But why did she think that she knew him?

'What's your name?' he asked, to make it clear that he didn't know her. Now she would realise she had mistaken him for someone else.

She didn't seem to. 'Nell,' she answered, as if the question was expected.

Nell. It rang in his head like a well-tuned bell. Dylan decided that he didn't care why she was here. He was too tired. He just wanted to look at that face, stare into those wide blue eyes.

'Can I get you a drink?'

Nell, who had been about to make the same offer, nodded hurriedly.

Waiting at the bar, Dylan found his gaze drawn back to the gleam of her hair. Who was she, this mysterious blonde from out of the blue?

Someone who thought he was somebody else, was the only answer that mattered. The decent thing would be to admit that he knew this.

But if he did she would only leave. And he wanted her to stay and tell him her story. He was sick of thinking about his own. He wanted to know all about her.

CHAPTER 6

'What *wines* do we have?' repeated the barman incredulously to Dylan as the barflies chortled. 'Just the two, mate. Red or white.'

'Oh. Right. Well, white then. Thanks.'

He returned, rather abashed, to the table with the drinks. Her smile of thanks made him feel better immediately.

'Do you work round here?' Dylan began, just before Nell could ask the same question.

'I work at home. I write.'

'Write?' Dylan repeated, suspicious again. Was that what this was about? She was a budding novelist, wanting tips?

'Only catalogues, it's pretty mundane really. Nothing like writing something like *that*.' She gestured at his copy of *All Smiles*.

'Oh, I don't know,' Dylan said feelingly, before he could stop himself. 'Writing novels can be pretty mundane. Um, or so I've heard. Er, what sort of catalogues?'

She rolled her eyes. 'They're pretty silly, some of them. About underpants with Latin mottoes and, uh, gramophones with horns on that look Thirties but are actually cutting edge technology.' She stopped, her face flaming. What had possessed her to talk about underpants and horns?

'But you want to do something else?' Dylan guessed, still braced for the declaration that she longed to be an author.

'Yes. But I don't know what.'

She wondered how it was that, a mere few minutes after meeting him, she was touching on such matters as this. She found herself waiting for his response as if he really had the answer.

If she really was a literary groupie, Dylan was thinking, she was taking her time to declare the fact. 'You hadn't thought of writing something else?' he prompted. 'Something a bit more . . . substantial?'

Nell shook her head. The most substantial catalogue she knew was the Argos one and that looked like a nightmare.

'Something more . . . creative?' Dylan suggested, still cautious but starting to feel more relaxed now.

'Maybe,' Nell sighed, thinking gloomily of Phoenix and the ever-receding possibility that it would rise from the ashes. Or that her life in general would.

'Why the sigh?' Dylan asked.

She eyed him. 'Nothing, really. I'm fine.' She gave him a bright smile and took a sip of wine. This was supposed to be a date, after all.

Dylan was intrigued. He batted away her attempts to be flippant. 'Tell me about your life,' he asked.

The pull of those dark eyes was irresistible. And he seemed so sincere. She found herself telling the truth.

'It's pretty lonely,' she concluded. 'I stay in too much. My friends have all got married. I've kind of lost touch with them. I've never been all that good with men . . . oh just listen to me. Urban cliché!'

She stopped, grinning but embarrassed. She had given away much too much. Time to return the conversation to more neutral territory. Time, in fact, to find out about him.

'So,' she said, glancing down at his copy of *All Smiles*. 'You like reading. What else, besides Dylan Eliot?'

They were soon deep in a conversation about their favourite books. Nell's reading, Dylan discovered, was impressively wide. She liked poetry as well as novels and she knew her Shakespeare. He laughed when she told him about the sock catalogue. His admiration grew as he listened, seeing her forget herself and glow with enthusiasm as she described her favourite literary heroes and heroines.

'I'm glad you haven't included Mr Darcy,' he remarked when she paused for breath. 'Everyone else always does. It's pretty boring, I think.'

'A bit hackneyed,' Nell agreed. 'Darcy's not my ideal sort of man anyway. Too cold and snobbish.' He watched her tuck a bright strand of hair behind an ear.

'Who is your ideal sort of man?' he asked before he could stop himself.

They looked at each other. Heat flashed through Nell's cheeks. Dylan, meanwhile, felt he wanted to take this woman in his arms and hold tightly on to her as if she were a rock in a rough sea.

They sat, locked in each other's gazes. They might have remained that way for ever had two dramatic events not followed each other in quick succession.

The first Nell knew of it was a loud, foreign-sounding female exclamation followed by a rush of overpowering scent. She blinked and realised that OutdoorsGuy was no longer there. Or, at least, was no longer visible.

Someone was between him and her. A woman who had come from nowhere and who seemed all heels and hair. She had leapt on OutdoorsGuy and began writhing on his knee;

straddling him in the tightest, blackest, shiniest trousers. Her arms were wrapped round his neck and her breasts – largely exposed in a half-buttoned blouse – practically in his face.

'Excuse me,' said a voice, even as Nell was taking all this in. She looked up to see a face peering down at her. A diffident, pasty face, attached to a skinny body which was clutching to it a copy of *All Smiles*.

'Are you CityGirl? Sorry I'm so late. The tube . . .' His voice was grating and his smile was a yellow grimace. There was a patch of spittle on his lower lip.

Nell sprang to her feet, the chair clattering to the floor. The long-haired woman was still writhing on OutdoorsGuy's knee. He was clutching her in response; at least that was what it looked like. 'Are you all right?' asked the real OutdoorsGuy. He was a good six inches smaller than her.

Nell's chest was tight and her breath was coming fast and hard. Non-OutdoorsGuy was staring at her now over the top of the woman's breasts, his features purple and contorted in what might have been laughter.

Laughing at *her*, Nell supposed. He had obviously been stringing her along for his own amusement. Killing time by getting the poor single woman to unburden herself while he waited for the predatory creature now grinding herself into his groin.

Hurling Dylan a glare straight from the red-hot heart of her anger, Nell wrenched herself around. Then, without so much as looking at OutdoorsGuy (the real one), she rushed out of the pub and into the crowd.

CHAPTER 7

Dylan watched helplessly from behind Beatrice's smothering breasts as Nell ran through the doorway and disappeared. Then, with a mighty effort, he wrestled free and shot on to the concourse.

He could see a teeming crowd, but no Nell. She had gone.

'Was it something I said?' a querulous voice asked beside him. Dylan glanced down. It was the weaselly little man who had turned up at the end.

'How do you know her?' Dylan asked. They seemed an unlikely pair.

The other shook his head. 'I don't. We met online. My first attempt. Not sure I'll be trying it again though.'

Dylan had spotted the book in his hand. Yet another copy of *All Smiles*. What was this? Some existential joke?

'It was the signal,' the weasel explained, raising the familiar volume. 'The way we'd recognise each other. Not the aptest of titles, as it turned out.'

As he watched the other walk off, Dylan wanted to kick himself. So the beautiful blonde had thought he was her date. If only he had been honest. If only he'd had the courage to put her right. She might even have seen the funny side.

How he wished she really had been his date, instead of Beatrice!

He turned glumly back into the pub. Where, waiting for him, and watched by an admiring audience of gawping barflies, was the furious Frenchwoman.

While Nell was there she had been laughing – the maddening, insincere theatrical laugh that he hated. But Beatrice was not laughing any more. Her eyes burned, the very ends of her hair flickered with fury.

'Who was zat?' she spat. The barflies all cheered; Act Two of the afternoon's unscheduled drama was about to begin.

Something snapped in Dylan. Enough was enough. He would not wait until after the book was finished to end it with Beatrice. He would end it now.

It was Beatrice who had ruined it all. Had she not turned up and forced his mouth into her cleavage so he could neither breathe nor speak, he would have been able to explain himself – at least to some extent. But the chance had gone and he would never see Nell again.

He took a deep breath and straightened his shoulders. He held the spark-spitting eyes with his own.

'I'm going back alone,' Dylan said steadily. 'You aren't coming with me, Beatrice. It's over.'

He waited for the explosion he felt sure must come. To his surprise, it did not. Beatrice merely picked up her handbag, flicked her hair over her shoulders and clacked out of the Apples and Pears. Dylan watched her melt into the hubbub of the concourse, expecting her, at any moment, to turn round, run back and hurl herself upon him, tooth and claw. But instead, crowds closed behind her, like water. Beatrice, like Nell before her, was gone.

That really was it. It really was over. He could go back to

Cornwall and finish his novel in peace and quiet.

That night, on the train, he slept deeply and dreamlessly. He did not even awake when Penzance was reached and everyone else got off. 'You seemed like you needed the kip,' said the guard, who woke him only when the train was being prepared to make the return journey.

Striding out of the station into the bright Cornish morning, Dylan looked up at the cawing gulls wheeling in the clear sky. He breathed deeply, pulling the tangy, sea-scented air into his lungs.

There was but one cloud in the blue; the shadow of yesterday's encounter with Nell. It felt like such a missed opportunity, but he would just have to let it go. There was nothing on earth he could do about it. The incident had, at least, spurred him to finally make the break with Beatrice.

And now, Dylan resolved as he unlocked his car in the station car park, he would return to the cottage and finish *Charm Itself.*

Back within sight of Bosun's Whistle, Dylan whistled himself as the car bumped up the sunny track, through the farm gate and over the glossy green grass to where the cottage crouched on the cliff edge.

For two days afterwards, resisting the call of the surf and the sea, he worked at his desk. In the afternoon of the third day he finished and emailed the document to Julian.

It was done! Dylan leaned back in his chair, stretched and enjoyed a rush of relief and elation. Now, finally, he could get on with the rest of his life.

And go out on his surfboard. It was the perfect afternoon for it: bright and wild with racing clouds and a buffeting, bracing wind.

As he parked at the beach he called his agent. Julian seemed less excited to hear him than he expected.

'Did you get it?' Dylan prompted eagerly.

'Get what?'

Dylan checked the email on his phone. His message to Julian, plus its precious attachment, had vanished without trace. There was nothing in the Sent box even. His system must have frozen, right at the crucial moment.

'Rural broadband,' he groaned, adding that he'd try again later.

'Send it now!' urged Julian, champing at the bit.

Dylan glanced through the windscreen at the great wide stretch of pale golden beach and the rearing waves bucking and plunging towards it. He could already feel the icy thrill of the water over his shoulders; the slap of salt spray in his face. There was no way he was turning his back on all this and returning to Bosun's Whistle.

'Later,' he repeated, grinning. 'Surf's up.'

It was, too, spectacularly. The waves were on excellent form; huge walls of water which picked him up and flung him down and gripped him with thick green muscles. They crashed in his ears, boomed in his heart, salted his eyes and sent agonising acid streams down his nose. Heaven.

Afterwards, he bumped into Neil, his former surf instructor. Neil was pleased to hear Dylan had finished his novel at last. 'Good for you, mate,' he drawled in his warm Australian accent. 'Never managed to finish one yet. Not much of a reader, me.' They went to celebrate at the Westward Ho, the pub nearest the beach.

The exertion of surfing, the whipping, sunny wind and the beer all combined to produce a feeling of simple good cheer that Dylan was reluctant to call time on.

He didn't want to go back to the cottage just yet. He wanted to stay, unwind, relax, and Neil had no plans either.

After a couple of beers they went up the hill overlooking the bay and sat in the spiky salt-grass by the old gun battery, smoking the joint Neil always had about his person. Even in his wetsuit, it seemed.

'Jeez, man, this is good.' Neil breathed out a thick and acrid plume of marijuana smoke.

The afternoon passed to early evening. Dylan was dimly aware of the sea turning from violet through forget-me-not to a shimmering white and the sun starting to dim rather than sink; no coral spectacular tonight.

The pot was overpoweringly strong, but so was Dylan's sense of relief. Beatrice was off his back – and every other part of his anatomy. The burden of the novel was finally off his shoulders. He had fulfilled his obligations to Julian and Eve and now he could think about what he wanted to do next. Although, with Neil's weed on board, it was hard to think of anything.

He had almost dozed off when he heard Neil give a whistle of appreciation.

Dylan stirred in the warm grass. 'What's up?'

Neil waved the joint between his fingers. Dylan looked out to sea. There were a number of black-clad figures in the waves, battling manfully to remain on their surfboards.

'That girl. Tasha.'

Dylan shifted in the grass a little, as if the mere adjusting of his position would help him to pick out one identical rubbered figure from another. Neil's ability to tell who someone was from this distance was one of the strange skills of a surf instructor, the same way a sailor knew his own ship on the horizon.

'She's hot,' Neil continued.

Dylan did not comment. He'd had enough of hot women in black rubber.

Wendy Holden

'From London.' Neil exhaled in a rush and handed the joint to Dylan. 'Poor woman.'

Dylan could only agree. 'Absolutely. Who'd want to live in London?'

Neil inhaled again. 'Nah, mate,' he said, holding his breath. 'That's not the point. Tasha got dumped at the altar. She was telling me about it yesterday.'

'Really?' Dylan squinted at the distant figure, surprised. He vaguely knew who Tasha was: a cheerful, pretty blonde. She didn't seem the type to get dumped, at the altar or anywhere else.

'The bloke she was marrying, he sent her a text on the morning. She was actually sitting in the register office. Told her he'd met someone else and couldn't marry her.' Neil shook his head, narrowed his eyes and sucked in another lungful of marijuana smoke.

'Poor thing,' said Dylan, although secretly he felt anyone considering marriage had to have a screw loose. Beatrice had hinted at it more than once. It didn't bear thinking about.

'Yeah, mate. And she's not the only one.' Neil shook his salt-roughened blond locks. 'Tash found out that she wasn't the first. He'd done it before.'

Dylan propped himself up on an elbow, frowning. 'What, you mean failed to show for his own wedding? He'd done it to someone else before her? Why?'

Neil blew out another plume of smoke. 'Some kind of revenge complex, Tasha thinks. She reckons he's probably in London now, doing it all over again to some poor unsuspecting woman who thinks he loves her.'

Dylan shook his head. Love was a dangerous thing. He thought ruefully of Beatrice again. And of Nell. While she seemed like a missed opportunity, perhaps he'd had a lucky

44

escape. She might have been crazy too. Certainly, she had been furious with him. She had obviously felt he had tricked her.

He remembered suddenly that he needed to go back to Bosun's Whistle and re-send the email. He returned to his car and drove back through the golden evening light and winding lanes. He regretted smoking so much now. His eyes were heavy and he felt sleepy and detached, as if someone else was driving and his own reflexes and instincts were slightly behind theirs.

But he also felt more mellow and relaxed than he ever had in his life. The fact that Bosun's Whistle would be empty when he got there was a blissful prospect.

He still could not entirely believe Beatrice had taken him at his word. Ever since his return from London his ear, even as he wrote, had been permanently cocked for the sound of a taxi grinding up the path followed by the slam of a car door and the sound of high heels on farm track. He had been braced, in addition, for some violent, punishing act that might happen at any time. Beatrice was terrifyingly vengeful.

But nothing had happened at all. It seemed that she really wasn't coming back. Perhaps she had returned to France. It was both strange and wonderful that she had left him so completely alone; no phone calls, no emails, nothing. And now he was free.

As he approached the track leading to his field, Dylan saw that the sun had, after all, decided to set in a blaze of glory. The sky over his cottage was a fierce orange, swirling with red and rolling with black. It looked incredible, especially to his semi-hallucinating vision. As if it were on fire, almost.

As he got closer Dylan slowly realised that it was not the sky over his cottage that looked on fire. The cottage itself actually was on fire.

The cottage containing the laptop on which his novel was stored. Of which there were no other copies, anywhere.

He slammed his foot on the brake, wrenched open the door and hurled himself out. The vehicle, un-handbraked, rolled serenely on, bumping over the grass down the slight incline to the cliff's edge. Dylan didn't even see it go over. He was racing towards Bosun's Whistle.

Seconds later he was bursting through the open door – had he really left it open? – into the choking, burning hell that had been his sitting room. There was no air; he seemed to be breathing fire; a wall of heat was melting his face and his burning hair smelt bitter in his nostrils.

The noise was unbelievable; he had not known that fire roared and screamed as it consumed and destroyed. Then he realised the screaming was himself, with the fire alarm in shrill counterpoint. But who was going to hear that? The cottage was at the edge of the cliff.

Dylan thrashed about, squinting blindly through boiling tears and stinging eyes. He could see Beatrice's surf boots, plastic cloven hoofs curling and melting in the yellow-hot centre of the blaze. By the time he realised his desk had been burned, and with it his papers and his novel, Dylan was on fire himself.

CHAPTER 8

Months had gone by since the Paddington Incident. Spring had passed into summer. Even dusty Gardiner Road had put forth its share of green on the privet hedges and the shady London planes whose trunks rose from the middle of the pavements. The Carrington & Co. board advertising the upstairs flat continued in full bloom too. No one seemed in any hurry to buy it.

Nell had not logged on to Elite Connections again. Neither, it seemed, had OutdoorsGuy. He had not messaged her, which was some relief at least. The circumstances of their meeting had permitted her only the briefest glance, but she had seen enough to know he was a non-starter.

As for Fake OutdoorsGuy, the one who, for perverse reasons of his own had pretended to be her date, Nell remained furious with him. He had made a fool of her; she had told him all sorts of things – things that embarrassment fanned in her imagination to seem far more intimate than they actually were. She knew that she should simply put him out of her mind, but couldn't. He had lodged there, damn him.

Never, ever again would she trust a man she met on the internet. Still less one pretending to be. The only comfort was that she need never see Fake OutdoorsGuy – or OutdoorsGuy – again.

It was Tuesday afternoon and Nell was out shopping. The market in Chapel Street was grinding to a halt. She smiled a no-thanks at the stallholder who offered her an entire box of avocados for a fiver. 'What would I do with them? I live on my own.'

The stallholder grinned. 'On yer own? Cracker like you? Blimey, what's wrong with blokes today?'

How long have you got? Nell thought. A cold prick on her cheek alerted her to the fact that it had started to rain; another prick came, and another. Curses erupted from the stall holders' vans; the pace of packing up quickened. Exposed beneath the unexpected and rapidly falling water, Nell's pace quickened too. Yet the rain fell harder and harder; soon it was a deluge. Nell abandoned her idea of going home; she would get soaked even trying. Instead she paused under the eaves of a building on the corner. Carrington & Co., estate agents.

She looked into its window, searching for the card advertising Choon's flat. She was surprised to see it now had a red triangle over the corner: 'SOLD Subject To Contract'.

A ray of optimism pierced her gloomy mood. Soon – perhaps very soon – she would have a new upstairs neighbour. Perhaps someone interesting that she could be friends with; perhaps even a single, eligible, nice man. Nell stopped that thought in its tracks. She was not looking for a man, single, eligible, nice or otherwise. Did they even exist?

As the rain still poured down, Nell gazed at Carrington's display of pricey stucco villas and elegant, light-filled flats. It would be wonderful to live somewhere like that: airy, fashionable, lovely. But these were places far above anything she could afford. She smiled as she read the descriptions. They were full of exaggerations, euphemisms and jargon; a branch of the art she practised herself.

Quite suddenly she caught the eye of the young man behind the desk. He was looking directly at her. Nell stopped grinning at the copywriting and felt herself flush red. She looked behind her, hoping the rain would have stopped and she could go. But no, it was coming down even harder, hurling itself at the pavement, spraying everywhere. Glancing back into the shop, Nell saw to her relief that the young man had left his desk.

Then came a rattling sound and the door right next to where she was standing opened. There he was, his smiling, handsome face mere inches from her own. His teeth were very white, Nell noticed, trying to contain her jangling nerves.

'Come in,' he invited. 'You look wet. Let me make you a coffee.'

'No thank you,' Nell said, politely but firmly. Why was her heart hammering?

'I make good coffee.'

'I'm fine, thanks.'

He was looking at the rain behind her, curtains of water through which it was difficult to see the street. 'You won't be if you stay out here. Come on. I try and do a good turn every day and I haven't done one today. So you'd be doing me a favour.'

Nell found herself following him in. He showed her to some modish brown cubed seating arranged before a small Gaggia machine.

'Cappuccino?' He flashed her that irresistible smile again. He was about her age; boyishly handsome with wide eyes and neat ears, his cropped dark hair with just the right degree of tousle. He looked like someone from one of her catalogues.

'Do you really do a good turn every day?' Nell asked. 'What did you do yesterday?'

She had asked partly from curiosity and partly to catch him out. But he seemed unfazed by the query. He looked over from frothing the boiled milk. 'Yesterday? Yesterday I sold a flat that had been on the market for, well.' He paused and grinned. 'Some time, you could say.'

Nell was immediately interested. 'It wouldn't be in Gardiner Road, would it? 19b? I live in 19a.'

He looked surprised. 'Yes, actually.'

The rain, she saw, was easing. She rose to her feet. 'Thanks for the coffee. I have to go.'

'Don't you want to know who's bought the place upstairs from you?'

'I suppose so,' Nell acknowledged.

'Well, before I tell you, you have to agree to another good turn.'

'What?'

'Let me take you out tonight for dinner.'

She stared. How brazen could you get? 'Fast mover, aren't you?'

He grinned, quite unabashed. 'Beautiful women like you don't just walk off the street every day.'

What a line, Nell thought. Yet she was flattered, despite herself. Not that she intended him to see. She didn't intend anything.

'I can't,' she said.

'Well, if not tonight, how about Friday?'

'Er . . .' Nell had not expected this level of persistence.

'Want to know about the person upstairs or not?' he asked, seizing on her hesitation.

She gave in then, and he shot her a triumphant grin. 'I'm Joey, by the way.'

CHAPTER 9

Joey had originally suggested La Cuillère Grasse, a hugely expensive local double-Michelin-starred French restaurant that occupied the site of a former greasy spoon. But Nell, alarmed at such a pricey prospect, particularly as she intended to pay her share, held out for somewhere less showy.

The compromise was the Modest Sausage, a modish bistro near the theatre. It had rows of very small tables very close together, like an exam hall. At the appointed hour, Nell walked towards it, as slowly and reluctantly as if she were actually sitting a test.

In the intervening few days, she had been on the point many times of cancelling the arrangement. She no longer cared who her upstairs neighbour was, what difference did it make? She would find out sooner or later. Nor did she want to meet Joey. What was she doing? She had no interest in him; in men full stop.

On the other hand, he was obviously the determined type and would make it hard to cancel. So it was probably best to go along with it. She had nothing else to do, anyway. She'd stay as little time as possible, then go home.

Joey was there when she arrived at the Modest Sausage,

waving at her from across a sea of people in black. Hipster theatregoers, bearded young men mostly, talking earnestly to women with red lipstick and ebony fringes.

Nell sat down, noting the two glasses of champagne on the table. He wasn't mean, she had to give him that.

'Cheers,' Joey said, raising his.

Nell took a sip, determined to pace herself. She was here only to get this over with. Although he was attractive, she had to admit. More so than she remembered. She liked his neat features and cropped hair, and the shirt that he was wearing, patterned with small flowers. Peeping from its cuff was what looked like a very expensive watch.

'So tell me,' she said, taking the retro-typed menu proffered by the waitress. 'Who's my new neighbour?'

Joey grinned and tapped his straight nose. 'First things first. I want to know all about you. Forgive me if this seems a bit forward, but are you single?'

Nell felt a mixture of offended at his cheek and embarrassed as the memory of the Apples and Pears swept over her. Joey was watching her closely. 'Did I say the wrong thing?'

Nell shook her head.

'OK, well let me tell you about me. I'm new round here. I used to be in South London but, well . . .' He hesitated.

'Didn't you like South London?' Nell was glad of this new conversational direction. The capital's geography was a safe enough subject.

He rubbed his hand over his chin. 'Things kind of didn't work out. Romance-wise, I mean.'

Oh no. They were back on romance again. She didn't want to hear about his love problems. She wanted to escape, to push back her chair and flee. She should go now, Nell thought, before the waitress came.

The waitress came.

Nell ordered the first things she set eyes on.

'You're sure?' the waitress said. 'Mussels to start with and then mussels as a main course?'

'I like mussels,' Nell said firmly.

'So it didn't work out in South London,' Joey resumed as the waitress left.

'I'm sorry,' Nell said shortly. She considered making a joke – North Londoners like her were traditionally rude about their neighbours over the river. But she didn't want to encourage him.

'It's OK. Plenty of people get dumped when they think they've found their partner for life, I guess.' He flicked her a nervous look from beneath his brows. 'I don't normally talk about it, to be honest. But . . .'

'You don't have to tell me any more,' Nell said quickly.

He gave her a rueful smile that was very different from the previous blazingly confident ones. 'I don't mind. You seem like you understand. Maybe you've been unlucky in love as well.'

Nell determinedly ignored this prompt.

'I sort of felt you had,' Joey continued. 'There's something in your eyes. I noticed it when I first saw you.'

Was it that obvious? Her mussels now arrived in a heap of dark blue shells and Nell seized on them as an excuse not to reply.

'Do you mind if I tell you all this?' he asked apologetically. 'It's just, well, a relief. It really helps.'

While she hadn't intended to play therapist to an unknown estate agent, Nell could not see what other option she had. She reminded herself that she didn't have to see him again, after this. And his story, whatever it was, was hardly likely to compare to her online dating disaster.

About this she was wrong, however.

'Left you at the altar?' she was echoing, some ten minutes later, as a heap of forgotten mussels cooled on the table before her.

Joey's story was so dramatically awful that it was impossible not to sympathise. After a whirlwind courtship, his girlfriend, Tasha, had failed to show at the register office. Later he had received a text from Italy, where she had gone with another man.

Joey looked at her over the candlelight. They had long since finished the champagne and nearly seen off a bottle of Soave. 'Now it's your turn.'

The combination of alcohol and sympathy had lowered what remained of her guard. Nell told him the whole story of the Paddington disaster.

They compared romantic misadventures for the rest of the meal. By the time they parted they had both ruefully admitted that neither of them were suitable mates for anyone else.

'So,' Joey said, suddenly drawing her close as they stood on Upper Street, 'that makes us perfect for each other.'

Nell drew back. She had not seen this coming. 'I don't think so.'

She had expected him to accept this and retreat, abashed, but Joey stood his ground. 'You're amazing, Nell,' he said, gazing deeply into her eyes. 'After everything that's happened, you deserve some happiness.'

His voice was low and cracked slightly, as if with emotion. She wanted to look away, but couldn't. She was aware of his strong shoulders, the curve of his thighs in his jeans. He pulled her to him and kissed her thoroughly and slowly. She felt lust now cloud a judgement already clouded by wine. 'What's the point of waiting?' Joey said when she made a last, feeble effort to send him home.

He was so confident, so sure, and she was so very ready to be swept off her feet. They kissed all the way back to his house in the taxi. Not long afterwards, in Joey's enormous bed, Nell found pure physical release from the sense of failure that had plagued her for so long.

The next morning, when she awoke to see sunlight falling on the polished wooden floor, it seemed to Nell that she had arrived in one of her own catalogues. His rumpled white bed with its enormous pillows only added to this effect, as did Joey, who now appeared at the bedroom door holding a tray complete with teapot and toast rack. 'Breakfast, milady.'

Nell sat up, shyly pulling the duvet over her naked breasts. 'Don't do that,' Joey said softly, putting the tray down and slipping back into bed beside her. Breakfast was never eaten.

Little was eaten that first weekend together. They spent most of it in bed, surfacing occasionally to make a cup of tea or open yet another bottle of champagne. Joey had a special fridge just for that, Nell discovered.

His circumstances were far more glamorous than she had expected. His flat, the spacious top floor of a beautiful Georgian house, was a dream of gracious living. It had lofty corniced ceilings, tall sash windows with the original shutters and polished pieces of antique furniture made of thin and delicate wood. He owned it, which must mean that he was fantastically successful at his job. Nell still hadn't found out who was moving into the flat above hers, but she no longer wanted to know. The thought of going back to the poky apartment in the drab road weighed on her. By contrast, Joey's big, light front windows overlooked an elegant street and those at the rear a long green lawn whose every blade seemed to shine.

Nor was there any comparison between Joey's neighbourhood and her own, she discovered, when they eventually emerged for a walk. The shops at the end of Gardiner Road were strictly utilitarian. There was a branch of Bargain Booze and the First Light Convenience Store, so called because of its opening hours. The windows of both shops were covered in iron mesh. At the end of Joey's street was Arcadia Walk.

In some areas of London, Arcadia Walk would be a ghastly irony. But here it more than lived up to its name. It was a succession of pretty, pastel-coloured shops selling elaborate cupcakes and high-end clutter such as toile de jouy lamps, patchwork cushions and leather pig footstools.

There was an old-fashioned ironmonger selling smart tools for smart gardening; Nell counted five different sizes and species of shovel. The newsagent stocked only the middle-class papers but all the glossy magazines. There was a traditional sweet shop (established 2005) called Just William's where bulls' eyes and pineapple chunks were poured out of glass jars on to weighing scales and sold in white paper bags with serrated edges. It had, Joey told Nell, featured in several Boden catalogue shoots.

Nell nodded; she knew just the ones. More than that, she had worked on some of them. She was enchanted but slightly disconcerted. She had always known that catalogues peddled dreams, but here the dreams were real. Arcadia Walk was perfect, just as Joey's road and flat were perfect. Most of all, he was perfect. It was as if, having been heavy, hopeless and slow, life had suddenly speeded up and acquired a bright shine. Everything was just as wonderful as it looked.

CHAPTER 10

'Marry me,' Joey repeated, as, yet again, they lay panting and tangled in the duvet. Every time she tried to get out, he pulled her back. She did not resist. There was a lot of lost time to make up for.

At first Nell had thought the proposal was a joke. At the third time of asking, she realised he meant it. 'Because – what are we waiting for?' Joey asked, nuzzling into her neck.

What indeed? Nell thought, wriggling pleasurably. Joey was like a champagne cocktail on an empty stomach. Having thought that nothing would ever happen, she now felt anything was possible.

And yet she could not quite bring herself to say yes. She had spent nearly thirty years considering things through carefully. She couldn't break the habit of a lifetime.

But Joey had clearly made up his mind. He took her hand and looked deep into her eyes. 'I want to make my commitment to you absolute. I want to be your husband.'

The flattering declaration knocked her steady head off course and sent it spinning with joy.

'We'd live here together at mine, of course,' Joey went on, throwing an arm out to include the gracious room.

Nell looked about her longingly, taking in the lovely details. 'But what about my flat?' Gardiner Road already seemed in a universe far, far away, an unimaginably dreary one.

'I'll sell it for you. I'm an estate agent, aren't I? I'll make it my business to get you an even better price than I got for that upstairs one.'

Everything was so easy to Joey, Nell thought. He had a way of cutting through complication and getting straight to the point. Perhaps things really were that simple.

'Say yes!' he pleaded. 'It's obvious we should be together. You are, quite simply, the most wonderful woman I've ever met in my life. And you seem to like me . . .'

'Oh, I do, I *do*.'

'So *carpe diem*. Seize the day,' Joey said, reaching over and seizing Nell instead.

Afterwards he returned to the subject. 'So – what do you say? What are we waiting for?'

Nell bit her lip. She just wasn't the impetuous type. It was useless pretending that she was. She tried to explain, but Joey clearly didn't understand. 'Perhaps I'd better go,' she said, and was heartbroken when he didn't try to stop her.

The following afternoon she sat in the Gardiner Road back bedroom, heart thumping in the heavy silence. Life here seemed even duller than before. Had it all been a dream? Joey hadn't been in touch at all; no calls, no texts, nothing. She felt a sense of rising panic.

She was working on *Rosey Posey*, a catalogue of stackable floral cake tins and rose-festooned ironing board covers. But it was hard to concentrate. Joey's offer was pingponging about in her mind. Perhaps she should accept it. He was right, she should seize the day.

In her agitation, Nell had started to pace about and now something outside the window caught her eye. There was a stranger in the scruffy back garden she shared with the upstairs flat. A woman, about her age but much shorter. She had a wild purplish bob and red lipstick. She wore calf-length Dr Marten boots and floaty layered skirts in shades of cinnamon and plum. She was digging with a garden fork, her face screwed up with the effort.

Nell was impressed. Her new neighbour, who presumably this was, had clearly decided the garden needed some work. Well, good for her. She must have arrived over the weekend, when Nell was at Joey's.

Come to think of it, there had been something big and strange parked outside the front of the house when Nell had arrived back. She had been too preoccupied to take in what, exactly.

She went into the sitting room. A large red Land Rover stood right in front of the projecting bay window. It blocked off most of the available light. Presumably it belonged to the woman in the garden. If she stayed here, Nell realised, this would be her view.

She went back into the bedroom, but the woman in the garden was gone. Nell was about to sit down at her desk again when she heard knocking on her door.

The woman with purple hair stood on her threshold. She was peeling off her gardening gloves.

'Sorry to bother you,' she said with a wide and radiant smile. 'I'm Rachel. I've just moved in upstairs.'

'Nell.' They shook hands. Nell was struck by the woman's eyes. They were a startling china-doll blue, fringed with long lashes. There was something piercing and determined about them.

'I just came to see if I could borrow some tea.'

'Tea?' Nell hesitated. Did she have tea? She had only been away a weekend, but she could hardly remember what she had in her flat now, or where. 'I might have some Earl Grey.'

'Great. I'm desperate for a cuppa. Been digging for *hours*. I thought there was no one in downstairs but then I saw you just now, heading out of the room.'

Nell remembered her manners. She would benefit from an overhauled garden too. 'Come in.' She looked doubtfully at Rachel's mud-clogged Dr Martens.

'I should have picked some tea up earlier.' Rachel dropped to one knee to unlace her dirty boots. 'I meant to, but I was taking Juno to her new school and everything else went clean out of my head. Juno's my daughter,' she added.

So a child had moved in too, or a teenager. A family, in other words. Three people would find it cramped upstairs, Nell thought.

She showed Rachel into the sitting room and went to switch the kettle on. She came back to find her neighbour yawning hugely. 'Sorry,' Rachel grinned. 'I've only got to sit down at the moment and I drop off. I get up at five, you see.'

'*Five?*' Nell gasped.

'To study.'

'You're a student?'

'Only at that time. At seven Juno gets up and then I work during the day. Normally, I mean. I'm having the day off today, because of Juno starting her new school. I wanted to go and meet the teachers, settle her in and all that.'

'Where do you work?' Nell asked. The purple hair suggested arts administration.

The answer was a surprise. 'In an insurance office.'

'Is it an insurance qualification you're studying for?'

Her new neighbour laughed and explained she was reading for a law degree. Her aim, she added, was to be a barrister.

The kettle clicked off in the kitchen and Nell hurried through. After hunting about for a tray, a plate, biscuits, she returned to find Rachel studying her bookshelves. She pulled out a volume, turned and grinned.

'I love this book.' Rachel waved *All Smiles*.

The tray shook in Nell's hand. It was the same copy she had taken to Paddington Station for the ill-fated blind date.

'Awful what happened to Dylan Eliot, isn't it?' Rachel was saying.

'What happened?' Nell wasn't sure she cared all that much. Dylan Eliot hadn't done a great deal for her recently.

'Almost died in a house fire.'

'How awful!' Nell had not expected a disaster of this magnitude. The poor man!

'His book was destroyed, his new one. It was on his computer.'

'What a nightmare!' Nell felt guilty about the blame she had heaped on *All Smiles*. What had occurred at the Apples and Pears was hardly its author's fault.

'Didn't you know?' Rachel was clearly surprised. 'It just happened, this weekend. He's in hospital. It's been in all the papers.'

'I didn't really read the papers this weekend.' She had had better things to do. Hurriedly, Nell poured the tea and handed a mug to Rachel.

'So what is it that you do?' Rachel reached for a chocolate chip cookie.

She laughed once Nell explained. 'So you're the reason I have a pair of snakeskin Birkenstocks I never wear. They looked great in *Driftwood* and awful on me. But I've never got round to sending them back.'

Nell hurriedly pointed out that *Driftwood* was not one of her contracts and was anyway notorious in catalogue copywriting circles for promising infinitely more than it could ever deliver. The images of elfin women in floating linens drifting like dryads through misty tree trunks sat ill with the fact that its actual customers were middle-aged commuters who needed clothes that still looked good after an hour on Southeastern trains.

'Enjoy it?' Rachel queried.

'Well, I enjoyed it more when I ran my PR business,' Nell confessed. 'But that went under in the recession. I'd like to start it up again, but . . .' She hesitated. She hadn't given Phoenix a thought for days, she realised.

'Can't you?'

'Well, I'd like to . . .' Even to her own ears Nell sounded half-hearted. And yet only a few days ago she had been determined to relaunch.

'Then you should,' Rachel said firmly. 'What's stopping you?'

Nell shrugged. 'I'll get it together eventually.'

'Oh God,' Rachel exclaimed suddenly. 'I'm so sorry!' She was looking at the window.

'What's the matter?' Nell asked, glad of the change of subject.

'The Baron! Out there!'

Nell looked. There was no sign of what the description suggested: an aristocratic gentleman in a topper, monocle and opera cloak. All that was visible in the window was the rusty side of the Land Rover. 'I can't see him.'

Rachel was laughing. 'The Baron's what Charlie called the Land Rover,' she explained. 'The Red Baron. Because it's red.'

Charlie, presumably, was Rachel's husband. Or partner.

'It's in the way, blocking your light. I'll move it. I didn't realise.'

'Is it difficult to drive?' Nell asked. The vehicle looked enormous and Rachel was pint-sized. Could she even see over the wheel?

'It's a bit of a truck. But I could never get rid of it. The Baron was Charlie's pride and joy.'

Why did she refer to him in the past tense? Nell wondered. 'He doesn't live with you?'

'He died,' Rachel said simply. 'I'm a widow.'

Nell thought of Rachel's Dr Martens. Her purple hair. Her relative youth. 'A *widow*?'

'We come in all shapes and sizes and ages, we relicts. We don't wear black veils any more.'

Nell's face was burning. 'I'm so sorry.' What had happened to Charlie? It would obviously be insensitive to ask.

'It was cancer,' Rachel said. She smiled at Nell. 'It's OK. I can talk about him. In fact, I quite like to.'

'He must have been very young,' Nell ventured.

'He was.' Rachel's dark eyebrows shot up ruefully. 'He might have survived if they'd caught it earlier, but there was a mess-up – I won't go into details, it's too tedious. Point was, by the time it got straightened out the tumours were everywhere.'

'How awful.' What else could she say? It *was* awful.

Rachel shrugged. 'They gave me compensation. That's how I managed to buy this flat. But,' she added, with a sigh, 'it doesn't compensate for Juno growing up without a father and me soldiering on without a husband.'

Nell sensed that her neighbour had decided to open up, to seize this chance to talk, as if she didn't often have one. She felt flattered to be the chosen confidante.

Rachel drained her mug. 'I have to second-guess what Charlie would have wanted. And he's missing all the milestones, like the new school today.'

'It must be lonely,' Nell offered, sympathetically. Lonely was something she knew a bit about, after all.

'It can be,' Rachel admitted. 'But I just have to get on with it.'

Nell drew in a breath. Getting on with it. She knew how that felt too.

Poor Rachel, alone upstairs with her daughter. It occurred to Nell now that if she turned down Joey's offer she would be alone too. But without a child. Probably with no hope of ever having one. The thought was the final push she needed.

Rachel was on her feet. 'I'd better go. Time to get Juno from school.' She raised a pair of crossed fingers. 'Hopefully it's gone well.'

'I'm sure it will have,' Nell said comfortingly.

She was rewarded with one of Rachel's warm smiles. 'Thanks for the tea. I'll return the favour soon.'

Nell saw her out, rather regretting she wouldn't be staying in Gardiner Road after all. It might have been nice to get to know Rachel better.

CHAPTER 11

Dylan opened his eyes. As ever, with the first glimpse of the hospital strip light, he experienced miserable disappointment. His eyes dropped to his bandaged arms, then across to the tubes and screens and drips and monitors. He was still here. It really had all happened.

He shifted slightly up the pillows, and a passing nurse, the fat, friendly one he liked, noticed his movement and came over. 'And how are we this morning, Mr Eliot?'

A good question, Dylan thought. How were we? Conscious, at least, which we hadn't always been. Dylan had been in hospital for several weeks before he'd even known he still existed; waking one morning to find himself plastered in bandages and immobilised on a bed with tubes emerging from every orifice.

He had been helicoptered from the burning cottage. The alarm had been raised by the farmer and the air ambulance had arrived just in time.

'Otherwise I'd not only have died, but saved everyone the trouble of a cremation,' Dylan quipped to Mr Davie, the consultant in charge of him.

'You could put it like that.'

He'd been found unconscious in the kitchen, having

managed somehow, possibly by rolling on the floor, to put out the flames on his clothes. But smoke inhalation had almost finished its deadly work.

The consultant had described how tubes had been inserted to pump oxygen down his damaged throat. There had been the matter of keeping his fluids up. And then, as Dylan had come round, there had been pain.

It had been of a level he had never previously suspected existed. Morphine had helped, but not dulled it entirely. It grumbled all day beneath his bandages and screamed when, every eight hours, he was put in the tub to have his dressings changed. He'd known, of course, that the skin was the largest organ in the body. But it had never really behaved like an organ before. He'd come to think of it as a protective shell, not the exposed, vulnerable and delicate thing it actually was.

Dylan had always been squeamish. He hadn't even seen his injuries, tightly closing his eyes when his dressings were changed. But the nurses' occasional sharp breath told him that what they were looking at wasn't pretty. Still, at least the prognosis was good. He should – eventually – make a full recovery.

Incredibly, there were jokes about burns units. Mr Davie had told him quite a good one. He'd wanted to repeat it to his parents but could see they thought his condition no laughing matter.

His mother and father assumed the fire was an awful accident. The idea that it was deliberate did not seem to have crossed their minds and Dylan had tried to stop it crossing his. The possibility that Beatrice had been responsible was too awful to contemplate.

He had not contemplated it at first, in fact. He had not contemplated anything. His mind had mostly been a blank. Shock, the consultant explained, and to be expected. But gradually, as the doors had opened in his memory, one of them had yielded up another door. The open door of the burning cottage.

Dylan had studied the remembered image, surprised. How could this have happened? Delighted though he'd been to finish his novel, in a hurry though he was to get down to the cove and surf, he would never have left his home unlocked. And then there was the companion image, of the fiery hollow in the centre of the blaze. And in that, the cloven hooves of Beatrice's surf boots. Curling and melting in the heat.

He tried to suppress these pictures burning in his mind. While the idea of Beatrice having murder in her soul was possible, he would not have imagined her capable of the organisation such an attack would involve. She must have watched the cottage. Waited for him to go out. She must have been intending to destroy his work. But that she had succeeded in eradicating an entire novel would have been beyond her wildest dreams. Had she read about it in the papers? he wondered. It had been all over them, according to his mother.

There was a police investigation under way, Dylan knew, but no conclusions as yet. With any luck they, like his parents, would decide it was an accident. He wanted to avoid a court case. Not because of any wish to protect Beatrice; the person he wanted to protect was himself. He wanted the Beatrice chapter to be as irrevocably closed as all the other chapters that had gone up in smoke.

An entire year's work had been wiped out, and with it his future. That *Charm Itself* would never see the light of day meant the definitive end of his career as an author. He had been thinking about doing something else anyway; something more challenging. Now the decision had been made for him.

'Visitor for you, Mr Eliot.' It was the friendly nurse again. Dylan opened his eyes, not sure if he had been asleep.

What visitor? His agent again, to spur him back to the

keyboard? Dylan's announcement about stopping writing had met with disbelief. 'Of course you'll write another book, dear boy,' Julian had said, in so exaggeratedly relaxed a tone Dylan knew he must be horrified. 'You'll bounce back. The best is yet to come.'

A glamorous brunette was now sitting down beside him. He did not recognise her. She was slimly elegant, with a delicate little face under a shining cap of short dark hair. She wore a navy blue shift dress and a big silver bangle that matched the silver hoops in her ears. She leaned towards him, dark cardigan slung over her shoulders, slim, tanned arms folded over the bag on her knee.

'Dylan,' she said softly. 'It's me. Eve.'

Dylan stared into the grave, dark gaze. Eve?

'Don't tell me you've forgotten me already.'

Dylan tried to shrug, which was not something he had done for a while. And perhaps this effort triggered another because quite suddenly, out of the blue, Dylan knew exactly who Eve was. His editor, at his publisher's.

A flurry of images appeared behind his eyes. A large, light office in the corner of a tall building. A view over some Central London park.

'Eve.' Dylan attempted to raise himself. Too quickly; pain knifed through him. After the spasm was over he said, 'It's nice of you to come.'

Eve wrinkled her elegant nose. 'You know "nice" isn't one of my favourite words.'

They'd had a conversation about favourite words, he could now remember. Over lunch, at some smart place in the West End. He recalled white tablecloths, shining cutlery, oysters. The taste of oysters! Salty, creamy, with a sharp shot of shallot vinegar. He felt his spirits lift. He decided to tell her a joke.

'Heard the one about the Serious Burns Unit?'

The shining cap of hair shook in a wary negative.

'So, an English doctor's being shown round a Scottish hospital, right?'

'Right.'

'He gets to a ward where the patients all look fine. No obvious signs of injury. Right?'

'Er . . . OK.'

'He goes to the first patient and has a look at him. The guy says . . .'

Dylan tried to imitate the consultant's Scottish accent for the next bit.

'Fair fa' your honest, sonsie face,

Great chieftain o' the puddin'-race!

Aboon them a' ye tak your place . . .'

Eve's face was a picture. Her fine black brows were drawn together in the effort to understand.

Dylan grinned. He was almost enjoying himself. 'So the English doctor's a bit surprised, right? He goes on to the next patient, who doesn't look injured either. And this guy turns to the doctor and says . . .'

Dylan took a deep breath. He hoped he'd remembered it correctly.

'Some hae meat and canna eat,

And some wad eat that want it

But we hae meat and we can eat

And sae the Lord be thankit.'

Sudden comprehension flashed over Eve's features. She rolled her eyes and clapped her hands. 'That's terrible, Dylan. The Serious *Burns* Unit. As in Rabbie Burns. My God, that's just about the worst joke ever.'

Their eyes held each other's and just for a split second, Dylan experienced the delicious sensation of being normal. More than normal. People didn't expect to come into places like this and laugh. He had surprised her, and that was a sort of power.

Eve was shaking her head. 'Glad to see you're still thinking in literary terms. That's what I want to talk to you about, actually.'

Dylan's smile faded. So Eve had an agenda. She wasn't here just for a social call. Of course she wasn't.

Eve had always been a friend to him, but even more, she was an editor. Without her, *All Smiles* would never have been so successful. She'd championed it from the start, pressed it into people's hands, got her marketing team behind it. She'd even come up with the way it looked, the Rolling Stones mouth.

But it didn't look that way now, of course. Something else was stirring in his memory. There was a new cover, a striped one. Orange and white. He'd seen it; but where? More pictures were struggling back. The inside of a taxi. The inside of a station. A grotty concourse pub; he'd sat in the corner. Then floating into his memory came a pale-haired woman, a woman who looked like an angel.

Who on earth was that?

He found himself looking up into Eve's face. She was leaning forward again. 'Dylan. About *Charm Itself* . . .'

'I'm sorry,' he muttered, meaning that he was sorry that he didn't want to talk about it. But he had moved too suddenly again. He closed his eyes as the pain flashed and throbbed.

Eve interpreted this as apology for his non-delivery. 'Don't be,' she said. 'Just put it behind you. For now. You can rewrite it, Dylan. When you're better.'

He spoke through gritted teeth, without opening his eyes. 'No. I won't.'

There was a silence from the side of the bed. Then he felt Eve's cool fingers tentatively touch his own. He opened his eyes;

she was looking straight at him. 'I can imagine that's the way it feels now—'

He cut savagely in. 'No. You can't imagine. You can't even begin to.'

He told her then. How angry he had felt after the fire. How he had been unable to accept that everything had gone. How his mind had clawed at the manuscript's loss as if sheer force of thought could bring it back. Frustration had been followed by helplessness, then, finally, acceptance. The grieving process after a death, he had heard, went much the same way. This was a death. The death of a novelist.

'You don't mean it,' Eve said gently. 'You have such great talent, Dylan. You're a great brand.'

'Brand!' He knew what she meant: a successful commercial entity. But the word also conjured up great burning beams crashing around him. Dylan felt that he didn't like either meaning.

'OK, maybe that wasn't the right word.' Eve hastened to undo the damage. 'But you'll write *Charm* again. You're an artist. Artists have to express themselves. You just need time, that's all.'

He glared at her from his pillows. What was it about the words 'it's over' that she didn't understand?

'I'm not an artist,' he said, grinding out the words. 'People think I am because I knocked out a book and it did well and caught the bloody zeitgeist or whatever.'

Eve was nodding. 'You did and it did and it was brilliant. And you'll do it again.'

He tried to raise himself up in his bed but a shaft of pain brought him down again. 'You're right,' Dylan began, getting a mordant satisfaction from seeing Eve look pleased. She wouldn't be looking pleased in a minute.

'You're right that an artist would want to carry on writing, That's how I know I'm not one. I can't think of anything worse.'

Bewilderment flashed in Eve's brown eyes. 'You don't mean that, Dylan. I can't believe you do.'

She paused, but as he didn't contradict her, she continued. 'Well, if that really is the case I have to say I'm disappointed. You're letting us down. Not just me and Julian, but your readers as well.'

Indignation was rising within Dylan. This was outrageous. He'd almost died in a fire! He opened his mouth to bluster, but she continued, in her steady tone, 'You have responsibilities.'

'If this is about the advance . . .' he interrupted rudely.

Eve rolled her eyes. 'It's not about the money, Dylan. It's about you. We all believed in you – we still do – and now you're going to let us down.'

It was too much, Dylan decided. Too much to make him feel responsible, when the person responsible was bloody Beatrice!

'I've heard you say before that you felt you needed more of a challenge,' Eve went on. 'Well, here is a challenge. Get out of hospital and back at your keyboard and give us the book we're all waiting for.'

Never, vowed Dylan. Silent and furious, he turned his face to the wall and would answer no more questions.

Eve had not finished, however. Her disappointed tones floated over from the far side of the bed. 'Look, Dylan. What's happened to you is dreadful. No one's saying it isn't. It's going to be very hard to write again after this. But that's the very reason you should do it, don't you see?'

Dylan glared at the wall and said nothing. Why didn't Eve see? Writing was over for him. He wanted nothing else to do with it. When he got out of here, if he ever did, and when he worked again, if he ever did, he was going to get a job as remote from a keyboard as was possible. In a place as different from Cornwall, as far from the sea as he could find.

CHAPTER 12

Within an hour of Nell's acceptance – by text, as he seemed unobtainable any other way – the flowers from Joey began to arrive. Arrangement after arrangement, in van after different van. There were large ones with lilies and small ones with rosebuds and everything in between. Her small sitting room billowed with blooms and colour, scent and cellophane, ribbons and small gold envelopes on sticks carrying messages. 'I Love You', 'I'm So Proud', 'Together For Ever' and, best of all, 'To My Wife'.

'I could open a florist's in Gardiner Road!' Nell exclaimed, when finally he answered his mobile. 'And how appropriate is that?'

'How do you mean?' His tone was indulgent, but puzzled.

'Gardiner. Like gardener,' Nell explained, laughing. It wasn't that good a joke but excitement had made her giddy.

Later that evening, in his flat, their reunion was ecstatic.

'We need to fix a date,' Joey declared. He was gazing at her from his pillow. 'As soon as possible!'

Nell felt a bubbling happiness. But it couldn't be that soon, not the actual wedding date. People took ages to get married. Years, sometimes. But they could start the ball rolling, definitely.

There was a beautiful church at the end of Joey's road. Elegant and Georgian, with a white wooden bell tower and a clock with golden hands. Her mind tumbled with white dresses, veils, bridesmaids.

Joey had propped himself upon his elbow. 'Register office, don't you think? Then we can do it really, really quickly.'

Part of Nell wondered what the rush was. But a much bigger part didn't want to puncture the moment and risk upsetting Joey again.

She quietly put aside the idea of marrying in church. She wasn't all that religious anyway and a London register office would be glamorous and romantic. Chic, in a Sixties black-and-white photo sort of way. And in a catalogue way too. She'd done a bridal one once on a Beatles wedding theme, all miniskirts and white plastic boots . . .

She snuggled up to Joey. 'When are you going to go and tell my father?' Dad would be amazed, she thought. Possibly disconcerted. 'Bit previous, isn't it?' she could imagine him saying.

But Joey would win him round. He could charm the birds from the trees. Convince anyone about anything.

Joey's reply took her by surprise. 'We don't need to tell anyone. It can be just us. Me and you!'

Nell tried to answer his smile with one of her own, but alarm was clanging through her. Getting married quickly was one thing. But doing so without telling her parents was quite another. They would want to be involved. She was their only daughter.

Nell rolled away and stared, worried, at the polished door of the antique wardrobe. She had not expected this.

'What's the matter?' Joey propped his face on her shoulder.

Nell felt nervous, but she had to tell him the truth. He

was to be her husband, after all. 'My mum would be devastated,' she admitted quietly. 'And my dad would probably be pretty cross.'

Joey did not reply. She had her back to him, so couldn't see his face.

'I guess we need to think about it,' Nell offered hurriedly, and to her relief, Joey took the olive branch. He wrapped his arms round her and gave her a big squeeze. 'Guess we do.'

They went out to celebrate with supper at the Pink Pirate, the local gastropub. Joey ordered a bottle of champagne, which arrived at the table in a shining bucket accompanied by two gleaming flutes. It was brought in person by Larry, the manager, a spry septuagenarian with gelled-up blue hair and jeans which fell off his bum like a teenager's. 'Enjoy!' he instructed them, before flouncing off into the bar.

Nell was eager to do just this, but Joey seemed quiet and withdrawn.

'What's the matter?' she asked softly. Perhaps he was tired.

He lifted troubled eyes to hers.

'Is everything OK?' Nell pressed, worried.

'Your parents,' he began.

This 'asking for her hand' thing again! 'Look, you'll love them,' Nell exclaimed. 'And they'll love you. You just have to meet them.'

He smiled ruefully, and reached for her fingers. 'I'm sure they're wonderful.'

Nell grinned. 'Well, they have their moments. Like everyone's mum and dad.'

'I wouldn't know.' Joey spoke quietly.

'What do you mean, you wouldn't know?' Something in his tone alarmed her. He was looking at her as if wondering whether to tell her something. Something momentous, evidently.

'Go on,' Nell urged, her heart hammering. 'Tell me. Why wouldn't you know about my parents?'

'Because I don't have any parents.' Joey clung hard to her hand.

'What . . . you mean they died?'

'Might have been better if they had.' He narrowed his eyes and looked, momentarily, like a different person from the one she knew. 'I was brought up in a children's home.' He now pulled his hand from hers, as if emphasising his loneliness in the world.

Nell's insides twisted with anguish. Poor Joey, he'd really been through it. Being dumped at the altar was bad enough without being dumped at birth as well.

'It doesn't matter. I'm a big grown-up boy now.' Joey gave her a brave smile. 'I made it without them.'

'Oh poor you. Poor, poor you.' Nell was passionate in her sympathy.

'So that's why I don't want to have family at the wedding,' Joey went on. 'Do you see?'

'Of *course* I do!'

'Do you mind?' His gaze was melting.

Nell shook her head. What choice did she have? She'd square it with her parents afterwards. Somehow.

She felt vindicated when she saw his eyes fill with tears. It was wonderful to make someone so happy. She told herself that it didn't matter about her parents, about Mum not being able to fuss over a hat. What mattered was that Joey wasn't afraid to show emotion and was so honest with her. Here was someone who would never let her down.

Afterwards, they walked back to the flat via the nearby heath, holding hands. It was a soft, early summer evening and the sun glowed brightly through the leaves. It was like a dream, Nell thought. A beautiful dream about the beautiful life she and Joey were going to have together. The golden future unfolded before her like a page from one of her own catalogues. But this was no fantasy spun with professional words and pictures. Her happiness was as solid and real as it was possible for happiness to be.

One evening midweek, Nell popped back to Gardiner Road. Her mission was to explain things to her new neighbour. It felt wrong to have had such a friendly meeting and then just to move out without a word.

She stood, awkwardly, on Rachel's threshold. 'I'm getting married,' she blurted.

It wasn't the most elegant of announcements but Rachel seemed thrilled for her. 'Congratulations! Have to say, though, I did slightly wonder what was going on. All those flower vans arriving at all hours.'

Nell wondered if Rachel thought it was strange that she had not mentioned the wedding when they met. She hoped not.

'And I'm moving out,' she added apologetically.

Rachel chuckled. 'I gathered that from the For Sale sign.'

According to Joey, Carrington's had already shown five interested parties round the flat. Selling it really was as easy as he'd said it would be.

'Come in!' Rachel invited. 'Have a drink!'

The upstairs flat was cluttered, yet had definite style. Rachel seemed to have a way of mixing vintage pieces with contemporary. Bright modernist prints in white wooden frames hung above a chaise longue covered with a fur throw. The kitchen table was new, but its surrounding chairs were mismatched and old.

Nell peered out into the rear garden. It looked different from up here, perhaps because Rachel had done so much. She and

Juno seemed to have lots of plans. They would put in lettuces immediately, plant bulbs in the autumn and, in spring, calendula and dahlias. By next summer, Rachel said happily, the back would be a riot of colour.

Juno was not in evidence. It was only eight o'clock but she was already asleep. 'She's finding the new school exhausting,' Rachel reported. Nell was impressed, as well as relieved. She wasn't sure what she would say to a child, and Juno, to judge from the photos around Rachel's flat, was a child with an unnervingly direct stare. She had a long, serious face and her side-parted hair, fixed neatly with a clasp, gave her an old-fashioned, Forties air.

The other notable photograph was that of a handsome, fair-haired man holding a baby. Charlie, presumably.

'Yes, that's him.' Rachel handed Nell a glass of wine. 'Isn't he lovely?' She spoke with as much fond ease as if Charlie were actually in the room, or had just stepped out. A wave of sympathy rippled through Nell, followed by one of relief that Joey was alive, well and indisputably hers.

'To your wedding!' Rachel raised her glass. 'So tell me all about it!'

'There's not much to tell.'

'Big? Small? Cathedral? Beach?'

Nell giggled. 'It's just going to be the two of us. Register office.'

'How romantic! Clever, as well.'

'Do you think so?' Nell was relieved. Rachel's opinion seemed important, especially as it was the only vote so far returned. For obvious reasons, her family were only going to be told afterwards. The only others in on the secret were the register office and the people booked to do her hair and make-up. She'd allowed herself that much ceremony, at least.

'*Very* clever,' Rachel confirmed. 'Organising weddings is such a faff. Especially if you have to do everything yourself. Charlie and I were so poor we literally had to butter the bread for the sandwiches.'

She described how they had married in the country near where Rachel's mother lived. Friends and family had pitched in with cakes, flowers and food. Even Rachel's dress had been made by a friend. It all sounded, Nell thought with a prick of envy, rather lovely.

'What are you going to wear?' Rachel poured her more wine. 'Meringue?' She looked at Nell critically. 'No, I can't see you in that. You're too stylish.'

Nell was pleased to be thought stylish by Rachel. She sipped happily from her glass. It was fun to have a girly conversation like this, one part and parcel of being a bride, especially as she hadn't thought it was going to be possible. Friends like Rose and Lucy were not being invited or informed.

She described the minidress, a simple shift made of lots of white crocheted daisies sewn together, worn with white PVC knee boots. Both were from a website called 'Lady Marmalade'. 'I loved the idea of that Swinging London thing,' Nell explained. 'I wanted lots of Sixties touches, even though it's just us two.'

Rachel got it immediately. 'Absolutely. Linda McCartney outside Marylebone Register Office. You'll look amazing. You've got those colt legs and I can just imagine those enormous eyes of yours with lashings of Twiggy mascara and eyeliner. And your hair will look wonderful all down and straight with a circlet of daisies.'

Nell was delighted. 'That's it exactly. You should be a stylist, not a lawyer.'

'I'd rather be a lawyer.' Rachel was beaming at her. 'Joey's a lucky man; I look forward to meeting him sometime.'

Something stirred in the back of Nell's brain: her first encounter with Joey at the estate agent's. 'But you *have* met him. He sold you this flat. Dark hair, lovely smile, really charming, really, *really* handsome . . . ?' She stopped herself, and blushed.

Rachel was laughing. 'You're crazy about him!' She knitted her brows slightly. 'Actually, it was a woman who showed me round. I'm not sure she smiled once.'

'Oh well,' said Nell, dismissing this insignificant misunderstanding. 'You'll meet him at some stage.'

Given their new intimacy, and all the details she had revealed, it was on the tip of Nell's tongue to ask Rachel to the wedding. But Joey, with his embargo on guests, might not approve. She felt the unasked question hang uncomfortably in the air.

Rachel, with her talent for ungluing sticky moments, swiftly changed the subject. 'What about the honeymoon?'

Nell relaxed immediately at the prospect of this wonderful treat. 'We're going to a gastropub in Leicestershire for a week. In a beautiful village in the grounds of an amazing stately home,' she revealed. 'Joey's organised the whole thing.'

'Groom's prerogative,' Rachel smiled. 'And lucky you. Charlie organised a week's camping on Skye. Sky was more or less all we saw – wet and grey for the most part. So we just stayed in the tent and . . . kept warm.' She flashed Nell a wicked grin.

She was so brave, Nell thought. And so cheerful and generous. 'You must miss him so much,' she found herself saying.

'I do, but I've got Juno. So part of him carries on. I'm lucky, really. She's a wonderful girl.'

'Well, she has a wonderful mother,' Nell said, then reddened, this being a lavish sort of compliment. Yet she already felt closer to Rachel than to, say, Rose and Lucy. That she had only just met her did not seem to matter, any more than it did with Joey. Clearly, this was the summer for making fast, firm friends, not to mention fiancés.

'Good. Well, I hope you'll be really, really happy.' Rachel was rising to her feet. 'But you'll have to excuse me. I've got to go to bed. I'm up at five, remember.'

Nell scrambled upwards.

'Good luck,' Rachel said warmly, at the door. 'You have to tell me all about it afterwards. We'll stay in touch, I hope.'

'Of course we will!' Nell assured her wholeheartedly.

The following evening, Nell and Joey visited the local register office to make the final arrangements. On the first floor of the Edwardian town hall, it was reached by a polished-wood staircase with fat, heavily carved banisters. The ceremony room was elegant, panelled and lit by windows leaded with municipal crests. There was a lot of civic hardware on the walls: an engraved silver spade used for some long-ago tree-planting, some chains of office spread out in a glass case and an ornate mace used for the type of civic processions that didn't happen any more. There was a dais, with a pair of imposing chairs. 'Disney thrones,' Joey whispered to Nell, making her giggle.

It really was all happening, although she still worried some-times that she was imagining it all. Sometimes she dreamed she was back in Gardiner Road and when she woke to find herself next to Joey, the sun pouring in through slatted white blinds, she felt weak with gratitude.

The registrar was large in biscuit-coloured occasion knitwear and a hairstyle reminiscent of an orange chrysanthemum. To Nell's secret relief she seemed unfazed by the idea of just the two of them getting married. 'But you'll need two witnesses,' she said. 'I can probably get one of the staff here to be one, but you'll need to find one yourselves.'

Joey and Nell looked at each other. An idea sprang into Nell's mind. 'How about Rachel?' she suggested suddenly. 'She'd be perfect.'

'Who's Rachel?'

'My upstairs neighbour in Gardiner Road. The one you . . .' Nell was about to say 'sold the flat to', before remembering that Rachel had said it was a woman. But, come to think of it, she was sure Joey had said he had done the deal.

Joey's mobile was ringing. He frowned at it. 'Got to take this,' he said. He glanced at Nell. 'Good idea. Call your friend.'

The flat sale business flew from her mind as Nell did just that. Rachel whooped with delight. 'I'd adore to! What an honour! And a great excuse to dress up. We love dressing up.'

'We?' Nell echoed, uncertain. Had Rachel got some new man in her life? She hadn't mentioned him, but there was a lot that Nell hadn't mentioned either.

'Me and Juno.'

'Oh yes. Of course.'

Nell was relieved, but nervous. Would Joey mind about Rachel's daughter? But she could hardly be left at home.

Joey was on his mobile with his back turned, so could not be asked. And by the time he had come off, some five minutes later, Nell was back in her world of blissful pre-bridal planning, and quite forgot to mention it.

CHAPTER 13

The sun poured cheerfully down and even the traffic roared its support as Nell emerged from the taxi outside the register office. It was her wedding morning and she felt like the luckiest girl in the world.

Rachel, as arranged, was waiting on the steps. She looked magnificent in a fitted sheath of deep cherry satin, with matching heels. Her burgundy curls were twisted up into a chignon, revealing her piquant little face with some previously unsuspected high cheekbones. A girl of about ten stood beside her.

'Fantastic dress,' Nell said admiringly.

Rachel looked down at herself. 'This old thing?'

'Don't give me that.'

'Seriously, it *is* an old thing. But date-perfect for your do. Vintage Dior,1965.'

Nell smiled at the child next to Rachel. 'And this must be Juno.'

The girl inclined her head gravely. With her long, pale face and mouse-coloured, side-parted hair, Juno looked even more serious in the flesh than in the photograph in Rachel's flat. Her clothes were a surprise.

If she had thought about what Juno might wear, which she

hadn't, Nell might have expected something along the lines of Rachel's own usual outfits: coloured layers, spots and stripes, something arty and shabby chic.

But the child wore a severe, old-fashioned, dark green two-piece tweed suit, set off with a small round brooch, white blouse and a pair of flat brown pumps. The effect, of a miniature headmistress from the wartime, was completed with a pair of round, gold-framed spectacles.

'Juno's channelling Miss Marple,' Rachel explained.

'Miss Marple?' Nell was puzzled. 'As in Agatha Christie?'

'Absolutely. Juno's mad about Agatha Christie.' Rachel patted her daughter's head. 'She loves mysteries.'

Juno's grey eyes, magnified by her glasses, met Nell's calmly. She seemed incredibly self-possessed. You probably had to be, if you were an only child whose father had died, Nell remembered sadly.

'She thought Miss Marple would be good for the Sixties theme,' Rachel went on. 'She found the outfit herself in a second-hand shop. It must have belonged to a very small old lady.'

'I love the brooch,' Nell said, dipping slightly to examine the circlet of woven metal flowers.

'It's got foxgloves in it,' Juno offered, speaking for the first time in a clear, assured voice. 'Which I think is very Marple. Foxgloves are poisonous.'

The magnified grey eyes remained steady. For Nell, the brilliance of the morning seemed to flicker slightly.

Rachel laughed. 'She's got quite a vivid – not to say morbid – imagination. You look *gorgeous*, by the way. I love the boots!'

Nell stuck out a leg to admire her gleaming footwear and smoothed down the white crochet minidress. She couldn't wait for Joey to see it. She forgot the foxgloves and felt about to burst with happiness and excitement.

'And your hair is beautiful,' Rachel was saying. Nell put her hand up to feel the circlet of freshly picked daisies that the hairdresser had woven in only that morning. As dawn broke she'd been scouring Queen's Park for them; '. . . and I can tell you,' the hairdresser had said, 'it's not all daisies in Queen's Park at sunrise.'

Perhaps, Nell thought, she should have got the hair daisies from the florist who had supplied the chic little bouquet of white marguerites she held in her gloved white hands. But one couldn't think of everything.

'Love the make-up too,' Rachel added, to Nell's secret relief. The make-up artist had ladled on eyeshadow of a Liz Taylor turquoise and Nell was worried she looked less Twiggy and Swinging London than Mrs Khrushchev at the Kremlin Christmas party. It was definitely something blue.

'Where's your husband?' Juno asked. Her voice, after her mother's friendly gush, sounded unemotional, almost accusing.

It sent a pang of anxiety through Nell, although she kept smiling. 'You haven't seen him?'

'Were we supposed to?' Rachel asked.

Joey was, Nell explained, meant to have been on the steps with the others when she arrived. He must have got there early and would be inside, checking last-minute arrangements.

'He must have got here *very* early in that case,' remarked Juno, her eyes through the round glasses fixed steadily on Nell. 'Because we've been here for *ages*.' There was, Nell decided, something rather relentless about her.

'Not *that* long, darling,' Rachel put in hurriedly.

Juno rounded on her mother. '*Ages*, Mum,' she insisted. 'You said we had to be here early in case Nell was.'

While rattled by Juno, Nell was touched by this evidence of Rachel's loyalty. 'Let's go in, anyway,' she suggested.

There was no sign of Joey inside, however. Nell, Rachel and Juno were shown to a side room off the main chamber by the assistant registrar, a small, bespectacled woman with thinning hair and a twittery manner. She was to be the other witness.

Muzak was playing softly in the background. 'Raindrops Keep Falling on my Head' was wonderfully inappropriate, given the golden weather outside.

Nell chattered to the others to keep her nerves at bay. All brides, she knew, felt the same churning anxiety. It was perfectly normal.

It was annoying of Joey not to be here, but understandable. The groom had a lot to do on a wedding morning, even one as minimal as theirs. No doubt he would be getting ready. The assistant registrar hadn't seen him either, but this was no cause for concern. Nell longed to call him, but getting out her mobile in front of Rachel and Juno – *especially* Juno – would make her look anxious. Which she wasn't. It might even make her look desperate, which she absolutely wasn't either.

She beamed happily at the others and shifted on her plastic chair.

'Perhaps he's forgotten something – the ring, maybe, ha ha – and gone back to the flat.'

Rachel smiled reassuringly, while Juno merely looked at Nell steadily.

Her heart was beating loud and fast – with excitement, Nell supposed. Inside her gloves, her hands were hot and sticky. To stop it wilting, she laid the bouquet on a seat next to the white patent clutch bag that matched the boots.

'We have these chairs at school,' Juno remarked suddenly.

Nell leapt on this with nervous relief. 'How *is* your new school?'

'It's not new any more,' Juno pointed out. 'It's OK, I s'pose. Though no one knows who Agatha Christie is. Someone asked me if she was on *X Factor*,' the girl added contemptuously.

Nell snorted and Juno gave her a stony look. Rachel, meanwhile, was twisting her fingers together nervously. Anyone would think she was the bride, not me, Nell thought.

Quiet fell. Traffic could be heard whooshing by on the road. Come on, Joey, Nell silently urged, wishing that she hadn't, after all, spent the previous night alone in a five-star hotel. It had been Joey's idea; his treat, too. Husbands and wives, he insisted, should spend the night before they got married apart. It was tradition.

Nell would have preferred to spend her last night at Gardiner Road. Her dislike of it had evaporated now she was leaving it to be married and there was Rachel upstairs to celebrate with. But the flat was under offer and all her things now in storage. The grand hotel with the pillared portico and glittering, golden chandeliers overlooking Hyde Park was the alternative.

Only after Joey had gone home did it occur to Nell that this tradition of spending the pre-wedding night apart had been honoured while many others had been ignored. Such as having her family attend.

Alone with the minibar and the marble-lined bathroom, she had passionately regretted giving in. She had paced around the suite, oblivious to its comforts and sophistications, seeing only, in her mind's eye, her parents' hurt faces when they found out. Why had she agreed not to tell them? Just because Joey had no mother or father didn't mean she should cut her own off too. On the contrary, it made her family potentially twice as important; they could also be his.

Why, she demanded of herself, had she not said any of this? If she'd stuck to her guns, Joey would surely have dropped his objections. He was so loving, so supportive, so concerned for her happiness. But perhaps it wasn't too late.

She had called him from the suite, seeking permission to tell her family after all. She would just have to apologise for the last-minute notice and beg them to come. They'd be alarmed, she knew. They would grumble. But they'd move hell and high water to be there.

Joey, however, had not been in. She had been unable to raise him on any of his numbers. Perhaps he had been out with a friend, celebrating. It occurred to her now, as it never had before, that she didn't really know who his friends were. After they were married, Nell resolved, it was the first thing she would find out.

'He's very late.' Juno's detached tones broke into Nell's thoughts.

'Shush, darling.' Rachel nudged her, and gave Nell a bright smile. 'Nell's right, he's probably just popped back to the flat. Or maybe he's overslept.'

Nell seized gratefully on this idea. Yes, that was it, his alarm had not gone off. Joey had probably woken in a rush and had scrabbled to get dressed. She pictured him bolting about his apartment, looking for his wedding cufflinks – special ones with Minis on so he had a Sixties touch too. She imagined him in the bathroom grabbing bottles – aftershave, mouthwash – dropping their caps in his panic.

A whole film was unreeling in her mind, one starring Joey which she was directing. Now he was leaving the flat and, with a machine-gun clatter of feet, hurtling down the stairs. Now, with an exploding slam of front door, he was outside, blinking in the North London sunlight, hastening to Arcadia Walk to grab a cab. Throwing himself in the back he now realised – with a slap of palm to forehead – that this morning of all mornings he had forgotten his phone! And to make things worse the traffic was terrible – sun bouncing off stationary car roofs as far as the eye could see. Distant traffic lights were turning from green to red to green again before his taxi could even move. Nell could picture it all so clearly she could actually feel the frustration grinding in his guts. Poor Joey!

The film in her head continued to play. Now, finally, the traffic was moving and he was getting close. The shining black taxi was coming along the road, the blocky orange indicator winking to announce the car's slow swerve into the kerb outside the register office. The car door had slammed; he was paying; if she strained her ears, right now, Nell thought, she could even hear the cheery salutation of the driver as the taxi pulled away.

And now, downstairs, Joey was pushing open the heavy, brass-fitted Edwardian double doors into the gloomy lobby. He was diving up the heavy carved staircase. Any minute now he would burst into the room, cheeks boyishly pink with exertion, eyes bright with love and apology. He would sweep her into his arms, then notice the municipal muzak. 'Bring Me Sunshine' was playing now. They would look at each other, and giggle. Nell giggled now, thinking about it.

'What's so funny?' asked Juno suspiciously. She clearly had a dim view of Nell's sense of humour since the *X Factor* remark.

'Nothing.' Nell looked down at her bouquet.

She could no longer suppress the urge to look at her phone. She had turned it off, but now she got it out of her clutch and turned it back on again. Her nerves had got the better of her tolerance, and while she wasn't worried, she was annoyed. Was it too much to ask that Joey could send a text, let her know that he was on his way?

'Bring Me Sunshine' had now faded out and 'Anyone Who Had a Heart' had taken up the baton. As Dionne Warwick paused after the first line, Nell's message box beeped.

Joey. Relief flooded her; all the same, her fingers shook as she opened the message. Words sprang on to her screen.

I've met someone else and I can't marry you. I'm sorry.

Nell read it a couple of times, not understanding. The phrase bounced against her brain like rain on an umbrella. She could hear the sound but felt none of the meaning.

Then, suddenly, she did. She felt something inside her shatter. She bent over as if sheltering from a bomb blast.

'Nell!' Suddenly Rachel was beside her, putting her arms around her.

'Oh no! I can't bear it!' The pain in Nell's heart was unbelievable. Perhaps she would die of it. *Who* had Joey met? It made no sense whatsoever. He'd never mentioned anyone. All he ever did was go to work and then come home again, to her. Didn't he?

She kept swallowing and rocking back and forth, emitting low moans. She kept covering her mouth, as if she might be sick. The shock was so absolute that she could not cry.

I want to kill myself. The thought slid into Nell's brain and gleamed there, sharp and seductive. Why not? It really seemed the easiest way out. She would never, ever get over this. She saw time moving slowly ahead, like a heavy river, into the future. She saw all the hours and days and weeks she must get through under the heavy burden of what had just happened. So many years would have to pass before she got even a distant glimpse of feeling normal again. It seemed to her that the wait was too long, and might not be worth it anyway. She should run out into the street and under the first car that came along.

As if guessing at all this, too, Rachel held her tightly. 'You poor thing,' she kept whispering. 'You poor, darling thing.'

The door of the little room now opened a crack and Nell heard the registrar clear her throat. 'We're ready to start . . . Oh dear. Is everything all right?'

Nell forced her skull up from her hands. It felt very heavy. Perhaps grief really did weigh down the brain. She had been worried that she might cry if she tried to speak, but now all she felt was a great weariness.

Rachel took charge. 'Not exactly,' she said, her tone capable but tense. 'The bridegroom's not here.'

The registrar's eyes bulged with panic. She looked at the narrow gold watch strapped to her plump and freckled wrist. 'Oh dear. Is he going to be long? I have another wedding at three.'

Nell suppressed a heaving sob at the thought of the wedding at three, and all the weddings after that, and all the weddings before as well. People got married all the time, all over the world, old, young, beautiful, ugly, for the first time or the twentieth. And yet she herself had been left in the lurch.

'Traffic, is it?' pressed the registrar.

'No,' Rachel said. 'He's not coming. At all.'

The registrar was blinking repeatedly, a serial viewing of gunmetal eyeshadow. 'Oh dear.' The air smelt of her sweet, thick perfume and an underwhiff of perspiration and fear.

Dean Martin had started on the muzak tape now, crooning about moons hitting your eye like a big pizza pie. But what hit Nell was the sheer farce of the situation and she bent over and burst uncontrollably into tears. She felt like crying for the rest of her life.

The registrar was alarmed. 'I'll be back in a minute,' she gasped, hurrying out of the room and closing the door behind her.

Bent over, her face in her knees, Nell heard Rachel murmur to Juno to go out too.

'Joey's dumped me,' Nell wailed into her lap.

She felt Rachel draw in a deep breath. 'Not necessarily the end of the world,' she said softly. 'If he's the type of guy to pull a stunt like this he's not really the guy you want to spend your life with.'

Nell spoke into her knees. 'I'm nearly thirty,' she said into her fingers, bleakly. The idea of having to resume her life where she had left off, start working on the catalogues again, all by herself, for ever, weighed on her like a ton of concrete.

She could feel the light pressure of Rachel's hand on her back. 'Yes,' she gently agreed. 'But you'd still have been nearly thirty if Joey had turned up.'

Nell clutched her hair, crushing the daisies in her fingers. How stupid the whole Sixties theme had been. Silly dressing-up, mere stage-setting for a production in which Joey, in the end, hadn't turned up to play his part. 'I'm on my own,' she whispered

'Join the club,' said Rachel. 'Although it's not quite the same club.'

Nell recognised that she was checkmated. Joey wasn't here, but at least he wasn't dead.

'No, but he's dead to you,' Rachel pointed out when she said this.

'I'm hardly going to venerate his memory, though,' Nell said tightly. 'Frankly, if he had a grave I'd dance on it.'

She looked up at Rachel in concern; was that going too far? But Rachel was smiling. 'That's the spirit.'

'I feel such a fool.'

'Don't,' Rachel said briskly. 'It isn't your fault. You were in love with someone different from the person you were marrying.'

'No, that was Joey. *He* was in love with someone different.'

Rachel patted her shoulder. 'I mean that the Joey you loved and the lying reptile he really is are two different people.'

A great hard lump was blocking Nell's throat and hot tears were stinging her eyes. She swallowed frantically and buried her face again.

Rachel patted her back. She opened a small silver handbag and produced a small silver flask. 'Brandy,' she said, proffering it. 'It might help.'

Nell stared at her. Rachel had come prepared. 'You knew, didn't you? You expected this.'

Rachel met her gaze sorrowfully. 'I didn't really *know*. Not for definite. But I did think he sounded too good to be true.' She shook her head. 'I never thought he would be as bad as this, though.'

The liquid burned down Nell's throat and settled into a glow in her stomach. She took another swig. And another. Gradually, she felt stronger.

'Go on,' Rachel encouraged her. 'You may as well finish it.' Nell drained the last few fiery drops.

'Better?' asked Rachel.

Nell nodded. The alcohol had numbed the sharp edges and added a helpful sense of distance. She felt now as if she were watching someone else. But what should this someone else now do?

'I'll tell you what I would do,' said Rachel, producing some wipes and proceeding to clean up Nell's streaked face.

CHAPTER 14

Rachel's idea was to carry on as if nothing had happened.

'But nothing has,' Nell pointed out. 'There wasn't a wedding, was there . . . ?' She gulped, and new, hot tears began to slide down her face. She tried not to care that Juno, squinting through her glasses in the bright sunlight, was staring at her curiously.

They were outside on the town hall steps. The plump registrar had expressed her deepest condolences yet was obviously relieved to get rid of them. Rachel was insisting they went to the Pink Pirate, where Joey had booked a lunchtime table for two to celebrate their wedding.

'I can't,' Nell said bluntly.

'You should,' Rachel replied, equally bluntly. 'It shows you have balls. That you're not going to give up and crawl away.'

'But that's exactly what I want to do,' Nell groaned. Why did Rachel not understand this? She of all people.

Rachel put an arm around Nell's trembling shoulders and squeezed them. 'My dear, as I'm in a uniquely informed position to tell you, life goes on. And lunch goes on, more to the point.'

'Yes . . . but . . .' Nell made a catch-all gesture intended to convey everything from the state of her hair to the great chasm of eternal misery yawning inside.

Rachel dismissed this kindly, but firmly. 'We need to eat somewhere. It's not as if everyone at the Pink whatsit will know what's happened.'

She had a point, Nell thought. No one knew, apart from themselves and the registrar. Most especially, her parents didn't know.

She felt the first glimmerings of something like relief. Thank God they hadn't come. They would never need to be told. There was something about the whole sorry mess to be thankful for after all.

'Well?' Rachel pressed.

'I suppose we may as well,' Nell allowed. She could do with a drink or three, at any rate.

'That's the spirit!' Rachel clapped her on the back. 'Now toss the bouquet!'

Nell had forgotten about this particular rite of bridal passage. As there were no bridesmaids or even any guests apart from a purple-haired widow and her eccentric small daughter, it seemed slightly pointless. Bouquets were traditionally tossed by brides so a single woman in the crowd could catch the posy and become the next up the aisle. But she, Nell, hadn't even got married herself and she doubted that Rachel, after her own bitter wifely experience, was planning to repeat the experiment.

She threw it anyway, and watched the white daisies wheel upwards into the bright blue sky. Rachel, sportingly, caught it and a car hooted as it passed.

'Goodbye to the scene of the crime,' Juno remarked darkly, once they were on their way in a taxi.

As the vehicle rattled through the leafy streets of Hampstead, Nell's misgivings returned. This was madness. She felt angry, despairing and desperately sorry for herself.

She was, despite this, half aware of a conversation that Juno and Rachel were having. '*What* did you say?' Rachel was exclaiming, her voice low, but urgent.

'That I called Carrington's,' Juno replied composedly, making no attempt to keep her own voice down. 'While you two were in that cupboard.'

Nell flashed back to the moment she and Rachel had emerged from the registrar's anteroom. Juno had not been, as expected, in the big ceremonial chamber with the maces and spades. She had been sitting outside on a bench in the lobby.

'I asked the registrar's assistant for a local telephone directory,' Juno was explaining calmly. 'Then I asked if I could make a call. She didn't mind at all.'

'And what did Carrington's say?' Rachel pressed. She still spoke in a murmur, apparently convinced that Nell was lost in her own dark thoughts. Now she glanced at her friend and saw Nell was following every word.

Juno rummaged in her pocket and produced a spiral-bound notebook. She licked the tip of her finger and flicked through the pages. 'They said that no one called Joey worked for them any more.'

'*What?*' Nell and Rachel exclaimed in unison.

'That can't be right!' Nell gasped. It was difficult to absorb this after all that had happened. She was so shaken up it was difficult to remember anything properly. But she was sure that Joey had said nothing about leaving his job.

'Well, it's what Carrington's said.' Juno was referring to her notebook. 'He left his job yesterday. The same day that the lease ended on his flat.'

'Lease?' But he'd told her he owned it. She had been going to move in there, it was to be her new home! Nell's hands were pressed against her mouth. She felt that she might be sick.

'Now, hang on a minute. He left his job *and* moved out of

his flat? *Yesterday?*' Rachel's head was twisting so fast between her daughter and her newly stricken friend that curls were detaching themselves from the chignon and flying about. 'But he took you to the hotel last night,' she directed at Nell, puzzled.

Nell could only stare back. She was numb, her every feeling masked by the same heavy, thick sensation that had followed Joey's text. There was something to understand here, something horrid and hurtful, but she couldn't grasp the edges of it. When she tried to, it slid away from her.

'But taking you to the hotel,' Rachel said slowly, brow clearing, 'meant that he could leave the flat without you knowing anything about it.'

In some distant part of her Nell could see that it was possible Joey had set her up, deliberately deserted her and never intended to marry her. But what possible reason could he have had to treat her like this?

'*Why?*' she burst out, looking at the others in utter bewilderment. '*Why* did he do it? It's so *cruel.*'

Rachel squeezed her hand. 'It makes no sense. But people can be cruel.'

Juno leaned forward and took her other hand. 'As Miss Marple's always saying,' she said gravely, 'there are some very bad people in the world.'

At the Pink Pirate, Larry was resplendent with his trademark gelled up hair and falling-down jeans. 'Where's that nice boyfriend of yours?' he demanded.

Rachel put her face close to his ear. 'Don't ask.'

'Like that, is it?' Larry rolled his eyes. 'Well, chin up, ducky,' he urged Nell. 'Don't let the bastards grind you down. Chance'd be a fine thing, eh? I like a good grind, myself. Table's this way, ladies.'

The Pirate was, as usual, full of wealthy, glamorous, successful-looking types who seemed to have stepped straight from the weekend supplements. Perhaps even more than usual; the place was packed. 'I wonder why there are so many people here,' Rachel mused, struggling between the punters.

'It's the dancing,' Juno said, pointing at a board on the wall advertising 'Larry's Larky Sixties Saturday Lunchtime Disco'.

They settled at their table. Over champagne, Rachel began to tell Nell that she could not let Joey beat her. So what if he had made a mockery out of her love and smashed her happiness into smithereens? That didn't mean she was giving in. She had her pride.

'But I don't,' Nell wailed. 'I've been entirely rejected and humiliated.'

The dancing had begun. 'Ticket To Ride' was now blaring out in the bar, and both the lounge and the bar were crowded with dancing families, all braying with laughter. The main event was Larry, who was tripping the light fantastic, leaping about with his mouth open in a permanent grin. He was clearly the type of manager who felt it incumbent on him to get events under his roof going with a swing.

'Come on, darling!' he shouted to Nell as 'Waterloo Sunset' struck up. 'Get up and dance! You've dressed for it!'

Nell closed her eyes. Being stood up at the altar was bad enough. That Larry assumed her wedding outfit was merely homage to his lunchtime disco added insult to injury.

Thankfully, the landlord had turned his attention elsewhere. 'Life's just one long party, don't you agree?' he shouted at a very old lady gamely doing the twist.

And you're invited, Nell thought, bitterly remembering the line she had written in so many catalogues.

'So what about the honeymoon?' Rachel broke in.

Nell's miserable thoughts suddenly came into focus. She had imagined the rest of her life a formless, planless blur. But there was, of course, one immediate plan that she had completely forgotten about. A week in a country gastropub.

'Shit. I should ring them.' Nell was on her feet now. 'I made the booking. I'd better cancel it.'

'But why?' Rachel drained her champagne glass. 'Why not go?'

Nell, incredulous, let the hand holding her smartphone flop to her side. '*What?*'

'So the wedding never happened,' Rachel went on cheerily. 'But you've had the wedding party. So why not go on the honeymoon too?'

Was Rachel joking? Drunk? Sticking to the lunch plan was one thing. But going on the honeymoon, a bride without a groom . . . Nell struggled to find words to express the strength of her objection. There was no possibility. No way on God's earth.

'Yay, a week in a honeymoon suite,' Rachel was saying. 'Whirlpool baths. Fancy bath things. Huge, comfortable bed. Piles of fluffy white towels. What could be nicer?'

'Almost anything,' said Nell tightly, turning on her white-PVC-booted heel and pushing through the pressing crowd now roaring along to 'Mustang Sally'.

Outside in the cool fresh air she sat under one of Larry's parasols and searched for the number of the pub with shaking hands. She had no idea what it was called but the name of the village stuck in her mind: Edenville. At the time, when Joey first mentioned it, it had seemed blissfully appropriate. Now it seemed horribly ironic and yet another good reason not to go.

There seemed to be only one pub in Edenville, the Edenville Arms. Much as she wanted to get the call over and done, Nell could not help stopping to examine the image that bloomed on her screen. It was of a small stone inn with roses round the door and white umbrellas outside. Tiny, ancient, diamond-paned windows winked in the sun, their frames painted a tasteful sage green and surrounded with clipped ivy. The ones on the upper storey were tucked away under little pointed gables whose edges were decorated with carved wood, like a Swiss chalet.

Nell felt the tears rushing to her eyes again. It would have been so nice. Paradise, in fact. As luxury country pubs went, it looked about the most luxurious, countrified and pubbish imaginable.

She took in a deep, galvanising breath and determinedly stabbed in the numbers.

'Good afternoon, the Edenville Arms,' answered a high-pitched, slightly nasal male voice.

Five minutes later, a disappointed and angry Nell threaded her way back through a bouncing crowd now bellowing along to 'Gimme Shelter'.

Rachel and Juno were still where she had left them. Rachel, smiling, was watching the increasingly silly dancing while Juno, demonstrating terrifying powers of concentration and a breathtaking capacity to block out all extraneous distraction, was reading *Death on the Nile*.

'All done?' Rachel greeted her.

Nell sighed. 'Not exactly. Basically I can't cancel the booking as it's less than twenty-four hours' notice.'

Rachel widened her eyes. 'So you have to pay for the whole week?'

'Dinner, bed and breakfast, every night,' Nell gloomily confirmed. The manager had been extremely polite about it, but also extremely firm.

'But my circumstances—' Nell had begun.

The manager had cut in. 'I'm afraid the circumstances make no difference, madam. I'm terribly sorry, but there it is. It was on the terms and conditions box you ticked when you made the online booking.'

'It's going to cost me over two thousand pounds,' she groaned to Rachel. That Joey had landed her with this bill as well as all the psychological pain he had inflicted made Nell feel that she actually hated him. He could have easily made the booking and cancelled it. Unlike her, he knew what was about to happen.

She swigged the champagne in her glass. It tasted as sour as she felt. What was it about her that made men want to humiliate her? Fake OutdoorsGuy in the station, now Joey.

'But that's great news!' Rachel was exclaiming, clapping her hands.

Nell looked at her. 'How do you figure that out?'

Rachel was smiling brightly. 'Because you *have* to go now. On honeymoon. Waste not, want not.'

'Want not. Definitely.'

Rachel raised her fine eyebrows. 'So what's the alternative? Moping around London?'

'Guess so.'

'And where, exactly, will you mope?'

Nell opened her mouth to snap that she'd mope at home, of course. In her flat. Then it hit her. She didn't have a home any more. Or a flat. Gardiner Road had been sold, or as good as. Her furniture was in storage. And Joey had moved out of the flat she had expected to be living in. Which had never belonged to him anyway.

She stared, shocked, at Rachel. 'I'm homeless.'

'Not quite,' Rachel pointed out. 'You've a week's worth of paid-for luxury roof over your head in Leicestershire.'

She had no clothes either, Nell was thinking, except for her pyjamas and the jeans and T-shirt she'd worn the day before. Expecting to return to Joey's flat, she had taken only her wedding outfit and sponge bag to the hotel.

'I don't want to be by myself in Leicestershire for a week!' Nell exclaimed. 'I've never been there. I don't even know where it is.'

'You won't be by yourself. Juno and I can come with you.'

'But . . . but . . .' Nell gasped. 'Juno's got school. You've got work.'

'Sure, but we'll just come for the weekend. I can get up early on Monday. If we set off now we'll be up there for teatime.'

How, Nell thought, could she possibly mean it? But the expression on Rachel's pixie face was utterly serious.

'But . . . how will we get there?' Nell flailed about for counter-arguments. 'I don't have a car.'

'We'll go in the Red Baron,' Rachel said decidedly.

Now she really was joking, Nell thought. While the vehicle was more or less red – in between the rust patches – it didn't look as if it would reach the end of the street.

She would not, Nell realised, win this argument with mere practical objections. A heartfelt emotional appeal was the only possibility. 'I *can't* go on honeymoon,' she wailed from the depths of her wounded soul. 'I didn't get *married*.'

'Thank goodness,' Rachel said briskly, signalling to the waitress struggling past for the bill.

'But . . . aren't you over the limit?' Nell gestured at the empty champagne bottle.

'Me?' Rachel cackled. 'I've had a glass and a half, at the most.'

Meaning I've drunk the rest, Nell thought, the tight feeling in her head increasing. Seeing Rachel entering her pin number into the waitress's handset, she tried to intervene.

'I'm getting this,' Rachel stated calmly. 'Come on, Juno.'

She really didn't, Nell saw, know the meaning of the word 'no'. There was clearly nothing else for it. They were going to Leicestershire and that was that.

CHAPTER 15

Nell was still objecting as they drove up the Euston Road in the Land Rover. They'd made a swift detour to Gardiner Road to pick up spare clothes for Rachel and Juno, and now they were on their way. 'But the honeymoon suite will be for two!' Nell complained. 'There won't be room for three of us.'

Rachel, handling the vehicle's big steering wheel with confidence, despite her diminutive size, shot this down immediately. 'Of course there will. This is 2016. Children from a previous relationship and all that. They'll have put-up beds.'

Nell subsided and looked out of the window. It being Saturday afternoon it was pretty busy: vans, trucks, cars, cyclists, taxis and buses all jostled for space. Some stared curiously in at them and Nell tried not to catch anyone's eye. She could imagine how strange they must look: the rusty, shabby Land Rover driven by a tiny woman in vintage Dior with another woman in a Sixties minidress and flowers in her hair in the passenger seat. Not to mention the ten-year-old girl in the back looking like an infant headmistress.

Instead, Nell tried to think about where all these other people might be going, and why. However bizarre a destination, and for however strange a reason, it could not possibly be as odd as what she was doing. Going on honeymoon without even being married.

'Can we have an Agatha Christie CD on?' Juno piped up now from the back, over the roar of the Land Rover engine.

Rachel tilted her Titian locks to survey her daughter in the driving mirror. 'Sure. Which one would you like?'

'*The Murder of Roger Ackroyd*, please.'

Rachel grinned at Nell from the steering wheel. 'That OK with you?'

'Sure,' Nell shrugged. She wondered, privately, whether exposure to all this murder was entirely healthy for someone Juno's age.

Rachel seemed to sense this. 'The stories are well written,' she said. 'And a lot less gory than anything you'd see on telly. Good for her vocabulary too.'

'I wrote a murder mystery the other day,' Juno put in from the back. 'For a school assignment.'

Nell turned her head to meet the clear, unfaltering gaze of the child. 'What happened in it?'

'All the school bullies died,' said Juno with relish.

Rachel cackled. 'Certain amount of wish fulfilment there. June has a hard time at school. She's a bit different, one could say.'

'What's so different?' Nell asked kindly, adding, untruthfully, 'You don't seem all that different to me.'

It was obviously the wrong thing to say. Above her glasses, Juno's dark brows scrunched together. 'I *am* different,' she said emphatically. 'I want to be. I don't want to be like *them*. Glittery nails. Long, messy, tossy hair.' She patted her smooth side-parted bob with bitten fingers.

'Absolutely,' said Nell, scrabbling to make amends. 'Much better to be your own person. To know what you believe in and not care what anyone else thinks. Be independent and live your life your way . . .' She stopped. Certainly, she had always believed all this and tried to live by these lights. But just where, exactly, had it got her?

'Right on, sister!' exclaimed Rachel, lifting one small fist off the steering wheel. 'Now, have a look in the box, will you? The one on the floor. See if Roger's there.'

Nell peered doubtfully down to the Land Rover's floor. The battered cardboard box with the CDs in it looked very far away. As she bent slowly forward her head started to pound and her stomach lurched nauseously.

'I can see *Lord Edgware Dies*,' she offered.

'I *quite* like that,' Juno said doubtfully. 'But *Roger Ackroyd*'s better. The denouement's amazing.'

Nell blinked. Juno was ten, and she knew words like denouement? Rachel was obviously right about Agatha Christie and vocabulary. Perhaps she should be taught in every school. 'Here it is,' she said, reaching for a cracked and obviously much-used CD case.

The engine was unbelievably noisy. Roger Ackroyd was going to have to be murdered very loudly.

They were going round the Outer Circle now. Nell looked out at the sunny green of the park: the grass and trees, the creamy-white Nash terraces topped with Classical figures. She thought about the park's beautiful rose garden, and the flower-heavy bowers where she had occasionally sat with Joey. She felt speared by a great javelin-thrust of misery.

They ground past the zoo, Rachel pointing out the giraffes excitedly.

'Shush, Mum,' admonished Juno. 'Poirot's talking.'

'The funny thing,' Rachel hissed to Nell, 'is that I've heard this CD loads of times. But I still couldn't tell you what happens in it. My attention drifts.'

'Mu-um!' exclaimed the rear, appalled. Juno's attention, Nell guessed, rarely drifted.

'But,' Rachel added, changing lanes as they chugged up Finchley Road, 'it's quite nice to drive along and have all these words just wash over you.'

'Can you turn it up a bit, please?' asked the back, pointedly.

It was Nell's first time following the demise of Roger Ackroyd and she meant to listen carefully, especially as conversation was so obviously discouraged. But there were strong indicators in favour of sleep. For one thing, she had drunk an awful lot of champagne. For another, they had reached the tangle of roads, signs and concrete that marked the bottom of the M1; visual interest would be in short supply from now on. There was, in addition, something surprisingly comforting about the fruity roar of the Land Rover engine.

As the Defender ground determinedly up the fast lane, doggedly overtaking a middle-lane-hogging Yaris and magnificently ignoring the flashing headlights of a Ferrari at the rear, Nell was overwhelmed by an almost painful urge to doze. Her last waking thought was that the 'Superb Offices To Let' sign strapped to a brown concrete block in Hendon looked like something of an overstatement.

She awoke to find that the signs had changed. Last time she looked, Hemel Hempstead, St Albans and Northampton had all been up ahead. Now the signs were reading Leicester.

'Welcome back,' said Rachel. 'You've been *very* asleep. You were snoring.'

Nell reddened. 'Loudly?'

Rachel grinned. 'Ish. But Juno poked you whenever it got too much for her to hear Roger Ackroyd.'

'Hasn't he been murdered yet?' Nell grumbled.

'Ages ago. But that's not the point, it's all about who did it. We don't know yet. Well, Juno probably does, but like I said, I never have the foggiest idea.'

'Shush!' warned the back.

She felt much better, Nell realised, as she completed checks on her physical state. Her headache had gone, and with it the sick feeling. The beginnings of hunger were now gnawing within her and visions of bacon sandwiches glowed in her mind. Would Rachel mind stopping at a service station?

Rachel would not, especially as Roger Ackroyd's assailant had now been revealed and Juno, big-eyed from following each twist and turn, declared herself hungry too.

'It doesn't spoil it a bit knowing the ending,' she told Nell over a ham and cheese panini in Costa Coffee. 'Because the characters are so interesting. Agatha Christie's all about character, you see. In *The Mysterious Affair at Styles*, Poirot straightens up a vase because he's such a tidy person. And then he notices something that helps him find out who the murderer is. I love that.'

Juno's pale face was glowing; her eyes shone through her glasses. Rachel ruffled her daughter's hair fondly. 'Juno wants to be a detective when she grows up. Don't you, darling?'

Juno nodded and scooped another teaspoonful of squirty cream from the top of her hot chocolate. 'Will Edenville be like St Mary Mead?'

'Where?' asked Nell.

The grey eyes turned on her, surprised. 'Where Miss Marple lives, of course.'

'Oh, right, the village where the vicar poisons everyone with his seed cake,' Nell joked.

'The murderer's hardly ever the vicar,' Juno corrected. 'Although sometimes it's the doctor. But mostly it's people who've been deceived and crossed in love, that sort of thing. Seeking revenge.'

'Is that so,' Nell said thoughtfully.

Juno was looking at her consideringly. 'You know, you'd make a great Agatha Christie character, Nell. You've got the motive for a really interesting murder.'

CHAPTER 16

Once upon a time, Pemberton Hall, Leicestershire had been a private fiefdom, over which a succession of Earls had held feudal sway. Their huge incomes from landholdings and mining minerals had once comfortably supported the vast estate with its hundreds of servants, but those days were long over. In line with other great estates the length and breadth of the country, Pemberton and its Earl had had to devise other ways of making money to survive.

This meant appealing to the visitor class that had replaced the servant one. Pemberton accordingly flung open the doors of the Hall to the tourist trade, installed room guides and shops and opened the stable yard to cafés and restaurants and yet more shops. As the years had gone by, the Big House had added more attractions and this year, in a bid to pull ahead of its competitors, Pemberton Hall was pioneering a new 'insider' tour in which former estate employees took visitors round and gave their own unique and frank perspective on the place.

There were other initiatives. A farm shop opened selling everything from apricot-stuffed chicken to designer chocolates. A wedding planning arm was launched, offering the house as a backdrop to 'that most special day of your life'. A catering arm was added to supplement the wedding arm.

Meanwhile, out in the great park surrounding the house, further income streams were tapped by converting buildings that had once been laundries, dairies and coal stores into tasteful holiday cottages. In Edenville, the 'model' estate village built at the edge of the park to house the workers of one of the Victorian Earls as well as to provide an opportunity for His Lordship to try out his fanciful architectural ideas, the former quite basic pub had been upgraded to within an inch of its life.

The Edenville Arms, designed to slake the thirst of estate labourers, had received a thorough makeover and had recently reopened. No stone had been left un-repointed, no inch of wood un-eggshell-painted, in its quest to attract as many punters as possible and put them up in a modish splendour for which quite eye-widening rates could be charged.

The new manager, Jason Twistle, had formerly been deputy manager of Ogthorpe's, a successful restaurant-with-rooms in a village on the outskirts of Melton Mowbray. The press release sent out on his arrival a month ago had described him as 'chief leisure experience curator in the ongoing hospitality journey of the Edenville Arms'.

All of which was bad enough. But Jason was now realising that Ros Downer, the Pemberton Estate's Director of Marketing and author of this gobbledegook, had perpetrated even worse crimes against good English in general and his establishment in particular in the latest brochure advertising, as it chose to put it, the Pemberton Estate's 'hospitality offer'. In other words, the estate hotels, holiday cottages, restaurants, cafés and pubs, including the Edenville Arms.

Jason had positively leapt at the bundle of brochures when they arrived from the Marketing Department, so desperate had he been to see his newly furbished fiefdom in print. As he read through, a horrid, cold feeling had increased its grip. The dead hand of Ros Downer was everywhere.

It wasn't just that the spelling was appalling and the words made no sense (his position as 'chief leisure experience curator' was reiterated). The pictures were uninspired too. Of the newly created rooms in particular. Was that really the most flattering angle of Spigots, the downstairs suite? Or Barrels, converted from a former beer store in the yard? The brochure's invitations to 'sleep in barrels and spigots' seemed directed to some drunk collapsing in the cellar.

And was that the best possible description of Kegs restaurant? Dismissing the chairs merely as 'candi-striped' when they were actually 'comfortable tub seating in bold contemporary colour-ways' seemed an opportunity missed to Jason. As for the gourmet menu, 'locally sauced' wasn't spelt like that, nor was pulled pork one word.

The worst outrage, however, was the description of the honeymoon suite as having 'a bordelo-like ambiance'. Did Ros Downer even know what a bordello – spelt with two l's, incidentally – actually was? Possibly not; she didn't seem like someone who knew much about the excitements of sex, although she'd evidently had it: there was a daughter, Rapunzal. The 'a' had always irritated Jason. If she couldn't even spell her own daughter's name, what hope was there for the estate literature?

However, the insinuation that the Edenville Arms was a knocking shop really could not be borne. Admittedly, the honeymoon suite looked like one. A professional 'interiors expert' called Buzzie Omelet had, Jason considered, gone some distance over the top with it.

While the room's pink wallpaper and black chandelier were startling, its overwhelming feature was a vast black and purple four-poster bed. This, given the smallness of the chamber itself, appeared like a room within a room. It was of an extraordinary height: the mattress was so far from the floor that assistance was required to reach it. A set of small black wooden steps stood against a violet valance to facilitate entry between brocade curtains lashed to the black painted bedposts with hot-pink tasselled ties.

Jason had confided to Mrs Poultney, the pub's formidable cleaner, that it all reminded him of the inside of an underwear drawer. Mrs Poultney's eyes had bulged and she'd said she didn't know what sort of underwear Jason had in his drawer, she was sure.

At the memory of the redoubtable cleaning operative, Jason took a swift nip from the half pint of beer he had concealed under the counter next to the telephone. It was past twelve and a busy lunchtime too. And the Earl, a fair employer, did not begrudge staff little treats like this to keep them going.

But it would take more than a free swig of beer to eradicate the effect of what Ros Downer had said about the Edenville Arms. 'Bordelo-like ambiance' indeed.

He would take action, Jason decided. He'd had more than enough of Ros Downer, with her flicky hair, lozenge glasses and psychotic passive aggression.

He would make an official complaint. He would pick up the telephone and call Angela Highwater.

He would, he knew, have to tread carefully. Angela might be the estate's Director of Human Resources but she was also Ros's close friend. Jason had not been in post very long, but it was long enough to know that the two of them were as thick as thieves. Though he doubted that even the dimmest thief was quite as thick as Ros.

He dialled. Angela was on answerphone. 'You hev reached

Ingila Haywater, Dayrector of Hewman Resources for the Pemberton Estate . . .'

'Angela? Jason here,' the manager began. He felt his resolve ebbing. Perhaps complaining about Ros was a bad idea after all and it was safer to just put up with it.

There was a clattering noise and Angela picked up. She had been monitoring the call, Jason realised with a stab of alarm. Now he was committed to the complaint he wondered whether he really wanted to make it.

'Jase!' exclaimed Angela, in her usual voice. 'Any news?'

Jason had been quick to grasp the Angela form. In order to get anything out of the Director of Human Resources you had first to offer her tribute in the form of gossip. And here Jason was at an advantage; his position as manager of the estate gastro-pub offered him the perfect opportunity to gather interesting information about guests.

He was therefore one of Angela's most valued contacts. However, as Jason well knew, he was only as good as his last story. Fortunately, quite a decent one had only just fallen into his hands.

'A woman from London rang up to cancel her honeymoon,' he told Angela. 'She was supposed to be coming today. Can you imagine?'

Jason, who had a soft heart, had felt sorry for the bride. She had sounded devastated about the collapse of her wedding.

'Well, I bloody well hope you told her she couldn't,' was Angela's robust response. 'All cancellations have to have twenty-four hours' notice.'

He should, Jason reflected, have known better than to expect sisterly feeling from this quarter. Angela was as hard as nails.

'I did tell her,' he said. 'And then she rang back and said that she'd decided to come after all and was bringing a friend with her instead.'

'What sort of a friend?' Angela's voice was suspicious.

'Another woman.'

There was a triumphant exclamation from the other end. 'A likely story! It's a gay wedding and it has been all along. She just didn't want to admit it. So she pretended her straight wedding had broken down and got her friend in that way.'

Jason marvelled, not for the first time, at Angela's ability to impute malign motives to the most innocent of people and situations.

'Why wouldn't she want to admit it?' he asked. 'This is 2016. It's perfectly legal for two women to get married and go on honeymoon.'

He was rewarded with a contemptuous snort of laughter. 'Hm,' Angela said, mock-wonderingly. 'Let's think, shall we? Let's say you were gay . . .'

Jason felt cold, suddenly. He had, he realised, walked straight into this. He had only himself to blame.

'Or that *one* was gay,' Angela apparently corrected herself. 'Might *one* necessarily want others to know? Or might *one* wish to conceal one's true, um, leanings? As it were? Hmm?'

Jason did not reply, even though it was horribly obvious what Angela was referring to. He was, he knew, widely suspected of homosexuality, although no one ever said so to his face.

And if he was gay, Jason felt, he would have no difficulty admitting as much. He would be out and proud. But his leanings were, even in his own mind, hopelessly confused. It was the not knowing that was the problem.

'They're also bringing a child,' Jason added, trying to set the train of the conversation back on its original rails.

'Two lesbians and a child!' Angela exclaimed excitedly. 'Must be a turkey baster job.'

Jason thought this remark as inaccurate as it was tasteless.

But he knew better than to say so. Disagreeing with Angela was fatal. At her worst, she was both thin-skinned and vindictive. This, combined with the undoubted power she wielded as Director of Human Resources, made her the original enemy who you had to keep closer than your friends.

He moved the conversation on to shopping, which Angela loved. She aimed to move with the times, and her clothes reflected this. Despite being north of forty, she invariably dressed like a partying teenager, with hair and make-up to match.

'I've found a great new site,' Jason said. 'Called *Urban Fox*. They do underpants with Latin mottoes.' He had slipped this in with the expectation of making Angela laugh, but he could tell from the momentary silence that it had fallen on stony ground.

Then she came back angrily: 'Don't talk to me about underpants. Don't talk to me about men full bloody stop.'

Jason guessed that Angela's repeated attempts to seduce the local lothario had still not met with success. Personally he wondered why she was bothering.

Angela was an influential woman, even if her personal style wasn't everyone's cup of tea. She had money and power, which she did not generally wield wisely. But at least she had it, whereas the man in her sights was a skint jobbing gardener whose jobs changed every five minutes.

The object of her affections, Dan Parker, lived in a battered council house on the local sink estate. Angela, meanwhile, lived in a flat in a converted mill in the nearby town of Chestlock. Hers was the penthouse and Angela was proud of having got it for a knockdown rate after the development ran into problems. The mill had, in its heyday (if that was the word), been noted for its cruelty to children, and the first wave of flat purchasers had complained about the gloomy atmosphere. Angela had been impervious to it and had therefore cleaned up.

'How dare bloody Dan not be interested in me?' Angela was fuming. 'I've got men queuing down the street.'

Jason politely let this gross exaggeration – if not outright untruth – pass. The person who had them queuing down the street was, for some unfathomable reason, Dan Parker. What so many women saw in someone who could at best be described as strong and silent, Jason could not imagine.

Jason's main objections to Dan were managerial, however. He was a pest so far as the Edenville Arms was concerned, parking his filthy old van in the car park and eating his sandwiches on the terrace in blatant contravention of the sign 'These Tables Are Reserved For Customers Eating Pub Food Only' – a sign which, as it happened, had been put up specifically to discourage Dan Parker.

'*And* I've heard he's carrying on with that Birch Hall woman,' Angela fumed. 'The scrawny one who looks like a dug-up corpse. What's she got that I haven't?'

Jason knew the woman in question. She was half of a couple who occasionally came in for a drink. Angela was right, the woman did look post-mortal: extremely pale and thin, with long black hair. 'Her husband's an actor, is that right?' he asked.

Grimly, Angela assented. 'He's on tour at the moment, which is why Madam's getting her oats.'

Jason decided to change the subject again. The preliminaries were now over; they could move on to the matter in hand.

He took a deep breath and crossed the fingers of his free hand.

'Angela, my darling,' he purred, employing the urbane manner he knew she appreciated, 'I've got a little teensy-weensy problem.'

'Join the effing club,' Angela responded tartly. 'How would you feel if Dan Parker passed up the chance to be with *you*? On second thoughts,' she added nastily, 'forget I said that.'

Jason's response to this was a dignified silence.

'Point is,' Angela went on, oblivious, 'he's supposed to be one hell of a shag. And I've got *needs*.'

Jason had heard about Angela's needs. Usually late at night after several large glasses of Chardonnay. He made another attempt to steer the conversation in the direction he wanted.

'I've got a complaint,' he said, deciding to stop beating about the bush. This got Angela's attention immediately. There was nothing she enjoyed more than a good complaint. Well, almost nothing.

'Tell me all about it,' the Director of Human Resources ordered. 'Ructions in the kitchen, is it?' It was obvious from her tone that she was anticipating the opportunity to unflatteringly dissect the characters of everyone who worked there.

'Ructions, yes,' Jason said evasively. 'But not in the kitchen.'

He knew that Angela would not appreciate criticism of her close friend. Yet there was nothing else for it. Bordelo-like ambiance indeed!

He steeled himself for the plunge. 'I'm afraid,' he said gingerly, 'that I've got issues with Ros's new brochure.'

He was immediately interrupted by an exclamation from Angela.

'Ros! Don't talk to me about bloody Ros,' she cried angrily.

Jason unfolded himself from the brace position he had automatically taken. His heart rose. Was Ros in trouble with Angela? 'What's happened?' he asked.

'Ros,' Angela ground out through evidently gritted teeth, 'has just had her job removed from her. That's all.'

Jason was amazed. 'You mean you've sacked her?'

'Not *me*!'

'Then who?'

'His bloody Lordship.'

'The *Earl*? He's sacked Ros?'

'Right over my head as well,' Angela snarled. '*I'm* the Director of Human Resources.'

'Well, he is the Earl,' Jason timidly pointed out. 'He does own it all.'

Angela ignored this. 'It's an insult to me!' she spat out. 'A resigning issue, frankly.'

Jason's heart shot up his throat. He could hardly breathe because of the great hope that filled him. 'Do you think you will?' he ventured, crossing his fingers, knees, even his eyes.

'I'm thinking about it,' Angela said tightly, but Jason could tell that she wasn't.

'What did he sack her for?' he asked, realising with relief that his own complaint was now redundant and he need not go into it.

'Said that she'd made a complete mess of the bumf,' Angela snarled. 'Said that she couldn't spell or write. That she was practically bloody illiterate.'

Jason was fighting the urge to cheer. He had always liked the Earl, who seemed just as Earls should be: dignified but understated, grand but un-pompous. Certainly a good deal less grand and pompous than Angela.

'The spelling is a bit hit and miss,' he ventured.

'Yes, but Ros is *dyslexic*!' Angela thundered back. 'Dyslexic people have issues with writing and spelling!'

It was the first Jason had heard of this and it rendered him briefly speechless. Why would you give a job which relied heavily on written communication to someone who could not write or spell? It turned out that the Earl had asked the same thing.

119

'I reminded him,' Angela said stiffly, 'that the Pemberton Estate is an equal opportunities employer.'

The Earl, Jason now learned, had singled out particular passages in the brochures to support the case for Ros's dismissal. 'Bordelo-like ambiance' was the main one.

'Was it Ros's fault if she didn't realise what a bordello was?' Angela demanded now.

Yes, thought Jason, but didn't say so. He was gratified to hear that the Earl had also taken exception to the description 'chief leisure experience curator'.

'He needs to move with the bloody times,' Angela raged. 'Ros was just using contemporary language, that's all.'

Jason said nothing.

'What's that noise?' Angela demanded. 'Sort of panting?'

It was Jason on the other end, punching the air.

CHAPTER 17

Dylan was finally out of hospital and in astonishingly good shape, considering. Thanks to the skill of his surgeons, the scars had healed amazingly well. You had to look closely to see that anything had happened at all. He was, Dylan knew, incredibly lucky.

Now he could pick up where he left off and get on with his life. Except that he couldn't. A black, angry gloom had descended.

People were constantly asking him what he would do next, but he could answer this only in terms of what he had no intention of ever doing again. Top of this list was writing.

'You can't mean it, dear boy,' Julian said, so purringly it was obvious he was worried. 'It's not possible that you're never penning another *mot*.'

'I've never meant anything so much in my entire life,' Dylan countered flatly.

'But think about it, dear boy. What am I to tell Eve?'

Since their acrimonious exchange in the hospital, Eve had not been in touch at all. She, at least, seemed to have got the message. He had imagined she had told Julian about it, but Julian had not mentioned it. Which did not mean that it hadn't

121

happened; Julian could be selective like that.

'Tell Eve whatever you like.' Dylan did not care if he sounded rude. He liked his agent, but Julian's refusal to accept his decision was as maddening as Eve's had been. He was never writing again, and that was that. He just wasn't an author; perhaps he never had been. The whole thing had been smoke and mirrors. Smoke, definitely.

The other thing that Dylan was definitely, under no circumstances, ever doing again was being involved with a woman. Mostly because of Beatrice. While the official verdict was that the fire was accidental, and he was outwardly content that it should be, Dylan secretly had no doubt that it was arson. Beatrice had been behind it and had tried to kill him from sheer jealous frustration. Not for nothing had she been smouldering and with a fiery temper. He had frequent nightmares in which she was strangling him whilst clad in a wetsuit, flames coming out of her eyes.

But there was also the blonde in the station. At first, when his memory of the events at Paddington was still unclear, he had been haunted by her face. He knew he had done something awful to her. He also knew that he had not meant to do it – whatever it was – but that she believed he had.

Gradually, as more of the details came back to him, Dylan's view changed. While Beatrice was clearly the villain of the piece, the blonde was far from blameless. She had made the first, disastrous move; coming up to his table and talking about *All Smiles*. He had genuinely thought she knew who he was, and by the time he realised that she didn't it was less embarrassing to carry on than to alert her to her mistake.

The blonde had been at the root of it, really. Had he and she not talked, Beatrice would never have found them together. She would not have put on that last, insupportable display of jealous rage and he would not have finished with her on the spot. Perhaps, had that not happened, Beatrice wouldn't have set his house on fire and he wouldn't have been in hospital at all. And *Charm Itself* would now be safely at the printers, about to launch on an expectant world.

Dylan wished he could tell the blonde what the consequences of her action had been. How he had suffered. While she, presumably, had got on with her life and forgotten all about him.

So work was over. Relationships were over. The only question remaining was where – or not – he was living. Not at home, definitely. His parents, much as he loved them, were driving him mad. His mother was obsessed with the idea of cheering him up, not understanding that he would never be cheerful again and it was unreasonable to expect him to be.

His father, meanwhile, was always trying to get him to do things. He was, Dylan sensed, inches away from giving him an Eve-style lecture on taking responsibility and getting back to work. That, Dylan resolved, he could not and would not stand.

His father's axiom, that activity improved the mood, only sent Dylan's spirits plunging further. He did not want his mood improved. His mood was dark and bitter and he intended to keep it that way. He wanted to stay up in his room with the curtains pulled, as he had when he'd been a teenager. Frankly, he felt like a teenager, but not in any good way. Only in the sense that, back with his mother and father, he felt trapped in his own past.

Trapped, too, by a ghastly new twist on fame. There had been wide newspaper coverage of the 'accident', meaning he was now a literary tragedy as well as a success. This had been followed by some doorstepping of his parents' home by journalists eager to learn the latest developments.

They hadn't quite reached the actual doorstep; the electric

gates had seen to that. But they were there at the end of the drive and people in the village had been asked for information. The phone rang at strange hours.

Although they had never complained about the disruption to them and were outraged only on his behalf, it was clearly unfair to expect his parents to put up with this situation. Another reason, Dylan decided, to disappear and let no one know where he was while he indulged his anger and depression. He could even make it look like consideration for others.

But where should he go? He did not, for obvious reasons, want to return to Cornwall. Or to London; he'd had enough of that too. He wanted to go somewhere he had never been before, where he knew no one and no one knew him. Somewhere, unlike the other places he had lived, that was neither attractive nor interesting. Miserable as he was, he wanted to live in a place that was miserable too, and where – unlike home – no one would be trying to cheer him up.

Dylan decided on the Midlands. He'd never been there and knew little about it. But – Birmingham, Coventry, the Potteries, the Black Country. The names suggested a post-industrial landscape, all depressed towns and motorways edged with litter. Perfect. Somewhere he could really revel in his hopelessness.

Presumably the very middle of these Midlands would be the grimmest bit of all. Dylan took a map of the UK and a very sharp pencil and drew a vertical line down the centre. Then he drew a horizontal line. He would move to the point where the two lines met.

They went through the E of somewhere called Edenville.

The name filled Dylan with a mordant satisfaction. He knew enough about industrial history to be aware that villages built in mill and mining areas had names that were at best euphemistic and at worst a mocking subversion of the miserable reality of their appearance. The area around this Edenville looked fairly empty, but that, Dylan reasoned, was because it was abandoned scrubland, littered with the spoil heaps of closed mines.

Edenville! He wanted to laugh out loud. The town centre would be all concrete multi-storey car parks, boarded-up shops and disaffected youth. The bleakness of it all would suit his current outlook exactly.

'But where are you going?' his mother kept demanding, right up until the moment he set off. She stood anxiously now in front of his concerned-looking father on the drive of the comfortable family home.

'I'll let you know,' he answered, deliberately vague. He did not want to hurt his parents; but nor did he want them coming to find him. He wanted to be alone.

He started up the little old hatchback he'd bought second-hand as a teenager and which had remained for years in his father's garage. Its back-to-basics lack of frills suited his purpose and outlook. It had just come back from being checked; it was, the mechanic said, running well, mostly because there was so little to go wrong. With its two doors, four gears, plastic seats and wind-down windows it was scarcely more complex than a bicycle. His bag, small as it was, with only minimal changes of clothes and a sponge bag, filled the entire back seat.

'You haven't even given us your mobile number,' his mother wailed as Dylan prepared to edge down the leafy drive.

He wound down the window with an effort. 'That's because I don't have one,' he said.

'But how will you keep in touch?' his father wanted to know.

'Old tech,' Dylan grinned. 'Phone boxes. Postcards.'

He drove off, waving cheerily to disguise his guilt and misgivings. He loved them, but he couldn't stay here.

He roared past the journalists waiting at the bottom of the

drive. There were only a couple; hopefully interest in his story was fading. He was two-days-from-now's chip paper, Dylan thought, and that suited him just fine. He was a piece of screwed-up newspaper blowing about in a deserted multi-storey car park in the post-industrial ruins of Edenville.

By the time he turned off the motorway, the Midlands had yet to come up to his expectations. Or down to them. Nothing so far remotely resembled the wrecked wasteland of his fantasies. Wretched towns and broken buildings, vast, smoke-belching power stations and ugly mechanical plants all seemed in depressingly short supply.

Dylan stabbed at the newly installed satnav – the car's one concession to the twenty-first century. But there was no mistake; he was definitely going in the right direction. He was approaching Edenville just now, in fact.

Perhaps the grim, *noir* bits would start soon. For the moment, the countryside was mellow, with fat fields of pinkish-brown earth and handsome red-brick Georgian residences with fanlights picked out in white. He had passed several attractive pubs whose shining windows were stickered with Good Food Guide labels while exterior blackboards listing the specials of the day stood invitingly outside.

Dylan hadn't realised the Midlands could look like this. The fields looked unbelievably green, under a sky of equally powerful blue. Well, hopefully they would stop soon and give way to some rackety, boarded-up suburbs leading to a brutalist concrete centre.

He had just been through a town called Chestlock, which hadn't been rackety at all. On the contrary: it had been an upright, well-kept sort of place. None of the businesses had been boarded up; the shops all looked prosperous and the town centre had bustled with people. There was a park of Edwardian tidiness that sported both a boating lake and a floral clock.

Aha, thought Dylan. According to his satnav, he was approaching something called the Pemberton Estate. Edenville seemed to be in the middle of it. He pictured a bleak expanse of public housing beset with social problems. At last!

But that he'd got the wrong end of the stick was evident even before he went over the ancient stone bridge and past the large green sign with 'The Pemberton Estate' painted on it in neat white letters. Beyond stretched a rolling emerald park through which a wide silver ribbon of river meandered between banks studded with elegant trees.

That Edenville village was going to be horribly attractive was glaringly obvious.

CHAPTER 18

Behind the managerial wooden flap of the Edenville Arms, Jason Twistle was worrying. It was possible that he hadn't sounded appalled enough about the sacking of Ros Downer.

Angela was clearly furious about it, but only partly because Ros was her friend and collaborator. The root of her indignation was that the Earl had acted over her head, without consultation, and this had made her look powerless. Appearing powerful, for Angela, took precedence over friendship every time.

Was his failure to sympathise a terrible mistake? Jason wondered. And might Angela Highwater make him pay for it, in some ghastly, yet undreamed of way?

He cast a glance into Pumps bar, and from there into the adjoining Kegs restaurant. His vantage point at the base of the stairs gave him a good view of both.

Nothing much was going on in either. The lunch service was drawing to a close and all that could be heard was the clink of cutlery and glassware as sets were put out for dinner. Outside, a few stragglers were drinking up at the sunny outside tables. It was all very peaceful. Not even Dan Parker had turned up to defy regulations by eating his home-made sandwiches on the pub's premises. Hopefully he had finally got the message and wouldn't.

Jason looked at his watch. The honeymooners should be here soon; the jilted bride and her female companion. And the child, of course.

Was Angela right and were they a same-sex couple? Jason found he was hoping so. Their example might help him face up to the tendencies he'd buried for years, but which were, he felt, steadily coming to the surface. There was a young barman he had hired, Ryan. He wasn't the sharpest knife in the drawer but there was definitely something about him . . .

Jason shoved the thought away and returned to flicking through the new estate brochure. Now Ros Downer had actually been sacked, Jason could enjoy her moronic descriptions. She had made a particularly impressive hash of the Pemberton Estate's holiday cottages.

The cottages had been converted from various estate buildings. 'Cobblers' was a former shoe mender's workshop, 'Sloppings' was an ex-pigsty and 'High Cheeses' an erstwhile dairy. The latest to come on stream was the rather more romantically named 'Bess's Tower'.

A one-time hunting lodge, it was named after an Elizabethan countess of Pemberton who had been especially partial to the chase. Once it would have afforded splendid views of the parkland below, but in the five centuries since it was built, woods had sprung up around it. The building now lay buried like Sleeping Beauty's castle amid a tangle of trees and rhododendron bushes.

Bess's Tower had been abandoned for many years, used mainly as a place for fag-breaks by the foresters working in the pine plantations at the top of the estate. But Buzzie Omelet, the famous interior designer, had recently taken the place in hand and given it an overhaul. Bess's Tower was now, Jason learned from the peerless Downer prose, 'transfoamed into a haven of piece and tranquility not to mention a shoecase for stunning locally sauced design'.

It was like reading a foreign language. Jason eventually translated details of the master bedroom's headboard made from ginkgo biloba branches and the Japanese toilet. He knew all about the toilet anyway. Thanks to the estate plumbers, who got everywhere, this convenience was famous throughout Pemberton. It apparently played music and sent up warm gusts of air after self-flushing.

Despite such attractions, Bess's Tower had as yet failed to catch on with the cottage-renting public as comprehensively as Cobblers, Sloppings and High Cheeses had. All were booked solidly throughout every holiday and many weekends besides – except for Bess's.

No one really knew why. Some thought it might be the remote location, others pointed to the lack of Wi-Fi. Possibly it was a combination of those factors and the exceptionally steep – even for the Pemberton Estate – weekly rental. The powers that be, it was felt, also had more faith in the pulling power of the Japanese toilet than perhaps, strictly, it merited.

Recent e-bulletins to managers in all areas of the estate had urged those in front-of-house positions to sell the new conversion hard. Jason knew this was an opportunity for him, the new kid on the Pemberton hospitality-offer block, as it were, to make an impression.

But it was a tough call. Only someone who really wanted to escape from the world would want to stay in Bess's Tower. A reclusive Howard Hughes type. And they'd need his money too if they intended to take advantage of the private chef option.

Edenville was a Best Kept Village on steroids. Worse than his worst fears. Dylan had drawn up in the car park of the pub and was sitting looking gloomily out through his windscreen.

The buildings were like nothing he had ever seen; certainly not in one place, all together, like this. While they had evidently all been built at the same time – early Victorian, at a guess – they were all different and all equally fantastical.

There was a house shaped like a tiny castle, complete with octagonal tower, cross-shaped arrow slit and white flagpole. There was a Tudor one with steep gables, barley-sugar chimneys and mullioned windows criss-crossed with diamond panes. Other houses had a Venetian look about them, with balconies and rows of pointed arched windows. Yet others had the big, projecting roofs of Swiss chalets.

It was all incredibly fanciful, ridiculously gorgeous, impossibly picturesque. And the gardens were even worse, exploding with traditional country colour: hollyhocks, roses, wisteria, delphiniums. There was a church with a green stretch of grass in front of it where a mirror-like pond reflected some majestic oaks and elms.

He stared at the pub, the Edenville Arms. It was built of the same golden stone as the rest of the village. There were twinkling windows and fresh white parasols above the terrace tables. Even the gravel in the car park had been raked like a Riviera beach.

Dylan would have liked to have driven off in search of the somewhere infinitely more miserable he had originally had in mind. But he had drawn his pencil line through this appallingly beautiful place. It was here, or hereabouts, that he'd vowed to live. He was stuck with it. And he was tired after his long journey; the least that was required was lunch. And maybe, after, a sleep in the car. He had to admit that the place was suitable for that at least; it was pretty quiet.

*

Jason was still absorbed in Ros's brochure. Perhaps he had been over-critical. In its way it was a masterpiece. So bad that it was good.

'Excuse me.'

Jason looked up. A gaunt young man in jeans and a white T-shirt stood before him. He looked drained, his wild dark hair accentuating his grey pallor and the shadows under his large, dark eyes.

'Do you have any sandwiches?'

Jason launched himself into full exuberant manager mode. 'Sandwiches! Indeed, sir. Absolutely. Allow me to get you a bar menu.'

Dylan watched the neat little bottom in its tight black trousers sashay off into Pumps bar. Jason returned waving a large grey sheet of paper. 'Here we are, sir. Allow me to recommend the crayfish, pea, mint and mango wrap.'

Dylan stared at the sandwich options printed in swirling script. 'I just wanted ham.'

'Certainly. Can I recommend the air-dried *jamón* from the Spanish black-footed mountain pig? It's fed entirely on acorns at an altitude of no less than three thousand feet and served with vanilla and green fig compote . . .'

Dylan groaned inwardly. He'd imagined he'd left this sort of thing behind him. Soho members' clubs had entire herds of black-footed mountain pigs air-dried into fashionable ham and washed down with boutique beers.

'Just normal ham, if that's OK.'

'Of course, sir. The black-footed pig isn't to everyone's taste. May I recommend one of our boutique ales to go with it? Tinker's Bottom is a particularly good fit.'

'Er, OK.'

Jason beamed. 'Please take a seat on the terrace, sir. Your

sandwich will be with you directly and I'll send someone out with your Bottom.'

Dylan wandered back out to the front of the pub and sat down at one of the wooden tables. They were clean, comfortable and well shaded. The honeycomb-coloured paving stones beneath them were entirely weed-free; free, too, of a single cigarette butt. This place was almost eerily well kept.

His eye caught the gold weathercock revolving cheerily atop the church steeple. It seemed to him that the sharp pencil shape might at any moment start scribbling on the sky.

Imagery, pshaw, Dylan thought, pushing away this glimmering of literary inspiration, his first since the accident. He didn't want literary inspiration, not any more. Along with everything else in the writer's bag of tricks – metaphor, allegory, rhythm, synecdoche, you name it – he no longer had any use for it.

He was here to *not* write. To not write in a place so depressing that he could abandon himself to nihilism and do nothing at all if he felt like it; where merely running away from writing was enough.

But it was hard not to recognise that things weren't quite working out that way. Instead of leading him to a miserable, post-industrial town, Fate had brought him to a village that looked like a living postcard. Edenville was all light and colour, beauty and tastefulness. It wasn't the kind of place where you could stare at a concrete wall whilst the people in the upstairs flat screamed and threw things and police sirens wailed all night long. It was the kind of place where you heard nightingales and stared at what were undoubtedly England's Best Views.

There was also something irrepressibly vital about it. From the singing birds to the blooming gardens to the thrusting trees, the village seemed full of natural get up and go. The few people

Dylan had seen were all busily occupied and the neat outsides of the cottages suggested that their inmates were both proud and happy to be there.

It was difficult, tired and dispirited though he was, not to feel stirred by all this life and activity. It occurred to him that just running away from writing might not, after all, be enough. Not for the rest of his days, anyway.

'Tinker's Bottom and a ham sandwich, sir?'

A pint of beer in a straight glass was put in front of him, plus a plate full of dazzlingly bright colours. An onion and tomato salad was topped with cress and chopped yellow pepper. Beside it, made of very fresh white bread and stuffed thickly with home-cured ham, the sandwich had been cut into quarters and carefully arranged along a narrow white plate. It was, Dylan had to admit, without doubt the finest ham sandwich he had ever seen.

As he ate, and despite his efforts not to let it, his unwanted mood of optimism gathered strength. He reluctantly accepted that perhaps his father had been right all along and he ought to find something to do.

But definitely not something where he worked with his brain, or used a keyboard. The something, whatever it was, would have to be far removed from the heated, esoteric world of letters.

Something practical, something outdoors. A building site, that sort of thing. Straightforward but boring and with a hard, backbreaking aspect to it. Dylan was reluctant to relinquish the idea of suffering.

He looked down at his plate, and was surprised to see both the salad and the sandwiches gone. He had finished the lot.

Warmed by sunshine just the right side of hot, Dylan now felt pleasantly full and sleepy. The air was full of soothing noises:

birds singing and leaves sighing, people on the terrace talking softly and sounds of sheep from the surrounding fields. He could smell cut grass and deep honey scents from the flowers in the cottage gardens. It would be so easy to rest his head on his arms and go to sleep . . .

But no. Dylan roused himself. He was not here to enjoy himself. He needed to find something to do. Something hard, outside and boring.

A newspaper lay on the table and he reached for it. It was a local freesheet, the *Edenville Advertiser*. Papers like this often had job sections. He could do worse than have a look.

A rustling noise now attracted his attention. A man was sitting himself down at the next table and removing what were ostensibly home-made sandwiches from a supermarket carrier bag. Behind him, affixed to the pub's sunny front, was a sign: 'These Tables Are Reserved For Customers Eating Pub Food Only', exquisitely lettered in white on a sage green background.

Dylan continued on to Situations Vacant. Till Operatives were needed at the supermarket and there was a caretaking opportunity at a primary school. They both sounded quite boring, which was good. But also quite indoorsy, which was bad.

'Lookin' fer a job?' enquired the man with the sandwiches.

Dylan, who had previously merely glanced at his neighbour, now found himself meeting a pair of deep-set eyes. His gaze widened to take in a pair of enormous shoulders. This guy was *huge*.

'Er, maybe,' Dylan admitted. He would have preferred the man to mind his own business but you didn't tell someone this size something like that. He looked as if he could wrench trees out by their roots and toss them effortlessly up in the air. As if he could pick up a tractor in each hand while balancing an articulated lorry on his head.

Flashing across Dylan's mind came the possibility that he had been recognised. But just as quickly he dismissed it. The stranger didn't look like the literary type. Besides, Dylan knew, he now looked quite different from the author picture in the back of his novels. He had maintained his clean-shaven chin and allowed his hair to grow longer. He had also, since the accident and despite his mother's efforts to feed him up again, lost a considerable amount of weight.

'What sorta job?'

The gaze of the huge stranger was trained intensely on him. An answer was evidently expected.

'A kind of, um, outdoorsy job,' Dylan said hurriedly.

'I do gardens,' the other offered, through his sandwich. 'Gard'nin'. Could do wi' some 'elp. You any good at gard'nin'?'

'Gardening?' Dylan repeated. He'd done a bit of it, he supposed. Occasionally, driven to distraction by his father's cajoling, he'd reluctantly gone outside to mow the lawn. He'd done the odd spot of weeding. But he'd never thought of doing gardening as a job. And yet it wasn't a bad idea. He knew more of the basics than he did about, say, building. And it would obviously be outside, very physical and presumably pretty boring, weeding and mowing all day. Exactly what he was looking for, in other words.

'Yeah, I'm OK at it.'

'Pay's not brilliant,' the other said shortly, naming a sum so pitiful Dylan was unsure whether to laugh or be shocked. But money, of course, did not matter. He had loads of the stuff.

Hang on a minute, though, he told himself. Being paid, even at these rates, might mean answering questions. Filling in forms, handing over numbers. Revealing the identity he wanted to put behind him. Dylan began to silently construct a defensive sentence about being ideologically opposed to giving personal information. If the guy didn't buy that, he'd have to turn it down.

'It's cash in 'and,' the other remarked, as if reading his mind.

No questions asked then, Dylan realised, with cautious relief.

'Reckon you're on for it?' He was being looked at questioningly.

Dylan reckoned he probably was. Apart from anything else, there was something appealingly rash about throwing his lot in with a stranger, particularly one like this. The guy was about as far as it was possible to imagine from a fashionable, neurotic London literary hipster.

'When do I start?'

The other finished chewing, screwed up his plastic bag and stuffed it in a back pocket. He rose to what, to the seated Dylan, looked like his full ten feet and picked up, from the bench beside him, a dirty denim baseball cap. He clapped it on his head and said, 'Monday. 'Arf seven. Meet you 'ere.'

Dylan blinked. He hadn't started work at seven thirty in his entire life, let alone for such bad pay.

'Or are yer livin' somewhere else?' his large new employer enquired, misunderstanding the hesitation.

He wasn't actually living anywhere, of course. Dylan's only permanent address was his car. He had noticed the pub had rooms; he could book into one of those.

'Here's fine,' Dylan assured his new employer. 'Seven thirty, Monday, then.'

He felt his right hand crushed in a painful grip. 'The name's Dan. Dan Parker.'

Dylan hesitated before giving his own name. He was no longer Dylan Eliot, the well-known writer, the literary *enfant terrible*. He was . . . who was he?

His eye caught one of the trees around the pond on the green. Huge trees, billowing with leaves.

'Greenleaf,' Dylan said.

'Greenleaf?' The big guy laughed. 'Good name for a gardener.'

'Yeah. Isn't it?' He was racking his brains for a first name. 'Adam,' he added, as it came out of the blue. 'Adam Greenleaf.'

It sounded quite plausible, he thought. Possibly even more than Dylan Eliot. Perhaps, in reality, he had always been Adam Greenleaf.

Dan nodded. 'Good stuff. See yer 'ere Monday, Adam.'

Dan was striding away on his enormously long legs when a flurry of activity from the pub entrance attracted Dylan's attention. The manager in the tight trousers now came skittering out in an obvious state of agitation. 'Excuse me,' he shouted, after Dan's vast retreating form. 'Could you please read the signs and not eat your *own* sandwiches at *our* tables?'

Dan gave no sign of having heard. Instead, he swung himself into a battered red van and shut the passenger side door with a mighty slam. After a couple of stutters, the vehicle spluttered into life. Dylan watched it exit the car park with a screech of brakes and a spray of gravel.

CHAPTER 19

Jason returned to his cubbyhole feeling intensely irritated. Quite apart from Dan Parker eating his sandwiches on pub premises *again*, the ladies and their daughter hadn't arrived yet.

This latter in particular concerned Jason. If the girls – as he'd started to think of them – didn't come, he would have nothing to tell Angela about. And given that she might still be angry about the Ros Downer business, he might be in for a bumpy ride.

There was a commotion in the doorway and Jason looked up. To his horror, Angela herself now came clomping in on her trademark six-inch heels. Her hot-pink mini wrap dress was yanked tightly round her waist and her thickly made-up black eyes sparked with fury.

Jason, frozen with fear, could only stare helplessly as Angela bore down on him like a juggernaut on a headlight-fixated rabbit. 'I've just missed him. His bloody van's just driven off.'

Jason realised that the object of the Director of Human Resources' ire was not himself but the jobbing gardener she had in her romantic sights. He hurried to redeem himself by assuring her that Dan Parker was plainly unworthy of her affection. 'He's just been eating his sandwiches outside again,' Jason reported, pursing his lips with disapproval.

He was perturbed when, instead of joining in his dissatis-faction, Angela looked indignant. 'Yes, but it's hardly *his* fault he does that, is it?'

Jason was confused. How could someone eat sandwiches in blatant contravention of the stated rules of the premises and it not be their fault? 'So whose fault is it?' he asked.

'That stupid old sod George Farley's, of course,' stormed Angela, tossing her stiffly sprayed ebony curls.

Jason was puzzled. George Farley was a widower in his late eighties who lived alone at the end of the village. He was quiet, law-abiding and fond of his garden, in which he spent long hours working. On no occasion, when Dan had been eating his sandwiches, had George been anywhere near the pub.

'That's the whole point,' Angela snapped accusingly, when Jason pointed this out. 'He *never* comes here any more. Dan says all the old guys think they're not welcome.'

Jason felt, inside his head, the clatter of a very big penny dropping. Angela was referring to the consequences of his new managership.

The Edenville Arms had, until last year, been a run-down village boozer with the letters falling off the sign. Its main customers had been ancient men who sat all night by a badly smoking fire cradling a half-pint of mild and playing dominoes. There had also been a widespread practice of locals using the outside benches to eat food not bought in the pub. Jason's instructions on the assumption of his duties had been to address both issues.

'Are you telling me,' Jason asked Angela, 'that Dan Parker's sandwich-eating has a political dimension?'

'Something like that,' Angela replied acidly. She turned her glittering eyes challengingly on his. 'And I have to say, I admire his commitment.'

Jason had to hold his jaw to stop it dropping. Admire Parker's commitment! In opposing a rule that Angela herself had wanted enforced!

It had been her idea, especially about the outside tables. Personally, Jason was happy to leave that arrangement the way it was. Most people with their own food at least drank his beer and wine, which was where the profit lay.

'Goodness,' he said, summoning up a tone somewhere between regret and admiration. 'I didn't realise Dan had such strong principles.'

'He's got strong *everything*,' Angela burst out longingly, with flared nostrils. 'I don't know what he sees in that Turner woman! How could he prefer *her*, when he could have me?' Her eyes filled with tears and her nose turned red.

Jason waited a couple of beats before saying anything else. He made a 'glass' gesture at Ryan, the handsome new barman.

Ryan looked puzzled. 'Wine!' Jason hissed urgently and was rewarded by a broad, understanding smile, brilliantly white in the middle of Ryan's lush dark beard. The sight of it filled Jason with a sudden, powerful joy.

'I was thinking,' Jason ventured later, when Angela had recovered somewhat and was halfway down her second large Chardonnay. 'Maybe we can do some offers for locals. It's a shame the old blokes don't come in any more. George especially. He's a nice old thing.'

'Troublemaking old bastard,' corrected Angela.

That seemed a bit unnecessary to Jason. George, or so the manager had heard, was a war hero. He had been a Dambuster, or something.

'Not a troublemaker?' Angela exclaimed, flashing her sharp yellow teeth. 'He made life hell for Ros before she left.'

Jason felt himself warm to the old man still more. Anyone who made Ros Downer's life hell was a friend of his.

'And Iggy's!' Angela added indignantly.

Iggy, Ros's partner and a house husband and part-time chainsaw artist, was someone the pub manager had found deeply irritating. He was always badgering Jason to let him cut down the trees in the Arms' car park – a row of fine, shady limes – so he could sculpt the stumps. Jason loathed chainsaw sculptures.

He wished he had known George Farley had upset these ghastly people. He would have given him a bar table all of his own. As well as free beer. 'So what did George actually do to make their lives hell?' he asked, doing his best to sound disapproving.

Angela began a heated account of the octogenarian's crimes. It was all about gardens, apparently. Jason knew the gardens involved. While George's was notable for its neatness, the Downers', from which it was divided by a broad leylandii hedge, was a chaos of hacked-up wood stumps and faded plastic play equipment for their absurdly named daughter, Rapunzal.

'But when Ros told him to cut down the hedge, he refused!' ranted Angela.

As well he might, thought Jason. Removing it would mean an unrelieved prospect of the Downers' mess. 'Well, surely it was up to him, if it was in his garden.'

'It was blocking the morning sun from their sitting room! Ros suffers from seasonal affective disorder! Selfish old sod,' was Angela's response.

Jason was relieved when, now, they were interrupted. The skinny, lank-haired young man who'd ordered the ham sandwich had reappeared.

Jason eyed him cagily. He'd observed that the young man had been talking to the troublesome Dan Parker.

'I hope the sandwiches were satisfactory?' he enquired, in a bid to draw attention to the Edenville Arms' strengths. The plate had been shining when it came back in; he'd eaten every last bit of pepper. And to noticeable effect; Jason was struck by how much better his customer looked. A sandwich and a beer had made all the difference.

He was actually rather handsome, with very good cheekbones and nice full lips. Now that awful, gaunt, drawn look had gone there was something appealingly soulful about those dark eyes, with their hint of tragedy.

'Very nice,' Dylan said, disconcerted by the other's stare. 'Er, do you have a room?'

Something now inserted itself between Jason and his customer. Something in a hot-pink dress with wild black hair. Angela pressed her buttocks against Jason's wooden flap, spread out her arms and faced the young man as an opera singer faces her audience: chest heaving, eyelids fluttering. 'Of course we have a room,' she declared huskily.

This was not the case, Jason knew. Every room at the moment was completely booked. But he did not dare gainsay Angela.

'Which room's free?' Angela hissed over her shoulder to Jason. 'Quick! Before he goes!'

Jason realised that, to add to his other challenges, the Director of Human Resources had fixed on his customer as an outlet for her thwarted, Chardonnay-fired affections. Perhaps it was just as well that he did not have a room. He leaned forward. 'I'm sorry,' he murmured into Angela's plump back. 'We're completely booked.'

Angela whipped round and the glare she now turned on him was vengeful and infernal. There would, Jason knew, be zero value in pointing out that filling every room of the inn was what he had been employed to do.

143

'What about the honeymoon suite?' Angela snarled. 'Those lesbians haven't come yet, have they?'

Jason regretted letting this slip earlier. He wished the lesbians – if they really were lesbians – would arrive soon. Where were they? He was under serious attack and wouldn't be able to hold the fort much longer.

CHAPTER 20

The Edenville Arms was not proving the easiest of places to find, especially with Google Maps constantly crashing.

They had turned off the motorway a while ago, but the countryside wasn't looking as it should. The mellow green fields Nell recalled from the pub's website hadn't yet put in an appearance.

Instead, they were going down ever narrower roads between stretches of moorland dotted with stunted trees and limping, blighted sheep with daggy bottoms. It was a landscape that seemed gloomy even in bright weather, absorbing the sunshine like a black hole, just as a series of enormous potholes threatened to absorb the Land Rover. Each one was filled with viscous mud which seemed to leap up of its own accord and spatter itself liberally over every window.

'Are you sure we're going the right way?' Rachel asked, wrenching the wheel round a steep corner and wincing as she hit yet another hole.

Nell frowned at the small screen in her palm, following the wiggling track. 'It should be somewhere around here.' She raised her head and looked round doubtfully. The countryside was as empty as it was desolate.

The Defender suddenly jerked to a halt, its engine juddering. Rachel leaned over the steering wheel. 'You're not seriously saying it's *that* place?'

At first glance it looked like a ruin, dark and half-collapsed. But more careful consideration revealed that the upstairs windows did have glass in them, albeit of a matt filthiness. And the rusty sign in front of it, hanging unpromisingly from a post shaped like a gallows, bore the remains of some complex illustration which might once have been a heraldic device.

'Evil Arms!' exclaimed Juno excitedly.

'What?' Nell gasped. But Juno was right. Nell found that if she really squinted hard, the remaining letters E VIL ARMS could be seen at the bottom of the sign.

'Bloody hell,' said Rachel.

Nell could not, for the moment, frame speech. Her gaze was fixed on the dirty upper casements. They were booked in the honeymoon suite, but this place didn't look as if it had any kind of suite. Even an en suite. 'It's gone downhill a bit since they took the website picture,' was all she could say.

Only Juno seemed inclined to look on the bright side. 'It's like *The Hound of the Baskervilles*,' she said happily.

It was, indeed, easy to imagine some bloodthirsty animal bounding towards them, jaws open and dripping with murderous intent. The Evil Arms, Nell thought, looked like a place where even the pub cat could kill. Except that there didn't seem to be one of those either. There was no sign of life whatsoever. She remembered the friendly, capable – if, as regarded the booking, disappointingly firm – manager. Where was he amid all this desolation?

Rachel had got out and was picking her way, in her red silk shoes, determinedly through the stagnant puddles and broken tarmac of what might once have been a car park.

Nell lingered in the Land Rover. She was not walking about here in her wedding dress! Up here you'd need thermals in July. And Arran jumpers on top of those. She hadn't even got wellies.

'Come on,' yelled Rachel, waving frantically as she disappeared round a corner. Of Juno there was no sign; presumably she had gone before.

With no option but to get out, Nell lowered herself gingerly in her white plastic boots and hurried after Rachel. A cold wind whipped around her bare legs.

Rachel stood before a dank aperture which might have been the inn entrance. Recessed into a green-streaked stone porch, a great, ill-fitting front door slumped sideways on its hinges. Rachel lifted the rusty handle – a circle of heavy iron – and twisted it, producing a creak as loud as a shout in the still air.

'Don't open it,' begged Nell.

This just couldn't be the Edenville Arms. Even allowing for the fact that this was where Google had sent her, and that hotel websites always made places look better than they were, there seemed no possibility this was the sunny, well-kept establishment she had seen online. Nell stared despairingly round at the black stumps of stone, the broken windows. It was a ruin, and not a romantic ruin at that.

She folded her arms decisively. 'Let's just go back to London.'

Rachel folded her arms as well. 'I've just driven for four hours up here. There's no bloody way I'm driving for four hours back. We're staying here tonight, at any rate.' She opened the door of the Evil Arms and called into the dark cave within. 'Hello?'

Nell looked back longingly towards the Red Baron. If they kept driving they might come across a B&B somewhere.

'It's raining,' said Juno, and it was. Hard. With incredible speed, a group of fat black clouds had gathered in the sky above.

A fat drop of cold water hit Nell hard on the nose. Then another. And another. The drops bounced off the broken ground, the size of a cherry tomato.

'It's hail!' Juno shouted, amazed.

Incredibly, it was. Everyone's ears filled with the roar of ice balls hitting tarmac and exploding into puddles. The whole sky was white and moving downwards. Then the hail abruptly changed direction and became horizontal. Cold, hard pellets lashed their faces. It was like being shot.

'My dress!' shouted Rachel and Nell in unison.

'Ow! *Ow!*' shrieked Juno.

Rachel yanked open the door and they hurried inside. The empty entrance hall, its rotting ceiling bristling with exposed cables, opened into a big, gloomy, stone-floored room. It was utterly empty, freezing cold and perceptibly damp; a situation that the tiny stove, set in a vast fireplace at the room's far end, would clearly never be able to address.

Hail rattled like bullets against the windows, setting Nell's nerves jangling. She felt like a refugee from a war, or an extra in the last scenes of a Bond film.

What light had managed to struggle through the small, dirty panes gleamed dully on rows of pewter pots hanging from great black ceiling beams. A pair of colossal bull horns was fixed to the nearest one.

Juno was the first to speak. 'It's like something from a Hammer Horror,' she said, delighted. 'Look at that suit of armour!'

Nell looked. The huge, helmeted figure was holding a pike whose axe-edge looked horribly sharp.

'And . . . next to it?' gasped Rachel, her fingers gripping Nell's bare arm. In a tall glass case beside the armour hung a jumble of something yellowish-white. It was a skeleton.

'It's not real,' Juno reported, skipping back from examining it. 'It's a facsimile of the bones of a highwayman who was hung on the gibbet near here. Apparently,' she continued cheerfully, 'he was a regular. Still is, in a way, because he haunts the place. Isn't that nice?'

'Lovely,' muttered Nell as Juno darted off to investigate the armour.

The freezing cold of the flagstones seeped through the thin soles of the women's footwear as they walked to what might, long ago, have been the bar. A counter made of thick black wood stood atop a great carved black panel. Behind stretched a grubby mirror, before which a couple of upside-down spirits bottles glimmered through the all-covering dust.

'Please let's go,' Nell begged. She could see, as if from a great distance, her dim reflection in the bar mirror, but she didn't want to look at it in case something creepy in a hood and carrying a scythe turned out to be standing behind her. Or a long-dead, gibbeted highwayman.

Rachel, however, had spotted the Gordon's bottle. 'Not without a gin,' she stated, in a tone which brooked no argument. She strode to the bar and banged her fist on it; some flakes of ceiling plaster floated gently down. 'Landlord!' Rachel called. The noise, in the lonely, eerie silence, sent panic shooting through Nell.

'There's no one here!' she gasped. 'Well, no one actually alive.'

'Don't be ridiculous. There's no such thing as ghosts,' Rachel replied briskly. 'Landlord!' she yelled again.

Nell wondered afterwards if, without Rachel's need for a stiff drink at just that point, any of what subsequently happened would have happened. It seemed amazing that so much could be contingent on a mere few distilled drops.

Nonetheless, when she looked back, of all the twists of Fate that could so easily have twisted the other way, or never have twisted at all, that drink seemed the most decisive.

Had Rachel not demanded refreshment in that peremptory manner, the owner of the establishment may well have chosen not to appear. The fact that he did gave them all a fright; the hunched, scowling figure appearing suddenly in the shadows behind the bar. Only the pungent smell that came with him indicated he was terrestrial rather than some awful apparition; he was accompanied by a powerful stench which quite bore out his claim to have been 'owt wi't pigs' and unaware that customers required his presence.

Once he had hunted about the dusty bar shelves for a small and rusting tin of tonic and jerked a smeared glass upwards into the Gordon's optic, mine host revealed that no booking in Nell's name for the honeymoon suite had been made online. There was no internet here. That, admittedly, was less of a surprise than the information, subsequently vouchsafed, that while this was indeed the Edenville Arms, it was not the only one. There was another pub of the same name in a village ten miles away.

CHAPTER 21

Dylan stood in the cramped lobby of the Edenville Arms waiting for the manager to finish his argument with the woman in the bright pink dress. The dispute was being conducted in whispers, so he could not hear what was being said, but it was clear it was both urgent and acrimonious. The woman's bottom, turned towards him, seemed to be getting more dangerously close all the time. Every time she made a point she stuck her rear out still further and there was a danger it was going to end up shoved into Dylan's midriff.

He had shrunk back against the wall as best he could, but, thin as he was, it was clearly only a matter of time. In any other circumstances he would have left; given it up as a bad job. But he needed a room here so he could start working with Dan on Monday. He allowed himself an audible sigh, hoping it might move matters on.

Jason, behind the flap, heard the sigh and the screw of anxiety within him tightened further. He and Angela had reached stalemate over the room business. They were quite unable to come to an accommodation over accommodation.

She wanted him to hand over the honeymoon suite but Jason was sticking to his guns. The lesbians – if indeed they were –

had paid in full, up front. He couldn't give their room away. What if they turned up?

Angela's response to this was to declare, in an aggressive, hissing slur, that she couldn't care less if they did. As a manifesto for innkeeping it lacked something, Jason felt.

Necessity, of course, is famously the mother of invention and now, just as Jason gave way to despair, an idea bounded into his mind. An idea about a Japanese toilet and a locally sauced headboard made of ginkgo biloba branches. An idea about a holiday cottage that no one wanted to rent. An idea that, if it worked, would not only satisfy Angela but earn him brownie points in the eyes of the Estate.

He scrabbled hurriedly under his counter for Ros Downer's brochure, found the page with Bess's Tower on it and shoved it over Angela's shoulder at his customer who, incredibly, hadn't fled yet.

'May I suggest, sir?' he yelped, proffering the little book.

'What the . . . ?' exclaimed Angela, following the publication's trajectory and twisting awkwardly back round. As she did so, her wrap dress caught on a hook in the flap and yanked itself partially unwrapped. 'Wassgoinon?' she demanded unsteadily, as Dylan politely avoided looking at her largely exposed chest.

He could not, Jason recognised, any longer afford to tolerate a drunken, partly undressed Angela in the main visitor welcome area of the inn. He leaned forward and whispered in her ear and Angela's suspicious, flushed, confused features settled. 'Ah,' she said, nodding. 'BeshesTower. SaverygoodideaJase. Yestis.'

As his customer was now reading the brochure, Jason took the opportunity to gently lead Angela into Pumps and settle her at a booth in the corner. Her head flopped against the padded seat and she regarded him through half-closed eyes. She was quite helpless, Jason saw. In this state, there was something almost vulnerable about her.

'Oozethatguyoutthere?' she slurred. 'Versexy, dontchathink?'

Jason sighed. There was a far sexier guy in the pub so far as he was concerned. But whether he would ever pluck up the courage to do anything about it was anyone's guess. Poor Angela, he thought. And poor me. We're just two lonely people, really, simply wanting to be loved.

'Bloodygorjusifyouaskme,' Angela was groaning. 'I would, I tell ya.'

Jason hoped she wasn't about to turn lewd. The bar dining tables were full of the gin-and-Jag couples that represented the Arms' customer base. Expensively understated clothes, ostentatious good manners and a tendency to converse in murmurs were their distinguishing characteristics. Angela's breasts were now almost fully dislodged from their moorings and her general deportment more suitable to some of Chestlock's less reputable establishments, such as Harlots or Knockers.

Jason was suddenly, electrically, aware of Ryan standing next to him. He swallowed a few times and breathed in deeply to control the racing of his heart. Then he looked up, straight into the melting eyes of his most junior barman.

'Can you get her some water?' he asked, hearing his voice come out rushed and panicked.

'Water?' Ryan repeated, his uncomprehending tone striking Jason's ear like the trumpets of angels.

'Clear stuff, non-alcoholic, comes in bottles,' the manager persisted. 'Or out of a tap.'

Ryan nodded, flashed another of his dazzling smiles, and with one final look into Jason's eyes, walked away. Jason stared after him, feeling as if all the breath had left his body.

A tower in the forest that you could rent, Dylan gathered,

having ploughed through Ros Downer's description. But what was that thing in the bathroom? There was something strange going on above the bed as well, a sort of bald hedge. Weariness was making it hard to focus.

'I'll take it,' he said, when Jason returned, raised his flap and entered the alcove behind it.

'Perfect, sir,' Jason nodded. 'If sir would give me a few moments, I'll phone through to the appropriate office. In the meantime, may I give sir a booking form?'

Dylan stared down at the many and varied demands for personal information on the paper Jason slid in front of him. He raised his head, looked steadily at the manager and let fly the sentence he had originally composed for Dan Parker.

'I'm sorry. I'm ideologically opposed to giving away information about myself. I'm happy to pay in cash up front, though.'

Jason's mouth dropped open. He'd never heard anything like this before. Most people he came across would tell you anything about themselves; were eager to. 'But sir, I'm afraid we have to have certain information. Credit card, date of birth, home address.'

Dylan shook his head. 'I don't see why, not if I'm paying cash in advance. My personal details are my own. I'd reveal them to the police, a court of law, a doctor, but no one else.'

One of those libertarian types, obviously. But he had a point, it *was* ridiculous the way you were expected to hand over everything from your blood group to your mother's maiden name on the flimsiest possible pretext. No, Jason didn't disagree with him. And he had good reasons for wanting this arrangement to work.

'I'd be prepared to pay a month's rent up front,' Dylan said, getting out his wallet. Luckily, he'd brought a great deal of cash.

It had seemed a sensible precaution as he was heading to unknown regions. Money always helped.

Jason needed no further convincing. 'Very well, sir.' He slid the prurient form away. 'I'll just give you a map and the code to get the key out of the safe at the cottage.'

'Great.' Dylan felt energised by his moral victory. His eyes sparkled.

'But may I at least have your name, sir?'

'Adam Greenleaf.'

Jason nodded. He was counting Dylan's notes. 'This all looks in order, Mr Greenleaf.'

He'd got away with it. Dylan was almost enjoying this now. He felt the urge to giggle tug at his lips. It was not a sensation he had ever imagined feeling again.

Jason looked up and bestowed on Dylan his best professional smile. 'Will sir be joining us for dinner tonight? Kegs is fully booked, I'm afraid, but if sir wishes to eat around eight, I can offer the best table in Pumps.'

'Er . . . OK.'

'Right next to the fireplace,' a smiling Jason went on. 'And as it's only early summer as yet, we light it in the evenings.'

He was puzzled at the expression of horror sweeping over his customer's face. Dylan reeled backwards. A lit fire! Flames roared in his imagination. He saw the devil surfing boots, shrinking and evaporating in the screaming heat.

'No thanks,' he stammered. He took the sheet of paper Jason now handed him and hurried towards the door.

Outside, the sunny afternoon was mellowing into golden evening and Edenville's fanciful buildings glowed in radiant light. Wall-ivy sparkled and shimmered and in the cottage gardens, the flowers glowed.

'This is more like it!' exclaimed Rachel as they hurried across the car park towards the Edenville Arms. The *real* Edenville Arms. Which, Nell was relieved to see, didn't merely look just like its website, but even better. The fields swelling gently behind it really were rolling and mellow. It was hard to believe that the stark moors with their twisted trees and blasted sheep were in the same country, let alone the same county a mere few miles away.

She felt fragile and very tired. The long journey, especially with the shock of the Evil Arms, had taken its toll. But Rachel, as ever, seemed to be firing on all cylinders. 'It's like a model village,' she exclaimed loudly, looking round. 'Except that all the houses are life-size.'

'Woo hoo!' Juno shouted from across the road. She was standing next to a pond on the village green. 'Ducks!'

'Come on!' Rachel yelled at her daughter. She was not, unlike Nell, even aware of the couple of drinkers sitting at the wooden tables on the sunny terrace who were staring in surprise at the women in party dresses and the little girl in a sober suit who had just emerged from the rusty red Land Rover.

While Rachel passed easily under the pub's low doorway, the much taller Nell had to stoop almost in half.

'It's lovely!' gasped Rachel, looking admiringly about her.

On one side of the entrance passage was a bar with small scrubbed-pine tables and a fake-antique figurehead with a chef's hat on it. On the other side was a restaurant with very brightly striped tub chairs. Rows of glasses and cutlery shone in the sun streaming through the polished windows. Everything was sparkling clean, and drifting through the warm air was a spicy, expensive smell of scented candles.

Nell was about to agree with Rachel when the words dried in her mouth. Someone was approaching rapidly in the entrance passage. A tall young man with dark hair and a preoccupied expression. He wore jeans and a white T-shirt and was studying a piece of paper in his hand.

Nell felt a shock like an explosion, followed by a strange, falling sensation, as if the atoms of her being had all been blown up into the air, floated back down and rearranged themselves.

He was thinner and looked scruffier, but there was no doubt that it was him. She would have been able to pick him out of a million. It was the man who had pretended to be OutdoorsGuy. Who had humiliated and embarrassed her at Paddington. Who, after Joey, was the source of all her troubles. Had it not been for him, she would never have fallen for Joey in the first place.

PART TWO

CHAPTER 22

The honeymoon suite's vast bed was draped in lilac and black.
It was scattered with hot-pink, heart-shaped cushions decorated
with black flounces, fringes and lace. Above it loomed a black-
draped half-tester and dangling in front of that was a black glass
chandelier.

'We've got to go,' Nell said grimly. 'We absolutely can't stay
here.'

'Oh come on,' said Rachel. 'It's a bit over the top, but it's
pretty comfortable. Juno likes it, don't you?'

Juno, seated at a side table tucking into room service bangers,
mash and onion gravy, nodded enthusiastically.

'And you've paid for it all,' Rachel added.

Nell turned her exasperated gaze on her friend. 'It's not the
bloody décor. And I don't care whether I've paid for it. I just
can't stay here, full stop.'

'Hey, less of the bloody, thanks. There are children present.'

'I've heard people say bloody before,' interjected Juno, with
a meaningful look at her mother.

Nell reddened guiltily. She shouldn't, she knew, have spoken
so sharply. 'I'm sorry. But it's just impossible for me to stay
here.'

'And why would that be?' Rachel asked, a touch impatiently.

Every reason, Nell thought. She was now convinced that she had only decided to marry Joey because of what Fake OutdoorsGuy had done. Joey was mainly to blame, obviously, but it was the man in the Apples and Pears who had driven her into his arms.

Explaining all this to Rachel would be too painful, though. After what Rachel had witnessed at the register office, describing her online romantic misadventures would be just too humiliating.

Nell decided to throw herself on Rachel's mercy, with an open-ended appeal. 'I just can't bear it,' she declared, turning wide, pained eyes to her friend and injecting into her voice all the drama she could summon. 'Surely you can understand? With the wedding not happening and everything? Being here is just . . . agony.' She ended with a sigh, and drooped her head pathetically.

But Rachel wasn't buying it. 'Yes, well, going back at this time of night will be pretty agonising as well,' she said tersely. 'We're all exhausted and Juno's about to have a bath. We haven't eaten either. And I've been drinking.' She raised a hand holding a half-drained glass of pink champagne. The bottle it had come from lolled in a silver bucket on a side table. 'This is my second.'

Before Nell could marshal a contrary argument, Rachel disappeared into the bathroom. Any further conversation would have to be shouted over the rushing water. The enormous claw-foot tub, a miracle of hydro-technology, had a long, rectangular single tap rather than two separate ones. A sheet of water slid out like Niagara Falls.

Nell drifted to the bedroom's diamond-pane window and stared hopelessly out. It was evening now and the pretty little village buildings were thickly painted with the golden brush of sunset. Their details were beautiful: barley-twist chimneys, scalloped roof-tiles, castellations, balconies. Nell, however, could not appreciate any of it.

He was downstairs!. Here, in the very same hotel. How that could possibly be the case she couldn't imagine. She had last seen him in London, and at a south-west-bound station too. So it was doubly unlikely that he would be up here in the Midlands. And yet, indubitably, he was. Presumably with that horrible harridan.

Well, she would obviously have to stay here tonight. But no more than that, Nell promised herself. Tomorrow, Rachel and Juno would be returning to London and she would go with them. Hopefully Rachel would let her stay in Gardiner Road while she found herself another flat.

Although . . .

Flashing across Nell's mind came the idea that she still might be able to stop the sale of 19a. She had signed nothing, after all. She could halt the whole proceeding, get her furniture out of storage and move back in there. She would call the estate agents about it on Monday.

But the estate agents were, of course, Carrington's. This flat business was only one of the messes Joey had landed her in. Calling them would be embarrassing; but did his colleagues even know about their relationship? It seemed that Joey had all sorts of lives, had told all sorts of lies.

In the bathroom, she could hear Juno enquiring about the bidet.

'The French use them for . . .' Rachel began.

'For?' prompted Juno, as the normally frank Rachel hesitated.

'For washing their socks in.'

Nell snorted, in spite of herself. It made her feel a little better and she reminded herself that, while she hated to think she and Fake OutdoorsGuy were under the same roof, there were ways of avoiding him. She and Rachel could stay in the suite and have room service. It looked good, judging from the empty plate of Juno's Rachel had put outside the door. There was no need to go downstairs at all.

'Why are the towels all black, Mummy?' Juno was asking now.

'They're not. Some of them are hot pink.'

'Hot? How hot? Too hot to touch?'

'It's just the name of the colour.'

'Oh.'

'Hey, Nell,' Rachel was calling from the bathroom. 'Why not go down and get a table for supper? I'm starving.'

'Downstairs?' Nell was dismayed. 'Wouldn't you rather stay here and have room service?'

There was a cackle from the bathroom. 'Are you joking? After what you said about the decoration? All that pink and black would put me off my food.'

'Yes, but—' Nell began.

'Besides,' Rachel swept on from the bathroom, 'Juno wants to go to sleep and it's been ages since I had a proper grown-up evening in a restaurant.'

She had no choice, Nell saw. She would really have to go downstairs and get a table.

On her way down the twisted stairs to the lobby, she fought to persuade herself she had been mistaken. That it was someone else she had seen. He hadn't been with the harridan, for one thing. And he hadn't seemed to recognise her. She wasn't sure he had even seen her.

But such efforts were in vain. There was no doubt that the person downstairs was the man she had opened her heart to in

Paddington Station. The one who had driven her, disastrously, towards Joey.

Kegs, the establishment's boutique restaurant, was full of busy diners. Nell hesitated, as instructed, by the 'Wait Here To Be Seated' sign. Feeling conspicuous, she studied the lobby carpet – a tasteful seagrass weave – so as not to catch anyone's eye. And in particular the eye of Fake OutdoorsGuy. If he was sitting at one of the tables, he could easily look up and see her.

Jason appeared and greeted her effusively. 'Mrs Simpson!'

'Miss,' Nell forced herself to smile bravely. 'I never got married, remember?'

Jason was disappointed. So the two ladies really were just friends and not the role models he sought. He snapped into smooth professional mode. 'A table? Yes, of course. This way, please.'

Nell took a deep breath and followed the manager through the restaurant. A quick, nervous look round reassured her that all the eyes meeting hers belonged to smart middle-aged couples. There were no long-haired young men in T-shirts.

But the sight also reminded her of the many financial brochures that were her clients, and the dreary inevitability of returning to this work. The clients had all been told she was taking a week's holiday; she had not given the real reason. Which was just as well, as it hadn't been the reason after all.

Nell decided to make absolutely sure. Jason, the manager, was fussing with menus and flicking napkins about.

'Can I ask you something?' she asked, trying her best to sound casual.

'Of course, madam.' Jason smoothed the napkin over her lap.

'There was a young man in the hotel this afternoon . . .'

Jason knew who she meant immediately. There were, after

all, few young men at the Edenville Arms. Early days as it was, it was already obvious that the client base was the silver pound.

'Dark hair, jeans?' he supplied, secretly dismayed at this conclusive evidence that Miss Simpson was heterosexual.

'That's the one.' Nell took a deep breath. 'He's not – staying in the hotel, is he?'

Jason interpreted her tremulous tones as ones of fragile hope. He had to hand it to her; she was resilient. To be giving a strange young man the glad eye the same day she'd been stood up at the altar was impressive. Talk about getting back on the horse.

She was, so far as he could see, still wearing her wedding outfit: a slightly muddy minidress teamed with rather dirty white boots. Her make-up was smudged, perhaps intentionally, and her hair was equally equivocal. Either it was the kind of tangle that was deliberately fashionable, or was the result of being out in a hailstorm. It seemed to have wilted flowers in it.

But how to answer her question? He thought for a minute. Adam Greenleaf was not staying in the hotel as such, but he was staying on the estate. So in a sense, Nell and he were under the same hospitality umbrella. 'Indeed,' Jason said.

He was perturbed to see an expression of absolute horror on the young woman's face. 'Oh no!' she exclaimed, leaping from her seat, scattering his napkin and knocking over a glass which, fortunately, was empty. A few diners at nearby tables looked round.

The hotel manager's eyes widened, but, consummate professional that he was, he moved swiftly to control the situation. 'I meant, indeed, he's *not* staying here,' Jason amended quickly.

'*Not* staying here?' Nell felt floppy with relief.

'The young man to whom you refer is definitely *not* a guest in this hotel.'

'He's not, um, staying locally, though?' Nell made herself ask. She braced herself for the answer.

Local, Jason was thinking. Was Bess's Tower local? It was right at the other side of the estate. For many people round here that practically counted as a foreign country. 'Not so far as I know, madam.'

He was rewarded with a smile from his guest. 'Good. Thank you. Um. Can I see the wine list, please?' Now all that was over she needed a large glass or three.

She was halfway down the first one and feeling much better when Rachel appeared, beaming, in the dining room. She had changed out of her vintage Dior and was wearing a smart black dress which was scarcely less elegant. She had fantastic taste, Nell thought, aware of the eyes following her friend. Aware, now, too, of her own grubby outfit.

'Juno OK?' she asked, as Rachel sat down.

Rachel was pouring herself a glass of wine. The candlelight played on her vivid little face. 'I've left her tucked up with *Why Didn't They Ask Evans?* She's having a lovely time.'

'She's a lovely girl,' Nell said warmly. Juno's tastes may not be those of other children her age, but Nell liked her all the more for it. Juno was definitely her own person. More her own person, in fact, than practically anyone Nell had ever come across.

Rachel's smile widened. 'I'm glad you think so. Most people think she's odd. You know, with her Agatha Christie fixation and everything.'

'Well, I guess that came in useful,' Nell admitted, thinking of the phone call to Carrington's. It had been an unquestioningly impressive piece of detective work. Painful though they were, Juno's discoveries had shed some light on the Joey mystery. Enough to make Nell not want to probe further when she called the agent's on Monday.

A handsome, bearded waiter had appeared to take their order. 'Today's special is pan-fried scallops with blasmatic drizzle and Maris Piper shepherd's pie infused with sake.' He pronounced it to rhyme with 'hake'.

Rachel stared up at him. 'Infused with *what*?'

The boy grinned. 'Some sorta Japanese wine. You drink it 'ot.'

'We'll have one of each,' Rachel said. 'They sound lovely.'

The waiter, looking gratified, went off. Rachel was so kind, Nell thought. It was one of her most striking characteristics. Hopefully she would be kind about what Nell now planned to ask her.

'Erm, about going back to London. Can I come back to London with you tomorrow? I thought that maybe I could sleep on your floor.'

'Sorry,' Rachel said mildly, not looking up from the menu. 'I would, but I've got the painters in. They're keeping all their stuff in my box room.'

Nell stared at her disbelievingly over the table. That Rachel would not meet her eye increased her doubts. This was the first she had heard of painters. It sounded like an excuse.

'It would only be for one night. I'm going to take my flat off the market. Move back in downstairs.'

If she had thought this would please Rachel, she was wrong. Her friend's face was a picture of indignation. 'You can't do that!'

'Why not?' Nell was puzzled. It was her flat, was it not? Mingled with her surprise was hurt. Didn't Rachel want her back? They could take up where they had left off. Develop their friendship.

'Because I met the couple who'd put the offer in. I didn't

want to say before, because they're this couple of lovey-dovey newlyweds.'

'Oh?' Nell was at a loss to see why she, of all people, should sympathise with lovey-dovey newlyweds.

'They're really sweet and they said 19a was their dream home. They'd looked all over London and they were so glad to find it.'

Nell frowned. 'But I'll be homeless if I sell it to them.'

Rachel met her gaze steadily. 'It's not their fault, what happened to you.'

Nell felt her insides twisting in irritation, as well as jealousy. How could Rachel side with a couple of anonymous drippy lovers against her? But there was something in Rachel's face that warned her to leave the argument for now.

However, she *was* going back to London tomorrow, Nell resolved, whatever her friend thought to the contrary. She'd just stay in a hotel. And if Rachel wouldn't give her a lift, she'd get the train.

CHAPTER 23

Even to the disenchanted Dylan, Bess's Tower, in its woodland clearing, looked like something out of a fairy tale. Built of pale stone, it was a tall, narrow fort formed by a quartet of towers that stood closely together like a group of pencils standing on end.

The pencils were fitted with leaded windows on three floors and were capped at the top with decorative lead domes. Between the front two pencils, at the base of the building, was a small, white, arched wooden door with black iron fittings. Rising up between the domes on the roof was a flagpole.

The way up to the tower was via a narrow tarmac road that wound blackly between the green trees. As Dylan had ascended he had noticed that visitors thinned out considerably once the terrain started to rise. The tourists tended to stay close to the cafés and shops, which was no doubt how the estate liked it. There were a few brave and energetic souls on the lower slopes, but once you got as high up as this, you were on your own.

He had not expected anything as dramatic as the building standing in the clearing at the end of the track, and now, as he parked his car, he felt a faint but nonetheless definite leap of excitement.

He was pleased to see that, sitting at the top of the shallow flight of stairs leading to the front door, was a jute shopper. This, presumably, was the 'Countess' hamper, chosen at random from the catalogue of holiday cottage catering options Jason had pressed on him, including a private chef. The estate had jumped to it, Dylan thought approvingly, to get the hamper up here so quickly.

He found the key safe and liberated the key. The white wooden door opened into a small hall. A pine dining table had some yellow roses in a vase. Everything was very clean. To the left was a plain stone fireplace, and a door led from the right into a kitchen. Dylan could see units and a mixer tap silhouetted against a lattice window. There was a pleasant, spicy scent of pot-pourri in the air.

Closing the front door behind him, Dylan felt a welcome sense of safety. He put the shopper on the table and went into the sitting room. A fire was made up ready for lighting in the fireplace; spills of newspaper poked between a neat pile of coal and there was a woven basket beside it filled with logs.

There was a pink velour armchair in one of the corners; Dylan went to it and sat down. Branches nodded outside the windows; their shadows and that of the criss-cross leading, cast by a fitfully gleaming sun, moved on the whitewashed wall. It was soothing to watch. Dylan felt peaceful, and his head heavy. Within minutes he was asleep.

What seemed like minutes later, he awoke. But several hours had evidently passed; the shadows were on a different wall and the light was a different colour. Formerly white and bright, it was now a rich amber. The sun was setting.

Hungry, Dylan unpacked the hamper he had left on the table. The 'Countess' contained a surprising amount: a bunch of sausages of stupendous fatness, smoked bacon in thick, lardy slices, a loaf of white bread, a bag of perfectly ripe tomatoes, butter, milk, tea and coffee. Further delving revealed fruit scones, a small pot of jam and a packet of biscuits, all with labels bearing the estate logo. There was also a box of a dozen eggs, a bottle of white wine, a bag of cashew nuts and a plastic-sealed joint of boiled ham. Plus a pork pie and a small jar of 'The Earl's Favourite Green Tomato Chutney'.

Dylan went into the small but functional kitchen. Every surface shone and sparkled. He pulled out a pan and placed on it some rashers of bacon. It was the sort that, cooked long and thoroughly, made superlative bacon sandwiches; he could dip the bread in the sizzling fat. And the tomatoes. He sliced them, stuck them under the bacon, and put the whole lot under the grill.

Then he set off to explore the bedrooms. Downstairs, reached by two twists of a shallow spiral flight, was a room with two white single beds, each with a pale blue cushion and a small pile of pale blue towels.

At the bottom of each bed was a vintage varnished pine trunk and on the wall was a large framed sepia photograph of a great line of children in pinafores and knickerbockers.

The first floor was reached via three twists of the spiral staircase, with its banister of rope attached to the wall with iron rings. The main bedroom contained a double bed topped with a peculiar headboard of contorted branches. The adjoining bathroom had a shiny new white bath with, above it, the broad silver head of a power shower. The loo was drum-shaped and of a black plastic material, faintly iridescent. As Dylan entered the room, the lid rose of its own accord and tinny classical music started to play.

Dylan gasped and took a step backwards before realising this was that example of trailblazing lavatory technology: a Japanese toilet. In the dark heart of a Midlands forest, such Far Eastern electronic attentions were unexpected.

The rope-banister wound upwards three more times before Dylan found himself facing a small wooden door, similar to the front entrance. It was unlocked and opened on to a flat leaded roof; after the cool shadows of the tower interior, the brilliant greens and blues of the outside world were dazzling, almost painful. There was a blast of metallic warmth from the heated leading.

Beside him, as he stepped out, was the thick base of the flagpole; much bigger and more substantial than it looked from below. It was screwed to the roof with thick bolts, its empty cable snapping and rattling in the breeze. What flag would he fly, Dylan wondered, if he had the choice? A black one? But no. A mere few hours ago he had arrived here, aiming to immerse himself in misery. Now he had a job and a place to live. Perhaps even the beginnings of a future.

A low wall edged the roof-top, connecting the quartet of lead-domed pepper-pot towers. Dylan leaned against the warm stone and peered down. The drop below plunged into the trees.

They clustered below him like bright green smoke, their leaves sticky with golden evening sunlight. Beyond them, at the foot of the hill, were the formal gardens surrounding Pemberton Hall. Dylan could see statues, lawns, paths, ponds, patches of colour that were flower beds.

From above, the great house appeared a jumble of roofs and chimneys and gilded parapet urns. Beside it was the stable yard, almost as big as the house from this angle, the gold arrow-top of its weathervane shooting light in all directions. Sun blazed from the bonnets of the few cars left in the car park. Beyond this the winding silver river slid through the electric green park. Following its contours was the accompanying grey curve of the road; Dylan could see the tiny cars as they moved along it and hear the occasional snarl of a motorbike.

Hear, too, a chorus of birdsong. Never had he heard so many. The air was thick with their music; it seemed to rise from every bough and ranged from loud and insistent chanting to rippling notes of an almost unbearable sweetness. Dylan listened intently.

He stood like this for some minutes, hands in his pockets, feeling the cooling air lapping his face. A plane was passing overhead, a white scribble on the blue. He inhaled the fresh scent of leaves and felt something approaching tranquillity for the first time he could remember. Certainly, since the fire.

He closed his eyes. Perhaps here, in this peaceful place, he might finally be able to come to terms with all that had happened to him. Rebuild. Renew. He had a new name, after all: Adam Greenleaf. Perhaps now he could become a new person.

The birdsong was getting louder and more insistent. It had a sharp, shrieky, tinny edge; one of them – a blackbird, presumably – seemed to be imitating some electronic device. Like an alarm. Very like an alarm. Then Dylan realised it wasn't a bird at all but was coming from within the tower, from down the stairs. Jerked abruptly from his reverie, he dashed over to the door and plunged down the spiral flight, the rope-banister burning his palm as he clung to it for support.

A rolling fog of grey smoke was coming up to meet him. Dylan's brain was dissolving in panic. History was repeating itself. Bess's Tower was on fire.

CHAPTER 24

It was the bacon. Dylan had left it under the grill and it had burned to a blackened, smoke-belching crisp.

It had taken a while to work this out, even so. His body had seized up in panic. Going back downstairs, his own legs and arms had fought him. They refused to move, staying so rigid and un-yielding that he had to seize each thigh with both hands to place his foot on the next downward step. Down he staggered in this robotic fashion, the smoke filling his throat and stinging his eyes.

In the dining room, a thick pall of stinking mist bounced and ebbed against the ceiling. In the kitchen, great black smoke-snakes poured and writhed from the front of the grill.

Yanking open the window behind the kitchen sink, he had hurled the grill pan through the lattice where it fell with a crash into the grass.

Then, to his surprise, he had heard something else.

A stifled cry. Dylan had gone back to the kitchen window and seen a surprising sight. A woman with wild black hair and a flapping pink dress was hobbling away rapidly, holding her leg. She looked like the woman he had seen in the Edenville Arms earlier on. But why would she be snooping around the tower, looking in his windows?

Dylan flew to the front door and round to the side, but there was no trace of his unexpected visitor. He stared around but the woman appeared to have gone. It was all very unsettling, and he was unsettled enough as it was.

He went back inside and, to calm his nerves, poured himself some of the Countess's wine. But his teeth chattered against the glass and he shivered as if it were January.

What the grill-pan fire had shown him was that he hadn't recovered from what had happened. Far from it; he was only ever a few burnt bacon rashers from recalling the Bosun's Whistle fire in all its terror. Those thundering flames cast long shadows and he would always smell their smoke. That oasis of calm on the roof had been an illusion. The moment of peace outside the pub, amid the birdsong, had been too. Trying to build a new life was pointless. A new name was pointless; Adam Greenleaf was the same useless waste of space that Dylan Eliot had been. There was nothing to be positive about.

When, much later that night, Dylan finally closed his eyes it was to see the cloven foot of Beatrice's surf boot melting in the heat. And when, worn and exhausted, he finally fell into fitful sleep, the wall of fire in Bosun's Whistle burned his face in his dreams.

It was Sunday morning in the Edenville Arms and Jason stood behind his shining flap. It had been, so far, a difficult morning.

The beautiful weather seemed to have got people up unexpectedly early. Which in turn seemed to be making them crabby. One woman had complained that the yolk of her egg was 'a really weird orange'. Jason had been obliged to explain that the Countess's Burford Browns produced eggs with yolks that particular colour and they were actually quite sought after. But the woman had not backed down and Jason had returned to the kitchen, agitated, tasked to find what the customer called a 'normal' egg. 'Pearls before swine,' he had sighed to the chef.

The matter had been solved by sending one of the sous-chefs round to a woman in the village who was known to buy everything from discount supermarkets. If the egg he came back with had ever seen a hen, Jason would have been surprised. Yet the customer had been delighted.

Now the crisis was over, Jason was allowing himself a few moments of self-congratulation. And a few more as he remembered the great triumph of yesterday: securing the first guest for Bess's Tower. He wondered how Mr Greenleaf was settling in, and from here Jason's mind leapt to the strange incident in the restaurant last night, when Miss Simpson from the honeymoon suite had been so keen to ensure that Greenleaf was not staying in the hotel.

In what context had the two met before? Clearly a dramatic one. Jason's curiosity was fired, but, for once, he wasn't going to speculate about it with Angela. Angela didn't need encouraging with regard to Mr Greenleaf; she was behaving in a very odd way as it was. Yesterday, once she'd sobered up with quantities of tap-water, she'd lurched off, and Jason had had the distinct impression that she was going up to the tower. He'd hoped she wouldn't make a nuisance of herself. But it was definitely good news that she had stopped obsessing over Dan Parker and the actor's wife.

Greenleaf, Jason reflected, had certainly caused havoc among the women of the Edenville Arms. Especially given that he was so skinny and exhausted-looking and had been on the estate less than twenty-four hours. Jason couldn't understand what they saw in him. He had eyes only for a certain bearded barman, but today, lamentably, was Ryan's day off. He was taking his mother to the garden centre, bless him, Jason thought fondly.

The manager's thoughts returned to Adam Greenleaf. He hoped he would keep his distance from now on. For the duration of Nell Simpson's stay, at least. Now he had assured her that Greenleaf was nowhere near, Jason could not risk him turning up in the breakfast room. Perish the thought!

He leaned over his flap and peered into Kegs. The ladies from the honeymoon suite were joining the early breakfasters, he saw.

Nell and Rachel had had no choice. Fired by the sample menus in the room information folder, Juno had been desperate to get downstairs as soon as she awoke.

Kegs, Nell thought, looked entirely different from the intimate, candlelit space of last night. In the full, strong daylight, the pink tub seats positively blazed and the neatly set tables of sparkling silver and snowy linen shone almost as white as Jason's teeth.

Was Fake OutdoorsGuy here? She didn't really think so, not after Jason's reassurance. She should forget about it. To carry on fretting would be both silly and self-indulgent; worse, Rachel might start to notice, and she would have to describe the whole ghastly episode. Nonetheless, as they followed the waitress to their table, she cast a searching, heart-thumping look around. No sign of him, thank goodness.

Juno ordered a kipper. 'I want to see what one is.' Then she went to explore the breakfast bar.

Rachel ordered porridge and Nell, at Juno's urging, something called 'The Earl's Breakfast'.

'I want to see what a real Earl has in the morning,' Juno said. 'Agatha Christie's always a bit vague about what Lord Edgware has, and while I have the highest possible opinion of her writing I do think you need to know what your characters have for breakfast.'

Juno was not wearing her Marple outfit today. Like the rest

of them she wore jeans and a T-shirt. Another thrift-shop find, it had three large curling moustaches printed on it. 'They reminded me of Poirot,' Juno explained.

'So,' said Rachel, as the waitress disappeared. 'About places for you to live. I've had an idea.'

Nell rubbed her face tiredly. Not this again. She was going back to London tonight and taking Gardiner Road off the market tomorrow. She didn't care whether Romeo and Juliet were trying to move in.

'This is a bit left field,' Rachel went on.

'Mmm?' Nell poured some tea, wondering what was coming.

'Why don't you just stay up here?'

'Here? You mean Pemberton?' The tea slopped in the saucer; Nell stared at her friend. Had Rachel lost her wits?

Rachel's sharp eyes looked more than usually focused, however. 'OK, so it's just a thought. But it solves all the problems. That couple I told you about can buy 19a.'

'You seem very keen on them,' Nell said sulkily.

Rachel extended a hand and squeezed Nell's. 'It's not that. I just think there's been enough suffering because of Joey. I don't want any more people made miserable because of him. Especially people in love.'

Nell stared at the tablecloth, thinking that people in love should be made especially miserable. Serve them right for being such idiots.

'And just think,' Rachel added brightly, 'how much further your money will go in a place like this. You could start again. Find a new job. Meet new people. Juno and I could come and visit you.'

'But-what-would-I-do-where-would-I-live-I-wouldn't-know-anyone-I-wouldn't-like-it.' Objections poured from Nell in a panicked stream.

'OK, OK.' Rachel was grinning and waving her hands. 'But just think about it, all right?'

Juno returned from the breakfast bar with a glass of apple juice balancing precariously on a plate heaped with pastries. 'What's that cage thing?' she asked.

'It's a toast rack,' Rachel explained. 'You never see them anywhere else but hotels.'

Nell had a sudden memory of the breakfast tray Joey had appeared with, that first morning in his flat. She forced it away.

Her cooked breakfast arrived. She stared at it, awed. Then she snatched up her knife and fork rebelliously. Who cared if this breakfast contained more calories than she had previously allowed herself in a week? She had never associated sausages with freedom, but the Earl's Breakfast was emancipation of a sort.

Rachel stared. 'You're really going to eat all that?'

'Don't tell me you're not tempted.' Nell dug her fork into the fattest, most glistening banger.

Rachel stuck her spoon into her oats. 'I never eat anything with a face.'

'Sausages don't have faces,' Juno pointed out. Her kipper was now placed before her and she contemplated the length of copper-coloured fish bristling with tiny bones. 'What's *this*?' She picked up the half-lemon wrapped in muslin that garnished the dish.

Rachel explained, and squeezed the lemon over her daughter's breakfast. 'You have to be very careful to get the bones out. Otherwise they might stick in your throat and choke you.'

Juno looked delighted. 'I've definitely got the most dangerous breakfast.'

'I wouldn't be so sure.' Rachel gazed pointedly at Nell's laden plate.

*

Up in Bess's Tower, Dylan had just woken. A hangover seethed in his head; he had, last night, downed the rest of the Countess's wine. His flailing hand hit something sharp. 'Ow!' He had bruised himself on one of the many prongs of the headboard.

Beneath his nausea and thumping brain was a clawing hunger. Not trusting himself to cook after the fire episode, Dylan had opened a bag of estate-labelled cashew nuts for dinner. That, patently, had not been enough and it now occurred to him that he could have breakfast at the pub. There was a menu in all the bumf Jason had given him. He remembered something about sausages from estate-reared pigs.

His clothes were all over the place and it took a while to find them. Eventually a crumpled and wincing Dylan staggered down the spiral stairs. His rioting, outraged stomach was the main focus of his attention as he got in the car. But even so he noticed the cold, mushroomy scent of morning and how the mud beneath his boots looked like chocolate. In the distance, the mist gathered between trees that looked like a silent army. The birds, by contrast, were their usual chorus of tuneful agitation: echoing, quarrelling, singing, swooping, hopping.

As he drove down through the woods, tall, straight pine trunks splintered the sunshine into spokes of light. Rabbits scampered across the road in front of him, white scuts bobbing in panic. There were pheasants with silly runs, weaving aimlessly from side to side. Darting squirrels, all fluid movement. Dylan found himself making mental notes but then he stopped himself. He had no use for the material. It wasn't as if he was going to write again.

Jason, behind his flap, glanced through the window and saw, approaching across the car park, Mr Greenleaf of Bess's Tower. His first reaction, alarm, was followed by the desperate hope that Greenleaf was just popping in briefly. Perhaps for a map of the estate or one of Ros Downer's terrible brochures. Yes, that would be it; he was planning a spot of sightseeing.

Jason's grin, as Dylan came in, was a rictus.

'Good morning, sir! I trust that all is well in Bess's Tower?'

Dylan nodded. Now was not the time to go into the fire in the grill pan and the stranger he might inadvertently have hit with it.

'Map, is it, sir?' In his eagerness, Jason lifted up the entire holder of maps on his desk.

He was very excitable for this time in the morning, Dylan thought. Much too excitable to be dealt with on an empty stomach. 'I want breakfast,' he said shortly.

'Breakfast?' Jason repeated, puzzled. The 'Countess' hamper had been full of breakfast items. Could Greenleaf not cook? Was there something wrong with the kitchen?

'Breakfast,' Dylan confirmed. He gestured at Kegs with his key fob. 'OK if I go in?'

Although Jason's eyes were fixed on Dylan he could see, in his peripheral vision, the white-blond back of Nell Simpson's head at a table halfway down the dining room. It would take only a half-turn for her to see him and the man whom, for whatever reason, she was so keen to avoid.

The prospect filled Jason's narrow chest with panic. There might follow a scene in the dining room. And then, who knew, some kind of embarrassing administrative fall-out to do with misrepresentations to guests which could stain his otherwise unblemished managerial reputation.

'OK if I go in?' Dylan repeated, louder. The hotel manager seemed to be in some sort of trance. But Jason was only racking his brains for a reason to keep Dylan out of Kegs. None were springing to mind.

Dylan decided to take matters into his own hands. He was starving, and a waiter had just gone past with a vast plate of sausages nestling up to a creamy yellow pile of scrambled egg. He felt as if he could eat the plate as well. But as he started towards the restaurant, a hand shot out and grabbed his arm.

Dylan found himself staring into Jason's agitated face. 'I'm awfully sorry,' the manager said, 'but I'm afraid you can't go in there.'

'Why not?' asked Dylan irritably. Another plate of bacon had just gone past and he felt himself almost swooning in its savoury slipstream. 'Because I'm not a guest in this place? Is that it?'

The suggestion struck Jason almost as divine intervention. As Greenleaf had on his usual trousers, he'd been about to go with 'no jeans in the restaurant'.

'That's it,' he said, shaking his neat head in mock sorrow. 'Kegs is for hotel guests only at breakfast, I'm afraid. I'll have to ask you to eat in Pumps.'

Dylan was about to object. He was paying a fortune to stay in Bess's Tower; he should be able to sit where he wanted. On the manager's knee if he liked. He let it pass, however. Dylan wanted food far more than he wanted an argument.

In Kegs, Juno was getting to grips with her fish knife. 'It's really clever, the way it slides under the skin.'

Her mother, meanwhile, was looking at the restaurant entrance. 'That man again,' Rachel said mildly.

'Who?' Juno looked up from her kipper.

Nell's head reared up from her sausages. 'What man?'

'*That* man. With the dark hair. The one we saw yesterday. When we got here.'

Nell had wrenched herself round, but there was no sign of Fake OutdoorsGuy. The lobby was empty. 'There's no man there,' she said fiercely.

Rachel stared at her. 'Calm down. What's the problem?'

Nell had no intention of saying. She reapplied herself to her sausages, although her appetite seemed to have gone.

'Why are you so red in the face?' Rachel probed.

The other side of the lobby, in Pumps, Dylan was finally ordering his breakfast. 'I'll have the full English,' he said to a plump teenage waitress.

'You mean the Earl's Breakfast.'

'Doesn't the Earl want it?' It was a silly joke, but he was feeling quite giddy with hunger. 'I bet everyone says that.'

'No, you're the first.' The waitress, rather surprisingly, seemed genuinely amused.

'What's in it?' Best to check that the Earl wasn't a grapefruit-loving muesli-eater.

'It's the, like, full English breakfast we serve here?' The waitress began to recite. 'The Earl's favourite herb pork sausages, eggs from the Countess's Burford Browns—'

'Great.' Dylan had no idea what Burford Browns were. 'Bring them on.'

In Kegs, Nell had regained her appetite. The soothing effects of a full English were amazing. She had quite calmed down from the agitation caused by Rachel's possible sighting of Fake OutdoorsGuy, and the earlier suggestion that she should leave London and move to Edenville.

'Do you think the Earl really eats that every day?' Juno was staring at Nell's plate. 'He must be very fat. I bet he bursts out of his waistcoats.'

'Do you think he wears waistcoats?' Nell threw herself into the exchange.

'Red ones with big gold buttons,' Juno said confidently. 'And a crown. Can we go and see him?'

'Well, we don't know him personally,' Rachel put in. 'But we could have a look at his house. It's open to the public and it's not far away. We could walk over after breakfast.'

'Is it a big house?' Juno wanted to know.

'Massive,' Nell assured her.

'Does it have those beds with curtains? Like we slept in last night?'

'Bound to have.'

'I like beds like that,' Juno said. 'When I grow up I want to marry a prince.'

Rachel rolled her eyes. 'So much for my efforts to bring her up as a feminist socialist,' she muttered to Nell. Aloud, she said to her daughter, 'You should want better things than that.'

'OK,' said Juno equably. 'I'll marry a king.'

Dylan's breakfast had arrived. He stared down at it, recognising a work of art. Two plump, glistening, tight-skinned sausages with lovely brown grill marks, a pile of magnificently oily-looking mushrooms and a heap of deep-yellow scrambled egg, marbled with white. The bacon, gloriously unburnt, was thick, pink and majestic, edged with perfectly frazzled rind.

Dylan reached for the jug of Worcestershire sauce and prepared to tuck in.

CHAPTER 25

Armed with one of Jason's maps, the girls had set off at a smart pace. Soon they had left Edenville behind; only the pointed church spire could still be seen over a shoulder of green hill. Now they stood at the top of a field of glossy grass sparkling with buttercups and daisies.

'Wow,' said Rachel. 'Imagine living here.'

Nell slid her a sharp glance, but the remark did not seem aimed in any particular direction. Rachel's eyes were on the wide river winding through stately groups of trees. The water shone like polished silver. Groups of very clean sheep stood expectantly about.

Juno was squinting through her spectacles. 'Even if I spend all day looking I won't be able to notice every different bit of loveliness.'

The women laughed. They walked on.

'There's the house!' Juno shouted, as they emerged from a small copse of oaks. Nell placed her hand over her eyes to look. The sun was beating down strongly now.

It spread before the water like a curtsey, sun flashing on the rows of long windows. There were pillars along the front and, on the roof, a pediment filled with lounging gods and a balustrade topped with urns.

'They've got gold flames in them,' Juno said wonderingly. 'They must have painted the stone.'

Behind and around them stretched the gardens. There were temples, statues, terraces, flights of steps.

Juno was up ahead, anxious to meet her prince or king as soon as humanly possible. The river curved round again and the house loomed once more before them. It was closer now. You could see the carving on the columns, the swags of stone fruit and flowers, the flowing robes of the gods and goddesses.

'Do you think the Earl's in there, looking out at us?' Juno wanted to know.

'Maybe.'

'What *do* Earls do all day?'

Nell and Rachel looked at each other.

'Count their piles of money?' Rachel suggested.

'Have baths in champagne?' grinned Nell.

'Go fox-hunting?'

'Polish their crowns?'

'Have lunch with the Queen?' Rachel again.

'Order their servants around?'

Juno considered all this. 'And then what do they do in the afternoon?'

The house itself was reached through a triumphal arch with a porter's lodge. There was even a porter in it. 'Hello, young lady,' he said to Juno.

'He was wearing a bowler hat,' she said wonderingly, as they walked up the drive. 'I didn't realise people really did that. Is that where he lives?'

A large, wide door admitted them to an entrance hall. It had a huge open fireplace and two rows of thick columns marching down the centre. The ceiling was painted with classical figures;

Juno was squinting up at it. 'What's going on up there?'

Rachel looked up. 'Something mythical. Not sure what.'

'Lots of bare bottoms,' Juno remarked with relish.

There were cash desks on each side, and, at the far end, a small group of people apparently waiting for something. Nell went to pay.

'It's just the Insider Tour this morning,' said the large woman behind the till whose badge read 'Visitor Welcome Operative Marlene'.

'Three for that, then. What's the Insider Tour?' Nell asked.

Marlene slammed the till drawer back in. 'It's a New Visitor Experience,' she said, emphasising the capitals. 'You're taken around by a former estate employee. Idea of our late lamented marketing director.'

'Late lamented?' gasped Juno eagerly. 'You mean she's dead?'

An expression of what might have been longing crossed Marlene's heavy face. 'She's been, um, moved on.'

'But that's a good idea, isn't it?' Nell asked.

'You're telling me. She were a disaster. Made a right mess of—'

'No, not the marketing person. I meant the former employee thing. Showing us round. It sounds fun.'

Marlene fixed her with a baleful eye. 'Depends which employee.'

A sharp sound rent the air. Someone was clapping.

'Ladies and gentlemen!'

'Here we go,' Marlene muttered, as Nell and Rachel turned round.

An old man had materialised and was standing at the top of the shallow flight of stone stairs. He wore a battered tweed jacket and had a large hooked nose. Mutton chop whiskers of a Victorian exuberance sprouted from each side of his weather-beaten face and the look was finished off with gap teeth and a hanging lip.

'Ladies and gentlemen!' repeated the old man in his grating voice. 'Let me introduce meself. I'm Bert Blood, retired estate carpenter. Worked on this estate forty-four year,' he added. 'Man and boy.'

'Why's *he* showing us round?' Juno hissed loudly. 'Why isn't it the Earl?'

'He's bathing in champagne, remember,' Rachel reminded her.

Bert Blood gazed fiercely at Juno. 'I'm warning you, you better bloody listen. And bloody keep up. I leave stragglers behind to get lost.'

'He said bloody!' stage-whispered Juno delightedly.

Something made Nell glance behind her. At the cash desk, Marlene had sunk her head in her hands.

Bert Blood marched them up some steps and across a marble-floored hall into a huge, high-ceilinged room. Gold blazed from the thick, heavy picture frames, furniture and cornices of the ceiling, which featured more plump and naked rears. 'That's four so far,' Juno said with satisfaction.

From among the tour group, a smart old gentleman in a sports jacket cleared his throat. 'Who's that?' He pointed at a portrait of a doe-eyed young Georgian in very tight white trousers.

Bert Blood curled his lip. 'Fifth Earl. Never married. Were of A Different Persuasion,' he added, his contemptuous tone showing exactly where he stood on such Persuasions.

Some other brave soul now asked about a painting over the fireplace. It was of a dark-eyed woman in a tight red dress and looked as if it were painted in the early twentieth century. 'Lady 'Arriet,' revealed Bert Blood.

'She's very beautiful,' ventured the brave soul.

Bert twitched his hanging lip. 'She were. Then. Right bloody misery when she got older, though. They say that whenever she smiled a donkey dropped dead in Blackpool.'

'Maybe it's counter-intuitive,' Nell whispered to Rachel. There seemed little explanation for Blood's grating voice, acid observations and ferocious gaze.

'How do you mean?'

'Refreshingly irreverent. A change from the usual forelock-tugging.'

'Possibly,' Rachel conceded doubtfully.

Bert had led them into the dining hall now. More paintings, more gold, more bottoms. 'Seven!' squeaked Juno. 'This is better than counting Christmas trees!'

A huge dining table was set for twelve. Bert was explaining the order of precedence. '. . . if you were at' back you could die o' starvation afore ye got sat down.'

Rachel nudged Nell. 'I wonder what they say about him on TripAdvisor?'

Afterwards they recovered at the café in the stable yard. This, they agreed, was much more the thing. A smart serving area dispensing soups in sunken tureens and sandwiches and cakes in refrigerated units filled the space formerly occupied by ducal carriages. The seating area was in the actual former stables, divided by wooden walls and with hayracks above.

'Such a shame,' Nell said, pushing her fork through the frosting on her cupcake. 'The house is beautiful and really interesting, and all you get is that horrible old man.'

'I counted twenty-six bare bottoms altogether,' Juno declared, plunging her spoon into the whorls of cream atop her hot chocolate. 'Mostly in the dining room.'

'They should do a Bottoms tour,' Nell said, smiling at Juno.

'It would be a lot better than Bert Blood.' She forked in some cake. 'They should do a lot of things, really. Rewrite all their brochures, for a start. I was looking at them in the hotel room. They're practically illiterate. If Pemberton was my client,' she added longingly, 'if I still had Vanilla up and running, we'd give them an entire overhaul. They need it. They've got to have good commercial literature here. Pemberton's a twenty-first-century retail enterprise and there's so much to sell. Shops, cafés, outdoor events, pubs, holiday cottages. And yet they're all being represented so badly. Outdated letter fonts, bad page design, off-putting colour, really boring and badly spelt copy.'

'Maybe that's why they've got rid of the marketing person,' Rachel remarked lightly, watching Juno skim off her frosting.

'What?'

'You heard that woman on the till. They've got rid of the Director of Marketing.'

Nell hadn't made the connection, but now she remembered.

'Could be an opportunity,' Rachel grinned. 'For you.'

'Don't be silly,' Nell exclaimed. 'They're hardly going to offer it to me.'

'You'd be perfect. You've got all the right experience. And all those ideas. Wouldn't you like to do it?'

'Oh, I would!' The project was so clear to Nell. If only she still had her own business and could pitch for the work! It was exactly the kind of branding job she had shone at. 'I wonder if they do it in-house or whether it's contracted out.'

'Why don't you ask them?'

Nell frowned at Rachel. 'You're not serious.'

Rachel smiled back. 'I am perfectly serious.'

Her friend, Nell thought, was gung-ho to an almost oppressive extent sometimes. She could never see the reason why not, even when, as here, it was glaringly obvious. 'Because they're bound to have someone else by now and—'

'They might not have.' Rachel popped in the rest of her cupcake.

'—and I live in London, not up here,' Nell finished, exasperated. It was impossible, why could Rachel not see? She did not work for the estate on the one hand, or live anywhere near it. And she no longer had her marketing business on the other. The state of the Pemberton literature was nothing to do with her.

Juno was begging to visit the stable-yard shops. 'It'll just be full of chutneys and teabags,' Rachel warned her. 'And kneelers for gardening in wipe-clean William Morris.'

'Why did William Morris need wiping clean?'

'Coming?' Rachel asked Nell, who shook her head and gestured at her unfinished cupcake. It was an excuse; she just wanted time to herself. The exchange about the marketing had been irritating.

She watched Rachel and Juno though the café windows as they made their way across the yard. Juno, serious in her spectacles, was almost the same size as her petite mother, who stood out from the elderly crowd with her jeans, layered plum-coloured tops and purple-red hair lifting gently as she walked.

'Excuse me.'

A man in late middle-age was standing before Nell. He was smartly dressed and very tall and thin. Strands of grey hair were combed across a freckled pate and he regarded her with mournful eyes which sloped to the sides of his face.

'I do hope you don't mind me interrupting you.' His voice was deep and fruity. 'But I just happened to overhear your conversation. Bottoms.' He flashed her a broad and unexpected smile which revealed wonky teeth.

Nell shrank to the wall and her interlocutor looked concerned.

'Please don't misunderstand me. I meant the tour your young friend was mentioning. Looking at the ceilings and so on. Jolly good idea.'

Nell nodded, still eyeing him cautiously.

'I was also interested in what you had to say about Bert Blood. Did you really not think he was terribly good?'

'Not really,' said Nell, wondering who this was. A fellow visitor, perhaps? 'He was pretty awful,' she added, in the interests of full disclosure.

Her companion sighed. 'We'll just have to put Bert Blood down to experience. I must say that I had my doubts all along. He used to terrify me as a child.'

Nell was surprised. 'You live here?'

'Yes. And I work here.'

He must, Nell concluded, be some sort of manager. Country estates were full of posh old chaps like this. They had tied cottages. Perhaps he lived in Edenville.

'Now there was something else that you mentioned I'd like to hear more about. The estate literature. How exactly do you feel it could be improved?'

Nell wondered how she felt about being so comprehensively eavesdropped. Especially on this subject, after the disagreement with Rachel.

'I'm not sure it's up to me to say,' she said, looking towards the courtyard shop and wishing she had gone with the others after all.

Her companion now produced a smart brown leather folder which he unzipped, producing from inside handfuls of brochures and flyers. He spread them out on the table and Nell was struck anew by the terrible photography, awful shoutlines and uninspired, badly spelt body copy.

'I'd be so grateful if you could tell me what you think,' he said with polite longing. 'Perhaps you could have a quick look through while I get you another coffee?'

Nell looked up; there was something almost pleading about the sloping, melancholy eyes. He really wanted her views. This, and his air of wonderful courtesy, was irresistible.

By the time he came back, carefully carrying her cappuccino, Nell had firm opinions on everything from the farm shop flyer to the booklet advertising the weddings service.

He listened to her intently, asked more questions and for a happy half hour Nell felt she was back at Vanilla PR, briefing a client. She was so good at this! She had not realised quite how much she missed it.

He took careful notes of everything she said, writing in a leather-bound notebook with a large black fountain pen. He had style, certainly.

A helicopter could be heard now, thrumming overhead. The sound seemed to trigger something in Nell's companion. He looked startled, glanced at his watch and leapt to his feet. 'Awfully sorry . . . have to dash . . . guests for lunch . . . please don't get up . . . it's been wonderful talking to you, Miss, er . . .'

'Simpson. Nell Simpson,' Nell said, wondering what sort of estate manager had lunch guests who arrived in a helicopter.

He was zipping up his folder. 'Thank you for all your insights. Hugely appreciated. I hope very much to see you again.'

Nell smiled, doubting it. She would be going back to London tonight. Whether Rachel wanted to take her or not.

She noticed, on his little finger, an old signet ring flash as he slipped a hand inside his jacket. He produced a card, wrote something on it and presented it to her with a smile.

'Our personnel department – which I must learn to call human resources – is looking for a new marketing and publicity person. I'd be honoured if you felt able to apply.' With that, he hurried off.

Nell stared at the card in her hand. Under a gold coronet were the words 'The Earl of Pemberton' and under that, in black ink, was scribbled a number and a name. 'Angela. HR.'

CHAPTER 26

They were sitting on the grass in the gardens of Pemberton Hall. A long strip of lake ran down the centre of a smooth lawn. Beneath the blue sky, it shone like stretched silk and at its far end rose the stately home; this side view scarcely less magnificent than the front. Nell, gazing down the water towards the domes and balustrades, wondered which of the long, elegant windows the Earl was behind, with his helicoptered lunch guests.

No doubt he had forgotten all about her now, as he poured the champagne or passed the peas. Which was fine, as she had pretty much decided that she didn't want the job.

Nearer to where Nell and Rachel sat, some children were playing skittles. A tall blonde girl was bowling and Juno, eyes round and longing behind her glasses, was standing just shy of the play area. Nell felt Rachel tensing beside her, but then the girl looked up, smiled, and asked Juno if she wanted to join in. Nell felt Rachel exhaling with relief.

'That would never happen in London,' she remarked.

Nell wasn't sure about the implications of that statement. London was where they were both going back to, after all. She decided that now was the time to tell Rachel about what had happened in the café.

'The *Earl*?' Rachel was amazed and excited in equal measures. 'The Earl's offered you a job?'

'Well, I didn't realise he was the Earl at the time.'

'But – a *job*? My God, what are you waiting for?'

Nell did not reply. She might have guessed that Rachel would be in favour.

Juno and her blonde friend were now dancing around in the spray being whipped from a nearby fountain by the breeze. Rachel's daughter was pointing into the shaggy trees crowning the escarpment behind the mansion.

'There's a tower! I can see a flagpole!'

'It's really nice,' the girl told Juno. 'We've just been walking in the woods up there.'

Rachel turned back to Nell. 'Seriously, this new job. It's just like I said. A new start. A new place. What's not to like?'

'They haven't offered it to me yet,' Nell pointed out. 'If I wanted it, which I don't. I've got to go and see the HR person.'

'A formality, surely,' Rachel breezed. 'If the Earl's asking you to apply and he owns the place, I'd say you had a pretty good chance.'

'I'm not sure about it,' Nell said stubbornly. She could feel the force of Rachel's will, pushing her in a direction she didn't want to go.

'Well, wouldn't you *like* to work here?' Rachel threw out an arm which encompassed the fountain, several sculptures and an expanse of manicured lawn.

Nell shook her head. 'I don't need a new job. I've got plenty of catalogue work.'

'But you hate that,' Rachel pointed out. 'You said you missed working with people.'

Nell said nothing. Silence was her only defence. Rachel would be bound to argue with anything she said.

'So what did you say?' Rachel pressed. 'To the Earl?'

Nell glanced towards the splendid house. 'Nothing. He went before I could.'

'But why wouldn't you want a job here?' Rachel repeated her earlier remark.

Nell looked at her steadily. 'Because I'm going back to London tonight. With you.'

'No, you're not,' said Rachel, equally steadily. 'I've already told you. I've got builders.'

Nell stared at the canal. The breeze was ruffling the previously still, blue surface. 'But I don't want to stay here.'

'Well, you've got nowhere else to go at the moment,' Rachel reminded her.

'Exactly. I need to go back and take my flat off the market.'

Rachel placed a persuasive hand on Nell's arm. 'Look. Why not stay for a couple of days? Go and talk to these HR people. You may as well hear what they have to say.'

A mallard was now pecking inquisitively about their feet.

'I don't want to,' Nell said, aware she sounded petulant.

'Here, ducky ducky!' enticed Juno.

Rachel waited a few beats before speaking. 'I worry about you.'

'You don't need to.'

'In particular I'm worried,' Rachel added gently, 'that you may be missing an opportunity.'

'And I think,' Nell returned, 'that I'm the best judge of that.'

Rachel sighed. 'Look, I realise your confidence is a bit low at the moment.'

'Low?' Nell said angrily. 'Why would it be low? I've been dumped by my fiancé at the register office, I'm potentially homeless, and now you're forcing me to make some snap decision about my whole future. One that would make me leave behind everything I know. What's there to feel low about?'

There was a pause. Then Rachel said, 'You're scared.'

'*Scared?*'

'You haven't been out in the world for a long time. You've been shut in that back bedroom. Writing about snakeskin Birkenstocks.'

Nell stared at her, mouth open. 'Can't you make *any* allowances for what I've been through?'

Another silence. They both stared at the water. While Rachel's expression remained calm, fury coursed through Nell.

Then Rachel spoke again. 'After Charlie died, I felt I'd been let down by everyone. The doctors, the hospital. I had enough cause for anger to last me the rest of my life.'

Nell stared at the grass. She resented the Charlie card being played; on the other hand, it was a strong one.

'And sometimes,' Rachel continued, 'that's all I wanted to do. Blame other people. Be negative. Feel sorry for myself and expect everyone else to feel sorry for me too.'

Nell's self-righteous anger was draining away. 'But you didn't,' she said slowly.

Rachel shook her purple-tinted curls. 'I wanted to. It was so tempting to turn my back on the world. To hate anyone who was happy. And everyone seemed to be.' She paused. 'Until you've lost your husband you have no idea how many happy couples there are out there.'

'So how did you not?' Nell asked, feeling a mixture of shame and curiosity. 'How did you keep going?'

'Because there's no way back from that anger. You think it's helping you but it isn't. It's your enemy, not your friend. Anger begets anger. You never get to the end of it. It just keeps generating more. You don't feel any better, you feel worse.'

Nell rubbed the heels of her hands into her eyes. She knew,

in her heart of hearts, that she no longer wanted to return to London. But did she have the courage, still less the energy, to stay here and start all over again?

Rachel was speaking again. 'And of course, I had Juno. I couldn't give in. I still have moments when I hate everyone, though.' She stopped, biting her lip.

Nell thought that it was impossible to imagine Rachel hating anyone. She was one of the most positive people she'd ever met. 'I'm sorry,' she muttered. 'I'm being an idiot. Of course you've suffered more than me.'

Rachel turned to her, eyes flashing. 'That's not what I'm saying! This isn't a competition! Your problems and disappointments are just as big to you as mine are to me. I'm just saying that you have to keep cheerful. And try and recognise an opportunity when it's staring you in the face. This job at Pemberton is exactly what you want. Writing, but with lots of people to interact with.'

Nell pulled a face. 'Maybe.'

Rachel gave her a nudge. 'No maybe about it. Come on, Nell. A new start, in a new place, where nobody knows anything about you. What are you waiting for?'

It was just before six that evening and Jason was settled happily behind his flap in the Edenville Arms. He sipped a decaf cappuccino as he prepared the bills for next morning's departures. He liked to write these out by hand, not just as an excuse to showcase his painstaking copperplate but in the belief that a bill on thick cream paper itemised in flowing Victorian script added a touch of old-fashioned class to the transaction. Handwriting made the eventual amounts – invariably enormous – look less stark; it also added to the establishment's USP. Few hotels had their bills raved about on TripAdvisor as his did.

The inn was quiet apart from the scratch of Jason's nib and the distant, comforting sounds of chefs preparing the service in the kitchen. The old grandfather clock in the hall ticked comfortably in its polished mahogany case. A scented candle on Jason's desk spread a warm, pleasant perfume through the air. He worked steadily on, pausing occasionally to reflect that tonight was Ryan's shift and he would be here in less than an hour.

Bursting, suddenly, into this order, industry and calm came a mighty roar from the vicinity of the Edenville Arms car park. It sent Jason's pen skittering messily across the foot of a newly completed account, one that had involved the computation of heavy use of the minibar over the space a week's stay, plus three meals a day washed down by wines from the south end of the list. The bill had been a work of art and now it was ruined.

Jason hurried to the window of Pumps and saw that the battered red Land Rover was pulling out of the car park. Nell Simpson's friend Rachel, the small woman with the purple hair, was leaving for London. They had informed him of this earlier; Nell had offered to move into a smaller room if it was more convenient for Jason. She had seemed almost disappointed when he had assured her she could stay in the honeymoon suite.

Jason was not sorry to see the Land Rover go. He liked Rachel, but her vehicle was no ornament to its surroundings. While by no means as bad as Dan Parker's, it had nonetheless stuck out like a scratched, unpolished thumb among the other gleaming conveyances in the car park.

Rachel seemed to be taking her time leaving. Nell remained beside the vehicle and there was a lot of shouting over the engine noise. The manager raised a slow, subtle hand and unfastened the catch on the pub's front window. The gesture was a practised one; he had overheard numerous conversations this way.

'Ring me as soon as you've seen Angela Highwater!' Rachel was yelling out of the driver window. 'I want to know *everything*!'

Jason stifled a squeal. Angela? Whyever was Nell seeing her? Suddenly, the manager wanted to know everything too.

He rushed back to his cubbyhole and lifted the phone. It was Sunday evening, and Angela would be at home in her Chestlock mill penthouse. Except that she wasn't; the answerphone clicked on. 'You hev reached Ingila Haywater . . .'

It was a sunny evening, warm and golden. She must be out on her roof terrace, which he had visited a few times. Given that the context was an eighteenth-century spinning mill, Jason had found it, with its patio heaters, palm trees and elaborate sunloungers, a tad anachronistic.

He looked up as the entrance now darkened. Someone was coming in; silhouetted against the brilliant evening sunshine and splitting it into rods of light. It was a woman, and Jason's first, alarmed impression was that it might be Angela. But it was Nell, looking preoccupied.

She gave Jason a distracted smile as she passed his cubbyhole and started to mount the stairs.

Her mind was tumbling with doubt. Had she really wanted to make an appointment with the Pemberton human resources department? But Rachel had refused to take no for an answer. Or acknowledge there were any difficulties in the way at all.

'But I haven't got a CV. I haven't needed one for years,' Nell had objected. 'I can't even remember what my GCSE results were.'

Rachel had brushed this aside. 'No one wants all that exam stuff,' she said. 'You just need to put a paragraph together about your experience.'

Nell could see that she had no choice. She would ring Angela Highwater first thing in the morning. She would go to the interview and see what happened. But for now, she was going to have a long, hot bath, a room-service supper and an early night.

It had taken almost an hour, but Jason had rewritten the spoilt bill. His pen was poised over it, preparing to administer the final detail, his own signature.

'Cooeee!' Someone now bustled noisily in through the door. Jason, startled, felt his pen slide and the nib dig into the paper, making a large and inky tear.

The estate's Director of Human Resources trotted over the age-worn flagstones of the doorway. Her progress, Jason noticed, was less commanding than usual. She appeared to be hobbling. 'Done something to your foot?'

Angela tossed her head. She had no intention of revealing that the previous afternoon's recce to Bess's Tower had ended in a painful encounter with a grill pan. Maintaining power was all about maintaining the fears of others. 'Is he here?' she demanded.

'Dan Parker?' Jason asked.

Angela's eyes flashed. 'Not *him*,' she snapped. 'I'm over him. Now he's gone off with *that woman*.'

There was something in her vehemence that made Jason doubt that she had got over it. He put it aside, however; he'd identified the person she was after now. 'Mr Greenleaf is up at Bess's Tower, I believe.'

Certainly, Greenleaf had left the inn after breakfast and had not been back. Hopefully he wouldn't be, ever, and to make extra sure of this, Jason had earlier sent an estate handyman up to check that all was well in the tower kitchen. He had come back reporting that he had been unable to gain entry; Greenleaf's car was outside, and presumably he was inside, but the door was locked. It was the handyman's guess that he was asleep.

The handyman had found a grill pan in the grass at the rear

of the building. Nearby had been some very burnt bacon. This intelligence had filled Jason with alarm; if Greenleaf really couldn't cook, he might be back tomorrow morning. Or even tonight.

He needed to come up with a plan for that. But for now he had a potentially disappointed Angela to deal with.

She had, Jason saw, made even more sartorial effort than usual, which, again, wasn't a good sign. Her hair was newly dyed a powerful black and crimped and scrunched into wild and writhing locks. She wore a dress cinched tightly at the waist and clinging to her hips and breasts. Brightly patterned in aqua and coral, it looked like something one might wear to the beach. Her toes were painted coral to match; two of them, Jason noticed, had plasters on them.

He decided to try and distract her. The story of the women shouting her name in the car park would do. Hurriedly, Jason told it, embellishing it as much as he could. He watched with dismay as Angela's eyes slitted with anger and her pout compressed to a hard, tight line.

'What's the matter?' Jason asked, realising he had only made things worse.

'The matter,' Angela said, biting out the words one by one, 'is that His Lordship has told me to interview that blonde one – Nell whatsit – for a job.'

Jason was bewildered. 'How on earth does he know her?'

'Met her in the café,' Angela growled.

'What café? I didn't know he went to cafés.'

'The stable-yard café.' Angela huffed. 'Doing his secret shopper bit.'

'Secret shopper?'

'*Oh, for God's sake,*' Angela shouted, with a suddenness, volume and fury that made Jason's head spin. 'Do you have to repeat everything I say? He goes into the café now and then to check it. Mingles with the cake-and-a-crap-crowd.'

'Cake and a . . . ?'

'*The tourists!*' Angela screamed.

Jason looked about him. It was clear that his colleague needed a drink. He could do with one himself. His heart tightened; had Ryan arrived yet? He craned his neck; it seemed not.

'Two large Chardonnays!' he hissed at a passing waitress, a newly hired local teenager called Georgia.

'Coming right up!' Georgia hissed back. She was as good as her word. She brought glasses, and also the bottle. Jason nodded at her approvingly. Where Angela was concerned, you needed to cut out the middleman.

'So,' Angela snarled, after a copious swig, 'His bloody Lordship met Nell whatsit having a cup of coffee. They talked and now he's got it into his bloody head that she'd be a good replacement for Ros. But I'm the best judge of that,' the Director of Human Resources stormed. 'I'm the personnel professional.'

'Yes,' Jason agreed hurriedly. 'Absolutely. You are.'

'Said he wanted to help,' Angela ranted, refilling her glass. 'But it would have helped a bloody sight more if he hadn't sacked Ros in the bloody first place.'

Jason could not agree with this statement, so asked more questions. 'Why does he think *Nell* could replace her? What does Nell even do for a living?'

'Marketing, apparently. PR. She was very rude about the estate bumf. The cheek!' Angela raged. 'Thinks she could do better, she said.'

Well, she certainly couldn't do worse, Jason reasoned. 'So you're going to interview her?'

'Haven't any choice.'

'When?'

Angela took another swig. 'God knows. She's supposed to be calling me to make an appointment. Which means tomorrow, I suppose. I can't bloody wait!'

Mercifully, at that moment, Ryan appeared in the restaurant and Jason's feeling that the world was a difficult place became the certain knowledge that it was a wonderful one, and no spot on it was more wonderful than this one.

CHAPTER 27

A shrill noise woke Dylan. He leapt out of bed instantly, his nerves juddering with panic. A fire alarm?

No, just an alarm. The face of the small plastic clock by the bedside was flashing blue. Six thirty on the first day of the rest of his life. The day he started working for Dan.

Well, the initial hurdle had been surmounted. He had woken up at least, thanks to the clock. He had bought it at the Chestlock supermarket the evening before, along with some food. Eating at the pub did not appeal, not least because it was miles away and therefore inconvenient, as well as incongruous. Now he was working for the minimum wage, taking his meals in a luxury hotel was pretty silly. And while, after the grill pan incident, he didn't quite trust himself with the Bess's Tower stove, Dylan felt he could manage the microwave. So he'd headed into town, found the supermarket and piled his trolley with ready meals.

Dylan shuffled down into the kitchen, where he breakfasted on a bowl of last night's cold noodles, eaten standing by the fridge. Curiously, they tasted better than the first time round. Packing what remained of the Countess hamper for his lunch – cheese, some pork pie – Dylan left the tower and drove down the track into Pemberton park.

A milky shroud of mist had risen from the river and lay thickly over the grass. The park had an unlit, mysterious air and the great house looked dim and unsubstantial through its veil of vapour, the delicate ghost of its normal solid self.

The fog was clearing as Dylan reached Edenville; something red loomed at the side of the road. A post box. He got out and shoved in the first of the cards he had promised his parents.

He drew up at the Edenville Arms at seven thirty on the dot. The clock on the church tower was still donging as he got out of the car.

He had expected to see Dan Parker's massive figure where he had seen it last, on the benches outside the pub. Yet, apart from a shimmering of morning dew, the benches were empty. Dylan crossed the car park, sat down and waited, surrounded by a chorus of birdsong and watching the mist continue to clear. It was going to be a beautiful day.

In the honeymoon suite, Nell heard the chimes of seven thirty. She was still in bed but she would, she told herself, get up in a minute. She had been telling herself this for the last ten minutes but was still lying there amid the soft swell of bedclothes. The four-poster was far more comfortable than it had first looked. She and Rachel had discovered on the first night that beneath the assertive black and pink surface was a duvet and pillows of a snowy whiteness.

At the foot of the bed, across the room, the diamond-pane windows were throwing shapes on the white walls. Dangling ivy, stirred by morning breeze, was dancing across the shapes. Nell watched this moving wallpaper, considering her plans for the day.

There was only one, really. She must go and see Angela, whoever she was, in the human resources office of the Pemberton estate.

She had promised Rachel. If she didn't go, she would never hear the end of it. The Earl, too, had been courtesy itself; it would be rude to let him down.

But afterwards, she'd head straight back to the capital. Once there, she would screw her courage to the sticking place, otherwise known as Carrington's, where she would get to the bottom of what was happening with the flat sale. Whilst avoiding any mention of Joey whatsoever.

And then she would either find somewhere temporary or persuade Rachel to let her sleep on the floor. If she turned up on her actual doorstep, Rachel could hardly refuse.

All of which meant, Nell concluded, that she needed to set up the HR meeting as soon as possible. Even though it was only twenty-five minutes to eight, she should get up and prepare herself so that she could ring Angela soon after nine. With a groan, she threw back the warm weight of duvet and swung her legs out of bed.

She walked to the window. It really was a beautiful morning. The early mist was dissolving and the Edenville cottages shone a pale gold in the sun. Light bounced off the windows, flowers glowed in the gardens and she could hear the birdsong even though the window was closed. Nell lifted the old and delicate wrought-iron latch to open it. A cool, grass-scented air drifted in, as refreshing as a perfume spritz. If you could bottle it, put a label on it saying 'Village Morning', you would make a fortune. She was, Nell thought wryly, already thinking in terms of Pemberton branding.

She looked down. The view from her window was of the tables outside the pub and someone was sitting there on the empty benches. A young man in jeans, with dark hair.

No. It couldn't be.

But it was. With every fibre of her body, she knew it. She

had stared at him for so long in the Apples and Pears she knew every contour, every gesture. The way his hands lay on the table, even.

A cold anger now gripped Nell. Fake OutdoorsGuy. Back again at the Edenville Arms. Whatever was going on? Was he waiting for her? Was this stalking? A joke?

Nell leaned further out of the window, too angry to worry about anyone else hearing. 'Hey!' she yelled. 'You down there.'

Dylan, who had been staring into space, looked up. He blinked. It was early, and he was tired. Why was a woman shouting at him from an upstairs window?

He narrowed his eyes and realised that he recognised her. That blond hair, almost white. That pale face, those wide eyes.

'Hello,' he called back. He had no idea what the girl he had met in the Apples and Pears was doing there. Had she followed him to Edenville to beard him about his behaviour in the pub? It seemed unlikely, for every imaginable reason. But what wasn't unlikely about his life at the moment?

Hello? Such a casual reply struck Nell as outrageous. 'Are you following me or something?' she accused.

Him following *her*? Dylan stared. 'Why would I do that?'

She was still angry with him, he could see. And he had been angry with her; had blamed her for the consequences of the split with Beatrice. But now it seemed all too much to think about. He felt he wanted to apologise, draw a line under it all. Now would seem to be a good time.

'I'm sorry,' he called. 'About what happened in the pub.'

Nell gripped the sill as if her fingers might drive through it. *Sorry!* Did he really think that was adequate? 'You deliberately pretended to be someone else!' she stormed. 'You made me look like an idiot!'

From below, Dylan could now see that windows were

opening. All over the front of the pub, sashes were lifting, casements were widening, heads were poking out.

'I didn't mean to,' he shouted back. 'I thought that you knew me. I didn't realise it was a blind date.'

'Knew you!' shouted Nell. 'How would I know you? I'd never seen you before in my life.'

Jason had been alarmed to hear shouting outside. Rushing to the inn's front door and seeing Adam Greenleaf, his heart sank. The man was a perfect pest. Wherever he went, trouble followed.

Glancing up at the windows to identify Greenleaf's interlocutor, Jason's sunken heart now came flying up into his throat. Framed by the weathered stone mullion and irradiated by the morning sun was Nell Simpson.

His fears had been realised. The two of them had found each other and now they were going at it hammer and tongs; it was like Romeo and Juliet's balcony scene in reverse. The whole village would be able to hear them. Not to mention the guests.

Terror gripped Jason: was anyone taking photographs on a smartphone? Posting them on social media? His establishment could be wrecked within hours. Jason shot back inside the hotel and pounded up the stairs to the honeymoon suite.

'Well, look, I'm sorry, anyway.' Dylan looked doubtfully up at Nell. 'It was all a misunderstanding.'

'Misunderstanding?!' came Nell's furious riposte. 'You can say that again!' How dare he act so casually? If it hadn't been for him, she wouldn't even be here.

He was wasting his time, Dylan could see. He was stung by the dislike in her tone. Who was she to shout at him? If it hadn't been for her he wouldn't be standing here at all. She had ruined his life.

'Do you live round here or something?' she was yelling now. 'Yes.'

This was greeted by a scream of rage. 'I knew it! Thank God I'm leaving this place!'

'You're leaving?' He felt relieved.

'You bet I am. Today. Mostly because I never want to see you again. You ruined my life!'

Nell slammed shut the window and leapt back just at the moment that the suite's entrance door gave way to reveal Jason, with broad-shouldered Ryan behind him, standing in the doorway.

CHAPTER 28

The silence that followed the slamming shut of Nell's window rang in Dylan's ears. He thrust his hands in his jeans pockets and turned his back on the heads which remained at the bedroom windows; not just in the Edenville Arms, but at several cottages nearby. Some front doors were open too but now, as Dylan met the eyes of the curious inhabitants, they started to close. 'Show's over,' he wanted to shout. 'Nothing to see.'

He knitted his brow, trying to make sense of what had just happened. That Nell was here, in the Edenville Arms, was a shock. She, on the other hand, seemed to have known he was in the vicinity. But how?

The situation reminded Dylan of the Apples and Pears meeting. There, he had known that Nell had thought he was someone else. Here, she had known that he was around. Were they doomed, Dylan wondered, to an endless series of acrimonious encounters in which one knew more than the other?

The crossed wires had got too tangled and tightly bound ever to be undone now. They would never agree. He would never persuade her, especially as she clearly felt herself the victim. What did she mean, he'd ruined her life? What about his? She had no idea what he had been through.

He wished Dan would come and take him away, so they could get on with the day's work and he could put this awful scene behind him. Although it was just as well his new employer hadn't turned up while Nell was shouting.

But Dan's van *was* here, Dylan now saw with a start. Among the car park's shiny vehicles was one that was red, filthy and dented.

And, very possibly, not working. Something was clearly the matter. Dylan hurried over to find the rear doors open and a pair of huge, soil-caked boots were protruding from under the vehicle. Dan's baseball cap lay on the ground by the left back tyre.

'What's up?' Dylan asked the boots.

'It's not starting,' came a voice from underneath.

'Oh dear.'

'Yer could say that.'

'Um, so what happens now?'

The mud-caked boots now became jeans, then a broad torso, followed by Dan's impassive features. He sat up, replaced his cap and looked at Dylan.

Dylan blinked before the steady stare. Dan could not have failed to hear what had gone on outside the pub. Would he now ask questions which might expose Dylan as at worst a liar and at best a fudger of the truth?

'We could use my car,' Dylan offered hastily, before the other man could say anything. 'Till yours gets patched up.'

Dan rose to his full six foot five in one seamless movement, and before he quite knew what was happening, Dylan was standing beside his own tiny two-door hatchback, watching Dan heap in the tools of his trade.

'It's fit in easy,' he declared with satisfaction. Dylan looked doubtfully at the mass of gnarled hoes, bent spades, two-pronged forks and broken plastic boxes crowding his boot. There were spilled seeds on the car floor and a strimmer and petrol mower on the back seat. He would have to drive with a rake either side of his head.

There were several bags of chippings and even one of manure. 'We'll just keep the winders down,' was Dan's solution to the associated stench.

Dylan minded less than he might have thought. He felt grateful to Dan for being so tactfully incurious. He still felt rattled after being shouted at, and the prospect of a day with his strong, silent new employer was strangely reassuring.

If perhaps not as silent as expected. As they drove, Dan switched on the radio and found some blaring music station.

'Down 'ere,' he yelled suddenly over the row, jabbing his finger at an entry they had almost driven past. It was on a steep bend. Dylan twisted the steering wheel and, with screeching tyres, just passed through the gateposts.

He was proceeding down a long drive, but under instruction from Dan, now veered left up a small track. This led between rhododendron bushes to a small parking area. According to a neat wooden sign, they had reached Kenilworth Lodge.

Dylan followed Dan down a flight of stone steps to a green-painted door. Kenilworth Lodge was in effect a little fort, with castellations along the roofline, reminiscent of the houses in Edenville village. 'Amazing place,' he remarked brightly.

Dan did not answer. The sound of rattling keys could be heard from within, then a scrabble and clatter as they engaged the lock. The door swung open and an elderly woman in a cardigan, pearls and checked skirt appeared.

'Mornin', Mrs P,' Dan said.

'Good morning, Daniel.' There was a cutting distaste in the woman's plummy tones, as if it had once been a good morning but wasn't any longer.

Dylan found himself being regarded coldly over her half-moon spectacles. 'And you are?'

'Me new partner, Mrs P,' Dan put in, before Dylan could say anything.

Mrs P folded her arms. The cuffs of her white shirt gleamed below the ginger wool of her cardigan. 'Bringing new people here, Daniel. I worry about the security aspects of it.'

Dan's tone was steadily pleasant. 'Oh, Adam here's OK, Mrs P.'

'Adam?' The old woman looked at Dylan sceptically.

He stepped forward, smiled, held out his hand and summoned the manners that had charmed everyone from Kirsty Young on *Desert Island Discs* to the Queen at a literary reception. 'How do you do. I'm Adam Greenleaf.'

'Are you indeed.' Mrs P, whose hands had stayed by her sides, now swept Dylan up and down with hooded eyes. 'I am Mrs Palethorpe.'

Something shiny and black now exploded behind the woman and hurled itself, barking, at Dan. 'Down,' Dan muttered, as the dog, ignoring him, continued to maul his thighs.

His owner made no attempt to address Dan's discomfort, or call the animal off. She merely handed Dan a list of jobs, which he took wordlessly. 'And mind you get through them all today.'

They walked round. It was on the tip of Dylan's tongue to criticise the old woman for her rudeness, but he sensed Dan would find it unwelcome. Perhaps he didn't notice. Or mind. Perhaps his exterior impassiveness went all the way through.

The garden and the house, Dylan decided, were rather more charming than their owner. The grounds were intensely detailed. There were two big lawns, their edges planted thickly with lavender. There was a woodland area, a vegetable plot and a formal parterre with rose trees and designs in box hedging. All surrounded by lovely old walls with wisteria and pear, both in full bloom, tangled up with climbing roses near the house. Lupins were shooting out, rocket-like, from big grey lead planters, each spiked leaf a setting for a fat diamond of dew. Kenilworth Lodge stood on a hillside, and the view across country from the woodland path was sublime.

Dan was still carefully reading Mrs Palethorpe's list. He passed the paper to Dylan.

Written in a cramped italic hand was:

Weed all flower beds
Pull all grass from lavender border
Weed all vegetable beds
Weed woodland area
Weed paths
Sweep all steps throughout garden
Clip box

'Wow,' said Dylan. 'That's quite a lot.'

'Aye,' was Dan's stoical response. He handed over an implement with two sharp pointed ends. Dylan took it and looked at it, unsure what exactly he was supposed to do with it.

'Weed,' said Dan, looking amused. 'Thought you said you done some gardening.'

Dylan reddened.

'You'll find a bucket down there. In't shed.' Dan pointed down the path.

Dylan fetched a bucket – for the weeds, presumably, although he had not dared ask – and began poking in the soil with the prong. Doing this while standing up, bum in the air, was uncomfortable. There was nothing for it but to kneel and feel the dirty earth soaking into his jeans. There was a washing machine at Bess's Tower, but he had no idea how to operate it. It looked like he'd better find out.

After a while Dylan realised that if you inserted the tool around the stem of a dandelion it gave you traction on the very thick, long root. He had never previously realised just how powerful the root of a dandelion was, nor how far down they went.

He began to rather enjoy himself; there was satisfaction in the feeling of the root resisting, then surrendering, then sliding out. The sun beat down, the birds sang and Dylan felt the agitations of earlier fading away. A sense of peace began to steal into his troubled soul.

From time to time, he looked at the view of the lovely valley. Hills folded into each other as far as the horizon, the furthest with a purple tinge and those nearer golden with hay. He could hear the grind of a tractor as it turned in the fields.

Bees hummed about him. He was surprised to find himself humming too. Never had he imagined that clearing a patch of weeds could feel rewarding. But results were instant, which could never be said of writing. Even writing as quickly acclaimed as his own had been.

Soon he had finished and sat back on his heels, satisfied with his efforts. He looked at the next item on the list. *Pull all grass from lavender border.*

Before starting on this, Dylan went to empty his bucket on the compost heap. Walking back, he saw that Mrs Palethorpe was standing in front of his recent theatre of operations. She turned to stare at him through her half-moon glasses.

Dylan smiled, expecting praise. The soil was not only weed-free but freshly dug over. It looked dark and inviting.

Mrs Palethorpe stabbed a finger downwards. 'You've missed some here. Look.'

Dylan looked. The few grass blades in question were so small he could hardly see them.

The old woman suddenly cocked her head. 'What's that *ghastly* noise?'

A faint crackling was coming from the direction of the woods: music interspersed with shouting people.

Mrs Palethorpe's eyes met his, aghast. 'Could it be a radio? I've told Daniel before that *I will not have* radios blaring out all over my garden. Kindly go and turn it off.' She strode away, the sharp pleats of her skirt quivering, her shoes crunching agitatedly on the gravel.

Dylan went to find his employer. Dan did not complain, or offer any comment. He merely shrugged and turned the radio off.

'She's horrible,' Dylan exploded, unable to keep it in any longer. 'Why do you work for her?'

Dan's impassive gaze met his. 'How much choice d'ya think I've got, mate? This game, you take whatever work comes. Gotta put up with it. Can't pick and choose.'

Dylan reddened as this lesson in the casual gardening economy filtered through. He'd had a charmed life before, only working when he wanted to, for vast sums, and for himself. All the same, strangely, he preferred what he was doing now.

He started to pull out long handfuls of bright grass from among the purple-topped lavender stems. This labour, while it lacked the visceral excitement of the earlier dandelion-pulling, was not without interest. The rasping stickiness of the blades was unexpected. And the sudden release of roots from soil sent the astringent, peppery lavender scent pouring into the air.

Dylan had a vague idea of the sun being to his left when he started but when next he looked up it was high in the sky. Surely it was lunchtime. His stomach certainly thought so. It was – or so it felt – cleaving to his backbone. The physical work and the fresh air had done exactly what physical work and fresh air were supposed to do. Dylan was starving, more so than he had ever been in his life.

He thought of his lunch in the bag in the car. That pork pie had looked exceptional, as had that creamy-looking piece of cheese, shot through with blue veins.

He rose and stretched, pushing his arms into the sunny air, enjoying the release of his muscles. He shoved back his hair from his perspiring brow and went in search of Dan, whose whereabouts were easy enough to guess at. The bottom of the garden was billowing with smoke.

At the sight and smell of flames, Dylan's heart began to thud. He tried to calm himself; this was just a small blaze for leaves and weeds. And he was a gardener now, for goodness' sake. Gardeners made bonfires.

Dan stood at the edge of a neat heap of burning debris, stoking with a garden fork a blaze from which smoke twisted rapidly out, unfurling itself into the air. Twigs snapped and crackled. Sparks flew. Dylan's breath was coming fast and panicked. He struggled for control.

'Aren't we stopping for lunch?' he managed to croak at last.

Dan turned to look at him. 'She don't like us to,' he said flatly. 'We're supposed to work all day.'

'Without a break?' Dylan exclaimed. Weren't there rules about this sort of thing? European Union directives?

'Aye.' Dan continued to fork the leaves on to the blaze. He had taken his top off and his muscled and naked torso shone with sweat. Underneath his baggy workwear, Dan cut a finer figure than one would imagine, although it was a sight wasted on Mrs Palethorpe, Dylan thought. With his huge muscles and massive height, he looked like some magus in an ancient grove. All he needed was a dryad or two. Dylan found himself wondering if Dan was married.

'Got nowt to eat, anyroad,' Dan added.

'You've brought nothing to eat?' Dylan remembered the doorstep sandwiches the last time they had met.

'Were in a bit of a rush this morning. Then t'van packed up.'

'I'll go and get mine. We can share it.'

Dylan hurried back up the path, relieved to escape the fire's heat and noise. Even a small, controlled bonfire brought it all back. His legs shook, his vision blurred and a band of iron was squeezing his chest.

Dan's level stare wobbled when Dylan returned with the pork pie and cheese. His eyes positively sparkled when Dylan fished out the small plastic tub of pickle that the Countess had so thoughtfully added. Watching the great jaw crash hungrily through the pie crust, Dylan felt a glow of satisfaction. It was good to help another human being. And Dan, he was sure, wouldn't sack him now.

After lunch, Dylan started on the vegetable beds. Some droning bees, heavy as bombers, kept him company. Plus a couple of appealingly cheeky robins whose beady black eyes were peeled for shining, writhing, purplish-pink worms in the soil.

The sun shone warmly on and Dylan felt pleasantly stunned with the power of it and the smell of earth-scented air eddying about him. A sense of deep peace was growing within him, as well as pleasure and pride at the ever-expanding frontier of clean, dark soil. Where there was chaos, he had brought order. This really was a good day's work. He had done the right thing, giving up writing.

Dylan was surprised to discover that Dan wanted to be taken straight home; the van, it seemed, was to be left in the pub car park. The question of whether the manager of the Edenville Arms would mind having the rotting wreck there was not addressed.

He dropped Dan at a house on a council estate which, while only a short distance from Edenville, might have been another world. The streets were lined with houses with broken fences; what had been gardens were now full of battered furniture and cars mounted on bricks. Dan's house, when they drew up outside it, did not look as if the occupant made his living from horticulture.

'I'll see yer tomorrer,' Dan said.

Various pale and villainous-looking boys, either very skinny or very fat, were kicking a football about. 'Shit car!' one of them yelled at Dylan.

They were spot on, Dylan had to admit. The smell of the manure had strengthened during the day.

The boys had now turned their attention to Dan and were shouting something at him. Dylan couldn't quite hear it but it sounded like 'All right, Shagger?'

But surely not, as Dan didn't seem offended in the least.

'Want me to pick you up here tomorrow?' Dylan asked, as Dan shut the passenger side door.

'Shagger!' shouted the boys. They were definitely addressing Dan, Dylan saw. 'Shag-*ger*! Shag-*ger*!'

Dan offered no explanation, however. He looked back steadily at Dylan as he started up his engine. The gang of youths roared and waved their middle fingers at him.

Dylan wound down the passenger window and leaned out. 'Here at seven thirty, yeah?'

'Reckon so,' Dan nodded, adding, deadpan, 'I'm not sure it's safe, meeting at t'pub any more.'

It was the only time all day that he had referred to the morning's scene. As, now, he turned his craggy head away, Dylan was almost sure he saw Dan grin.

CHAPTER 29

After shutting the door of the honeymoon suite on Jason and Ryan, Nell began to pack her things.

Jason had not asked her to leave; far from it. He had fallen on his managerial sword and apologised profusely for having misled her. He had sincerely believed Adam Greenleaf to be nowhere near the pub and had no idea why he had returned.

Adam Greenleaf! That was Fake OutdoorsGuy's real name? It seemed all wrong to Nell. It sounded so pleasant, entirely unlike its owner.

She had tuned back in to hear Jason ending his spiel by promising all manner of luxurious extras to make up for the distress caused. Champagne, spa treatments and a free cream tea had been among the reparation offered.

For her part, she had apologised for hanging, shouting, out of her bedroom window in a manner likely to embarrass the establishment. But Jason had assured her it couldn't matter less.

They had parted friends, all ruffled feathers smoothed, and Jason's last act before leaving the honeymoon suite was to go to the window and assure her that Greenleaf had gone.

Nell had not wanted to upset Jason by telling him that,

despite his efforts, she intended to leave on the first train back to London, wherever it went from. She had had enough of Edenville. She had no intention of going to see Angela in HR. She was finished with the whole place.

And so she was packing her few items – her wedding outfit, basically. The jeans and T-shirt that had been her one change of clothes had now been laundered – beautifully – by the hotel. While comfortable, they were hardly suitable attire for a job interview, which seemed yet another good reason not to bother. Nell zipped up her bag and opened the door of the suite. She was going, going . . .

But not quite gone. Just before she could shut the door behind her, the mobile in her bag rang. Nell fished it out and saw that Rachel was calling.

She groaned and went back into the suite. More comfortable to talk in there than the corridor.

Rachel, as ever, got straight to the point. 'You'll never guess,' she said.

'You're right. I won't.'

'Juno's found out – don't ask me how – that there's a touring production of *Murderous Death* coming to Chestlock.'

'What's *Murderous Death*?'

'One of those Agatha Christie-type murder mystery plays,' Rachel's tone was amused resignation.

Nell, on the other end, rolled her eyes. 'Well, that would have been great, but the thing is, Rach, I'm—'

'She's desperate to see it,' Rachel cut in.

'Won't it come to London?'

'No chance. It's one of those really cheesy touring productions you only get in the provinces.'

'Well, great, but as I say, it's not very convenient because—'

Rachel was obviously not listening. 'And, hang on a minute,

Juno's here, she's telling me that it's the last night. The production finishes in Chestlock on Saturday.'

'The thing is—'

'So you see, you've got to get tickets. And by my calculations, Saturday is your last night in the honeymoon suite. So we could come up again and stay.'

'Er . . .' She had it all mapped out, Nell realised. And gainsaying Rachel in full determined flow was not for the faint-hearted. Nonetheless, she had to try. 'Look, Rach, I'd love to but the thing is, you see, I'm leaving.'

There was a short, disbelieving silence.

'Leaving?' shrieked Rachel. 'You're leaving Edenville?'

'Er, yes. You see, I have to come back to London, because . . . um . . .'

'Why? *Why?*' the other end demanded fiercely. 'You can't possibly have a good reason! There's nothing for you to come back for! You were going to that job interview today, weren't you?'

'Yes, but . . .' Nell battled, trying to keep her end up. But she was no match for Rachel.

'It drives me *mad*,' the other end stormed. 'I do my best to support you, to point you in the right direction, and the minute I turn my back it all crumbles. You just dissolve and give up. I don't know why I bother, I really don't.'

She sounded angrier than Nell had ever heard her. Determinedly, she rallied her defences. 'Look, Rach, I have to leave. I've run into someone I want to avoid.'

'*Joey?*' Rachel gasped, her anger now all concern. 'God, I'm sorry. I never imagined you meant Joey.'

For a second, Nell was tempted to lie. Then: 'No, not Joey.'

'So *who?*' Rachel's tone was climbing the anger register again.

'I'd rather not say.'

'You'd rather not say?' came Rachel's mocking echo. 'Well, I'd rather not tell my small daughter – *my small, fatherless daughter* – that she can't see something she desperately wants to because you're getting the hell out of Edenville for no very good reason that I can see.'

There was another silence, then Nell cracked. 'OK then!' she shouted into the void. 'Have it your own way! So I won't go! I'll stay! I'll go to the interview! I'll get tickets for *Murdered By Death*, or whatever.'

There was a giggle from the other end. 'That's more like it,' said Rachel. 'Oh, hang on a minute,' she added, 'what was that, Juno? Oh, right. Juno says please can you get seats in the front row?'

The call over, Nell flopped back, arms above her head, and stared at the lilac pleats on the inside of the bed canopy. So she was stuck here. Stuck here with an unmade bed and a bath full of black towels: she'd thrown them in the empty tub as her last act before leaving.

She groped for her smartphone, now lost among the sheet folds, and consulted the website of the Pavilion Theatre, Chestlock. Unexpectedly, seats for *Murderous Death* seemed to be selling out fast. There were only four left in the front row. Nell fished out her credit card.

The production was being put on by something called the Backstabbers Theatre Company. The synopsis was suitably bloodcurdling. *A group of friends come to a country house for the owner's birthday party. But when they start to die, one by one, a damper is put on the celebrations. In a thrilling two-hander, world-famous detectives Miss Mandrake and Hercules Pierrot arrive to solve the mystery.*

Looking down the cast list, Nell could well believe Rachel's assertion that the ensemble rarely trod the boards inside the

M25. The Backstabbers Theatre Company seemed to be made up of 'stars' which had long since faded.

Nell had never heard of Gilly Davenport, the actress playing Miss Mandrake. Gilly's pouty, airbrushed photo showed a vintage sexpot; she was also, the website explained, the actress who had for many years played Karenza in *Bodwithian*, a Seventies TV drama series set in Cornwall. While the company's male star, Pete Leather, who played someone called Major Wilderbeest, had apparently once been a rival to Elvis.

The other leading man, Caradoc Turner, who played Pierrot the Poirot-like detective, had evidently seen better days too. He seemed to have a more serious thespian background than the others; his finest hour was a play called *Strangling Percy*, a West End hit in 1996. But things had evidently been on a downhill slide since: panto in Richmond and stints in *Holby City* and *The Bill* were among Caradoc's more recent achievements. Everyone in the entire cast had done *Doctors*.

The Backstabbers Theatre Company had toured *Murderous Death* for six months, Nell read. Their itinerary, which was astonishing, had touched almost every point of the national compass. They had been from Glasgow to Gillingham and all points in between and to the sides. They were, she guessed, relieved to be winding it up this week, although the Pavilion Theatre, Chestlock, hardly seemed to equate to going out with a bang.

Afterwards she called the human resources department. Angela Highwater was not available in person, but a pleasant-sounding assistant went to consult her and returned with the news that the Director's earliest available slot was four o'clock.

Four o'clock was six hours away. It was going to be a long, tedious day. Should she, Nell wondered, kill time by going into Chestlock to buy clothes for the interview? But she didn't want the job, so why bother?

Instead, she dealt with the other item on her to-do list, which was to ring up Carrington's and take her flat off the market. The salesperson, disconcerted, put on the manager, who tried to change Nell's mind: the price achieved was an excellent one given the state of the market and the location and state of the flat (Nell bridled at this). He added that the buyers, newlyweds, would be disappointed.

Nell, who had been through all this with Rachel anyway, did not care about the disappointment of the newlyweds. Nor did she care about Carrington's. Had Carrington's not existed, she herself would have been spared a great deal of disappointment. 19a was to be taken off the market, and she was moving back in. No one, throughout the whole exchange, mentioned Joey.

She told the agency she would be back next week, when she would complete the formalities and get the key to the flat. Nell pushed to the back of her mind what Rachel would have to say about the disappointed newlyweds.

Slipping the 'Please Tidy My Room' sign on the doorknob of the honeymoon suite, Nell now set off for a walk through the village.

But so frustrated and resentful was her mood that the delightful, neat little houses; the pretty, tidy little gardens; the glorious setting on the edge of the splendid stately park had no power to soothe or impress her.

She was here against her will. She had not wanted to come and she did not want to stay. But behind all that was something else, something Nell was trying to suppress: the fact that she didn't really want to go back either. It wasn't just a matter of facing Rachel, it was the thought of facing and re-establishing the dreary routine in the back bedroom.

Pacing glumly on, Nell found herself walking up towards the

church and lifting the wrought-iron gate into the churchyard. A smooth gravelled path on the other side led through carefully tended plots. There seemed not a single slumped gravestone, weed or broken cross. In Edenville, the resting places of the dead were as well cared for as the houses of the living.

Nell wandered through the neat lines of stones and reached a slightly raised area set aside from the rest. It seemed to be the personal plot of the Earls of Pemberton. There they were, planted next to each other, their final resting places marked by imposing yet simple gravestones. No vast tombs or mausoleums, as one might have expected given the splendours of where they dwelt in life. When it's over, it's over, seemed to be the view taken by the Pembertons.

The suggestion, by extension, was that you should enjoy life while it lasted. Nell felt her inner screw of discontent take another twist. She would love to enjoy life, except that life seemed bent on being as unenjoyable as possible. She was hemmed in by the actions of others, unable to do anything for herself. How had that happened? Since when had she lost control?

She entered the church and breathed in the musty-cold smell of age, wood and hymn books. The door swung shut behind her and the sound boomed through the dark interior.

It was a perfect English country church, with everything where it should be. Tudor tombs in the chancel, Georgian memorials on the walls and Victorian colour and carving round the altar. Drawings of some cataclysmic biblical event by the children of the local school were pinned to a padded board by the font. Every pew had tapestried kneelers; there were ones with tractors on, as well as animals and birds. Quite a few had the by-now-familiar Pemberton coat of arms.

Nell sat down and found herself closing her eyes, clasping

her hands, dipping her head and silently asking for help in straightening the tangled threads of her life.

Feeling vaguely soothed, she retraced her steps along the aisle and back out into the porch. The churchyard, which had been empty, now had one other person in it. An old man, crouching before a grave just opposite the porch, was setting out garden tools, clearly preparing to do some work there.

For all his evident advanced age, there was something very proud, clean and tidy about him. His thick white hair was ploughed neatly with comb-lines and the sleeves of his pressed white shirt were rolled up very precisely at the elbows. He wore brown trousers with braces, and a fawn-coloured cardigan was folded up beside his gardening tool bag.

He had brought some small flowering plants in pots to add to the grave which was, Nell now saw, a garden in miniature. Tiny early roses flowered in pink and red profusion but not so high as to obscure what was spelt out neatly in black capitals on the weathered grey granite of the simple arched head-stone: EDWINA MARGARET HARRINGTON FARLEY 1926–2004. BELOVED WIFE OF GEORGE ERNEST FARLEY.

His wife's, Nell thought. Meaning that the man before her was George Ernest Farley. She was about to step out of the porch when she heard a low, steady voice. Mr Farley, she realised, was talking.

'Well, Edwina, love,' he was saying. 'I'm sorry it's been a while since I came.'

Nell, who had not been intending to listen, was struck by his strong northern accent. It sounded unexpected for what was presumably the husband of the magnificent-sounding Edwina Margaret Harrington Farley. Had they married across the classes, back in the 1940s or whenever it was?

'But I do have a bit of good news for you,' Mr Farley continued. 'Those rotten people next door have finally gone. You can imagine how relieved I am. You know I don't drink these days – not since the pub went all posh, like. But I did wish I could nip down the Edenville as it used to be and celebrate with a few pints.'

Nell absorbed this glimpse of village politics. So the gentrification of the Edenville Arms had not been without its consequences.

'Now you know I don't like to moan owermuch in case you worry about me,' Mr Farley continued. He spoke to Edwina as if she were really lying there, listening.

'But next door, they really were pretty dreadful and I doubt that even you, who could find the good in anyone, could have found any in them.'

Should she show herself? Nell wondered. This was all so intimate that eavesdropping seemed wrong. On the other hand, if she suddenly appeared, the old man might be embarrassed. Or shocked. Better to stay where she was.

'The noise, Edwina!' Mr Farley was exclaiming. 'Now, I'm used to noise, as you know. The racket in a night-flying Lancaster isn't something you forget in a hurry! Especially after you open fire. But there was a good reason for that. And there was no excuse for that screaming, shrieking child next door.'

Mr Farley paused and pressed the earth round the base of one of the new little plants. Then he sat back on his heels again. 'At first, as you know, I tried to put up with it. Then I asked them to tone it down. I was never asking for complete silence, of course. That would be unrealistic, and even unfair. But a bit of consideration would have been nice. We were living very close to each other, after all.'

He was bedding in another plant now, pressing the soil down with the tines of his fork. 'But then the mother turns up! So aggressive, Edwina, you wouldn't have believed it. Flouncing round, bristling with fury. Swearing. Asking me who the beeping beep I thought I was. Telling me that this was a free country.' The old man sighed. 'Well, I knew *that* of course. None better. Hadn't I helped to make it that way?'

From the porch, Nell watched the old man taking his trowel and scooping a hole for another little plant. 'And after that, Edwina, she started playing this terrible music really loudly in her garden. Booming, pounding row, it was. Like the fall of distant bombs. I couldn't bear it, so I went round again and saw the husband. Or partner or whatever they call them these days. He was useless. Puny, weaselly little creature, who wouldn't look me in the eye.'

Mr Farley had turned to tackle another part of the grave and was now directly facing Nell. She pressed herself against the porch wall where the shadow fell, hoping that he wouldn't look up and see her. It felt very wrong to be listening, but it was also terribly touching. The old man had clearly adored Edwina, who must have been his wife for many years. And equally obviously he missed her terribly.

He was still talking; about the noisy child, Nell gathered. 'I'd even find her in the house!' he was exclaiming. 'She'd come wandering in while I was out in the back garden. Through that hole I told you about, that one she hacked in the hedge. I'd find her raiding my blooming biscuit tin!'

An agitated cough now shook the elderly frame. Then the old man continued.

'I'd ask her to go away, and she'd say she'd go where she beeping well liked. It was her human right. When I said that I had rights as well, including not having people wandering into my house and helping themselves to my things, she said go on then, sue me.'

Nell was listening indignantly. What appalling people, to treat this decent old man like that!

'I ask you, Edwina love. How does a child that age know about suing? How has life got so . . . degraded? What was that war we fought all for?'

Nell bit her lip.

'I don't know, love. Everything's gone. It's all different. That world we lived in together has nothing in common with this one, where I'm on my own.'

Nell felt her throat tighten. Her eyes pricked and tears brimmed over her lashes. 'Oh Edwina,' the old man was saying as, tenderly, he pressed the earth back down around the roses. 'I miss you so much, my love. I miss you every minute of every day.'

CHAPTER 30

The human resources office of the Pemberton estate was a palatial establishment. It was housed in a gracious Georgian house in the estate park and entered via a shining black front door with a white-painted fanlight and brass fittings. Inside was a double-height stone-floored hall whose terracotta walls were hung with large paintings of oversized cows and colourful game birds.

A panelled corridor with a herringbone wooden floor led off this hall. It was punctuated by broad mahogany doors. A sign on one of these read: 'Angela Highwater. Director'.

Angela sat within, staring at her computer screen. She was reading the e-mailed CV sent through by Nell Simpson, the woman she was to interview later that day. As late as humanly possible, after Angela's appointments at the beauty salon, after she had ordered her groceries online. Of all today's priorities, Nell Simpson was Angela's last and lowest.

'This isn't a CV,' Angela snapped at her timid assistant, Gail. 'It's just a paragraph about her catalogue work. What about her exam results, the schools she went to?' Angela felt she had a right to know these things. Where someone had grown up, what their background was. She vehemently disagreed with the latest school of HR thought: that personal information such as addresses and exam results encouraged preconceived ideas about applicants. Preconceived ideas were the whole point.

'It doesn't even have an address on,' she complained.

'It doesn't have to,' ventured Gail. 'If someone's of no fixed abode and has to say so on their application it might prejudice people against them.'

'Exactly! Save us wasting our time.'

'But it's not always their own fault that people are homeless,' pointed out Gail, whose timidity concealed an ineradicable sense of fairness.

'Of course it bloody is.'

Gail hesitated, but realised there was no point arguing with Angela. She had clearly had a difficult weekend and intended to take it out on whoever came to hand. Her boss had had a lot of difficult weekends recently; her moods, always unpredictable, were now predictably black.

Gail guessed that, underneath all the bluster and spite, Angela was simply lonely. She knew from the estate tom-tom about the failure of Angela's recent efforts to establish a relationship with Dan Parker. Gail felt sorry for her boss. Her highhanded, bullying ways made her as unpopular as her outlandish appearance made her the subject of mockery. But Gail, unlike most other staff, could remember a different Angela. Years ago, when Gail had first come to work with her, Angela had been funny and clever. That humour and insight had now sharpened into something mean and aggressive, and yet Gail felt sure the original Angela remained somewhere within.

'She's obviously completely unsuitable,' the Director of Human Resources grumbled now, re-reading Nell's summary of her experience.

Gail disagreed. 'She's done a lot of commercial writing,' she ventured, 'which is a large part of this job.'

Angela glared at her assistant. Gail's own job, as Assistant Director of Human Resources, was to make Angela's coffee and answer Angela's phone. Not to have opinions about the suitability – or otherwise – of applicants.

'I thought the Earl told you to give it to her anyway,' Gail added, knowing she was pushing her luck, but unable to resist.

Angela thumped the top of her desk. A photograph fell over.

'Whether she gets the job is up to *me*. And I don't mind telling you that, as things stand, she won't.'

Gail propped the picture back up – it was one of His Lordship with Angela – and tried not to look as surprised as she felt. That Angela thought herself more powerful than the Earl was a new development. She had, up until now, always seemed to have a grasp of realpolitik.

'She's never worked on a big estate, for a start,' Angela added.

Neither had Ros Downer, thought Gail. Ros had been a freelance, although freelance what was anyone's guess.

'She's also gay, of course,' Angela continued. Jason had not had the heart to disabuse her of this illusion.

Gail wondered what on earth that had to do with anything. Surely it was Nell's business.

Angela could always tell when her assistant was thinking subversive thoughts. 'Go and get me a bloody coffee!' she yelled. 'I'll get rid of Nell Simpson somehow,' she vowed, as Gail scurried out. 'There's no way she's coming to work here.'

Nell, still killing time, lunched in the same café in which she had met the Earl. But there was no sign of him today. It ebbed and flowed with tourists instead; a low, cheerful buzz of chatter accompanied Nell's thoughtful chewing of her salmon sandwich. Her thoughts kept returning to Mr Farley tending his wife's grave. Nell felt a strange affinity with the lonely old man. She wondered who would move in next door to replace his nasty neighbours. In other circumstances, she would rather have liked to herself. Then she could have kept an eye on him. They could have become friends.

It was now afternoon, but some hours yet from four. Nell had wandered into the gardens of Pemberton Hall. The day had remained sunnily cheerful. The trees were burgeoning with new summer growth and the warm grass glittered and shone.

The great sweep of green was full of people enjoying themselves. Dogs bounded towards her, pursued by their owners. Groups of older walkers strode along purposefully under broad-brimmed white cotton hats.

It was all, Nell thought, so active, so positive. So why couldn't she feel positive too? Yet the feeling of being neither here nor there persisted. Edenville. London. She didn't want to stay here, she didn't want to return there. She didn't want to be interviewed for a new job but nor did she want to carry on with her old one. As a plane roared overhead, dragging the noise through the sky behind, Nell wished she were on it.

Her mobile rang. It was not, as she had expected, Rachel. So who was this Unknown Caller? Her heart jumped painfully. Not Joey. Anyone but him.

But the accents of the young man on the other end were unfamiliar. He sounded anxious and upset. 'You don't know me,' he gasped, 'but my name is Ben and me and my wife Dora are trying to buy your flat.'

'Oh.' Nell was disconcerted. The newlyweds.

'We had our hearts set on it,' Ben continued. 'Dora's pregnant. We thought we'd be moving in to Gardiner Road in the next few weeks, but Carrington's have just rung us and said that you've taken it off the market.'

'Yes,' Nell said slowly. 'I have.'

'I don't know your reasons,' the young man continued. 'And I'm sure you have good ones. But if there was any possibility at all that you could still sell the flat to us we'd be grateful for ever. We'd looked all over London and we'd given up hope until we saw 19a. We loved it as soon as we walked in.'

Nell remembered how much she had come to dislike the place, how confining it had come to seem. Clearly, one man's prison was another man's paradise.

'That garden,' Ben continued with what sounded like genuine longing. 'It had such potential.'

'It certainly had that,' Nell conceded. Until Rachel had turned up, that was pretty much all it had. She could imagine how much Rachel would appreciate help with the digging. And how much Juno would enjoy a new baby downstairs.

'Do you think you might change your mind?' Ben sounded quite desperate. 'It's just that I don't know how Dora will cope, in her state, if we have to start looking again.'

Nell hesitated. Deciding to take the flat off the market had seemed so easy. Less so now she could see the potentially devastating consequences. There was a parallel between this situation and what Joey had done to her on their wedding day. She knew what it was like to be dealt a bolt from the blue. To lose something precious and feel betrayed.

She felt herself crumbling, and tried to rally. 'It's just that, well, my circumstances changed. I was moving somewhere else, but it fell through.'

The young man on the other end sighed. 'Well, I can't argue with that,' he said resignedly. 'That's fair enough. I just wanted to talk to you, see if there was anything that could be done. But I absolutely understand.'

To Nell's guilty ear Ben's polite acceptance seemed so much worse than any amount of angry ranting would have. Was it really fair for her to place such a great obstacle in the way of this sweet couple and their baby? Did they deserve it, when they had offered for her flat in good faith? She had broken a promise, just as Joey had. By denying them the flat, she was perpetuating Joey's legacy of misery. Would it not be better just to sell Gardiner Road and find somewhere else?

'These things happen,' Ben was saying cheerfully, trying to mask his obvious disappointment. 'It was good to speak, anyway. Thanks for talking to me.'

'Yeah, thanks,' Nell was about to say, when she stopped. 'Hang on,' she gasped. 'I don't think I was thinking straight before. I'll get on to the estate agents and see if we can get things started again.'

CHAPTER 31

It was five past four and Nell was waiting in the lobby of the human resources office.

'Miss Simpson?' A woman had appeared: short, brown-haired and dark-suited. Nell recognised the soft voice she had spoken to on the phone. 'Ms Highwater won't be a moment. She's just tied up with something.'

Gail's voice was shaking. Angela had been in the foulest of moods all day. At the moment, what she was tied up with was flicking through *Hello!* magazine.

Gail was struck by how friendly and pretty Nell looked. She hated to think of what would happen. Angela, with her ruthless cunning, would tease out personal revelations which she would twist into reasons against employment.

Gail had seen it happen many times to good-looking women applying for jobs at Pemberton. And these were women Angela hadn't even been told to employ. Nell's attractiveness, plus the directive from the Earl, could only end one way.

'Perhaps you'd like to look at these.' Gail presented Nell with a sheaf of estate promotional literature. She felt she wanted to give this candidate every chance.

Nell thanked her and took it, even though she'd already

looked through it all in detail. There had been plenty of time after ringing Carrington's and instructing them to re-activate the selling process with Ben and Dora. It had been a slightly embarrassing business but no more embarrassing than anything else that had happened recently. And Nell had rung off with the uplifting conviction of being firmly back on the moral high ground.

This, in turn, made her decide to take the interview more seriously and approach it more positively. For reasons of personal dignity, if nothing else. And so she had gone into the various estate shops and cafés and gathered up every Pemberton-related brochure she could find. In the dank, shady corner of a garden grotto she had squinted at the website on her smartphone. There was no getting away from the fact – especially given her new, positive frame of mind – that there was a real job to do here, and it was right up her street. She had exactly the right skills to make a wonderful success of it.

Even if she didn't have the right clothes. Nell now regretted not going into Chestlock to find something smarter to wear than a T-shirt and jeans. Ought she to have worn her wedding dress after all, dirty though it was, and odd though the plastic boots would have looked?

But perhaps clothes didn't matter too much now that Fate seemed to be driving the whole business. Every plan she had made for herself, after all, had been countermanded. She had wanted to leave Edenville but was, thanks to Rachel, staying the rest of the week. Now, thanks to Ben's intervention, she had nowhere to live in London when that week was up.

Everything seemed to be pointing towards what Rachel had urged all along: giving this whole Pemberton job idea a go. For the time being, at least. Was there a good reason not to?

Well there was Adam Greenleaf. The fact that he lived in the area was not ideal. But she would just have to keep out of his way. She couldn't spend her life running away from people. Especially when she had nowhere to run to.

And she had, at least, had the satisfaction of telling Greenleaf what she thought of him. He would probably be as keen to avoid her in future as she was to avoid him.

Gail appeared again and Nell followed her down the corridor. Gail knocked on Angela's door. 'Nell Simpson for you, Miss Highwater,' she said, heart sinking in the knowledge this was another lamb to the slaughter.

Nell's experience of directors of human resources had been that they tended to be of conservative appearance. The woman behind the desk looked the opposite, with her crazy hair and tight clothes.

Angela was, as Gail had anticipated, all friendly brightness. She always was, to start with. It was after she got them comfortable that she stuck the knife into her victims. 'Hello, Nell! Come in, it's great to see you. I'm Angela, Director of Human Resources for the Pemberton Estate. Tall, aren't you? *Love* the jeans!'

Nell reddened. 'I'm sorry about my clothes. I didn't expect to be coming for an interview when—'

'Couldn't matter less! It's great you feel so comfortable with us already,' Angela exclaimed, untruthfully, as Gail knew. Angela was obsessed with people looking smart at interviews and regarded anything less as a personal insult. Nell's outfit would count against her, there was no doubt about that.

Once Nell sat down, Angela wasted no time getting to the bottom of things. 'So where are you from, Nell?' she beamed. 'There wasn't an address on your CV.'

'Er . . .' Nell had been intending to give Gardiner Road as her home, but that was obviously not an option now. She might be back on the moral high ground, but it didn't provide anywhere for her to live on.

'I don't really have a place at the moment,' Nell confessed. 'I'm staying at the Edenville Arms.'

Homeless, Angela thought with satisfaction. A vagrant lesbian. Marvellous. 'Of course, you're the lady newlyweds! Congratulations.'

Nell concealed her surprise with a smile. 'We're not actually *together*. Not in that way.'

Angela stared. 'Not . . . together? You're *not* married, then?' Bloody Jason. How could he have got this wrong?

Nell smiled. 'My friend Rachel is a widow. And I'm . . .' She stopped. Angela Highwater was obviously a warm and sympathetic person, but that didn't mean she needed to go into the whole Joey business.

'A widow!' Angela shook her head, tutting. 'Poor lady. So you brought her up here for a treat, did you?'

Nell hesitated. 'Not exactly,' she began, and again wanted to leave it at that. But the kindness and sympathy in the other woman's face encouraged her onwards.

'Not exactly?' prompted Angela, with her warmest smile and most confidante-worthy tones.

Nell's resolve not to say anything splintered and collapsed. Angela listened with an expression of compassionate understanding. But her nails were positively gouging her palms with excitement. Forget the lesbianism; this was miles better. Jilted at the altar with nowhere to live! Homeless and emotionally unstable! Eminently unsuitable for estate employment!

Nell came to the end of the tale. 'So there it is. That's what's brought me up here.' Well, some of what had brought her up there. The Adam Greenleaf business remained unbroached. Even Rachel didn't know about that.

'It's a terrible story.' Angela shook her head sorrowfully. 'You poor thing. I can't bear to think what you've been through.'

She had not meant a word of it but was surprised to feel that, actually, she did. Somewhere deep within her serially romantically disappointed soul was a stirring of sympathy for everything this woman in front of her had experienced at the hands of a man. It reminded her of what she had suffered over Dan Parker, who in the end preferred that living corpse Juliet Turner. Men were so bloody destructive, so bloody heedless of the chaos they caused! But it was only a stirring, and Angela was swift to remove the heat beneath it and put the lid back on. She wasn't here to sympathise with Nell Simpson. She was here to dispatch her back to where she had come from.

Though grateful for the relief of unburdening herself, Nell sensed she had rather overshared. 'I'm sorry,' she began. 'You'll have to excuse me talking about myself so much. I hadn't meant to but it's all rather complicated. I know I can count on your discretion, though.'

'*Tell* anyone!' Angela's red fingernails flew to her blancmange-like white breast. 'I wouldn't *dream* of it! Wild *horses* wouldn't drag it from me! I'm Director of Human Resources, remember!'

Nell felt instantly reassured. It was true that Angela's position guaranteed confidentiality. She was hardly likely to go out and start gossiping about interview candidates, was she?

She watched Angela stand up and smooth down her tight dress. Something was missing, Nell realised. 'Aren't we going to talk about the job?'

Angela looked blank. 'The job?' There was no job for this woman. Not once the Earl heard she was an unreliable vagrant who'd just left her fiancé at the altar. 'Oh, er, leave it with me.'

'So you'll get back to me?' Nell rose to her feet now as well. She felt worried.

'Course I will.' Angela snuck a glance at her watch. Just coming up to five. If she could wind this up in the next few minutes and then call the Earl, she could head over to the Edenville Arms and see Jason. She had a bone to pick with him.

'Is everything all right?' Nell searched Angela's features, which somehow looked less friendly than before. She was reassured to some extent by the dazzling beam the other woman now trained on her. 'Everything's fine. Couldn't be better!'

Nell was hardly out of the door when Angela pressed the speed-dial link to the Earl. It took some time to get through, even so. Angela suspected that Margaret, the secretary, had put her on hold on purpose. They had crossed swords in the past; there had been a misunderstanding over Margaret's husband. Eventually, however, His Lordship's patrician tones floated down the line. 'Good afternoon, Angela. What can I do for you? Interviewed that young lady, have you?'

It was best, Angela knew, to come straight to the point; the Earl was famously unkeen on beating about the bush. 'Yes, and I really don't think Nell Simpson is a good choice.' She tried her best to sound regretful.

'Well, I disagree,' the Earl returned robustly. 'Her experience is spot on. She's just what we need.'

'She's a destabilising influence,' Angela countered vehemently.

'A what?'

Angela drew in a deep breath. 'Nell Simpson,' she said with all the pomp and circumstance she could summon, 'turns out to be a vagrant with a history of emotional instability, deceit and untrustworthiness.'

The Earl let a few beats pass. 'What is the evidence for this?' he asked.

His very calmness exacerbated Angela's hysteria. 'She left her fiancé standing at the altar! How can we possibly give a position of such enormous responsibility to someone like that?'

'Leaving one's betrothed at the altar might in some circumstances be a wise thing to do. People have second thoughts.'

Angela was getting desperate now. 'She was dressed appallingly! Turned up for the interview in jeans and a creased T-shirt.'

'She was wearing that when I saw her,' His Lordship mused. 'She looked very nice, I thought.' And certainly better than how Angela Highwater normally looked, with her strangely coloured clothes and bizarre hair.

Angela flailed for another negative. 'She's much too good-looking,' she said censoriously.

'Is she really?' the Earl said innocently. 'I must say I hadn't noticed. What has that got to do with it, anyway? You've just said she was badly dressed.'

'Attractive women lower productivity,' Angela ignored the last remark. 'It's a proven fact.'

'Whatever can you mean?' the Earl asked. Personally, he'd always preferred to be served by a pretty girl in a shop, or at least someone with a smile. This reflection led on to the realisation that there were very few smiles or pretty girls in his shops, if anywhere on his estate. Why was that?

'They're seen as social magnets. People go over and talk to them, men try to impress them, that sort of thing,' said Angela, trotting out the one piece of theory she had agreed with at the recent human resources training day.

'Absolute twaddle,' said the Earl. 'I absolutely want you to hire Nell Simpson. Indeed, I insist on it. We need someone good in that position, and we need them now. As a matter of urgency.'

Angela was about to tartly observe that it was only urgent because His Lordship had seen fit to sack Ros, but she thought better of it. One of Angela's few genuine personnel skills was recognising when her own job might be in danger.

She tried one final tack. 'But Your Lordship, she's of no fixed abode. She's living at the Edenville Arms.'

'I don't object to that. On the contrary, it shows excellent taste. The Edenville Arms is a very good pub.'

'Well, she can't stay there,' Angela said ominously. 'She's only got the room for the rest of this week. Jason's got it booked solid all summer.'

'Has he now?' mused the other end, approvingly. Angela could have kicked herself for inadvertently ushering the hotel manager into the limelight. 'Perhaps she can rent somewhere,' the Earl suggested.

'There isn't anywhere for rent,' Angela stated quickly, and in the face of the plethora of ads to the contrary in all the local estate agents' windows. 'Summer's coming. All the local places have gone.'

The Earl, who tended not to look in estate agents' windows, was silent, as Angela had expected. Then he said something she did not expect at all.

'Well, she can always stay at Pemberton. Plenty of spare bedrooms here.'

The possibility of Nell Simpson taking up residence in the Earl's actual home was so far-fetched, so ghastly, it had never so much as crossed Angela's mind. She imagined her now, the cool, tall blonde, beneath the pleated canopy of one of the state bedrooms, looking out over a view of the park. She imagined her in one of the bathrooms with their polished copper pipes and mahogany fittings. Furious, murderous jealousy filled Angela. It could not be tolerated, it would not be borne. It absolutely could not happen.

'I've got another idea,' she said desperately.

247

'And what is that?'

'There's Ros's old cottage. Just outside the village. Beggar's Roost.'

'Didn't they leave it in rather a mess?' The Earl had heard from the estate maintenance men of drawings on walls and a garden like a bomb site. Ros Downer, it appeared, had had rather a free-range child.

'It's not so bad,' Angela maintained, although she had privately been shocked by Rapunzal's biologically explicit depictions of the human form. 'Iggy and I believe that nakedness is beautiful,' Ros had explained. 'We don't feel the need to cover up at home.'

'Well, perhaps we can get it repainted for her,' the Earl said. 'Did all that business with the old chap next door get sorted out, by the way? It sounded very unpleasant.'

'Dreadful!' Angela agreed, seizing on an outlet for her pent-up ire. 'It was very stressful.'

'Yes, I understand old George had a very difficult time.'

But Angela's loyalties – so far as they went – were with the other side. 'He was a very difficult neighbour,' she countered.

'Didn't they want to cut his hedge down? Seemed rather unreasonable. Old George Farley has been there for as long as I can remember.'

'On a peppercorn rent!' Angela put in, even though rents were not her business. She had, at one stage, attempted to get close to the estate manager, whose business they were and who was Margaret's husband.

'Lovely man. So gentle,' the Earl was saying thoughtfully. 'War hero too. You know he flew a Lancaster bomber, don't you?'

Angela suppressed a yawn.

'Yes, awfully brave. So few of them survived. But you'd never

248

know it, he's so modest. Never talks about it . . . Poor old chap, his wife died a few years ago. Rather retreated into himself after that.'

'Must have been a welcome release for her,' Angela muttered uncharitably.

The Earl didn't quite hear this, but the sound nudged him from his reverie. 'I'm afraid I have to go,' he said. 'So can I take it that Nell Simpson will be offered the job as Director of PR and Marketing, with the option of Beggar's Roost with the job?'

Angela, through gritted teeth, agreed that he could.

Afterwards, she slammed the phone down hard and yelled for Gail. As Angela thundered out the latest unwelcome human resources developments, Gail did her best to look as appalled as she was clearly expected to, and not, as she actually felt, that it would be a relief to have someone nice about the place.

As her boss continued to rage behind the desk, Gail remembered she had a piece of meat to throw the ravening beast. She had just read it in the local newspaper. She hurried off to her desk to fetch it.

Angela seized it from her minion's trembling hands. The item concerned Caradoc Turner, actor husband of the corpse-like temptress who Dan Parker had preferred to her. He was returning home from his latest tour. The play was *Murderous Death*, an Agatha Christie-esque mystery.

Angela skimmed the article before shoving the paper back at Gail, her eyes sparkling through her clogged mascara. The final night of *Murderous Death* was to be this weekend, at the local theatre in Chestlock. Well, Angela planned to be at the stage door afterwards. She had news for Caradoc Turner.

CHAPTER 32

Caradoc Turner sat in his dressing room at the Woking Hippodrome. He was manically pressing and re-pressing the redial on his mobile. His wife, however, was not picking up.

What was she doing? When he had spoken to Juliet earlier that morning, she had not said she was going out. So far as he was aware, she rarely left their home, Birch Hall. What was there to go out for, in Chestlock?

Caradoc breathed deeply in the manner he had been taught at theatre school to combat stage fright. But it had been months since he had feared walking out of the wings; he knew his part so well he could perform it in his sleep. On at least one occasion he had. It was not stage fright that was exercising Caradoc now.

It was Juliet.

For some reason, the gnawing anxiety Caradoc felt whenever he thought of his young, attractive wife had worsened as the tour's end drew nearer. He had longed for her every day for the past six months, as the Backstabbers Theatre Company moved from Gaiety to Hippodrome to Palace to Civic Theatre in towns he had never even known existed and would have been happy to remain ignorant of. But now he was finally coming home, and the very last performance loomed. It was on Saturday, a mere three days from today. A mere six performances left, three matinees and three evening.

Caradoc felt a palpitating excitement. The moment he had been looking forward to for six months was almost upon him. Soon, hopefully, Juliet would be upon him too. Would his wife, after the long absence, finally agree to have sex with him?

When his agent had first called to offer a six months' stint in a touring provincial production of *Murderous Death*, Caradoc had laughed in his face. He, who had once played Hamlet at the National (admittedly, as understudy to the understudy; his actual part had been Guildenstern)! He, playing a character called Hercules Pierrot in an Agatha Christie-style mystery with a washed-up bunch of old soap-stars!

True, his career was some way past its zenith. But it had not, or at least so Caradoc thought, yet reached the nadir that sent actors out into the wild to be shot, stabbed or poisoned in dusty provincial theatres in front of ancient audiences sucking Mintoes.

His agent's response had been frank and crushing. His view was that not only was Caradoc's career at just such a nadir, but that he was lucky to have even this opportunity. As he absorbed this it had occurred to Caradoc that *Murderous Death* might be the break he and Juliet needed to reinvigorate their marriage. Or simply invigorate it, full stop.

In fact, their marriage had started pretty well. Full-bloodedly, quite literally. Juliet had been a set designer when Caradoc met her. She was in charge of painting gore all over the stage in a production of *Titus Andronicus* which was sanguinous even by Globe standards.

Her very black hair and very white face had beautifully set off the bright red she was professionally concerned with. She was also fabulously wraithlike, wafting about the stage in floaty garments that clung to her narrow hips and small, firm breasts. It seemed to Caradoc, who had always found Gothic women a turn-on, that Juliet, in her clinging, bloodstained clothes, pulsed with a repressed yet powerful sexuality. It was in the hope of liberating it that he began to pay serious court to her on the *Andronicus* press night.

By the time the *Andronicus* cast filed out for the last time (curtains did not fall at the Globe; it had none), Caradoc and Juliet were definitely an item. He had found her refusal to sleep with him until after they were married delightfully novel; Caradoc was – or at least had been – a man used to finding keen young actresses falling to their knees. And so they had married, but the expected unleashing of Juliet's spectacular libido had never happened.

Caradoc was at a loss as to why – he was a vigorous man in the bloom of middle age – and Juliet offered no explanation either. She would just look at him with her fathomless dark pools of eyes and murmur that the time was not yet right. She would then roll away in her shroud-like white nightgown to the distant wastes of the other side of the bed while Caradoc felt his balls might explode.

The actor tried Juliet another ten times and then put the phone back in his jacket pocket. He'd call again after the matinee which was coming up fast on the inside. But even if he got her, he knew he'd call her again after that. Something was making him call her a lot these days.

As he stuck on his Pierrot moustache, Caradoc thought how glad he would be to say goodbye to the beastly thing. He'd got a nasty sore on his upper lip now.

He'd be even gladder to say goodbye to Pierrot himself. The part was depressing, as was the play. Being called a 'poisonous little potato-faced beast' by Gilly every night – she seemed to say it with particular emphasis – had had a cumulatively demoralising effect.

The horrible deaths suffered by so many of the characters in the play were depressing as well. Before taking the role, Caradoc had had no idea there were so many different ways to kill people. But now he knew several methods in psychopathic detail.

Plant-related ones in particular. Gardens were a death trap; he'd never realised to what extent. The entire conceit of the play was that almost all the characters were killed by poisons grown by the murderer in his own herbaceous borders, right under the noses of his victims.

Monkshood, otherwise known as *aconitum*, was responsible for two of the play's deaths. The plant, which could cause multiple organ failure, looked uncomfortably like a large clump that Caradoc remembered was growing in a dank corner of the Birch Hall garden. And deadly nightshade, which carried off another main character, looked familiar as well.

It made Caradoc uncomfortable to think of his frail young wife alone in the dark old house surrounded by a poisonous garden. Strange old house, too; Birch Hall wasn't a place that he knew especially well. An uncle had died and left it to Caradoc when his courtship of Juliet was at its height. He had at the time been renting in Muswell Hill, so an ancestral Elizabethan hall coming unexpectedly on-stream had been useful.

But now he'd had Birch Hall twelve months, Caradoc was beginning to realise its downsides. Quite apart from the general gloom and the potentially fatal garden, the place ate money. It was huge, with millions of bedrooms. The heating system was Jurassic. The water came from a spring, and not a terribly clean one at that. Simply keeping it all standing cost more than he earned in a year. In two years. Five.

He had been wondering about selling it, although God only

knew who to. But Juliet, unexpectedly, seemed happy at Birch Hall. Caradoc had feared that she would be bored on her own in the middle of the Leicestershire countryside after years of the light fantastic in the capital. The nearest town, Chestlock, didn't even have a Waitrose.

But Juliet said she wasn't bored and didn't need a Waitrose. She was perfectly happy sketching. And perhaps, Caradoc thought, that really was enough. Juliet looked so frail and ate so little that perhaps it only took a few strokes of the pencil to wear her out.

The actor's thoughts returned to the poisonous plants. Maybe he'd get that new gardener of Juliet's to dig them out. She had said he was a good worker – 'amazingly strong' were her words. Yes, Caradoc thought, he'd ring the guy. Or talk to him himself once he got home. 'You only have to brush yourself against a monkshood.' It was one of his lines in the play and it always made Gilly corpse; she thought it sounded like a prophylactic.

He'd be glad to see the back of bloody Gilly, Caradoc thought. She was so obsessed with double entendres it was impossible to have the simplest conversation, and such a tiresomely randy old trout too. Itinerant theatre troupes were famously promiscuous and Gilly regarded it as a point of honour to live up to the clichés. She was always cackling suggestively that 'what goes on tour goes on Twitter'.

As the tour had progressed, so had Gilly, round the cast and crew. Only Caradoc had resisted her, though there'd been a near miss in Nuneaton. He'd overdone it on the Sauvignon at a Friends of the Theatre event and Gilly was unhooking a fearsome-looking girdle by the time Caradoc remembered Juliet. He had fled and for some days afterwards the performance reviews had noted 'a distinct froideur between the two lead actors'.

But as someone else – some actor, was it? – had once said,

why go out for a burger when you had steak at home? The only problem was that the steak at home was frozen.

Night after night, as he lay in Grimsby or Grimethorpe, Caradoc would think longingly of his wife's graceful body; her long, sexy hair. Why wouldn't Juliet allow him to introduce her to the pleasures of lovemaking? She was young, she was lithe. She really didn't know what she was missing. He, on the other hand, did, all too well.

He hadn't spoken specifically about her frigidity to his fellow thespians. But a late-night pub session in Peterborough had got dangerously near the mark.

'Aren't you worried your wife might be having it away when you're on tour?' Pete Leather had asked with his usual subtlety.

'No,' Caradoc had said. The thought had never even crossed his mind.

'Blimey, mate,' Pete had remarked in his throaty Cockney. 'Either you're kidding yourself or you're a very lucky man.'

'The latter,' Caradoc had replied tightly.

'But seriously, mate,' Pete had said, once he had recovered from his inexplicable paroxysm of laughter, 'what would you do if you found out she was?'

It was not an eventuality that Caradoc had ever pondered, but he was surprised to find the answer coming, swift and clear. 'I'd kill him,' he said, simply.

Now, in his Woking dressing room, Caradoc finished drawing in his eyebrows and hoped that, come Saturday night, absence would have made Juliet's heart grow fonder. Her heart, and all the other bits of her. He hoped that he wouldn't reach out for his wife only to have her roll away in her shroudlike nightgown across the chill acres of sheets, murmuring 'Not now.'

He tried the mobile one last time before heading down the cramped stairs and behind the curtain on to the stage. Still no answer. What was Juliet *doing*?

CHAPTER 33

Working for Dan was nothing if not varied, Dylan was finding. If Mondays was Kenilworth Lodge, Tuesdays was Birch Hall.

This turned out to be a great Elizabethan wilderness of a place owned, according to Dan, by an actor called Caradoc Turner. He had recently inherited the property and intended to restore it to its former glory.

Which would cost a fortune, Dylan imagined. And did Turner have a fortune? It was always hard to get information out of Dan and more so than usual in the case of Birch Hall. But by dint of determined questioning Dylan discovered that Caradoc Turner was an actor in a touring company. He was away a lot. He was away at the moment.

Dan had seemed to get fed up with being asked questions. He had disappeared to the other end of the garden where he could be heard pulling branches around in order to build up the inevitable fire. Dylan, meanwhile, busied himself collecting up mountains of dead rhododendron leaves. There was layer upon layer of them, those at the bottom presumably being the great-great-grandparents of the ones on top. The whole garden was basically a three-acre rhododendron bush, with occasional small clearings from which, if one stood on tiptoe, the triangular points of the house's gaunt gables could be spotted.

Dylan was not expecting to come across Mrs Turner in one of these clearings. Her appearance was even more of a surprise. Actors' wives, in his London members' club experience, were a skittish bunch much given to the foxy-rock-chick look. But the woman in the clearing looked as if she had stepped from the frame of a particularly gloomy pre-Raphaelite painting. She was pale as death, paper-thin and had huge, wild, dark eyes which, as he had blundered in with his wheelbarrow, had turned on Dylan with a burning, theatrical terror.

Mrs Turner had been sketching, her white hand scraping feverishly at a big pad of white paper. But once Dylan appeared she dropped it and rushed wordlessly away, her dark hair flowing dankly behind her.

He had not known what to make of this except to pick up the drawing and inspect it. It was of a bundle of knotted root and stem, of a Dürer-like detail, full of nervous energy. It was delicate and highly wrought, possibly even crazy. It was signed 'Juliet'.

At lunchtime – which the Turners seemed to permit – Dylan had tried to press Dan about the mysterious lady of the house. She had seemed so fey and wraithlike, he wondered if he had imagined her. But trying to get Dan to talk was like trying to start a car whose battery had failed.

Later that afternoon, when it started raining lightly, Dylan remembered Juliet Turner's sketchbook, left on the bench in the clearing. As she might not have come back for it he decided to check. It was where she had left it; Dylan took it and headed to the house.

Dylan tiptoed in, intending only to slip the sketchpad on a table. The hall, however, was arrestingly strange and he could not prevent himself looking round. It was huge, stone-floored and gloomy with two fireplaces yawning vastly at each other from facing walls. It looked as if the Tudors who had built it had only just left. But it wasn't just this that had riveted Dylan's attention.

In a dark wooden screen at the end, two archways led off into the rest of the house. Coming through these apertures was a terrible sound. It was like Conan Doyle's description of The Hound of the Baskervilles. A dreadful low moaning rising to a shrieking that froze the blood.

Logic told Dylan, as it had told Sherlock Holmes, that the sound was not a phantom dog. But Sherlock Holmes would have blushed to know what Dylan now guessed it was.

He hurried back outside. The bonfire had died back to a smoulder and the space around it was empty. Empty, that was, apart from Dan's discarded top.

Dylan continued to work, methodically raking up great piles of sharp-edged brown leaves and heaping them into the wheelbarrows. Inwardly, however, he was struggling to believe that Dan and Juliet Turner were having an affair. It just seemed so unlikely. She so insubstantial and artistic and he built like a prop forward with all the emotional range of a cliff face. Or did Dan have hidden depths? Dylan could never be quite sure.

He tried to picture how it had happened. Had unspoken, passionate agreement flashed between Juliet's dark eyes and Dan's flinty recesses? Feeling his imagination taking flight, Dylan stopped himself. He didn't have to invent this sort of thing any more. Writing was no longer his job.

Later that day, as afternoon slipped into evening, Jason, in his manager's cubbyhole, leapt to his feet. A woman was entering the Edenville Arms. One he was expecting. 'Miss Simpson!'

He had the estate brochure in his hand, opened at the

offending section. If the new Director of PR and Marketing was about to embark upon a rewrite, Jason intended the Edenville Arms to be the first beneficiary.

'May I congratulate you on your new position?'

Nell was astonished. 'How do you know?' His obvious pleasure was touching, but she had been offered the job less than half an hour ago. Even Rachel did not know yet.

Jason tapped his nose. 'Estate tom-tom. You'll get used to it.'

Actually, it had been Angela herself, ringing to rage at him for getting his lesbian facts wrong. He had not minded in the least; that someone with half a brain was now in charge of marketing was what Jason had focused on.

Nell went upstairs, wondering about the estate tom-tom. She was not entirely sure that she wanted to get used to it. She planned to keep herself to herself. Fortunately, it looked as if she would be able to. To move out of the spotlight that was the Edenville Arms, at any rate.

'There's a house comes with the job,' she told Rachel a few minutes later. She was curled up in the pink armchair in the corner of the honeymoon suite. She realised that she felt relaxed for the first time since arriving here.

'A house! How fantastic!'

'Well, a cottage.'

'Even more fantastic. We can come and stay!'

'Of course you can. Whenever you like.'

'How about Friday? We could come up the night before the play. Make the most of it.'

'Great idea!' Nell was excited because Rachel was so excited. It was wonderful to be able to give people pleasure. Especially people like Rachel, who so deserved it.

'How brilliant! Juno's so thrilled about the play already, this will send her over the edge. Where is it, your place?'

'Just outside the village, apparently.'

'Ooh. Lattice windows and roses round the door!'

'I don't know what it's like. It's called Beggar's Roost.'

'I didn't realise beggars roosted. You learn something every day.'

Nell hesitated. 'There's a man next door, Angela says.'

Rachel gave a gasp of excitement. 'Woo-hoo. Single, I hope.'

Nell moved to crush this with all speed. 'Are you joking? I'm not interested in men.'

'OK, OK, so you say. So who's the hottie next door?'

Nell snorted. 'He's in his mid-eighties.'

'Hotties can be old. Look at Bill Nighy.'

'Apparently he's completely horrible.'

'Really?' Rachel sounded surprised. 'He doesn't look it. I love his glasses.'

'Not Bill Nighy. The guy next door. He's supposed to be the neighbour from hell.'

'So much for friendly chats over the garden fence with an apple-cheeked old countryman, then.'

'Looks like it. According to Angela he forced the people before me out of their cottage. Made their lives a misery.'

'Are you sure she wasn't exaggerating?' Rachel asked.

'Of course not. Why would she do that?'

'Oh well,' Rachel said, 'you've got the job. That's the main thing. When do you start?'

'Tomorrow. Angela suggested that I start by looking at the weddings department and rewriting all their stuff.'

'Not hugely tactful of her,' Rachel remarked evenly. 'There must be loads of other departments she could have sent you to.'

'She was very apologetic about it,' Nell conceded. Angela had, indeed, been very gushing. 'And besides . . .'

'Besides what?'

'I think that in a funny way it might help.'

'*Help?* How do you work that out?'

Nell wasn't quite sure how to put it. Her theory was that working in weddings might fast-forward her through whatever deep-seated misery remained to be faced. Which surely it did. The whole Joey fiasco hadn't even been a week ago and had been the most tremendous shock. She could not possibly have absorbed it all already and moved on.

'I suppose I get what you mean,' Rachel said doubtfully, when Nell had explained this. 'It's pretty brave of you to see it that way. I'm not sure I could.'

Nell glowed. Being called brave by Rachel was quite a compliment. 'It sounds quite funny in some ways. Apparently there's a very demanding couple from Florida driving the wedding department mad.'

Rachel snorted. 'Good for you,' she said briskly. 'Now you can move on. It's a new start. And you get a cottage, even if it's got the neighbour from hell there. Just wait until I tell Juno about him.'

'Do you think you should?' Nell was worried. 'She might be too scared to come up.'

Rachel laughed. 'She'll be fascinated. She'll immediately start casting him in one of her Agatha Christie fantasies. What's he called?'

'I don't know,' Nell said. 'Guess I'll find out when I get there.'

'Will you move in today?'

'Ooh. I hadn't thought of that.' Nell considered. The prospect was thrilling, but she had other priorities. 'I might go along later, but I haven't got the key. The main thing today is to buy some clothes. I've only got what I'm standing up in.'

'Well, make sure you're moved in when we get there,' Rachel ordered.

'Don't worry. There'll be a cheerful fire flickering in the grate and lavender-scented linen sheets in your small white bedrooms.'

'Yay. Perfect.'

CHAPTER 34

The next morning, sun poured down from a brilliant blue sky. It was hot, and about to get hotter. As she crossed the park, Nell's eyes burned heavily in their sockets. She had slept badly. The potential difficulties of the wedding department, dismissed so breezily when talking to Rachel, seemed less easy to overlook during the silent small hours. Might not an entire office dedicated to arranging people's special days cause the dam within her to burst?

With the daylight, however, her courage had returned. While she felt tired, she felt better. The pressure against the dam wall seemed less than in the night. Perhaps, Nell thought, she had learned self-control at last. It might simply be that Joey wasn't worth getting upset about.

Or perhaps the loveliness of Pemberton was working its magic on her soul. As Nell paced along, feeling the spring of the grass beneath her feet, she watched a slight breeze wrinkle the river's molten-silver surface. The great pale front of the house was now sliding into view; a sight which never failed to lift the heart. On the stable-yard tower, the weathercock blazed gold.

The Weddings Manager, a woman called Julie with an

understanding voice, had instructed her to go into the stable yard. 'Look for a small green door in the corner.'

Nell strode up the main drive and past the first visitors emerging from their huge white coaches. They were fanning their faces with their travel itineraries and gasping about how warm it was.

In the stable yard, she found the green door without difficulty. Behind it was a steep flight of narrow wooden stairs which, Nell guessed, the stable staff of old had used to access their quarters.

Standing at the top was a plump young woman with long dark hair. Her full, freckled face was flushed with the day's warmth already.

'Nell? I'm Julie. And this,' she added, smilingly waving a hand into the room where two people were seated before a desk, 'is Jed and Carly. They're from Florida but they're getting married at Pemberton. They're staying at the Pemberton Hotel.'

The demanding Americans, Nell realised as she shook hands. She was clearly hitting the ground running. She hadn't intended to turn up in the middle of a meeting. Was she late?

She glanced furtively at her watch at exactly the moment that the stable clock donged nine.

'No, no, you're not late,' Julie smilingly assured her. 'Jed and Carly are here . . . um . . . in very good time.' Nell guessed that the couple had been there for the last half hour. At least.

Jed had remained on his feet. He was massive and broad-shouldered. 'We had a real good chat with your director Angela in the bar last night,' he boomed.

This triggered a slight exhalation from Julie. 'Angela's the human resources director,' she pointed out gently to Jed. 'Not the director of the whole of Pemberton.'

Jed ignored this and continued addressing Nell. 'She told us all about what you're doing, redoing the bumf and stuff. She thought you might write about us for the estate newsletter. And the wedding brochures, as a case history sort of thing.'

Surely it was up to her what went into the newsletter, Nell thought. As well as the brochures. She looked at Julie, who rolled her eyes.

'You see, our wedding's somewhat different.' Carly shifted round in her chair to face Nell. She was tiny, blonde and possessed of a doelike prettiness. Her outward fragility, however, was belied by the intensity of her stare and the determination in her voice. 'It's on a *Pride and Prejudice* theme.'

Nell dredged around for some bright remark. 'Pemberton will be the perfect background,' she conceded. 'It's almost spelt the same as Pemberley.'

'Well, of course Pemberley in the novel was based on Chatsworth,' Carly said. 'But they were fully booked on our chosen date. We looked around the internet a bit and eventually found Pemberton. It's a great little place.'

Nell thought wryly of the rolling green acres outside. Just how little was it?

'So our wedding would make a great article for you,' Jed stated, his eyes locking Nell's.

'Or series of articles,' Carly put in. 'You could follow us as we prepare. As we fly back and forth. And Skype Julie here.'

Julie's smile was looking strained.

'And let's not stop at the newsletter,' Jed added. 'Hell, you might be able to get a TV series out of it.'

'Yeah! Like fly on the wall!' Carly clapped her hands. Light shot out of a diamond the size of a sugar cube.

As Carly and Jed now began to discuss TV rights, Nell saw that Julie was gripping the desk-edge so hard her fingers were white.

Jed had produced a tablet and was flicking it with his thick red fingers. 'Take a look at this.' He handed it over. 'This was the proposal scene.'

Nell looked.

'It was awesome,' Carly reminisced. 'I came home for the weekend and my mom and sisters were, like, in those bonnets and gowns?'

Four women in Georgian caps and gowns sat in a modern kitchen. Three of them bore a detectable resemblance to Carly. The other, an older brunette, might have done once, before the facelifts.

'And I was in the closet,' Jed added. 'In my Darcy gear. For the surprise. Y'know?'

He swiped the tablet. The next image was of Carly and an older man, presumably her father. He was in a tailcoat and wore a white shirt and stock. Carly herself was now in an empire gown with her hair in ringlets. They were in a sitting room with a huge widescreen TV.

'Dad and I did that scene between Mr Bennet and Lizzie,' Carly reminisced rapturously. 'And then Jed came out of the closet . . .'

Nell and Julie exchanged glances.

'. . . in his tailcoat.'

Nell considered Jed's huge size. It must, she thought, have been one hell of a big closet.

'We did the proposal scene in the backyard.' Jed took up the story just as Nell found the picture of them gazing into each other's eyes. The location was the edge of a zingingly blue swimming pool with a diving board.

Nell passed the tablet back to Jed. 'It all looks lovely,' she said diplomatically.

Julie cleared her throat. 'Jed and Carly are certainly doing it by the book. They want every detail to be perfect.'

'Yes, we want white soup,' said Carly proudly.

'White soup?' Nell blinked. She had not heard of white soup. Perhaps it was a Florida thing.

Jed leaned forward. 'It's mentioned fifty-four times in *Pride and Prejudice*.'

'It's proving quite a challenge for the chef at Pemberton,' Julie said brightly.

'It's kind of a mixture of meat stock, egg yolks, ground almonds, cream and negus,' elucidated Carly.

'I see,' Nell said, wondering what negus was.

'We're also having mood boards. With quotes from *Pride and Prejudice* on them?' Jed took a deep breath and grasped Carly's tiny hands in his own vast bear paws. 'You must allow me to tell you how ardently I admire and love you.'

He and Carly looked at each other, then back at Nell, starry-eyed.

Dylan had picked Dan up at his house again this morning. It seemed that the gardener's van was to be left to rot in the car park of the Edenville Arms.

Dan had said nothing about that, however. He appeared lost in thought as they drove off, not even seeming to notice the salutations of the estate children. But at least Dylan now knew what 'Shagger' referred to. And who.

Dan, for his part, evidently realised this. Their eyes briefly met as Dan directed him out of a junction. The big man's massive chest pressed upwards in a sigh. 'It's not right, I know,' he said.

Dylan shrugged. With his disastrous romantic history, who was he to judge other people's emotional arrangements? He had given the Edenville Arms a wide berth since encountering the angry Nell there, driving straight past the village, through the park and up to the woods at the end of yesterday's work. Nell had said she was leaving, but he was taking no chances.

The only other thing Dan had revealed was that Wednesday's garden was somewhere called Byron House. For all the swashbuckle of its name, this turned out to be an old people's home in the suburbs of Chestlock. It was entirely modern and of yellow brick. The front was all car park; this, along with the flat windows and sliding glass front doors, gave the place an officey appearance.

There was a receptionist behind the front desk, a large lady with spiked purple hair and red glasses. She beamed at Dan. 'Eh up, love.'

'Eh up, Mandy.'

'They're all waiting for you!'

Who, Dylan wondered, were they?

Mandy, grinning, thumped a big green button on the wall behind her and a set of sliding doors opened. The corridor they now entered was very warm and smelt of gravy and an undertow of something chemically sweet. Directly opposite the sliding doors was the large aluminium front of a lift. A short, plump woman in a blue overall was pushing a large white laundry bin towards them.

Her face lit up when she saw Dan. 'Eeh, love! Talk about a sight for sore eyes!'

Dan was evidently highly popular here. It was an interesting contrast with Mrs Palethorpe, Dylan thought. Of course, Dan was popular with Juliet Turner too, but for a different reason.

They passed the open door of a lounge. Old people sat on red chairs and waved as Dan, strimmer over his shoulder, hoved into view. He paused at the door. 'Morning, ladies and gents.'

They exclaimed back, evidently wildly excited. Dylan, walking behind with a spade, a fork and a rake which had a mind of its own, was revising his initial assessment. Dan wasn't just popular, he was adored. It was as if Elvis had entered the building.

Dylan had never set foot in a care home before. He had imagined they were depressing places, full of medicated ancients waiting to die. But the old people here seemed much less miserable than others he could think of. Mrs Palethorpe, for example.

At the end of the corridor, Dan opened a pair of white French windows into the garden. Given the arid, leafless front, Dylan had been expecting something small and scrubby at the rear; he was surprised now to see that it was both large and pleasant.

A big green lawn spread generously in front of him, dotted with bushes and bordered by trees. It was divided by curving gravelled paths which twisted between the bushes and past various points of interest such as a small wooden windmill and a little red post box. There was a paved area with wooden benches and another area under shade where some black wire chairs abutted a good-sized matching table. Beyond that was a greenhouse and a shed, which Dan was now opening.

Dylan took the tools and received his instructions. He settled himself and began to work. In the distance, Dan's strimmer flashed like a sword in the sun.

Some of the old people were coming outside, Dylan noticed. Some on their own legs, some on Zimmer frames and some pushed in wheelchairs by the care assistants. They gathered round a large garden table near the door, underneath a big parasol. They were all looking at Dan, Dylan realised. It was almost as if they were waiting for something. A show of some kind.

An almighty noise now ripped through the quiet morning. It

was the roar of Dan's strimmer, which he was revving hard. He began to stride up and down the greensward in front of his audience, flashing his mighty blade as it whizzed over the grass.

As Dan now peeled off his top and tossed it casually to the side, flexing his mighty chest and biceps and grinning at his audience, Dylan was no longer in any doubt that this was the show the old people, and the old ladies in particular, had been waiting for.

An old lady with a stick now came past Dylan as he knelt in the weeds. 'Dan's a marvel, he really is,' she told him, round-eyed with admiration. 'We all love him here. He keeps this garden beautifully.'

Dylan nodded. Dan was clearly a man of parts, and one of the biggest seemed to be a kind heart.

CHAPTER 35

The strimmer show was now over and the entertainment baton had been passed on. An elderly man in a Johnny Cash black shirt with contrast stitching was holding a karaoke session in the day room.

Dan was digging quietly at the other side of the garden and Dylan was still weeding. Visitors to the home came frequently past, some pushing their nearest and dearest in wheelchairs, others with their arms linked with someone making slow progress on a stick. They all greeted Dylan, said how wonderful the garden was looking and how much they loved Dan. 'He keeps us going,' they said.

Dylan's admiration for his boss was increasing. Dan might be having an affair, but that was far from unusual. Whereas the ability to spread such happiness was rare indeed.

Occasionally the inmates came past alone. At one stage a man with a bristling moustache and black nylon tracksuit bottoms appeared. He stood by Dylan in complete silence, just watching. Then, quite suddenly, he looked at his watch and hurried off, like the White Rabbit.

''E's 'armless enough,' Dan remarked, pushing past with a wheelbarrow. 'They all are. Just livin' in their own worlds, that's all.'

The home's manager had stopped to introduced herself. Anne was a medium-sized woman with short grey hair. She wore pixie boots and a purple dress.

'The garden's massively important to my ladies and gentlemen,' she told Dylan. 'Does them the world of good. Dan's a bloomin' miracle, he really is.'

Dylan felt he wanted to become a part of that same miracle. Just as the warm sun beat on his back, he sensed it stealing into his soul, warming it up. He, too, wanted to contribute.

'I'm always trying to dream up new ways to improve the garden, so if you have any ideas, let me know,' Anne was saying. 'So long as it doesn't cost a fortune, we'll do it.'

Dylan did have an idea, as it happened. He had noticed the greenhouse was empty. 'We could grow some flowers from seed in it,' he suggested. 'The old people might like to see them.'

Anne beamed. 'Brilliant!'

Dylan felt something sing inside him. It felt so uplifting to do something good. Why hadn't he worked to help others before?

Later, still weeding, Dylan glanced up to see an old lady with white hair looking down at him. She wore a pale blue belted raincoat and carried a large white handbag. 'Can you lend me a pound?' she asked.

'A pound?' Dylan raised himself on his knees and felt in his back pocket. His wallet was in his jacket in the car, but he might have some change.

'I need a pound for the bus fare,' the old lady explained earnestly.

Dylan felt a small coin, pulled it out and handed it over.

The old lady's face lit up. 'Thank you, love,' she exclaimed delightedly.

Dan loomed behind them. 'You don't want to be catching your bus today, Mavis,' he said.

Apprehension clutched Dylan. He hadn't realised the old lady was a resident. Now he had created a difficulty.

The old lady glared at Dan. 'Yes, I do.'

'But look at it up there.' Dan raised his arm to where grey clouds now bloomed in the sky. 'It's going to pour down, Mavis. You don't want to get your nice coat wet.'

The fire was draining from Mavis. She looked doubtfully at her coat.

'Come on, Mavis.' Dan bent from his massive height and propelled her along with infinite gentleness. 'You can get your bus tomorrow. Let's go and have a nice cup of tea.'

Mavis allowed herself to be led away. It was, Dylan thought, a touching sight; the huge man with his arm slipped through the little, frail old lady's.

Lunch was at the table under the shade. Anne brought them out plates of what the old people were having: beef goulash and rice. 'And it's jam roly-poly for pud!' the manager called over her shoulder as she walked away.

'She seems nice,' Dylan ventured.

Dan's great chewing jaw stopped its motion. 'She's a diamond. Looked after my old gran like she were a queen.'

Dylan's fork paused on its journey. 'Your gran was in here?'

'Died in 'ere a few year ago. They were good to 'er. She were good to me,' Dan added, resuming his lunch.

Dylan suddenly imagined the huge man as a boy in shorts, petted by a pair of wrinkled hands.

'So I'm good to them. That's 'ow it works. Ain't it?'

Dylan nodded. Yes, indeed. That was how it worked.

'I'd ask you for a drink,' Julie said to Nell at the end of the day. 'But I've got to pick the kids up from nursery.'

'It's all right,' Nell said, although actually she would have enjoyed a drink. She liked Julie and her subversive sense of humour.

Still, she had plenty of other things to do, top of the list being exploring her new home and getting it ready for her weekend visitors. Jason had undertaken, during the day, to get hold of the keys to Beggar's Roost, so they should be waiting for her when she returned.

There would be beds to make up, Nell imagined, so she needed to get some sheets from somewhere. But hopefully there wouldn't be too much cleaning to do. According to Angela, the former occupants had been model tenants and had left only a mere few weeks before – entirely because of the vicious old man next door. The thought of him was one Nell was doing her best not to dwell on. Hopefully she could keep out of his way.

As she entered the Edenville Arms Jason picked up some keys and waved them at her. He explained where in the village the cottage was to be found, then made his excuses and disappeared. He wanted to be involved as little as possible; getting the keys had been nightmare enough.

Prising them out of Angela was like pulling teeth; she had affected not to know where they were. In the end it was Gail who'd come up with the goods. Jason had had to go and fetch them, however, which meant leaving the inn in the delicious but not especially experienced hands of Ryan. Jason was glad, on his return, to find that a few bungled bills and a double booking were the worst that had befallen the place.

Nell approached Beggar's Roost excitedly. It was one of two cottages, Jason had said, which stood quite close to each other. They were the very last in Edenville, at the point where the houses began to straggle out before giving way to fields. These, Nell thought, must be the ones.

The pair of cottages before her were low, grey-stone buildings with thick stone-tiled roofs and small mullioned windows. They differed in that one was clearly well kept and the other wasn't. Neither had a nameplate on the gate and Jason hadn't said which was which. Nell naturally assumed the one with the white-painted door, white picket gate and neat garden with a greenhouse was Beggar's Roost.

It stood to reason. The previous occupants had been model tenants, and model tenants would never have lived at the next-door cottage, with its gate like broken teeth and overgrown garden where piles of plastic rubbish showed between the nettles.

Nell had hoped Angela was exaggerating about the neighbour, but this did look horribly like a place where some nasty old man would peer scornfully at the world through windows which, even from here, had a smeared look to them. A big laylandii hedge divided the two gardens: shaggy and wild on the messy side, neatly cropped on the other.

Nell headed for the picket gate and opened it. The stone path was neatly swept and entirely clear of the dandelions which infested the next-door garden.

She decided to delay the excitement of opening the little white front door. Instead she went to the front window. It was scrupulously clean and looked into a cosy sitting room.

She was relieved to see that it was furnished. There was a small, comfortable sofa and a couple of chairs. A small TV stood in the corner. There was a large, flat, rustic stone fireplace, clearly very old, into which a wood-fired stove had been fitted. Nell imagined herself opening the little glass doors and putting logs inside and was warmed by the very thought.

On the wall was a black-and white photograph. It was of a couple: a wartime wedding, by the look of it, a handsome young man in air force uniform and a beautiful, smiling blonde with a flower pinned to her jacket. It seemed to Nell that there was something familiar about her.

But mainly she thought that it was odd, to leave a wedding photo behind. Especially an old one like this; the previous tenant's grandparents, presumably. Had they departed in such a rush they hadn't even taken their family pictures? Had the antipathy of their elderly neighbour been so unbearable they had cut and run that suddenly? She forced the thought away; nonetheless, a disquieting shadow had been cast on her sunny imaginings. She moved round the corner to explore the garden.

It shone in the sun, orderly and colourful, even by Edenville's zinging standards. Nell buried her nose in a flowery bush next to the wall. The petals, white and waxy, packed a punch so sweet and powerful it made her head spin.

Her ears were full of birdsong, which seemed to get louder and more excitable all the time. Were they talking about her, and what she was doing? She could almost feel them watching with their little black eyes, feel their birdy interest.

Nell looked happily around. She was wondering what the various flowers were called. She thought she could identify some snapdragons. Some sunflowers were leaning up against the greenhouse and looking very cheerful. And that was definitely lavender over there by the wall. But these blazing yellow and orange flowers by the path, what were they? She would buy a flower identification book, Nell resolved, moving into the greenhouse.

My, but it was hot in here. The air was close and thick and smelt tangy. Nell spotted with delight, among some pale and hairy leaves, the red shining globes of tomatoes. And was that really a vine, growing all along one side? Big, crinkly leaves were hiding clusters of little green dots. Were they grape bunches in embryo? And, on the shelf which stretched round all three sides, were lots of little orange plastic pots, each holding a small green spurt of leaves.

It all looked so amazingly well kept. Not remotely as if the inhabitants had driven off for ever with all their chattels. Rather, it looked as if they had just stepped away.

CHAPTER 36

This, did Nell but know it, was exactly what had happened.

George Farley had just watered his lettuce bed. The tidy leaves sparkled in the light. The sun was slanting through the polished panes of his greenhouse from whose open door the warmed air pulsed, tangy with the sharp tomato smell of geraniums, the sharp geranium smell of tomatoes.

His old upright aluminium sun-chair, its blue cotton seat weather-faded, its white plastic arms cracked and warped, had stood invitingly behind the greenhouse. The house wall nearby was radiating heat. Perhaps just five minutes then, George had thought to himself, sitting down and tipping his hat over his face.

It was so peaceful in the garden. So gloriously calm now that those dreadful people next door had gone. The old man drifted into sleep.

Beneath his faded cotton sunhat, he dreamed of his wife. As always in his dreams she looked young and beautiful, the way she had when they met. Tall and pale like a lily; a gilded one too. Her pale gold hair rippling with the Lincolnshire breeze, her eyes as blue as his RAF uniform. He'd just arrived from training in London as a rear gunner. She had just arrived too, as a volunteer. The base was the nearest to where she was spending the war with her aunt, away from the London bombs. The particular London bomb that was Edwina had blown him to smithereens. He had never had a chance.

She had a tinkling, well-bred laugh and her smile was like a sunburst. He felt its heat both within and without. There was a rosy tinge to her creamy cheeks.

And she had always looked that way to him, ever after. The old lady, the ill lady, he had never really believed it, even when it was there before him. And now, in his dreams, she was young again, and would be for ever. He wished he could join her. He was so weary, so lonely. They said it would get better with time but it had only got worse.

The sun shone red through the blood in his tightly shut eyelids. He was waking up. Time, George realised, to go and shut the greenhouse. He took a deep breath, opened his eyes and, with a heaving grunt, raised himself out of his chair.

Someone, he realised, was in the greenhouse. He stumped over, summoning his breath. The hideous possibility that it was his former next-door neighbours flashed through him. Last year the child had picked all the grapes long before they had ripened. Then stamped them into the floor because they tasted sour.

He could see someone through the tangled green of the tomato plants. Not the little girl, thank God. Nor her mother. They were both dark-haired.

This person was very fair. Tall, like Edwina, and with his wife's pale hair.

The old man stopped. Through the vine leaves pressed against the greenhouse window, it was hard to make her out. He could see a curve of pale cheek. A flash of pink lip. The resemblance made his heart hammer. Was it her? Come to fetch him, at last?

He stretched out both hands imploringly. 'My darling.' She heard him, and turned. Looked out, smiled.

The first Nell knew of it was when she heard the voice. A sort of cry. She looked up from examining the grape bunches to see a man flailing around in the garden.

She rushed outside. Her hazy, immediate impression that she knew him strengthened into certainty. This was the old man she had seen in the graveyard. Lovingly tending his wife's grave. Telling her his news and how much he missed her.

'Mr Farley!' Nell exclaimed. What was the old man doing in her garden? Was he a friend of the horrid man who lived next door?

He lunged at her, his eyes fixed and wild. Their hands met in mid-air. Then he fell to the ground, so suddenly and heavily it was all she could do not to fall with him.

Nell fought for her balance, then felt his pulse. Faint, slow, but there. She dragged out her mobile and punched in 999.

'Heart attack?' The operator sounded sceptical. 'I'll get someone to call you. Can you confirm the telephone number I can see on my screen?'

The old man's breathing was rasping and laboured. 'But why does someone have to call me?' Nell's voice was sharp with panic.

'Just to run through a few questions.'

For all his weak heartbeat, George Farley was clinging powerfully to her hand. His face was grey but the bright hazel eyes were trained on her. They were longing and pleading, as if she were the only hope of saving him.

'Look, he's really ill,' Nell told the operator. 'He'll die if you don't do something.'

The other end sighed. 'We'll send an ambulance as soon as we can. But I should warn you, they're busy this afternoon. It might take a while.'

Nell patted the old hand. He resisted as she tried to peel off his fingers. The bright eyes widened anxiously and a faint whimper came from the wrinkled old throat.

'I'm not going far,' she told him. 'Just to get help.'

She charged to the edge of the garden, to where it overlooked the road. She would flag someone down. The very next person who came along.

Dan and Dylan were driving back from Byron House when Dan's mobile rang. As Dan was driving, Dylan answered. He hoped it wasn't Mrs Turner.

It was not. An imperious voice now boomed into his ear. 'This is the Lady President of the Chestlock Golf Club. I need you tomorrow. The man who mows our course has let us down and I hear from several of my lady members that you provide a good service.'

Dylan took down the details. By the time he had finished they were approaching Edenville.

The return from the Byron House end of Chestlock came through the back of the village. It had a different feel to the rest of the settlement. Possibly it was the oldest. The straggle of houses here were plainer and smaller, ending in a couple of cottages which were plainest of all. As they approached, Dylan noticed that while one of them had a beautiful cottage garden, the other was the opposite extreme, an utter bomb site.

Trees heavy with summer growth overhung the quiet, green lane. Banks of summer flowers filled the hedgerows. It was all very peaceful. So when a woman suddenly appeared in the middle of the road it took both Dylan and Dan by surprise.

'Who the 'ell's *that*?' asked Dan.

Dylan knew exactly who the hell. He had last seen her screaming at him out of a pub window. His first instinct was to swerve round her and speed on.

'Bloody 'ell, slow down,' Dan advised. 'She might want a lift or summat.' He wound down the window. 'You all right, love?'

Nell hurried over. Surprise and anger flared within her as she recognised Adam Greenleaf. '*You!*'

Yet there was nothing for it but to call a truce. For now, anyway. At the moment, all that mattered was George. 'I need you to help get someone to the hospital,' she gasped. 'He's in the garden. It's going to take both of you to carry him.'

Dan leapt out immediately, his long legs eating up the few feet between the car and the garden gate. Dylan scurried after. The sight of a large old man on the grass was unexpected.

'George Farley,' Dan muttered, crouching down beside him.

'You know him?' Dylan asked.

'Yeah. Good bloke.'

'I think it's a heart attack,' Nell bleated from behind. 'But they say that the ambulance will take a while. We'll have to put him in your car.'

Dylan thought of his car. Not only was it tiny but the back seat was crowded with garden equipment. They could hardly lay the old man on top of the strimmer.

'We can't move 'im,' Dan said flatly. 'If 'e's 'ad an 'eart attack, it'll strain 'is 'eart even more.'

The old man's face was now a sickly yellow. Beneath his jutting eyebrows, the bright hazel eyes were closed.

'We can't just leave him here!' Nell wailed, watching Dan link his enormous fingers, place the heel of his right hand on the old man's chest and start to push down with the full weight of his massive body.

283

'We'll have to,' Dylan said, glancing at Nell over his shoulder. Her eyes were round and blue and he could see the dislike in them. But also the anxiety, which made something turn within him. 'Until the ambulance gets here. And it'll be on its way, don't worry.'

Who was he to sound so sure, Nell wondered angrily. To sound so *anything*? Adam Greenleaf looked much dirtier than he had outside the pub. His shirt was grubby, his dark hair tangled, his jeans filthy. He looked sweaty, stubbly and unshaven.

'Come on, lad. Come *on*.' Dan, pushing, was muttering to George. Dylan could tell that he was flagging, losing hope.

'I'll take over,' he offered. 'I know what to do.'

He'd picked up all sorts of things during his time in the burns unit, and afterwards on the general wards. The ability to perform CPR was one of them. It was hard work; soon he, too, was gasping with the effort. Beneath him, the old man seemed still.

'Do you really know what you're doing?' Nell asked, tersely.

Oh, where was the ambulance? Did either of these men have a clue?

Dylan pumped harder, more determinedly. He intended not just to save the old man but also to prove to Nell that she had got him wrong, that there was good in him and he was not the contemptible creature she obviously thought him.

He looked at her, and she at him. As their eyes locked, Dylan felt a great force surge within him and roar down his arms into the old man's chest. This was followed by a movement, a flicker, then a definite ripple below his down-pressing hand. This resolved itself into a faint but steady beat. The old man's heart had started again.

'He's alive,' Dylan said. As George Farley coughed in

confirmation he sat back on his heels, panting. He did not look at Nell.

The wail of an ambulance siren could now, finally, be heard in the distance. 'Oh, thank God.' Nell rushed to the wall to flag it down.

Thundering through her body, besides her relief, was the knowledge that Adam Greenleaf had performed this miraculous deed. He had saved George right before her eyes. She had seen him do it.

A pair of cheery paramedics hurried up the path. 'That's all right, we'll take over.'

Within seconds, or so it seemed, they had buckled the old man into a stretcher and were loading him into the waiting vehicle. Dylan was watching, but all he was really seeing was the way Nell's hair rippled and flashed in the sunshine and breeze.

Dan nudged him. 'Come on. They don't need us now.'

CHAPTER 37

Nell sat with one of the paramedics at the back of the ambulance. George, across the small aisle, lay strapped to a bed in an oxygen mask. His eyes remained shut but his face was pink now. He was also breathing regularly. He would live, the paramedic said.

The vehicle was grinding and swaying along, and Nell was staring at the floor. But she was not seeing it. Instead, she was back in the old man's garden, examining what had happened, replaying the dramas of the last half hour in her mind.

George's against-the-odds survival was of course the main event. But scarcely less extraordinary was Adam Greenleaf's role in the proceedings. The man Nell had written off as a bounder and a cad had proved to be a hero of the first water. He had acted decisively and saved a life. Which changed things, of course. How was she to think of him from now on?

The ideal answer to this would have been – not at all. But he kept turning up; he obviously lived somewhere in the area. It seemed likely that she would see him again, and if so, what would she do, or say?

Nell lined up her new knowledge of Adam Greenleaf against what she already knew. Had she somehow misjudged him? Got it all wrong?

But no. She could not have misinterpreted what had happened in the Apples and Pears. He had acted deliberately to deceive her. She had absolutely no doubt about that.

The novel was the proof. He had had a copy of *All Smiles*, as had she. Somehow he had known that was the prearranged signal. Perhaps he had cyberstalked her? It was the first time that this thought had occurred to Nell and it seemed suddenly horribly likely. What other explanation was there? How else could he have known about the book?

The only possible conclusion, Nell decided, was that Adam Greenleaf was good and bad at the same time. He had been deceptive towards her and heroic to George. His heroics were obviously much more important than the deception, but it didn't mean that the deception hadn't happened. And if he'd really stalked her online, it had been worse than she first thought. She had, Nell decided, not without a certain relief, been right all along to avoid him.

That was definitely the safest way, not least because there was something about those dark eyes and that tall, rangy body that she was finding it rather hard to forget. It was as if Adam Greenleaf had found the chink of doubt in her mind, slipped through it and lodged himself there.

The paramedic was speaking to her. Nell looked up, confused, into the cheerful face above the green boiler suit. 'Sorry?'

'I was just saying that they did well there, your friends,' he said.

'They're not my friends,' Nell answered quickly.

The paramedic looked surprised. 'I thought he were your boyfriend. The dark-haired one. Or your husband.'

'Absolutely not,' gasped Nell, horrified at precisely how unhorrified this suggestion made her feel.

'Sorry, I'm sure.' The paramedic raised his eyebrows.

Nell rushed to make amends. 'I didn't mean to snap. It's just that . . .' She hesitated. 'I guess I'm not really in the market for romance at the moment.'

'Broken heart, eh?'

'Something like that.'

'But not like his?' The paramedic nodded at George. 'Different sort of broken heart, that.'

Nell agreed, and was grateful when the ambulance man said no more. It was not long before he started chatting again, however.

'Know him, do you?' He nodded at George.

Nell smiled and shook her head. 'I think he's a friend of the man who lives next door.'

The paramedic's easy grin had faded. 'Man who lives next door? Just moved in there, have you?'

Nell nodded, choosing her words carefully. 'Yes, and I've heard the neighbour's quite difficult.'

'That man's gone,' said her companion. 'And difficult was the word, from what I hear.'

Nell felt a warm wash of relief.

'Him and his wife and the kid,' the paramedic added.

'I hadn't realised he was married,' Nell said, surprised. Wasn't the difficult neighbour over eighty? She wished this garrulous man would shut up. He seemed to have a genius for difficult topics.

He continued, however. 'The state that place is in. Beggar's Roost.'

Nell was confused. What did he mean? Beggar's Roost was a dream cottage: the simple house with its sparkling windows, the colourful garden like something off a calendar. Or a postcard.

And wasn't the difficult man the one next door, anyway?

Her body seemed to understand before her brain did, because something hard and cold now clasped her insides. She realised that what the paramedic was saying was that Beggar's Roost was not the neat house with the white door. Rather, it was the bomb site next to it.

The second great shock of the afternoon now crashed like a wave over Nell, followed by the third. If the difficult man lived in the neat house, he was, presumably, George Farley. But how could *that* be? Angela had said he was the neighbour from hell.

'Shocking, the way them Downers left it,' the paramedic tutted.

'The Downers?'

'Rotten family, they were. She used to work at Pemberton. Some sort of PR person.'

Nell took a long breath. There was always the possibility that he was wrong. How would a paramedic from Chestlock know so much about village affairs?

'She were useless at her job. Useless. I've got a friend in the Pemberton Estate office,' he added; his source, Nell realised, was a depressingly authoritative one. 'And that Ros Downer were a disgrace. Couldn't even spell.'

It had the ring of truth, Nell had to accept. The estate bumf she had inherited was certainly the work of an illiterate. She was now feeling distinctly nauseous, and not just because of the jolting movement of the ambulance.

'And they made a right mess of that cottage. Her and her kid and her other half.' The paramedic shook his head in disgust before looking Nell frankly in the eye. 'You're going to have your work cut out there, love.'

They had now arrived at the hospital and Nell could escape. As the men in the green boiler suits hurried George into A&E, she wandered into the reception area they had pointed out to her and sat down to wait.

There were lots of other people waiting too. Or perhaps

they were just here for the sake of it. The place had a strangely sociable atmosphere. People were happily browsing the stationers, florists and coffee shops that surrounded the main seating area.

Others watched the enormous flat-screen telly suspended above the waiting area as they ate chips from polystyrene boxes or drank giant lattes. Both chips and lattes seemed incongruous given the hospital context, but perhaps the café wished to ensure a steady stream of clients for its parent institution.

The TV – which had a great dent in it, as if someone had hurled a heavy object – was showing a property programme. Nell had been trying not to think about Beggar's Roost, but she couldn't avoid it now. The neat house that the TV blonde was showing the doubtful-looking couple round reminded her by its very contrast of her new home and its cruel disappointments.

Nell summoned her courage. The cottage couldn't possibly be as bad as she remembered. It was the shock of George Farley's heart attack; it had cast a pall over everything. Beggar's Roost was just a bit messy, that was all.

She clung to the memory of Angela Highwater's assurance that the former residents had been model tenants. The friendly Angela would not deliberately give her somewhere disgusting to live. The outside might be a bit untidy, but she would soon be able to clear it up. And the inside would be fine; it had to be. Not least because Rachel and Juno were coming on Friday.

Eventually a nurse came to find her in reception. Jasjit was friendly but efficient and Nell found herself swiftly appraised of the situation. George had had a massive heart attack. The hospital was trying to trace his relatives. He had been lucky to survive; the prompt action of the man at the scene had undoubtedly saved him.

'What a hero,' Jasjit enthused. 'Friend of yours?' She seemed to think there was only one of them.

Nell shook her head hurriedly. It was nothing less than the truth. She didn't know Dan, and Adam was no friend.

'Ooh! Think I'd get to know him if I was you.'

A pair of dark eyes again swam in Nell's memory, along with a full mouth and dark hair curling on the collar of an open shirt.

She got back to Edenville much later than expected. The hospital bus stop had a good service to Chestlock but buses from there to Edenville were few and far between. By the time she returned, a bright stripe of yellow sunset was glowing through the trees on the edge of the village with a heavy lid of darkness above it. Shouldn't she just leave the visit to Beggar's Roost until tomorrow?

No, Nell told herself resolutely. She should face up to it; be brave. Get it over with. Not least because she would imagine the worst if she hadn't seen with her own eyes that it really wasn't so bad.

It was, though. And, actually, much, much worse. She was of course prepared for an untidy garden, and in the few hours since last seeing it, had even persuaded herself that it was actually only marginally dishevelled. The reality was dramatically different.

Even with a mellow summer sunset showing it in quite literally the best possible light, there was no escaping the accumulated horror of the pile of broken fencing, the dented plastic play equipment and the heap of smashed bricks and concrete. This discordant and ugly main melody was counter-pointed by bulging plastic bags with sinister and unguessable contents. And, above, between and beneath it all, rampaging nettles, knotweed, willowherb and every other invasive, impossible-to-remove shrub known to horticulture.

Nell fought through this horrible debris to the front window of Beggar's Roost and the reassuring order she was confident of finding within. The filthy condition of the windows, however – equally dirty both inside and out, it seemed – and the generous heaps of dead flies on the interior sill, indicated that her optimism was misplaced.

While within was theoretically a sitting room, Nell could see that it would be some time before she was sitting in it. There was, for a start, no furniture. No anything. The former tenants seemed to have taken it all. Even the wall light fittings had been yanked out, leaving wires sprouting from walls like the roots of some invisible electric plant growing the other side of the crackled plaster and ripped paper.

The damage done to these walls seemed so recent and extensive it could only be deliberate. There were crude drawings and spray-painted graffiti that Juno certainly could not be allowed to see. Even the carpets had been taken; uneven and dusty boards lined the floor. Rubbish was liberally scattered over this: crushed drinks cans, paper, fast food cartons. This room needed not just a thorough cleaning, but fumigating.

Nell stared for a while in the hope that familiarity with the carnage would ease the shock. As it made it worse, if anything, she trailed round to the back.

The garden here was more of a mess than the one at the front. A collection of cracked and broken toilets were lying on their side and a wrecked bathtub full of silt and stagnant yellow water continued the incongruous ablutionary theme.

As the first thing to meet her eye through the kitchen window was a sink heaped with mouldy dishes, Nell turned away.

Determinedly, she forced back tears. Crying would not help. Only work would, but even if she spent every spare hour she had here, there was no possibility that it would be ready for the weekend. Or any weekend over the next ten years.

The temptation – in as much as anything associated with such a wreck could be tempting – was to throw the towel in on the whole place. But if she did, where would she live? In the Edenville Arms? But she had only two more nights there. One of which, the Friday, she had already promised Juno and Rachel would be spent in Beggar's Roost. They would be so disappointed.

Nell walked slowly back to the Edenville Arms. It had been a confusing, perplexing, distressing day. The house she had had such high hopes for was a disgusting ruin. Added to which, the man she'd had such a low opinion of had turned out to be a hero. Her world was in disarray again.

CHAPTER 38

'Is something the matter?' It was the next day and Julie was looking keenly at Nell from over the spreadsheet. Despite her phone pinging constantly with texts from Carly, the Weddings Manager was trying to explain the four other celebrations the department was currently handling.

'No, I'm fine,' Nell assured her, determinedly yanking back her wandering mind. But in truth she was distracted; nothing Julie was saying was going in. If she was asked any questions, she would be in serious trouble.

The state of Beggar's Roost and the question of Adam Greenleaf were chasing each other round her mind. Of the two, the cottage was clearly the most important, so why was the other taking up so much bandwidth? Yet again, Nell tried to focus on what Julie was saying.

The Weddings Manager paused. It seemed a meaningful pause, and apprehension gripped Nell. 'I heard about that business at the hospital yesterday,' Julie said, tapping her pen against her teeth. 'Old George Farley.'

Nell found herself reddening. 'How did you hear?'

Julie grinned. 'Estate tom-tom.'

That again. Nell had a feeling the paramedic might have had something to do with it too.

'You were quite the hero, I hear,' Julie added, confirming Nell's suspicions. Who but the paramedic would know? She felt irritated, as well as embarrassed, but Julie's voice was warm with approval. 'You and those guys. Dan Parker and that other one. Who was he again?'

Nell shook her head wildly. 'I don't know.' As Julie was looking at her, her expression speculative, she decided it was time to move things on. She no longer wanted to think about the event in George Farley's garden.

'Look, sorry, you were saying . . . ?'

Julie looked down at her spreadsheet again. 'Oh yeah.' She tapped her pen on her teeth again. 'Where were we? Here we go. Hannah wants the food to be pie and mash in brown paper boxes.'

Hannah. Nell tried to remember. *Hannah.* What had Julie told her about Hannah? Oh yes. Hannah was in PR and her fiancé – Jake, was it? – was a solicitor. They wanted a 'festival feel' for their wedding.

'. . . and to have a dressing-up chest at the reception next to the photo-booth.'

'Are they sure?' Nell was doubtful. 'Some of the photos might not be ones they'd want to keep. Especially when people have had a few.'

'That's more or less how Josh sees it.'

Josh, not Jake. *Josh.*

'Apart from anything else, he keeps reminding Hannah that some of his relatives are in their nineties and might not get it.'

'How stressful.'

The word sent Nell's thoughts straight back to her new home. She had rung Angela and left a message, first thing. She had expected a call, probably an apologetic one, straight away. But Angela had not been in touch at all.

Nell now considered the possibility that Angela was out at

meetings all day. Or even away somewhere. Both scenarios were disastrous because every hour that passed was crucial. There was so little time between now and Rachel and Juno arriving. Of course, they could all sleep in the honeymoon suite, but Rachel and Juno were so excited about coming to the cottage, and she wanted them at least to be able to visit it first. She needed help, although from whom or where Nell couldn't imagine. It would take something akin to a biblical miracle to sort things out in time.

Shooting through her mind now came the idea that they could stay next door at George Farley's. She had access, after all; she had locked up before getting into the ambulance. The key had been in the kitchen door and Nell, glancing casually in, had seen that the place was just as neat and cosy as it had looked from the other side of the window.

But she knew George only slightly – even though that small amount of knowledge was so positive – and he didn't know her or her friends at all. And she could hardly ask his permission, as he was in intensive care in hospital. She would visit him tonight, though; just so she could bow out respectably. See how he was and check that his family had been tracked down. Give them the key, too, for that matter.

'. . . a twinkle dance floor,' Julie was saying now, her voice serious, frowning over the spreadsheet. Nell tuned hurriedly back in, trying to catch up. Julie was talking about the wedding of some people called Sam and Will. Oh yes. Nell remembered now. Julie had mentioned them earlier. 'Sam and Will. Sound like men but one of them's a girl.'

'Sam?' Nell had guessed.

'No, Will,' grinned Julie. 'It's short for Wilhelmina.'

So what was this about a twinkle dance floor? 'How does it twinkle?'

'Lights up with lots of little sparkling lights. They're also having a coach and four with a liveried footman and ambient swing at the reception.'

'Sounds like something you sit on.' This was nothing if not an education.

'Yes, but it's a close-harmony singing group called the Ellington Sisters who do Hollywood jazz interspersed with Justin Bieber. The food's going to be haggis bonbons and—'

'Did you say haggis bonbons?'

'I did, yes.'

'What are they?'

Julie giggled. 'I've no idea. Will saw them in some glossy magazine. They're also having champagne from personalised bottles. Oh, and did I mention the ice-cream bike? Nell? Are you listening to me?'

Nell's guilty eyes met Julie's. She could no longer lie to her. 'Not really,' she confessed.

Julie rolled her eyes and put down her pen. 'I knew it. Something's on your mind, isn't it? Is it that hospital business? Look, you can tell me. If you need a day or two off, that's fine. It must have been an awful shock, finding George like that.'

Julie was obviously not going to give up. Nell could see there was nothing for it but to tell her about Beggar's Roost. 'And my friends are supposed to be coming to stay in it tomorrow,' she finished hopelessly.

The eyes of the Weddings Manager narrowed. 'Bloody Angela,' she hissed.

Nell was surprised. 'Why bloody Angela? I'm sure she didn't send me there on purpose.'

Julie fixed her with a stare. 'Believe me, Angela does *everything* on purpose. Usually for a nasty purpose.'

Nell's eyes were wide. 'But why would she want to be nasty to me?'

The other woman snorted. 'Well, you're young, pretty, clever, funny, stylish and interesting. That's six things Angela isn't. So I'm guessing them for starters. I'm also guessing that Angela wants you out of here.'

'Here? You mean the estate?' Nell was not certain she believed Julie. Angela knew, as Julie didn't, about Nell's unfortunate romantic history. No one in command of those facts would envy her, surely. And Angela had been so friendly, seemed so nice. Why would she want to make things more difficult?

'Like I say, I'm just guessing. But you wouldn't be the first one. I mean, I'm glad that she sent you here, but there's probably a reason. She probably intended you not to like it.'

It had certainly been less than tactful. But was it really deliberately cruel? Nell put her hands to her forehead. A headache was threatening.

Julie seemed suddenly to have swung into action. She was now on the phone but the call did not seem to be about weddings. Julie was talking about a house.

'Yes, that one,' she was saying. 'Where the Downers used to live. In Edenville.'

'What are you doing?' Nell asked when Julie put down the receiver.

Her colleague smiled. 'Just hurrying things along a bit with Works.'

'Works?'

'The works department. My hubby runs it.' Julie looked briefly and winningly self-conscious. 'Turns out that Beggar's Roost is on the list to be done up.'

Nell brightened. That was something at any rate.

Julie went on. 'But it can take Works a long time. Years, sometimes. Especially when it's someone as unpopular as Ros Downer living there.'

Nell's spirits sank again.

'However, once you mention that Angela Highwater won't like the work being done straight away, it can have a miraculous effect.' Julie gave her a meaningful look.

Nell gasped, understanding. Of course, the work could not possibly be done by tomorrow. It would take weeks, months, years. But at least she could tell Rachel and Juno that refurbishment was under way. Things were moving. 'Thank you so, so much,' she added, gratefully.

'Hey, come on,' Julie grinned. 'You deserve a break. You saved an old man's life, after all. One good turn and all that.'

Meanwhile, a few miles away in Chestlock, Dan and Dylan were trying to find the golf course.

Dan, unsurprisingly, was not a golfer and had no idea where it was. Dylan drove hopelessly around as Dan tried with decreasing success to field increasingly irate calls from the Lady President. Her directions only confused them more, and her bossiness gave the lie to the idea that the game promoted relaxation and a balanced outlook.

Eventually they got on the right track; a road bordered by large detached houses set in mature, tree-filled gardens. The golf club was announced by a large painted sign behind which stretched a car park filled with gleaming Audis, Range Rovers and sports cars.

Behind the cars was the clubhouse and behind that were the greens and fairways, their flags merrily fluttering.

'It looks big,' Dylan said doubtfully.

'It'll be all reight,' Dan said confidently. 'They'll 'ave one o' them big tractor mowers.'

The Lady President came striding over in her green padded gilet and fixed Dan with a gimlet eye.

'Oh yeah, no problem,' Dan said in reply to the questions about golf-course-mowing now being rained down upon him. But Dylan knew for a fact that Dan had never mowed a golf course in his life.

The Lady President finally wound up her inquisition. 'Come on. Let's get started.'

They followed her as she strode off across the car park. 'Play golf, do you?' she barked over her quilted green shoulder.

As Dan remained mute, Dylan felt bound to answer. 'I don't, actually,' he said. 'I never have.'

The quilted back stopped suddenly. '*Never?*'

'I played crazy golf when I was a kid,' was all Dylan, under pressure, could dredge up. 'It had a cannon at the end that fired if you got your ball in the hole.' He smiled. He hadn't thought about that particular course for years.

A whole host of other memories rushed back with it. What the madeleine was to Marcel Proust, Dylan reflected, the crazy golf course was to him. Except that it wasn't, because he wasn't writing any more.

The Lady President strode swiftly ahead, pausing at a small creosoted shed down the side of the clubhouse. 'The mower,' she announced, handing Dan a key.

Dan opened the door to reveal, not the gleaming red tractor of his fond imaginings, but an ordinary manual model, and not the newest at that. He turned to look quizzically at his latest employer. 'You want me to get round eighteen 'oles with that?'

The Lady President tipped her chin challengingly upwards. 'Our former groundsman was perfectly happy with it. He never,' she added warningly, 'complained.'

Dylan eyed her disbelievingly. Had not the former grounds-man just resigned? He remembered the fee, briefly discussed in the car park. Its skinflint nature had contrasted with the displays of motorised wealth all around.

'I suppose,' he said to Dan as the Lady President stalked off, 'that we'd better get our mower out of the car as well. Then at least we'll have two.'

They started mowing at the back of the course, at the furthest hole, so Dylan, who had been landed with it, could master the ancient machine in relative privacy. None of the golfers had got this far round the course yet, although some were getting near. Dylan could hear them shouting encouragement at each other.

'Tosser!'

'Twat! Call that a shot?'

There was much worse, and Dylan was surprised. While he had always thought golf was boring, he had at least imagined it was civilised.

They worked, as usual, in silence for some time. Then Dan paused and leaned on the mower. 'So,' he said, shooting Dylan a glance from the depths of his recessed brows. 'What you going to do about it?'

'About what?' Dylan looked at his mowing. Admittedly, it wasn't textbook. The ancient machine either gouged up the grass or slid over it without touching.

'That blonde.'

'What blonde?'

Perhaps he had said it too quickly. Dan's tanned and massive forehead creased quizzically. 'I don't know how many blondes you've met lately. But the one I mean's the one in the garden. Yesterday. With the old bloke.'

Dylan surrendered. 'What *should* I do?'

Dan shrugged his huge shoulders. 'Something. She thinks you're a hero, mate.'

'It was a joint effort,' Dylan said. Yet he could feel, again, the great energy flashing through his hand. And, beneath it, the old heart starting again. Amazing.

'Whatever. Get in there. Make hay while the sun shines.'

'I don't want to get in there,' Dylan said primly.

Dan stared. 'Why not? She's bloody gorgeous.'

'Is she?'

Dan cackled. 'Come on. You can't fool me. I saw her give you that look, and I saw you give 'er a look back an' all.'

'But she hates me,' Dylan sighed.

'They say it's a thin line, mate.'

CHAPTER 39

George was in a small room by himself, propped up in a bed with barriers on each side. The plastic mask was no longer attached to his face, but he remained hooked up to a bank of machines. Wires spilled out of them, some going into George under pieces of tape fixed to his skin.

On the other side, a television was suspended from an overhead swivel stand. It was not on. The old man's eyes were closed. But he was not asleep; the jutting brows were moving, and he was muttering. Nell couldn't make out the words. She leaned over.

'Mr Farley?'

The voice was a woman's, low and soft. It entered the old man's troubled consciousness. Was it his wife? He opened his eyes slowly.

A pair of blue eyes were looking into his and blonde hair hung around her pale face. 'Edwina?'

Edwina! A hot, prickly feeling rushed through Nell. She realised now why the woman in the photo on the old man's wall had seemed familiar. Did she not glimpse her, daily, in the mirror?

The reason he had gripped her hand so hard was now clear too. Mr Farley thought she was his wife.

Nell sat down hard and sudden on the plastic chair at the bedside. That day in the garden, he must have really believed Edwina had come back from the dead. That all that talking to her grave had finally raised her from it.

Did that mean, Nell wondered, pushing the thought to its logical conclusion, that she had actually caused George Farley's heart attack? Had the shock of seeing her, of thinking her his wife, almost killed him?

What an awful responsibility! What unhappy, one-in-a-million coincidence could have made this happen? The same bad luck, of course, that seemed to dog her everywhere these days. This poor old man was the latest victim of the disaster and destruction she wrought wherever she went.

'You all right, love?' The friendly nurse from the night before stood before her.

Nell shook her head and explained what had just happened.

The nurse regarded her steadily. Then she walked off, out of the room. The gesture confirmed Nell's worst fears about her own culpability. She sat on at the old man's bedside, sadly regarding the old body propped upon the pillows, empty hands roped with veins spread on the covers; green hospital gown tied at his wrinkled neck.

George's eyes were closed and sunk in thin folds below jutting brows. They were still dark, as they must have been when he was young. As Edwina would have known them, when they first met.

'Here she is, doctor.' It was the nurse's voice. Nell now looked up to see a tall man standing in the doorway and looking at her testily. He had cropped grey hair, very clean glasses and, it seemed, not very much time. 'I'll get straight to the point,' he said shortly. 'Jasjit here tells me that you think you caused this old gentleman's heart attack.'

Nell nodded. Her primary emotion remained guilt, but there was something about the doctor that made her feel silly as well.

'Well, you didn't,' the doctor stated. 'I won't go into the medical reasons, I haven't got time. But if you want to see my secretary, make an appointment.'

And with that he was gone.

'So there you have it,' twinkled Jasjit. 'Not guilty, your honour.' She bent over and squeezed the old man's papery hand. 'You're all right, aren't you, George, love? Doing well. Promote you to the general ward soon, won't we?'

'Has his family visited?' Nell asked. The key to the old man's cottage was in the front pocket of her handbag. Now that the burden of responsibility for his condition had been lifted, she wanted to hand this lesser burden over too.

The nurse pulled a face and she shook her head. 'No, no one else has come.' She added that George Farley seemed to have no relations. There were none on his records and he hadn't had a mobile phone, which was how they usually informed people.

'Maybe there's one in his house,' Nell suggested. 'Or an address book or something. I could go and look.'

Returning to the wreck of Beggar's Roost would not be fun. But it would be a whole lot less heart-sinking now. Julie's husband and his team were about to start.

'She could go in the morning, before work,' Nell decided. Then, if she visited George again tomorrow, she could bring what she had found. She looked up at the nurse, who was adjusting the machinery by the bed. 'Will he be ready to go home soon?'

'Difficult to say.' Jasjit finished her fiddling, then bent over the old man. 'Bye, love. I've got to go now but I'll be back to check on you later. Shepherd's pie for dinner. Your favourite!'

The room felt empty without the friendly presence of the nurse. The machinery hummed and beeped. Nell looked around the pale yellow walls, and at the view out of the window. When she looked back at the old man his eyes had opened and he was staring at her. But it was immediately obvious that he no longer thought she was his wife. The adoration had gone. This stare was cautious, even suspicious.

'Who are you?' His voice was gravelly, phlegmy. He cleared his throat.

Nell gave him her best reassuring smile. 'I'm your new neighbour.'

The eyes blazed with alarm, as if the word had bad associations. '*New* neighbour,' Nell repeated. 'The Downers have gone, remember?'

She was pleased to see the fear fade from his expression. 'I'm looking after your garden,' Nell added, as the idea came into her head.

This word obviously meant something very different. The old face smiled.

'For the time being,' Nell added. 'Until your family come.'

The old brow gathered in puzzled lines. The lips moved, as if trying to find the words. He murmured something, and Nell bent forward. 'Say that again?' she asked kindly. 'Didn't quite catch it.'

'Don't have a family,' said Mr Farley.

Nell sat back. She thought of the key in her bag. Who would she give it to now?

The old chest beneath the hospital gown rose and fell. 'We never had children, Edwina and me. It were the great sorrow of her life.' The old man sighed again, a rasping breath. 'Aye, it were. Nowt to be done about it, though.'

Nell bit her lip. There were greater difficulties and tragedies in the world than her own, than any she could ever know. 'Tell me about Edwina,' she said impulsively.

She was curious about this woman she so strongly resembled; who had inspired, and continued to inspire, such devotion.

But as the large old head with the rumpled white hair turned away, she feared she had said the wrong thing. Perhaps the subject was too sensitive. Or personal; George was, after all, from a more private and circumspect generation.

But no, he was speaking. Talking in his soft northern burr, apparently to himself. Lying on his back, his words were directed upwards rather than at anyone in particular. Nell bent forward. What was George saying?

'I knew I wanted to marry her, straight away.' His voice was low, but audible. 'Soon as I met her, I knew. She knew, an' all. We were both only eighteen, but we knew all right.'

It was surprisingly easy to imagine the sick and ancient figure before her as an ardent young man fired with romantic determination. Nell blinked her suddenly swimming eyes.

'We just had to persuade everyone else,' George went on. He was now turning his head towards her, smiling. 'My family were fine about it. It were hers that were the problem.'

'Why?'

The old man chuckled. 'It would have been easy enough if she'd been an ordinary girl. Everyone wanted a uniform on their arm. But Edwina's family were the sort who would only want particular *types* of uniform.' He paused, and coughed.

'They were very posh, you know. The *Harringtons*.' He gave the name a comic emphasis and his mouth stretched in a roguish grin.

Nell bent further forward. 'So how did you persuade them? The *Harringtons*?'

Because, self-evidently, he had. Had it been an impassioned speech? A brave act? A stroke of luck?

Talking seemed to have been too much for the old man,

however. His eyes were closed now. His breathing was regular. He seemed to be asleep.

Nell patted the old hand. 'I'm going now. I'll be back tomorrow.' Not least, she thought as she left, because she wanted to hear the next part of the story.

Outside, behind the nurses' station, Jasjit was laughing with a colleague. As Nell passed, she stopped. 'Hang on a minute, love. Want a word with you.'

Nell waited obediently. 'Just to remind you about going to his house,' the nurse went on. 'To get his mobile or whatever.'

'Actually, there's no point. He told me that he doesn't have any family.'

Nell had imagined that the nurse would be surprised, but Jasjit looked rather as if she had expected this. 'Another one,' she said.

'Another what?'

'Lonely old person. It's a real epidemic. I worry about them, I really do.' The nurse shook her head sorrowfully, her big brown eyes troubled. 'But you could go into his house anyway, get him a few things, couldn't you?'

'What things?' Nell asked cagily. She had vaguely assumed that now there was no family, some hospital official would take responsibility. Perhaps even ask for the cottage key.

'Well, pyjamas, so he doesn't have to wear those horrible gowns. Some clothes, and maybe a photo or two. Make him feel a bit more at home.'

'Oh. Right.' Well, that wasn't too onerous. Nell nodded. 'OK.'

She began to walk away. The nurse's voice stopped her, however.

'Ooh, and one other thing.'

Nell turned.

'Have you seen that dishy bloke again? The one who rescued George?'

Nell was annoyed to find herself blushing furiously. She had been trying not to think about it, but the glance that had passed between herself and Adam Greenleaf had been endlessly replaying in the back of her mind. 'No.'

CHAPTER 40

At the exact same moment Caradoc Turner sat in the dressing room of the Festival Theatre, Tunbridge Wells. It wasn't especially festive, but he hadn't expected it to be. Six months of touring provincial playhouses had left him with a morbid appreciation of the distance between such names and the grim reality. The Grand, Ipswich, wasn't all that grand, and what sort of Royal thought the theatres bearing that adjective deserved the name was anyone's guess.

But perhaps these old-fashioned statements of civic over-confidence were better than names like the Congress, Eastbourne, which had got Gilly all fired up with its overtones of sexual permissiveness. On the other hand, it was at the Churchill, Malvern, with its resolute, spine-stiffening associations, that he'd managed conclusively to fend her off.

Caradoc stuck on his Pierrot moustache and winced as the nylon bristles pressed down on the sores. Only one more night to go, thank God.

People often said how fascinating it must be to see so many different towns. But people, Caradoc thought, should get out more. If they did they would see that it was anything but fascinating; these towns were all absolutely the same. Especially in the rain, which there had been an inordinate amount of. There had been a lot of black clouds doing the same tour as them.

Leeds. Aberdeen. Bath. Dublin. Cambridge. Newcastle. Blackpool. Ring roads on the outside and multi-storeys on the inside. And boxy glass buildings – flats, offices, whatever – which made everywhere from Swindon to Sheffield look the same. Small wonder they had all blended into one in his memory. The theatres had too, apart from what was really important about each of them. Caradoc knew the locations of the fridges, microwaves and toilets in every provincial playhouse in the country.

He was quite desperate now to get home and see his wife. Tomorrow she would be in his arms. At last he would be able to introduce her to love's pleasures. Awaken her dormant sensuality as the kiss of the handsome prince had woken the Sleeping Beauty. Make her his and introduce her to all she had been missing. All he had been missing too. After all these long months of waiting it made him ache to think about it.

Caradoc stood up, turned side on and regarded himself in the mirror, sucking his tummy in hard. OK, so no one could accuse him of being tall. But from certain angles and in certain lights, he still looked young. Agile, strong – and more than capable of satisfying a young wife.

He hoped Juliet was looking forward to it too, but it was difficult to be sure. She was more elusive than ever; last night the phone had rung and rung before, eventually, she'd answered sounding quite out of breath. She'd been in the garden, she said.

The thought of her out there left Caradoc feeling unhinged. He was almost as obsessed with the fatal potential of the Birch Hall garden as with finally possessing his wife. Reiterating the dangers of all its poisonous plants every night in *Murderous Death* left him in a frenzy of anxiety by the end. His dreams were a disturbing melange of wild sex and agonising death. He hadn't slept an entire night for weeks.

But then, nor had anyone else. The quality of the digs they'd stayed in had been even lower than he'd been led to expect. The nicest places had been snapped up by Gilly and Pete, who were old hands on national tours, while this was Caradoc's first. Old hands had certainly been the word, especially with some of the friskier elderly landladies. It had been a baptism of fire, although in that sense only. Some of the rooms had been so cold and basic that the pee in his chamber pot had frozen overnight. Well, perhaps that was an exaggeration. But he had definitely wished on countless occasions that he'd taken his agent's advice to bring his own pillow.

Never again, Caradoc thought. Nevermore, like that raven in the poem. He wouldn't miss anything about this bloody tour. He certainly wouldn't miss the cast. If he ever saw Gilly and Pete again it would be too soon and as for the others, it was difficult to know which of them he disliked most.

Actually, it wasn't. He didn't like Gary Burley, who played Strangle the gamekeeper and had been in a muscly ITV drama called *Squaddie*. But Burley was not the main focus of his loathing, for all he kept farting in the cast minibus and then denying it. Nor was the equally disliked Simon Fey, who played floppy-haired Bertie Spiffing and hailed from that arena of uncertain sexual orientation known as children's TV. Caradoc hadn't liked the unbearably boring Marmaduke Grey either, who played Curate Segg. He had spent years in *Heartbeat* and talked about Nick Berry as other people talked about Robert de Niro.

But none of his co-stars – or co-failures, given the state of their careers – annoyed Caradoc as much as Candice Floss, who played the mysterious femme fatale Signora Stiletto.

While the Backstabbers as a whole lacked esprit de corps, Candice was the worst team-player of the lot. Everyone hated the way she hogged the bows at the end; doing a little jump when she came on to draw the audience's attention her way and then doing a little pat on her heart as she bent over – so low that her forehead touched her toes. Those cast members whose backs were too stiff to do more than nod resented this last in particular. They felt it was showing off. Candice also followed the dictum that when bowing you should look at everyone in the audience. Unfortunately, on some nights, this had not taken very long at all.

But the very particular reason that Caradoc hated Candice was that unlike the rest of them she had work lined up. This very weekend she was flying out to join *Fifty Shades Of Grey, The Musical*, in Orlando. Whereas he could look forward to doing voiceovers for local radio if he was lucky. Which wouldn't even begin to approach the expense of running Birch Hall.

He might simply have to wait for another *Murderous Death*. Gilly certainly was; quite happily too. 'I used to be a tour de force,' she liked to trill over her gin and tonic. 'But now I'm just forced to tour.'

Should he resign himself to a similar fate? Caradoc doubted it, and not just because the thought of traipsing round for months in the same (thanks to Gary) smelly minibus made his blood run cold.

The notices of the tour hadn't been great, particularly his own performance. 'The verdict is unanimous' (*Hexham Gazette*), while cryptic, had probably been the best one, compared to which 'thoroughly executed' (*Bristol Chronicle*) seemed only a statement of fact. 'Slick . . .', from the *Harrogate Post*, had started well, but had ended badly: '. . . in the oil sense: sluggish, sticky and miserable'.

Oh well. If his theatrical career was at an end, it might be a good thing. He could simply stay at home at Birch Hall with Juliet. Open a B&B for touring actors, ha ha. Or maybe . . .

Caradoc's brow furrowed as the thought began to form, to take flight . . . Yes! He could open a residential centre for acting training. There were enough bloody bedrooms at Birch Hall and its slightly collapsed state would only add to the theatrical ambience. They might even be able to do productions in the garden once that new gardener of Juliet's had got rid of the poisonous plants.

Other ideas now tumbled into his excitable brain. Juliet had set-dressing experience; she could run a stage design course! Caradoc clasped his hands to his heart; the prospect was thrilling. They could stay at home together for ever, the Laurence Olivier and Vivien Leigh of theatrical training. He could hardly wait to see her, to tell her about it.

After their first, passionate physical encounter, of course.

Caradoc took out his mobile once more, but then saw the time on it. He'd try Juliet again afterwards. He'd better step on it. The Festival Theatre's curtain was about to rise.

In the bar of the Edenville Arms, Angela was halfway down her third large Chardonnay. Jason decided that now might be a safe time to report The George Farley Incident.

He had hoped that she might have already heard about it and he would not, after all, have to be the messenger. But Angela had been away the day before – on a course, or so she had said – and been out of the loop.

'So come on,' Angela commanded, as Jason had known she would. 'Give us the goss.'

Her tone was even more bumptious than usual. Perhaps, behind it, there was a new nervousness. Angela had not been away on a course the day before, but at the hospital, where she had been undergoing tests at the behest of her GP. Her last check-up had revealed a lump; something and nothing, Angela was certain. Either way, she did not plan to tell her colleagues about it. While wallowing in those of others, she kept her problems to herself.

She was looking at him expectantly, but how should he begin? The trick with Angela, as Jason well knew, was to present things in the right way. Angle a story to play to her prejudices. And there was plenty in this she would be happy to hear. That George Farley, who she hated, was ill, was the obvious headline.

But he could hardly tell her that without revealing the heroics of the others involved. Without mentioning Dan Parker, the man who had thrown her over for Juliet Turner. Or Adam Greenleaf, who seemed similarly uninterested in her overtures. And worst of all, Nell Simpson, who Angela had been forced to employ, had been the one to call the ambulance.

Jason gestured at Ryan for another gin and tonic. He had a feeling he was going to need it. Even Ryan's blazing smile, and the electric touch of their fingertips as the glass was handed over, failed to cheer him in the usual way.

Angela listened, the muscles of her face working as she absorbed the news. Her various expressions did not fill Jason with confidence. 'What a moron,' she snarled, when he had finished.

It was not clear who was meant. 'Which one?' Jason ventured.

'All of them,' slurred Angela, swiping a hand across the bar and knocking over Jason's bottle of tonic. It was practically full; neat gin had suited the occasion better.

Angela's inebriated mind ping-ponged among the *dramatis personae*. Saving the life of George Farley had been idiotic of Adam Greenleaf. On the other hand, he was very good-looking. Sexy and stupid was a good combination.

As Jason well knew. She slid a look of teasing contempt to the manager, who shifted on his stool, silently wondering what it meant. What it means, Angela silently answered him, is that I know you've got the hots for your barman. And one day I'll use that information.

She dragged her thoughts back to Greenleaf. He was the least to blame, she decided, because he was hers. Had she not hand-picked him to replace Dan? Their meetings hadn't yet gone according to plan. But Angela hadn't given up hope yet.

Nell Simpson was a different matter, however, mooning around the estate with her blonde hair, long legs and dangerously single status. Angela had hoped to discourage her, even send her packing, by putting her, a just-jilted woman, in the weddings department to face the Americans from hell. But it seemed to be going maddeningly well. A chance encounter with Julie in the staff car park had revealed that Nell was a dream to have about the place.

A dream with the nightmare of Beggar's Roost to sort out. Ha ha! Angela twisted her lips with satisfaction at the thought of the mess that place was in. The Earl had mentioned a refurbishment, but the works department would take years to get round to it. By the time they did, Nell Simpson would be long gone.

Jason was now outlining Dan's role in George's rescue. Angela felt a cold fury sweep her. As she picked up, and replaced, her empty glass, Jason caught Ryan's eye. The barman looked blankly back at him.

'Bloody Dan,' Angela snarled as Jason, admitting defeat, got up and went round the back of the bar to fetch the wine bottle himself.

'Don't you think he was a little bit heroic?' Jason asked, his sense of fair play for once trumping his cowardice. He rose a little too quickly from the fridge and felt his head spin.

'Bloody stupid,' Angela countered fiercely. 'George Farley was a horrible old man.'

'He fought in the war,' Jason pointed out. He knew it was madness, but he couldn't quite bear to let Angela get away with such gross misrepresentation. Not in front of Ryan, anyway.

But Angela didn't give two hoots about the war. Her campaign against Dan Parker and Juliet Turner, however, was another matter.

Here was one plan that could not possibly go wrong.

Hell, after all, hath no fury like a woman scorned. And Angela's scorned fury was about to express itself. On Saturday night, Caradoc Turner would be in town with *Murderous Death*. Angela was looking forward to the play very much. But only because she had planned her own special private little drama at the stage door afterwards, in which Caradoc would find out what Juliet had been up to in his absence.

CHAPTER 41

On Friday morning, Nell got up early to go to George's house and pick up his things. There would be time to fit in a quick visit to the hospital before Rachel and Juno arrived in the evening.

The prospect was not cheerful, neither the hospital nor the clothes-gathering. The idea of poking around his property did not feel right. As for the hospital visit, she didn't resent it, exactly; Nell was too kind-hearted for that. But there was no doubt this was an extra complication. Despite not intending or wanting to be, she had become responsible for an old man she hardly knew. At least for the time being. Until George got better and came home.

It was a beautiful blue and gold morning as she left the Edenville Arms and set off through the village. Steam was rising gently from the village green and, as she passed, droplets of dew flashed in the hearts of the flowers. The hedgerows were full of squawking sparrows, and the herby scent of grass played around her nostrils.

Despite all this beauty, Nell was prepared for her heart to sink as she rounded the bend and caught the first glimpse of Beggar's Roost. She had, last night, felt compelled to warn

Rachel of what was waiting for her when she arrived on Friday. 'Don't worry, I'm sorting it out,' she had reassured her.

Just as she was sorting out George, and the job she was actually here to do, the estate literature. She was sorting out a lot at the moment, Nell reflected as she braced herself for the first sight of her new home. She could not see it, however. Something big was between her and the cottage. A skip, being unloaded from a lorry. What did that mean?

She hurried forward. The skip chains were rattling, slapping metallically against the big container's hollow interior. She could hear voices too; men shouting. She caught the glow of hi-vis jackets. Sun bounced off a couple of hard hats. Whatever was going on?

The men were everywhere, in the garden and in her house. She could see them at the upstairs windows. They were all wearing dark blue overalls, and now she was nearer she could see they had a logo on the chest. It was a logo she recognised: the line of pillars of the Pemberton house front. These men were from the estate.

And now it all fell into place. 'You're from Works!' Nell exclaimed to the first man she came across. He was young and freckled and grinned at her from under his hard hat. 'That's right. Emergency job, this.'

Julie, Nell realised joyfully, had been as good as her word.

'You Nell?' She twisted round to find herself looking into a pair of frank grey eyes set in a tanned and square-jawed face. 'Pleased to meet you. I'm Tim, Julie's husband.'

She felt like falling on his neck, but instead wrung his hand and thanked him profusely.

He brushed it off with a grin. 'You're all right, love. It's the missus really. Word is law and all that.'

The skip was now positioned and a succession of thuds begun

as the debris from the garden was hurled into it. Tim steered Nell out of danger. 'We'll be out of your way soon,' he said. 'Don't worry.'

'Oh, I'm sure it'll take a while,' Nell said. 'It's such a horrible mess.'

The team of men in dark boiler suits was working extremely fast. A gang in the garden were passing the rubbish out to another gang in the road. The heaps were disappearing before her eyes.

She could not see what was happening in the house, but she could hear banging within, and shouting. Men were hurrying in with big white pails, roller brushes and trays. Others were brandishing brooms and shovels. They all seemed very cheerful, shouting at each other and singing. Big, burly and boiler-suited as they were, they put Nell in mind of the little birds that helped Cinderella.

'We'll get it done today,' Tim assured her.

Nell gasped. 'You're joking.'

The hard hat twisted from side to side. 'We've been at it since six. Halfway there already. Like I say, t'missus's word is law.'

There was a sharp sensation in the tip of her nose and Nell suddenly felt the overpowering urge to cry. She swallowed hard. 'I can't even offer you a cup of tea.'

'Not sure I'd want one, from that kitchen.' He moved off. 'See you later, love. Should be done by the time you knock off work.'

Nell doubted it, profoundly. But she did not want to sound discouraging. 'I'll just be next door for a while,' she called to him, thinking she should cover herself lest the builders thought anything amiss. 'The hospital's asked me to get a few things.'

She watched Tim's burly form stop and turn. 'For old

George. Yeah, I heard about that. You did well there, love. One good turn deserves another.'

He touched his hard hat and continued on his way. Nell proceeded on hers, hurrying up George's path as, next door, Tim's team, flashing her the occasional grin, rushed up and down hers, carrying boxes, bags and all manner of rotting and broken things she neither could nor wanted to identify.

One good turn deserves another. Both Julie and Tim had said it to her now. And so, Nell thought as she turned the key in George's pristine front door, why not do yet another? Bring the old man's things to him in hospital without feeling she'd been asked to bring the moon.

The hallway was practically silent. The cheerful shouting and the blare of radios sounded very faint from in here. The outside world felt quite sealed off, and yet the place was not sepulchral. It had a pleasant, firewoody smell, no doubt from the solid-fuel stove in the sitting room that she had seen through the window that day which now seemed a lifetime ago. She had had no idea what was about to happen.

The interior was very plain and quite masculine, which was unsurprising given that Edwina had not lived here for many years. How many? She could remember the gravestone had said 2004. Over a decade, then.

And yet Edwina had lived here; it had been her home. The thought made Nell feel intrusive, and rather shy. What if Edwina were looking down from wherever she might be, at this unknown woman in her intimate space?

The old man's clothes would be in his bedroom. It still seemed awfully personal, this rummaging through his possessions. Better make it as quick as possible.

A flight of varnished wooden stairs led to the next floor. Nell scurried up them, hearing her feet on the treads and thinking how familiar the sound must have been to the Farleys. Each stair would have its special creak.

It crossed her mind, as she reached the landing, that the cottage had the same layout as Beggar's Roost next door. Three bedrooms led off the top of the steps, and a bathroom. The place was bigger than it looked.

For a second she was tempted to peep in the bathroom. But she was not here to compare and contrast architectural features. She was on a mission. Guessing that the front-facing bedroom would be George's, Nell pushed open the white-painted, panelled door.

Her first impression was that it was cool, shadowy and smelt of something woody, faint and delicious. Her second was that it was a complete Forties period piece; the wallpaper printed with small pink flowers; the net curtains; the brass-framed bed spread with the patchwork quilt; the washstand with the basin; the small shaving mirror propped up beside it.

A handsome mahogany wardrobe expanded across most of one wall. It had not one but two oval mirrors, let into the doors and throwing the light from the window into the mirror of the dressing table opposite. This was in the same style and same wood as the wardrobe; they were obviously a set and evidently quite a grand one.

Nell immediately thought of the posh Harringtons the old man had mentioned. Perhaps this bedroom furniture had been their wedding present. If so it had been appreciated; it was beautifully polished and cared for. She could not see a speck of dust anywhere.

She crossed to the dressing table. In the muted light from the deep-set, net-draped windows, the mirror gave an intensely flattering reflection. Nell thought of Edwina sitting here, looking at herself. Applying her make-up; that deep red Forties lipstick.

On an embroidered cloth – very clean and carefully ironed – spread across the dressing table's glass surface were arranged a brush, mirror and comb, all backed and mounted in silver.

In the centre of the brush and mirror backs was the engraved letter 'E'. This must be the very set Edwina had used, pulling those very bristles through hair that must, given her husband's confusion, have been a similar colour to her own. Nell bent to look at herself again, wondering how alike she and Edwina really had looked.

Each of the two small bedside tables, of solid brown polished oak, held a framed photograph. Nell went over to look at them. One was a smaller version of the wedding picture, and now, with more opportunity to study it, Nell could see that the resemblance between herself and Edwina was closer even than she had thought. She wondered what colour the bride's wedding coat had been, and the little flower pinned to the lapel.

George, proudly clasping his wife's hand on his arm, looked like a younger version of himself. The white hair had been dark and sharply parted, but the brows were the same. And while she had never seen him smile quite this widely, she had seen an echo.

The other picture was of seven young men in RAF uniform standing beneath an enormous aeroplane. You didn't have to be a genius to guess that this was George's wartime crew. Nell slipped the two pictures into her bag to take to the old man in hospital, and went to find the clothes.

In George's cedar-scented cupboards, everything was neatly in its place. Pull-out drawers held pyjamas and underwear; larger items were suspended from wooden hangers. In a matter of minutes Nell had located shirts, cardigans and trousers. She went into the small, very clean bathroom and filled a spongebag. But what to put it all in?

In the very bottom of the wardrobe was a snap-lock case. It, too, bore not a speck of dust. Nell wondered what holidays it had been on. Laying it on top of the patchwork quilt and placing the old man's things in it, she felt as if she were about to go somewhere herself. She snapped the locks together, hurried back down and locked the front door.

'You won't recognise this place later!' Tim called from an upper window of Beggar's Roost as she hurried back up George's path. Nell waved back. It was sweet of him to say so, but there could be no chance the cottage would be finished today. Even Rome wasn't built in a day and Beggar's Roost was a much bigger job than that.

CHAPTER 42

As she was to visit the hospital straight after work, Nell took George's case into the weddings department. When Julie found out what it was for, she insisted Nell must take the afternoon off for the visit.

'Are you sure?' Nell asked. This was undoubtedly helpful. Getting the visit to George out of the way meant she would be able to see Beggar's Roost before dark and before her guests arrived.

They would not be staying there, obviously – Jason had already reinstalled Juno's put-up bed in the honeymoon suite. But it would be useful to assess the extent of what remained to be done. There was also George's garden to water.

'You don't need me for anything?' she pressed Julie. 'No Carly and Jed?'

'Don't get me started. Got here this morning to find an email from them asking about a father of the bride make-up package.'

'*Father?*'

'You heard me. Here, check out these two, could you?' She handed Nell a couple of flyers. 'Have a look at their online offer, see if they're worth adding to our files.'

'These two' were string ensembles who played at receptions. Nell studied the websites. The first, 'Handel with Care', was a foursome of fetching female violinists in tiny silver dresses. They pouted kittenishly out of the screen, flicking their long blonde hair. The cellist took full advantage of her instrument's leg-parting potential.

'Debussy Galore' was the other, rival act. They were brunettes with tinier dresses even than Handel with Care. They too could play Michael Bublé and Adele as well as Vivaldi.

There didn't seem much to choose between them, Nell concluded. 'I think they're both fine, if that's the kind of thing you like,' she said to Julie.

Julie rolled her eyes. 'Those string groups are notorious for getting off with every man in sight. Sometimes even with the groom. Personally, I wouldn't touch any of them with a bargepole. Oh *no*!'

'What's the matter?'

'Will's changed her mind *again*,' Julie exclaimed in annoyance. 'Wants party food stations now. Hot dogs, candyfloss and crêpe stalls. Oh, and fruit machines.'

'Why don't they just hold it at a fairground?'

'Well, if they did,' Julie pointed out sagely, 'I'd be out of a job and Pemberton would make a lot less money. Don't worry,' she added, disappearing behind her desk and re-emerging holding a file. 'I've got lists of crêpe stalls and fruit machine hirers coming out of my ears.'

Nell made a note. Brides at fruit machines would make a striking image for the wedding brochures she had started to redesign. Work was beginning to take on a definite shape now; an enjoyable one. Sharing an office with Julie was fun and setting up photoshoots and liaising with designers felt almost like old Vanilla times.

*

Later, Nell arrived at the hospital to find that George was still in his single room. Jasjit bore away the clothes while Nell showed the old man the photographs. His face lit up in delight.

'Nobby,' the old man said, pointing at the man in the centre of the group. He had a broad grin and looked very good-humoured.

'Tell me about Nobby,' Nell said, feeling for the chair and sitting down.

'He were the pilot in my Lanc.'

'Lanc?'

The old fingers tapped at the image of the enormous plane. 'Lancaster bomber.' He was watching her closely. Nell was almost certain she could see a flicker of amusement.

'Oh, yes, of course. Sorry.'

George had sunk back against his pillows again. He held the photograph in his hand and was studying it. The one of himself and Edwina had gone straight up on the bedside table.

'I trained as a rear gunner. I wanted to be a pilot,' George said, 'but the RAF told me there were too many of them. It were Nobby that put me right.'

'How do you mean?'

'Nobby said, is that what they told you? That old "too many pilots" line?'

'So it wasn't true?' Nell prompted.

The bright eyes locked hers. 'That's what I asked Nobby. And he said, it's not a case of too many pilots, mate. It's not enough rear gunners. And you know why that is, don't you?'

The old man paused. 'Why was it?' Nell asked.

George patted his chest, wheezing slightly. 'Because rear gunners didn't last more than six missions. And you had a life expectancy of twenty-two seconds if you were shot at.'

Nell gasped. '*That's* what Nobby told you?'

'And it got me thinking,' George said.

'I'm sure it did!'

'I thought, right, as soon as I'm free today I'll go and get Edwina. We were getting married, no matter what. We obviously weren't going to have long together. Pass me the picture, will you?'

Nell obliged, feeling pleasurable anticipation. She had been wondering how to get to the second part of the wedding story.

'So you managed to deal with the posh Harringtons?' she prompted.

George did not reply immediately. Nell was just wondering whether she had offended him when she heard him take a deep breath. 'I never expected them to let us get married. The *Harringtons*. But for some reason they didn't stand in our way. Perhaps they had other things to worry about. One of Edwina's sisters, her husband were a Spitfire pilot. Shot down over the Channel.' The old man paused, drew another breath. 'They probably all thought I'd be next.'

'Well, they got that wrong,' Nell put in.

The old man chuckled. It turned into a wheeze. 'They did.'

'What was the wedding like?' Nell asked, studying the picture of the happy couple.

'Very simple. About as simple as it gets, I reckon. Me in me uniform and Edwina in her best suit with a rose from the local park pinned on it.'

'Ah, so that's where it came from.'

'Pale pink, it were. I remember, I picked it myself.'

He stopped and Nell saw the bright eyes momentarily mist over. 'We just went to the local register office. Dragged a couple of witnesses off o' t'street. No one had asked any questions.

There were a lot of laughter, in fact.' A smile now stretched the old face.

Nell's thoughts had flown to her own register office experience with impromptu witnesses. There had not been much laughter at that. And far too many questions. She took a deep breath.

'No honeymoon, I'm guessing,' she prompted.

A look from the bright hazel eyes. 'Nothing like! I were off on a mission that very same night.'

Nell tried to imagine it. To be a just-married teenager, wrenched from the side of the girl you loved. To go out and drop bombs on Hitler.

'What was a rear gunner, actually? What did you do?'

'Eyes and ears of the pilot, at the back of the plane. You'd tell him to dive to port or starboard and he did. And the first thing you'd do, when you got in your turret, was knock out the Perspex in the central panel.'

'So you could get out?' Nell guessed.

The old man's burst of laughter turned into another burst of coughing. 'At twenty thousand feet? Not likely! You knocked it out because if there were a speck of oil on there, or a dead fly, it might look like an enemy plane. You might put the crew in danger by trying to get away from it.'

'But didn't you get cold?'

George was smiling broadly now. 'Edwina used to ask the exact same question. 'And I used to tell her about the ice beards we grew on our oxygen masks. There were serious competition to see who could grow the longest.'

Nell chuckled. 'So it wasn't all doom and gloom up there.'

'Not at all. There were a lot of laughter. The lads in the parachute room had a sign up: "If it Fails to Open, Bring it Back".'

'No!' The war was always presented so very soberly and

seriously. You forgot that it had been fought, in the main, by teenagers, and high-spirited ones at that.

'But you survived,' she said gently.

The old chest, under the striped flannel pyjamas, rose in a deep sigh. 'Because of my wife. We'd be flying over Berlin, caught in the master searchlight. The dazzle hurt your eyes, you couldn't see anything. But everyone on the plane knew they'd be out there. German fighters, circling in the dark, ready to swoop in and kill.' He paused. Nell looked down at her hands. They were clenching the bedclothes.

'And I'd think of Edwina, so far away. I hoped she'd be asleep and I'd think about her, with her lovely hair spread over the pillow, and I'd think, thank God she can't see me now.'

Nell watched the soft, bright eyes harden suddenly, and the droopy jaw jut firmly forward. The nostrils flared with resolve. 'And then,' the old man rasped, 'and then I'd think, I'm not going to bloody well die. Not here, not now. Why the hell should I?'

Tears were pricking Nell's eyes now. It seemed to her that all the wedding theming she had witnessed in Julie's department, all the accessorising on which the participants placed such emphasis, was merely so much stage-setting. Mere background, a sideshow, not the main event. There was nothing genuinely romantic about a festival food box, still less a fruit machine or Debussy Galore. What George was describing, unadorned as it was, was the real thing.

For all he was old, ill and lonely, he had been lucky. Luckier than her. Yet again, Nell forced her thoughts away from Joey. Incredible to think how recent all that had been; it seemed like years ago, in the life of someone else.

Worn out by talking, George now fell asleep. Nell got up to go. It was time to go and see Jasjit.

'He seems really well,' she began optimistically. 'Very chatty.'

'He is,' the nurse cheerfully agreed.

'Do you, um, think he'll be ready to go home soon?'

The warm brown eyes looked wary. 'To be honest with you, we're not sure he's going to be able to.'

Nell stared at her in horror. 'Not going to be able to go home?'

'No.'

'Not ever?'

'To be honest, the way things are looking right now, no.'

It was hard, after hearing this, to go and water George's beloved garden. Nell decided, on the bus, that she would just have to hope for the best, that Jasjit was wrong. The old man had only been in for a few days, after all. His condition might well improve. Because if it didn't, where would he go?

It was in this preoccupied state that she hurried down the lane from the bus stop. But then something caught her eye that shot George and his problems straight out of her head.

Beggar's Roost looked entirely different. A transformation had taken place.

The garden, while far from pristine, looked considerably tidier. The piles of bent and broken plastic had disappeared and the split black sacks of rubbish had gone too. The logs were still there, but stacked neatly in a corner. Albeit yellow and starved-looking, grass was actually visible.

Nell rubbed her eyes. Tim and his team had been even better than their word; they had performed the impossible. She hurried to the cottage windows; they were clean. Not only the glass; the woodwork had been washed too. Underneath all the grime it was white. Looking through the sparkling pane, Nell saw that yet greater wonders had been wrought.

The bomb site inside was no more. The floor had been swept to expose varnished oak boards and the walls had been whitewashed. The graffiti had disappeared.

Nell gasped and ran round to the rear. Here, too, the formerly chaotic garden had been made orderly. The toilets had all disappeared, as had the bath. Nell looked round, frowning. Had she imagined it? Had it all really been there?

The mouldy dishes in the kitchen sink had gone. The sink had been scoured and now shone. Nose pressed to the clean kitchen window, Nell could see right into the room. The walls were white; freshly painted. There was no furniture, but nor was there any rubbish.

Stunned, she inserted one of the two keys into the back door. It opened easily and a smell of paint and bleach rushed into her nostrils. She felt that she preferred it to a million scented candles.

The excavation – there was no other word for it – had uncovered some pretty architectural features. There were some nice old fireplaces in the downstairs rooms which were easy to picture in the winter with flames leaping romantically in the hearths. Someone had even left a piece of paper in each grate saying 'Swept'. They had thought of everything.

Any fears that the work did not extend upstairs vanished as soon as Nell set foot on the little twisting staircase. Varnished, as George Farley's was, it was just as clean and led up to the same higgledy-piggledy landing where steps at different levels led off in different directions to three bedrooms.

One of the bedrooms was tiny; perfect for Juno, Nell thought. Another was bigger, with a sloping roof. That could be Rachel's. Yet another, the counterpart to George's, had a view of the Beggar's Roost garden. This would be hers, Nell vowed; from here she would watch as the lawn re-greened itself and the flowers she would plant grew and flowered.

All the rooms had deep-set windowsills and little casements with hand-wrought clasps. The bathroom was sparkling clean and seemed entirely fit for purpose. It had a wooden floor and exposed beams in the roof.

Nell felt a great rush of joy. What had been uninhabitable was now a dream home. It was a miracle. And just in time.

CHAPTER 43

So late had Juno and Rachel arrived from London, the fact that they were staying in the honeymoon suite of the Edenville Arms was actually the preferable option. But Beggar's Roost was, at least, in a state to show them now and they spent a happy Saturday morning exploring it.

Juno rushed from room to room. She loved her tiny bedroom. But her real focus throughout was the Chestlock Pavilion Theatre and the moment that night, at 7.30 p.m. precisely, that the curtain was to rise on *Murderous Death*. Her excitement was palpable and she was quite obviously despairing at ever living that long.

Rachel, meanwhile, was taking notes and drawing maps.

'What are you doing?' Nell asked her.

'Thinking about furniture. A fridge and some sort of cooker's top of the list.'

Nell, who'd been unsure where to start, felt grateful for her friend's practical input.

She left her to it while she and Juno went out to tend to George's garden. Juno immediately busied herself filling the two green watering cans at the outside tap. 'I've never seen so many flowers,' she said, with a city dweller's awe.

Nell smiled. She was almost used to it now, this profusion of beauty at Edenville and Pemberton. But it was still new enough to fill her with wonder too and she looked round now at the sheer range the old man had called into being. Rainbow banks of pompom dahlias blended into firework displays of red-hot pokers mixed with coral-pink gladioli and delphiniums ranging from palest powder blue to a deep and royal purple. Bushes rioted with raspberry-ripple roses and and their extravagant pink heads of peonies erupted between dark green leaves. Orange blossom was everywhere, pouring over the walls and fences like sweet-scented cream.

She forced to the back of her mind the possibility that George would never work in his garden again. Jasjit had to be wrong. He had to recover and come home.

She watched Juno exploring the vegetable garden and the neat rows of lettuce. 'He has five different types,' she reported, hopping about between the lollo rosso and the oak leaf.

So exciting had been the garden, Nell noticed, she hadn't mentioned *Murderous Death* once.

Afterwards, they headed for Chestlock, where the local superstore provided the cooker and fridge, plus all the required glassware, cookware, cutlery and bed linen. Before long, Nell's trolley was piled high and she handed over her credit card at the checkout with a shaking hand. Even at supermarket prices, and on the principle of only buying bare necessities, equipping Beggar's Roost wasn't cheap. Thank goodness the sale of Gardiner Road was back on and she could afford it.

'Now for the fun bit,' said Rachel. 'The dining chairs, table, armchairs. Lamps. Sofa.'

Doubt filled Nell. Interiors had never been her strongest point. The ability to fling a few cushions about and link a room together was one she conspicuously lacked. 'IKEA?'

Rachel looked appalled. 'No. The antiques shop. There's a brilliant one in Chestlock.'

'Is there?' It was somehow typical of Rachel to know her local town better than she knew it herself. 'I can't afford antiques, though,' Nell warned.

'Not antiquey antiques,' Rachel corrected. 'More, you know, *vintage*. Pine tables, chipped enamel buckets, carpet beaters.'

'I don't want a carpet beater. I don't have a carpet.' Nor did she want a chipped enamel bucket.

Rachel nudged her. 'You know what I mean. I looked online and they had some great things. I saw a kitchen table and chairs that would be perfect. Mix up your supermarket stuff with a few vintage pieces and it'll look wonderful.'

The vintage furniture shop stood in the centre of town. Nell could not imagine how she had missed it. It was the most conspicuous in the street: a double-fronted emporium whose windows were filled with pictures, hat stands, bowls, chairs and all manner of bric-a-brac.

'Yippee,' said Rachel. 'This is my absolute favourite sort of place.'

Nell felt less certain, and could not work out why. She knew about shabby chic of course. Even 19a Gardiner Road had sported a stack of Cath Kidston cake tins, a crocheted throw on the sofa and a couple of distressed storm lanterns. Perhaps this shop's sheer convolution of random objects made her feel claustrophobic. All those guitars, post horns, clocks, barometers, milk churns and carved wooden chairs shoved haphazardly together behind the glass.

'What's up?' Rachel, as ever, had recognised something was wrong.

'I don't know where to start.' Which was true. But even as she said it Nell knew that it wasn't just that.

'Leave it to me,' Rachel declared. 'Inside this frustrated lawyer lurks a frustrated interior designer.'

She dived through the doors of the shop, Juno at her heels. Nell followed and found Rachel excitedly examining sewing machines and milking stools. She was lifting up painted plates and staring assessingly at pictures that had slipped sideways in their frames. She was clearly in her element.

Nell stood awkwardly and uselessly as Rachel picked up carpets and candlesticks and old chapel collection boxes. She watched her peering at patchwork quilts and rocking chairs and walking sticks and fur coats. Some of these things she gave to Juno and told her to take them to the front desk.

'Hang on,' Nell said, seeing a standard lamp with an outlandish fringed shade being selected.

Rachel turned to her. 'Trust me. We can change the shade. But look at this lovely woodwork.' The base of the lamp was slender and graceful. 'It's oak,' Rachel added. 'It will polish up beautifully. And it's so *cheap*!'

Before Nell could argue, Rachel sent Juno off with the lamp and hurried to examine a corner full of chairs and tables. She looked at them, and back at the notes she had taken in the cottage. She had a plan, Nell realised. Somehow Rachel could see past the clutter to pick out exactly what would work in Beggar's Roost.

Nell followed her past radios and handbags with rusty clasps. Royal mugs by the dozen stood on shelves beside lines of dusty glassware. One corner had a collection of gloomily slow-ticking grandfather clocks. Another had oak furniture and smelt pleasantly of beeswax. 'Perfect!' Rachel said, lifting the lid of a dark oak carved chest big enough for a man to hide in. 'That will look brilliant at the back of your sitting room. Ooh, and so will these!'

Nell watched her friend swoop on a couple of small armchairs. 'Look! Distressed leather! You'd pay a fortune for these in London!'

And in the catalogues she used to work on, Nell thought. An Englishman's Castle had charged infinitely more for chairs that were inferior to the ones Rachel was now poking and prodding. 'We'll have these,' she told a passing assistant, whilst whipping a pile of framed prints from beneath the very noses of a couple stooping to examine them. Then she disappeared, only to reappear with an armful of antique jugs of different shapes, colours and sizes. 'For your kitchen shelves!' Next she materialised with a box of assorted crockery: flower-print cups and saucers with gilt rims and tiny, delicate handles. 'For your cupboards!'

Nell lost her again, until a familiar purple-clad, pink-faced figure hoved into view waving a couple of lamps and saying that she had spotted the perfect bookcase. Then she returned with a small desk. Another table appeared, then a bench. Then a chest and another standard lamp. The pile beside the front desk was growing.

The women behind it, a purse-lipped pair, eyed the heap of purchases. 'Going to need a removal van to carry this lot.'

Nell was feeling distinctly anxious now. There was a limit to the Land Rover's capacity, not to mention that of her own funds. 'We've probably got enough stuff,' she said, discovering Rachel flicking through a box of Edwardian postcards.

She had now, also, realised that disturbed her about the place. With its vintage radiograms, Utility furniture, faded cushions, cabinets of ornaments and black-and-white photographs in thin wooden frames – especially those – it reminded her powerfully of George's cottage. It was like an extended, rambling, much less tidy version of his home.

The things that she was looking at, the things that, Rachel

had piled up by the counter, had belonged to old people like him. They had been bought in particular circumstances, for particular reasons. A lot of them – the old dolls, say – had been bought with love and other items – the vintage dresses, the worn-heeled shoes – with hope.

It seemed to Nell both possible and unbearable that the home George had shared with Edwina, all the things in it that they had bought together and loved, should end up somewhere like this. Edwina's silver brushes. George's shaving mirror. Being picked over by strangers, commented on, rejected. All these treasured, personal, dignified things.

'Listen to this!' Rachel, still rummaging in the postcards, pulled out a black-and-white view of 'The Valley Gardens, Mablethorpe'. '"Mother sends her best regards and hopes that you received the parcel."'

'Sounds like code.' Juno admiring herself in a top hat in front of a long mirror. 'Mother is obviously the mastermind of an evil gang. The parcel is probably drugs. Or a dead body.'

Rachel laughed. She looked at Nell, who had sunk down on to a stool and was sitting there silently.

'Whatever's the matter?' Rachel's lively dark eyes were full of concern. She called to Juno. 'We'd better go.'

Outside, Nell tried to explain about George. But it was difficult to give the full picture without bringing Adam Greenleaf into it. She finished with the feeling that her hasty, broad-brush version of events had failed to convince the others.

'But everything we've bought is going to a good home,' Juno pointed out. 'We're not treating any of it with disrespect.'

'She's right,' Rachel said. 'I think you're being a bit mawkish, to be honest. It's people that matter, not the things they leave behind.'

This was, of course, unarguable. Especially coming from

Rachel. 'You can't stop time,' she counselled. 'And you shouldn't get upset about places like this.' She waved a hand towards the cluttered shop. 'They do everyone a service. The stuff all gets mixed up and moved on and people like us buy it and give it a new home.'

'But George,' Nell wailed. 'What if he can't go back home?'

'George sounds like he's moving into a different part of his life now. He needs a lot of care. And he'll get it, I'm sure.'

Nell glanced back through the windows to their pile of purchases by the till. Rachel had arranged to come back with the Land Rover to pick it all up. She knew Juno was right. Every item, once in Beggar's Roost, would be cherished.

'You're being very kind to him by the sound of it,' Rachel assured her. 'But you're worrying about him too much.'

'But where will he go if they throw him out of the hospital?'

'They won't throw him out. He'll be well looked after.'

'But *where*?' Nell's tone was almost fierce now. She could not let it go.

'I don't know. Ask the doctors. Look, Nell. You're not responsible for everything that happens to him.' She paused. 'I have to say, this all seems a bit disproportionate. Don't you think you might be dragging a few other issues in here as well?'

Nell could see this was a possibility. The antiques centre was, in its way, a temple of rejection, a storehouse of discarded things deemed no longer useful by their owners. Perhaps she was projecting some of her own buried feelings of abandonment, her anger at being deserted by Joey. Or was it all to do with a tall man with dark eyes she couldn't make up her mind about and who made her feel nervous and out of control?

Maybe this was all a bit deep for a Saturday morning. 'I'm sorry,' she muttered. She was being self-indulgent, and the weekend was Rachel and Juno's treat.

'You are forgiven,' Rachel said. 'Now do you mind if I go back in because I haven't quite finished.'

'Nor me,' Juno said quickly. 'I'd just found a Ladybird *Book of Spies*.'

They remained another entire hour. Rachel had by then added to the pile a silver tray, the entire leather-bound works of Dickens, a Venetian mirror intended for the bathroom, some apparently unused embroidered linen napkins and a set of champagne glasses. Juno, meanwhile, had bought the code post-card from Mablethorpe, the *Book of Spies* and a fob watch that had one of its hands missing. She wore this proudly tucked round one of the belt loops of her jeans.

Everything Rachel had chosen was perfect for the cottage. Nell could see this even as they unpacked the back of the Land Rover. She was already sorting the items out into piles for different rooms.

With what seemed amazing speed, the armchairs were positioned, the pictures hung, the chest pushed against the wall, the jugs and glasses arranged on the shelves, the rugs put down and the Venetian mirror placed in the bathroom. In the course of a morning, the formerly empty-feeling Beggar's Roost had taken on the aspect of a home.

There was plenty more to do; beds, for example. But as starts went, it was a good one. The cottage already felt more welcoming than Gardiner Road ever had.

'Next week, when you come up, it will be ready,' Nell promised the others.

That afternoon, Rachel drove her to the hospital in the Red Baron, warning her not to get too upset or too involved.

Nell went alone to George's private room. Rachel claimed she had some coursework reading to do but Nell sensed she wanted to avoid the situation. She felt she had done George a disfavour somehow with her half-description of what had happened; the harmless old man was now cast as the villain of the piece.

There were no stories from George today. He was asleep. Nell went over to Jasjit. She was behind the nurses' station frowning into a computer.

'How are things?' Nell crossed her fingers behind her back.

Jasjit looked up and smiled. 'We're moving him from his room on to the main ward.'

Nell's face lit up. 'But isn't that great news?'

The nurse pulled a face. 'It doesn't mean much, to be honest. Just that he can survive without the machines now.'

Nell, nonetheless determined to see this as a positive development, went back to George's bedside and softly pressed the vein-roped hand. 'See you later,' she whispered.

'Dive, Nobby,' George muttered. 'Dive right down into the master searchlight. It's the only way. Get below the level of Messerschmitts. Then they'll leave us alone.'

CHAPTER 44

It was the interval, and Nell, Rachel and Juno stood in the bar of the Pavilion Theatre, Chestlock.

Juno, resplendent in her Marple costume, was sipping a Coke and expounding her theories as to who'd dunnit. 'It's never who you think. And almost always it's a crime of passion.'

'My money's on Bertie Spiffing,' Rachel declared. 'He's definitely got something to hide. No one could be quite that stupid.'

Juno consulted her copious notes. 'It could be Curate Segg. That business with the coffee cups was suspicious. But I'm pretty certain it's Signora Stiletto.' She glanced up at Nell. 'What do you think?'

Nell, hand clamped round a large glass of chilled rosé, shrugged. All she thought was that things, finally, seemed to be going well.

Beggar's Roost, with all its new-old furniture, felt so homely now that in their usual impetuous fashion Rachel and Juno had insisted on staying there tonight rather than the honeymoon suite. Jason had willingly lent them the put-up bed for Juno, plus two others. It would be basic, but fun. They had even bought logs and coal for the fire.

'Strangle the gamekeeper's a definite possibility too,' Juno was musing. 'I wish they'd murder Pierrot, though; he's the worst actor I've ever seen.'

Nell was surprised how busy the place was; Agatha Christie-type murder mysteries were clearly very popular. She'd never heard of any of the actors, although Juno had. According to her, Gilly Davenport, the actress playing Miss Mandrake, had been in lots of similar productions, as had Pete Leather, who played Major Wilderbeest and had been shot in the first act.

Nell had to agree with Juno's assessment of Caradoc Turner. He was hopelessly miscast as a sleuth, having none of the requisite calm and calculation. Rather, he seemed to radiate agitation with his insanely staring eyes, glistening bared teeth and manic walk. The ends of his fingers twitched ominously.

Elsewhere in the bar, Angela Highwater swigged the rest of her sweet white wine. She felt like a fish out of water; this was emphatically not her scene. She hadn't thought the audience for murder would be so ancient. When you were that close to the grave, you might want to avoid so many references to it.

She took another swig and yawned. She was wearing a tight lemon dress teamed with a clinging leather jacket in dusty pink. Her heels were their usual skyscraper height and her hair wound wildly around her head. Her latest handbag, encrusted with diamanté, swung from her manicured hand on twisted silk cords. She looked fabulous, she knew, but she was aware of dressing at least fifty years younger than everyone else present. There were an awful lot of white Crimplene pleats and sandals that put bunions before beauty. And that was just the men.

Everywhere Angela looked, bespectacled eyes were narrowed in her direction. Pursed, wrinkled lips muttered to each other behind programmes. The old bats were staring at her as if she had designs on the husbands who stood or slumped beside them like wrecked ships. Dream on, Angela thought.

Even the women behind the bar – maternal types who seemed to know their customers by name ('of course I'll pop some ice in that for you, Doris'), were looking at her disapprovingly as they dispensed large plastic bags of boiled sweets in advance of the second half. The deafening volume of her neighbour working his way through some chocolate limes had made it hard, at times, for Angela to hear the first couple of acts.

The prospect of yet more crackling plastic in the second half, not to mention the chomping and grinding of dentures mere inches from her ears, made Angela briefly consider getting the whole business over with now. Was there time to rush round to the stage door and deliver the message she had come with?

Possibly not, she was forced to accept. The interval was only fifteen minutes and she'd spent half of that trying to get served. The stage door, moreover, was round the other side of the building.

As soon as the play ended, she'd be round there like a shot, as it were, ha ha. Until then, there was the whole of the second act to endure. She'd lost the plot ages ago; there were at least ten possible murderers although she couldn't remember their motives. Only the Major had bitten the dust by the interval, which meant nine to go. Would it ever end?

She avoided the condemning gazes by pretending to study the programme again. In his photograph, Caradoc Turner looked defeated. Having to stick on a moustache every night and drive the length and breadth of Britain probably got you that way.

She pictured Caradoc in his dressing room now, reapplying his make-up in a mirror framed with blazing bulbs. What a shock he had coming to him! But what would he do with the information that his young wife had been unfaithful to him with the local Lothario – or Lawn-thario, given Dan's occupation?

Physical reprisals looked unlikely. Angela had scrutinised Pierrot in the first half and concluded that, while his Belgian accent was touch and go, it was typecasting on the shortness front.

As Caradoc was hardly a size to tackle a man-mountain like Dan, he'd have to come up with something more ingenious than mere violence. But that was his problem. Angela didn't care. She would have got her revenge by then.

The front of house manager, his white shirt straining across his belly, now came through ringing his bell. 'Layzandgennelmen, please take your seats, the second act of *Murderous Death* is about to begin . . .'

Shuffling back down the corridor from the bar with the rest of the elderly crowd, Angela was surprised when her gaze fell on three people whose hair was not the permed white frizz of most other attendees.

There was a tall blonde, a small brunette and a child. She recognised the blonde, but who were these other people? Angela, for whom knowledge was power, had to find out.

She darted forward, skewering several elderly bunions on the way. Plastering on her sweetest smile, she tapped Nell on the back, summoning her best friendly manner. 'Nell! How are you? How's it going?'

Nell jumped, turned and found herself looking at the Director of Human Resources. This was the first time she had seen Angela since the transformation of Beggar's Roost. Nell was still not certain that she shared Julie's trenchant views as to her motives – why *would* Angela dislike her so much? But she was certainly more suspicious now.

As Angela was gazing expectantly at her, Nell waved cautiously at her two companions. 'This is my friend Rachel and her daughter Juno.'

Angela nodded curtly. They looked frankly bizarre to her. The woman had strange purple hair and what *was* that child wearing? She returned her attention to Nell. 'So how's the local heroine? And the local heroes? The lovely Mr Greenleaf?'

Angela was fishing. She hadn't seen Adam Greenleaf for some days now. Had he been with this wretched woman?

Seeing that Nell did not reply, Rachel seized on the name. 'Mr Greenleaf?'

Angela, with her nose for intrigue, sensed she had hit on something. Something, by the look on Nell Simpson's face, that she didn't want her friend to know about. Bingo!

'Ooh yes,' Angela cackled. 'The lovely Adam! She hasn't told you about him? And his kiss of life!'

'Layzangennelmen . . .' The bell was ringing. Only the four of them stood outside the auditorium now.

'Who does he think is the gentleman?' Juno hissed.

As they were ushered hurriedly to their seats, and Angela sashayed off into the gloom, Rachel nudged Nell. '*Adam Greenleaf?*'

'I'll tell you later,' Nell muttered.

'You've gone bright red,' Juno said loudly. 'I can even see it in the dark.'

Murderous Death was finally over. The last bow had been hogged by Candice Floss and Caradoc was free to go. Home, to Juliet at Birch Hall. His taxi would be waiting outside, even now.

Perhaps it was disappointing that she hadn't been to his last night. But the play was hardly one to increase his stature in her eyes; a stature which, as it was, needed all the help it could get.

But he made up for it in other ways, as she was about to find out.

He would possess her at last!

So excited was Caradoc that his clothes slipped in his hands as he changed and he kept dropping things. But at last he was packed and ready to go home. His last act was to grind the Pierrot moustache very hard into the gritty dressing-room floor.

Gripping the handle of his rolling suitcase, he paused at the door and took one unregretful last look around. Then he strode out in his built-up heels and made his way down the murky corridor to the front of house.

The bar, to his surprise, was empty. The hideous pattern of the uninhabited carpet blared up at him. The rest of the cast, the barlady informed him, had already departed in the minibus.

'But they've left you these, love.' The barlady, whose badge read 'Ivy', handed over a wrapped rectangular box with a ribbon round it. A label dangled from it: *To Caradoc, from your fellow Backstabbers. Let's stay in touch, it's been a pleasure.*

'Aw,' said Ivy, craning her neck to read. 'That's nice of 'em.'

Caradoc remembered the old theatrical adage. 'When you say let's stay in touch and it's been a pleasure, chances are that you won't and it wasn't.'

'Go on,' Ivy urged. 'Open it.'

Caradoc peeled off the paper. It was a box of chocolates: a black and pink box tied with black grosgrain ribbon.

'Ooh,' said Ivy longingly.

Reluctantly, Caradoc opened the box and offered her one. It took some time for Ivy to read each description on the lid before making her selection. 'I'm going for this one!' she exclaimed. 'Salted Caramel Surprise. A tongue-tingling tangle of toffee and smoked Himalayan salt enrobed in rich chocolate made with organic Welsh milk!'

'Delicious,' said Caradoc, thinking impatiently of the taxi outside.

Ivy, meanwhile, had alighted on another option. 'Ooh, hang on. Maybe I'll have Eton Mess Sundae! A decadent explosion of meringue-studded raspberry ripple chocolate filled with raspberry ganache!' As she looked up at him, eyes shining, Caradoc reflected that this was probably the only genuinely pleasurable moment to occur in the theatre all night.

'I forgot to tell you,' Ivy murmured, eyes swivelling between Eton Mess and Salted Caramel. 'There's someone waiting for you outside.'

'The taxi,' Caradoc said.

'No, love. It's a woman. She were at the stage door but I sent her round the front.'

'*What?*'

His wife! Caradoc's heart lifted; more than that, it soared. Juliet had done better than come to see him in the play, she had actually come to meet him at the stage door! Could there be any clearer sign that this was the beginning of a whole new phase in their marriage? Now, tonight, at last . . .

A great rush of lust surged through him. His own Juliet! Pure and unsullied, whatever that bastard Leather had insinuated in Peterborough. And had insinuated again, last night, in Tunbridge Wells.

Of course Juliet had not been unfaithful. She would never dream of such a thing. Which was just as well, Caradoc thought, now swirling with violent desire, as he really would not hesitate to kill anyone who usurped his bed. The bed from which he had been kept for so long but which, tonight, like a returning hero, he would triumphantly conquer.

'I think I'll go for the Salted Caramel,' Ivy said, her digits poised to dive.

But it was too late; Caradoc had shoved the lid back on the chocolates, grabbed his suitcase and rushed out.

A woman was there, sure enough, but despite the lamplit gloom he could see immediately that it wasn't Juliet with her long hair and tight yet floaty clothes. This woman wore clumsy high heels and a tarty dress. Her hair stuck out in all directions.

Caradoc was confused. A fan? She didn't look like one. Most stage-door Johnnies had six fingers and tea-cosy hats. He fumbled for his pen. 'Shall I sign your programme?'

'You can if you like,' came the unexpected reply. 'But I've come here to give you some information. It's about your wife.'

'My *wife*?' Caradoc gasped, thinking immediately of the garden full of poison. 'What's happened to her?'

'Dan Parker,' was the grim response.

Later that night, glass of wine in hand, before the fireplace of Beggar's Roost, Nell described her various encounters with Adam Greenleaf. She had hoped to feel relief in the unburdening, but Rachel's face was giving nothing away.

Rachel spoke only after Nell had finished. 'Gotta hand it to you,' she remarked. 'You do like a drama. First Joey, and now this.'

'There's no resemblance,' Nell replied sharply, stung by the suggestion. 'I'm not involved with Adam, for a start.'

Rachel narrowed her eyes. 'I hope not.'

'He's just a bloke who works round here. Who I've met before.'

'Yes. In pubs in peculiar circumstances.'

Nell stared into the flames, blushing. Rachel had asked some very probing questions, especially about the scene in Paddington. 'Why didn't you say anything about that before?' she asked accusingly.

'Because I thought it made me look stupid,' Nell admitted.

Rachel, diplomatically, did not reply to this. 'It all sounds very complicated,' she concluded. 'But I have to say this Adam Greenleaf sounds slightly, well . . .'

'What?'

'Weird.'

'The first time you see him inside a pub he pretends to be someone else. The second time you see him outside a pub you row with him. Then he turns up in an old man's garden out of the blue . . .'

'Saving his life,' Nell felt compelled to point out.

'I think you should keep away from him,' Rachel said sternly.

'I wasn't planning to do anything else,' Nell said indignantly. 'He did save George's life, though,' she couldn't resist repeating.

Rachel rolled her eyes. 'Granted. And that was great, obviously. Amazing, admirable, heroic.' She paused. 'But that doesn't make him sound any less dubious. I'd definitely give him a wide berth if I were you.'

CHAPTER 45

'Feeling bloody awful, mate,' Dan groaned.

'What's the matter?' Dylan yawned into the mobile. It was early Monday morning and he wasn't quite conscious.

''Orrible stomach ache.' Dan took a rasping, painful breath before continuing, as if with his last effort. 'Don't think I'm going to make it today, mate.'

When Dylan arrived at Kenilworth Lodge alone, Mrs Palethorpe was unimpressed to hear about Dan's malady. 'Well, he had better recover soon,' she said curtly. 'There's a great deal to do in this garden and I can't have people letting me down.' She handed over the inevitable list and strode off, the sharp pleats of her skirt slicing the air.

The list, Dylan saw, was even longer than the previous week's. But as most of it was weeding, that suited him. The repetitive task freed up the mind. He could think about Nell, as much as he wanted.

And he hadn't wanted to, but he couldn't help it. Dan's words kept coming back to him. *She's bloody gorgeous. Come on. You can't fool me. I saw her give you that look, and I saw you give 'er a look back an' all.*

He should keep out of her way, even so. It wasn't as if their encounters so far had been particularly straightforward. And he'd vowed never to get involved with women again.

I'd definitely give him a wide berth . . . Rachel and Juno had left on the Sunday afternoon, but her friend's warnings were still ringing in Nell's ears when she arrived at Weddings on Monday.

She resolved to throw herself into her work and forget about Adam Greenleaf. There was plenty else to occupy her anyway. Julie wanted to know all about the weekend at Beggar's Roost, the furniture that had been bought, Nell's plans for the garden. It was touching to see, as Nell heaped praise on her husband, Julie's proud blushes. Good, solid men like Tim were a much better bet than mysterious gardeners.

'Right,' Julie said eventually, putting down her 'Bridezilla' coffee mug. 'To work. And the first thing you need to know about the weddings department on Monday is that it means a full inbox. Brides spend the weekend talking to people, looking online, going to other weddings, even. They've usually got a few, um, *thoughts.* Come and see.'

Nell went round to the back of Julie's chair. As she had predicted, her inbox was black with unopened mail. There were ten from Carly, fifteen from Hannah and twenty-one from Will.

As Julie began to open them. Nell read them over her shoulder. 'They've all completely changed their minds! I can't believe it. They all seemed so sure.'

'They always do,' Julie said wearily. 'The sure ones are the worst, in fact. What I've learned in this job is that there's nothing sure about a wedding until it's over.'

'You're not joking,' Nell said, with an emphasis she rather regretted. Fortunately, Julie was too deep in the emails to notice.

Nell read on. Josh and Hannah's festival-themed wedding

was now nudging into pagan territory. Hannah was wondering about a shaman and a tarot reader.

'They want a cake to throw over Hannah's head,' Julie mused, several emails further down. 'It's all about fertility, apparently. Pagans used to throw or crumble the cake over the bride.'

'Messy. Imagine all those crumbs down your front.'

Julie was reading on. 'It's got to be flat and round. And have fruit and nuts in it.'

'Sounds as if a packet of biscuits would do. How do you cope with this? It's madness.'

Julie looked up, grinning. 'The secret of this job is to get round things. It gets a lot worse than this. Oooh . . . speak of the devil. New email from Carly!'

Nell had gone back to her desk now. She watched Julie's face change from apprehension to amazement as she read the communication. 'You're not going to believe this . . .'

'Go on.'

'They want a period dance instructor. I thought I'd heard it all, but . . .'

'A what?'

'Someone who can teach them to waltz, polka, whatever. Carly mentions the mazurka.'

'They're planning a ball now?'

'Yup. A *Pride and Prejudice* candlelit ball. And get this, they want it in the house.'

'In Pemberton?'

Julie nodded. 'To get the full Pemberley effect, they say.'

'Surely that's not possible. What about the fire risk? And all the antiques?'

Julie smiled at her. Her unending cheeriness was amazing, Nell thought. 'At Pemberton, anything's possible. Although this is a bit left field, I'll give you that. We'll have to see what His Lordship has to say.'

At lunchtime they went down to the stable-yard café for chicken, basil and avocado salad. The food was delicious and staff discounts, Nell had discovered, were generous.

'Oh look,' she said, spotting a familiar figure in the distance. 'We can ask him about Carly's candles right now.'

The Earl was earnestly engaging a pair of old ladies over a cup of tea. Spotting Nell and Julie, he hurried towards them.

'Ladies over there have just been telling me there's too much jam in the Victoria sponge. And not enough raisins in the scones.' The Earl shook his head before looking impishly at Julie. 'Bridezillas behaving themselves?'

Julie grinned. 'Much the same.'

'Still changing their minds all the time?'

As Julie explained the latest *Pride and Prejudice* development, Nell watched the Earl's face, anticipating horror as he contemplated blazing candles among his treasures. He looked, instead, thoughtful.

'House is licensed for weddings, of course. Not sure about naked flames, though. Housekeeper might have something to say, all that wax dropping on her floors.'

Julie was nodding in agreement.

'On the other hand,' said the Earl, 'houses like Pemberton are meant to be used. They were built for parties, for big events.' He paused. 'How much did you say they were prepared to pay?'

Julie named the sum. 'Hmm. Not bad. Could get two whole paintings restored for that.' He stood up. 'Leave it with me, ladies.' He smiled again, raised his hand and walked off.

CHAPTER 46

When Dan was no better on the Tuesday morning, Dylan knew it must be serious. Tuesday was Birch Hall and Mrs Turner. Yet it was obvious from his voice that Dan could hardly stand up, let alone perform to the level that Dylan had overheard.

'Shouldn't you go and see a doctor?' he suggested.

'Nah, mate,' came the choked and agonised reply. 'I'll be reight enough.'

'You sound awful, though.' It seemed to Dylan that his boss was being ludicrously stoical. He pictured him, alone in the scruffy house on the bleak estate.

'I'll be reight,' Dan repeated.

'You must have eaten something.'

'Nowt out o' t'ordinary.'

The ordinary was quite bad enough. From what Dylan could gather, Dan lived on a diet of fish and chips alternated with pizza and kebabs.

'OK,' Dylan said resignedly. 'I'll go to Birch Hall on my own.'

He thought gloomily of the dark and knotty grounds.

'What?' Dan was saying something. Dylan pressed his ear closer to the phone.

'They don't want us there any more.'

'Why not?'

'Mr Turner. Says he's going to. Do it from now on,' Dan could only managed a few words at a time.

'*Mr Turner?*' The actor husband, Dylan recalled. The peripatetic star of touring murder mystery productions. 'He's back home then?'

Dan gave an affirmitive grunt.

'And he's going to do all the gardening?'

Dan grunted again.

It made no sense to Dylan. Why would Turner – why would anyone – want to take on that Forth Bridge of a garden all by himself? It was too much work for two people, let alone one. Dylan pictured the thespian squire of Birch Hall as a small man in spats with a Poirot moustache gingerly approaching the rhododendrons with a hacksaw.

But why? It could hardly be expense; Birch Hall, like Mrs Palethorpe, paid the minimum wage. There must be something else.

And of course, potentially, there was. If Mr Turner had found out about Dan and his wife, he would obviously be furious and wouldn't hesitate to sack him. So, had he found out. Did he know?

'Came to tell me in person, he did, Mr Turner,' Dan croaked. 'Very nice about it, he was.'

'He came to your house?' Dylan now abandoned the angry cuckold theory. While it wasn't beyond the bounds of possibility that the deceived Turner might have confronted Dan, it really wasn't likely that he would have been nice about it.

'Very friendly, 'e were. Thanked me and gave me some chocolates. Said it were for everything I'd done. *Oooohhh,*' Dan groaned, as if the effort of talking had doubled his agony.

The sound was so awful that Dylan decided firm action was necessary. 'I'm taking you to the hospital. Now.'

He slammed out of Bess's Tower and leapt into the hatchback. As he tore down the track between the trees he told himself there was nothing to worry about. Dan had probably just had a dodgy kebab. But as the ghastly groaning echoed in his mind, Dylan put his foot down.

He drove like the wind to Dan's house, playing fast and loose with the speed cameras. He roared through the ramshackle estate, narrowly avoiding a paper boy simultaneously smoking, consulting his mobile and staggering under a bag of tabloids.

Dylan drew up with a screech of brakes and leapt out of the car almost before he had turned the engine off. Dan's smashed gate slammed back against the wrecked fence as he shoved it open and sped up the broken path. Urgently, he thumped on the dirty front door with its boarded-up window.

Dan took some minutes to shuffle to the door, but it took only one look for all Dylan's fears to be realised. His employer's eyes burned feverishly in his face and his huge jaw had a sickly yellow tinge. He hung over his feet, rocking slightly as if he might collapse at any moment.

Glancing down the hall, Dylan could see a shabby sitting room containing a battered sofa.

He helped Dan out to the car. The usual boys were roistering past, smoking, shoving each other and swearing.

'Awright, Shagger?' one of them called.

'Shag-*ger*, Shag-*ger*!' chanted the others.

Dylan was touched to see that even in extremis Dan was capable of an appreciative, if weak, thumbs-up.

He went back into the house to get Dan a change of clothes. Admittedly, he'd never seen him in one but there might be something clean somewhere.

Spotting a chocolate box on the sitting room's grubby carpet, he picked it up. Presumably these were the ones Turner had brought for Dan. The box was empty. Was it this that had made Dan sick?

Dylan studied the lid. Eton Mess Sundae sounded pretty sickly. As did Salted Caramel Surprise. But even eating the whole lot in one go wouldn't make you that ill, surely?

Dylan put the box back down and went into Dan's bedroom. Black flowery paper was peeling off the wall. The bed was just a mattress on the floor covered by a crumpled, dirty sheet. Dylan's heart twisted. The room shouted grottiness, but it also shouted loneliness and neglect.

He decided not to rummage in the drawers. There was no telling what might be in them. Fresh and laundered underwear seemed unlikely. Instead he shut up the house and went out to the car.

They set off. Dylan had no idea where the hospital was, but figured that Chestlock was bound to have one somewhere. After driving round a couple of the out-of-town roundabouts he spotted what he had been looking for: the red sign with the white H in the middle.

Chestlock Hospital looked about the size of a small town; a row of distant buildings fronted by vast acres of car park. All of which seemed solidly full. But eventually Dylan reversed into a vacant spot and began the by-no-means-simple task of getting Dan across the miles between Car Park Q and the hospital front entrance.

Dan had given up protesting now. He was evidently fading fast and his massive frame weighed heavily on the slighter Dylan as they staggered past the hospital bus shelters in which vastly overweight people, presumably recent beneficiaries of expert medical attention, sucked violently on cigarettes.

The hospital building itself, a sprawling glass-and-steel erection, reminded Dylan unpleasantly of the place he had spent so many months in following the fire. He took his déjà vu strongly in hand, however. This was no time for self-indulgence.

Settling Dan flat out on a row of burgundy plastic seats in the reception area, Dylan hurried to the welcome desk. 'It's an emergency,' he told the bull-necked woman behind the computer monitor.

She flicked him the briefest glance before frowning back into her screen and tapping keys. There was a chugging, grinding noise. A plump hand thrust a piece of paper at him on which was printed a number. 'Wait until you see that on the screen,' she said.

There were screens hanging above the seating areas, on which large numbers appeared. The one showing at the moment was 44. The number on Dylan's paper was 86.

He cast a look over his shoulder. Dan was lying on his back on the seats, one arm dangling to the floor. He turned back to the receptionist. 'I'm not sure he's going to live that long. He's very ill.'

The woman gave a weary sigh. 'Name? NHS number?'

'I don't know about the number. But his name's Dan Parker.'

A miraculous transformation now occurred. An expression best described as dreamy now softened the receptionist's harsh features. She raised herself from her chair slightly and stared at Dan over the counter-top. 'Bloody 'ell. It's Shagger!'

She spoke with a certain wistfulness. Dylan blinked.

'You're right. He doesn't look good. Go back to yer seat, love. I'll see what I can do.' She picked up the phone and muttered into it.

Dylan returned to what remained of his employer. Dan

seemed to be ebbing fast. His breathing was rapid and rasping. Dylan had heard of a death rattle: was this it? He patted the massive, grubby hand, its nails edged with dirt, surprised at the fondness he felt for him. 'Come on Dan,' he muttered. 'Fight it.'

CHAPTER 47

A few miles from where Dylan sat, Julie and Nell were at a Wedding Fayre. It was held in a run-down Victorian hotel whose large ballroom, which must have been the scene of many a proud nineteenth-century civic gathering, was now packed with stalls offering contemporary wedding essentials.

Nell walked around, fascinated. Her first stop, Sassy Seating, displayed chairs wearing skirts of organdie and damask teamed with contrasting bows and sashes. 'They look better than most of the brides,' Julie muttered.

No detail had been overlooked. There were white post boxes for party venues into which guests could slip cards for the happy couple. There were chocolates on sticks on which names could be handwritten for table placements. There were any number of complex invitation options; the 'Save the Date' industry in particular was growing apace. 'Thistle with Custard on top is the most popular combination at the moment,' the stallholder told Nell. Custard and Thistle were both ink colours.

Through the ballroom's huge windows, beribboned VW camper vans by the score stood in the car park. 'From Colombia,' a florist told Nell when she asked where the white hydrangeas arranged in jam jars had originated. It seemed a long way to go for that casual English hedgerow look. Another florist displayed vases of dead roses: 'The Gothic vibe is really in at the moment.'

Huge men who looked like bouncers were selling discos. They were surrounded by so many laptops and other technical devices they looked as if they were launching a space programme.

The First Dances Company offered to immortalise that special moment of the wedding reception in forms ranging from DVDs to oil paintings to specially created perfumes. 'It's one of the key decisions of the whole wedding,' Nell was told.

A photographer with floppy auburn hair specialised in the 'engagement' photo album. This, he explained, was the essential adjunct to the wedding album; the prequel, as it were. The recording of the actual proposal moment.

Nell looked through a sample album featuring a happy couple-to-be posed in a sunlit meadow next to an artfully arranged bicycle whose wicker basket overflowed with daisies. She suppressed a sigh. In her case, the prequel had been the happiest period of the whole ghastly business.

'Why do people want pictures of the proposal?' Julie was asking. 'It's a private moment.'

'It's the hashtag selfie effect,' the photographer enlightened them. 'People are used to having every moment of their lives immortalised on Instagram.'

'But what if the bride said no?'

'Well, she's unlikely to do that because the groom will have had a persuasion masterclass with someone from *The Apprentice*.' Nell laughed.

'Doing anything later?' the photographer asked her.

She recoiled instantly; made an excuse. 'But why?' Julie demanded, as they moved off.

Nell was defensive. 'Isn't it a bit sleazy, picking people up at wedding fairs?'

'Don't see why. Maybe it makes them feel romantic.'

This idea seemed to Nell as fantastic as the sassy seating and as unlikely as custard combined with thistle.

As they passed the hospital on the way back to Edenville, Julie dropped Nell off at the entrance. Making her way through the reception preoccupied with thoughts of George, she did not notice the two men at the back of the vast space, one lying along the seat and the other watching him. Nor did they notice her.

Was George's move to a general ward a good thing, Nell wondered. She was less certain now. It seemed very noisy. Children were running up and down. Large mothers in straining trousers were rebuking them loudly. 'Tiffany-Grace! Carlsberg! Will you come and bloody well sit down *now*?'

George's eyes were closed but he seemed restless. He had been fretting, Jasjit told Nell. 'Been lying there with his eyes shut, muttering to himself about beards and lanks and whatnot. What are lanks anyway?'

'Planes,' Nell said. 'The ones he flew during the war.'

Jasjit whistled. 'Quite the hero.'

'Definitely.'

'You been in touch with your hero yet? The one who rescued George?' The nurse's voice was teasing.

'No,' Nell said firmly.

Jasjit cackled. 'You're blushing!'

The old man's eyes had been shut, but now they opened and Nell experienced the usual surprise of seeing how very bright they were. He looked directly at her and for a second she could see the usual amazed hope in them, followed by the realisation that she was not, after all, his wife. 'Garden?' he managed, after a few attempts to speak.

Nell thought of all the beauty the old man was missing. 'It's fine. I'm looking after it.'

Had George any idea that he would probably never work in it again?

She talked to him about his vegetable beds, how Juno had enjoyed watering them. But George did not seem in the mood for a chat. He kept closing his eyes and seemed more tired. He was muttering; she bent over to hear.

'It were thrilling . . . I never expected in a million years to go up in a plane; no one from my background did. It were like being in a film . . . and Edwina looked like a film star. Blonde. Her hair were parted in the centre and curled into her neck. Her smile . . .'

War and love, love and war. They were wired together in his mind. The two significant moments of his life. What, Nell wondered, had been the defining event of hers?

'I need to tell you something.' As Nell left, Jasjit came out from behind the nurses' station. Her eyes were grave. This was obviously bad news.

'He's not getting any stronger. He made a good start but he seems to have slipped back. He needs full-time care. It looks like he's going to have to go into a home.'

Nell bit her lip.

'He hasn't got any family, you see. No kids to look after him.'

Nell thought of Edwina. If the sorrow of her life had been her inability to have children, how much sadder she would be to think that lack of children had condemned George to a care home.

Skidding across Nell's mind now came the idea that she could somehow step in. Keep an eye on him. On the other hand, she worked all day. And George needed more than an eye, he needed full-time care. What if he fell, or had another heart attack?

She looked bleakly at Jasjit. 'Is a home the only option?'

'It's looking that way. But they're not all bad places. Some are pretty good.'

'It's just that he'll miss his garden so much.'

Jasjit looked sympathetic. 'I know. We're trying to find him somewhere with a nice one.'

Nell went out to the bus stop with a heavy heart.

Dylan, in the reception area, was starting to lose hope. The receptionist who had recognised Dan and who had seemed to promise so much, had not followed through. No doctor had yet appeared.

Dan, stretched out on the seats beside him, appeared to be groaning his last. The numbers on the large screen had been stuck at 53 for ages. Perhaps the system had broken down.

Meanwhile, on another large screen nearby – a half-smashed plasma – *Location, Location, Location* was getting under way. Dylan tried to forget about his own location and resigned himself to watching it.

'Mr Parker?'

An intelligent-looking young man in a green overall had appeared. 'I'm Dr Akim.' Behind him were two male nurses and a trolley. The former proceeded to heave Dan on to the latter and wheel him off.

'He's been very sick for two days,' Dylan said as he hurried along with the little group. It seemed to be all systems go, suddenly. 'It's all a bit mysterious.'

Dr Akim raised his handsome eyebrows. 'What does he do for a living?'

'He's a gardener.'

'Is he up to date on his tetanus, do you know?'

They had arrived in a small ward. The nurses were busily hooking Dan up to various monitors, chatting about last night's football results as they did so.

'I don't know.'

'It's because of the soil.' Dr Akim pushed back Dan's eyelid with a thumb and examined the colour of his eyeball.

'The soil?'

Dr Akim was squinting at the monitors now. 'The earth is full of unpleasant viruses that can make people very ill. Especially if they're exposed to them a lot.'

Dr Akim sent Dylan back to the reception area to wait. He gave no indication of how long things might take. On the other hand, as Birch Hall was no longer on the agenda, it wasn't as if Dylan had anything else to do.

He settled himself as well as he could on the hard plastic chair under the telly. Another daytime property programme had started. An apprehensive couple were being shown a blue-painted kitchen by a tanned and excitable blonde. The house seemed to be in Cornwall; cliffs and sea were visible through the windows.

Dylan decided to go outside, get some fresh air.

On the pavement overlooking the A&E arrival area, the air was blue. A cloud of smoke rose from a crowd of puffing patients. Some of the smokers had casts on their legs, others slings round their arms. Others had sticks; either one or two. They were all talking about online poker.

Dylan found himself fighting a sudden, sweeping nausea. The smoke smell had whisked him back to Bosun's Whistle.

He returned, shaken, to the reception area. 'Dr Akim came to look for you,' the receptionist told him.

Dylan slapped his forehead in frustration. He must have missed the doctor by seconds.

'I told him you must have popped out for a fag.'

'I certainly did not.' Dylan was indignant.

'Doctor told me to give you a message, anyway. They're keeping him in. For observation.'

'What does that mean?'

The receptionist shrugged. 'He didn't say. But what it usually means is . . .'

'Yes?' prompted Dylan urgently.

'That we should keep our fingers crossed.'

There was a blonde at one of the hospital bus stops, Dylan noticed as he passed en route to the car park. A blonde he felt he recognised. Then, as she turned and looked at him, he realised that not only did he recognise her, he had resolved to keep right away from her.

I'd give him a wide berth if I were you. Rachel's words rushed back to Nell as she stared into those eyes she had been seeing so often in her mind. But he was far too close to give him any berth, wide or otherwise.

'How's it going?' Dylan asked cautiously.

'Um. Fine. Fine, thanks.' She looked around for an escape. Not by bus, it seemed. According to the timetable, at least two should have been and gone by now.

'How's your neighbour?' he asked, and saw her face fall.

'Not well at all,' Nell admitted. 'They don't think he'll ever go back home.'

'That's a shame.'

'You could say that.' Nell wished he would go away. George's predicament made her feel emotionally volatile and she didn't want to lose control. Least of all and yet again in front of this person.

'That was a great garden.'

Nell looked at him. He'd been there in that garden, he knew what it was like, how beautiful the old man had made it. He had been there on the last occasion George had been there himself. 'I can't bear to think of him never going back there,' she said, feeling all her pent-up emotion rushing, suddenly, irresistably, to the surface.

Dylan watched her standing there, sobbing into her fingers. He felt he should do something, but what? He reached for her shoulder, gingerly, as if she were made of something that might melt at his touch, or explode. As he did so, a sense of wonder filled him. He had forgotten what it was like to touch a woman. Dylan reached out his other hand and let his shaking fingers make contact with her hair.

It juddered through Nell with the force of a thousand volts. It brought her back to her senses. She sprang back, embarrassed. 'I'm sorry!'

'It's fine.' Dylan said, feeling dazed. His finger-ends burned and his head was spinning.

She was hurrying away from him, down past the bus stops. Her hair was streaming behind her like a white flame. He was wondering whether to run after her, and what he would say if he did, when someone cut into his thoughts.

'Well!' came a deep, suggestive female voice. 'Fancy seeing you here! Our very own home-grown hero!'

It was the second time that afternoon that Dylan had had sudden, surprising contact with a woman he only vaguely knew. But this encounter was much less strange and magical. He found himself staring now, not into Nell's wide sapphire gaze, but the mascaraed Venus flytraps of Angela Highwater.

CHAPTER 48

A letter from the oncology department had called Angela to the hospital. They wanted to discuss with her the results of the tests she had recently undergone.

Of course it would be fine, Angela told herself. Nonetheless she had, on the drive there, felt uncharacteristically apprehensive.

Oncology departments brought back bad memories. As did hospitals. Her mother had died in one, years before, from breast cancer. This had marked a low point in Angela's life, one she never talked about. This did not mean that she never thought about it, however.

She was thinking about it now as she parked in one of the hospital car parks and walked up past the long line of bus stops.

A couple were clinging to each other, Angela noticed. And while there were plenty of couples clinging on to each other outside the hospital entrance, mostly for the purposes of standing upright, these ones caught Angela's eye. Not only were they doing it for seemingly romantic reasons, there was also something familiar about them.

It was only when, suddenly, the woman sprang back and dashed off, that Angela realised what the something was. The girl who now rushed unseeingly past her, blonde hair flying agitatedly about, was none other than that wretched Nell Simpson, bane of Angela's life.

While the man staring after her, arms still open in a bereft sort of fashion, was, to Angela's rage, Adam Greenleaf. Saviour of local pensioners, all-round hunk and the man she intended to be Dan Parker's successor in the supplying of sexual services.

She quickened her pace and greeted him in her best seductive voice. He gazed at her, seemingly baffled, but she soldiered on.

'Mr Greenleaf! Or can I call you Adam . . .'

'I've got to go,' Dylan gasped. His instinct, the first time he had met Angela, was that she was mad. And possibly dangerous. While there was no resemblance in looks, she had the same unhinged air as Beatrice. The contrast with the just-departed Nell was profound.

'Didn't realise you knew Nell *that* well,' Angela beamed. 'The way you were kissing her just then,' she prompted, caustically.

'I wasn't kissing her,' Dylan indignantly rebutted.

'Could have fooled me.' Angela maintained a mask of gay admonishment. But she really needed to get rid of Nell Simpson, and as soon as possible. Make her life such a misery that she'd have no option but to leave. The weddings department idea had misfired; as had the cottage. She would just have to think of something else.

As the conversation was not going well, and Dylan's desire to get away from her was depressingly obvious, Angela sought to show herself in a better light. 'I suppose you were visiting poor George Farley?' she asked sweetly. 'How is he, the dear?'

She saw a cloud pass over Dylan's handsome face. 'I was here with Dan, actually,' he said.

Angela's eyes bulged and she swayed on her heels, feeling, for a minute, the world spin about her.

What had happened to Dan had been the most tremendous shock. She had intended, when apprehending Caradoc at the theatre, only to expose his wife's affair and spoil things for the lovers. Supplying the actor with a motive for murder had been the very last thing on her mind. She had never dreamed Caradoc would go so far or do such a stupid and dangerous thing.

She had bumped into him in the local Sainsbury's, in the housewares aisle. Angela knew Caradoc only slightly, but it was clear even from this vague acquaintance that he had undergone a change for the worse.

Caradoc seemed to have gone quite mad. His short frame had quivered with a manic intensity and his eyes had blazed feverishly as he told her about the chocolates he had filled with lethal garden substances and given to Dan Parker.

The words 'complete organ failure' had almost caused Angela to drop her basket. She had wanted revenge, and to kill two birds with one stone. But not literally.

'People recover from that, don't they?' she had croaked, through a suddenly dry throat.

'Hopefully not,' Caradoc snapped, stalking off to a newly vacated self-checkout till.

Now, as she looked at Dylan, she felt her face drain of blood. 'How is Dan?' she asked, trying to stop her voice from shaking.

'That's what I'm hoping to find out.' Dylan was struck by Angela's evident agitation; he had not realised she was a friend of Dan's. The fact she cared was to her credit. 'We'll just have to keep our fingers crossed,' he added more gently.

Angela swallowed fiercely and turned away. There was a hot, unfamiliar sensation in her eyes, which she eventually recognised was tears.

She felt suddenly desperate for Dan to survive. He was a man she had been passionately attached to, and that he might be dying in hospital because of her was hideous. No, she had not actually administered the poison. But she had definitely pulled the lever that had started the deadly machine. She thought again of Caradoc's crazed and burning stare by the bathroom sprays.

Angela was not usually much given to pondering the consequences of her actions, but the consequence of this one was too awful to ignore. And yet there was nothing she could do about it.

She flicked a glance towards the impassive block of the hospital building. Now she was going in there she felt, frankly, vulnerable. Here, she had no dominion. No one cared that she was Director of Human Resources for the Pemberton Estate. Her power, which seemed so great when she was behind her desk, was pitifully small and inconsequential compared to the power of life and death.

Nell hurried through the sea of cars in the hospital car park. She was completely disorientated and had no idea where she was going. Her main aim was to get away from Adam Greenleaf. He was dangerous; dangerously attractive. He'd burned her fingers once, and to let him do so again would be madness.

Her head was whirling and her heart galloped. Through the blood thundering in her head, she heard the sound of wheels.

'Want a lift?' Dylan asked. 'Only, I'm going back to Chestlock and I can drop you at Edenville on the way.'

He hadn't intended to say this. It just came out, as if some force other than himself was speaking. The same force had made him change direction when he saw her at the other end of the car park. The force was irresistible, or he would have resisted it.

Nell's mouth opened and shut. Her first instinct was to say no, her second was to point out that Edenville was the other side of Chestlock and miles out of his way.

But something stronger than instinct was kicking in, opening her mouth and replying, 'Yes, please.'

As she settled herself in the passenger seat he found himself looking at her smooth, pale knees below the hem of her summer dress. He was immediately aware of the state of the footwell: a flotsam of rubbish, leaves, dust and mud. What must she think?

Nell hadn't noticed. She was staring out of the window at the passing scene – lamp-posts, kerbs, pubs, small roundabouts. And yet she took none of it in. Her entire being seemed concentrated on the long, strong hands twisting the steering wheel beside her. Hands whose touch she had felt already. She was suppressing with all her might the idea that she wanted to feel them again.

Dylan's task was even harder. He had to drive along the road despite not really believing any more that he was in a car on a road. He felt strangely detached from reality but was, at the same time, hyper-aware of Nell's every breath.

He was building up to seize the moment, the moment that might not come again. He had to say his piece. Make his peace. Apologise.

He decided to get straight to the point. Beating about the bush was not an option.

'About that pub in Paddington,' he began.

He heard her draw in a deep, angry breath. 'I just thought you were so beautiful,' he added hurriedly, 'and I didn't mean to, um, mislead you. But by the time I realised you thought I was someone else, it was too late.'

He glanced at her pleadingly. But the eyes that that met his were hard and disbelieving. 'How can that be?' Nell said coldly. 'You even had a Dylan Eliot book on the table. It was as if you knew I'd be coming in with one.'

Dylan gripped the steering wheel in despair. He had hoped

to avoid having to identify himself. But the past was like a roadblock. Whatever avenue he turned down, it reared in the distance. He saw that he could either allow it to halt him, or he could simply remove it. He could, quite obviously, no longer go round it.

Perhaps it was better to remove it, once and for all. He didn't want to lie to her, especially not now she was looking at him with those beautiful, accusing blue eyes. But how, exactly, was he going to tell her? What could he say?

How about nothing, a small voice inside urged him. Love had cost him so much in the past. He had built a new carapace and was successfully hidden inside it. Why break out and reveal himself?

Because, he answered the voice, he couldn't bear her thinking that he was a liar any more. Or that he had deliberately set out to humiliate her.

'My ex-girlfriend burned my house down,' he said abruptly.

Nell was confused. Why was he telling her this? 'Like Dylan Eliot's house burned down?' They'd just been talking about the books. Was he drawing some parallel with the author?

Dylan took a deep breath. This was it. 'Dylan Eliot,' he began.

'Yes?' She looked doubtful. It was likely that she wouldn't believe him. That she would think he was mad.

Was it a risk worth taking? He didn't have to tell her. He could stop here, on the edge, where it was still safe.

But he knew that he couldn't. This was a pivotal moment. Not just in love, but in life. A crucial turning point. He was taking a risk, and it might all go wrong. But she had to know the truth. She was the sort of person with whom complete honesty was the only option.

'Dylan Eliot is me.'

'*You?* You're joking.'

It was worse than even Rachel had thought. She had described him as peculiar, but he was far more than that, he was a liar, and a crazy one too. 'I'd like to get out, please,' Nell said.

He slowed down, then drew into a lay-by and stopped. He turned towards her from the steering wheel. 'But just before you do,' Dylan said, 'there's something else I'd like to tell you.'

There was something so broken and hopeless about his expression that Nell's urge to run started to fade. Just at that moment, a faint tattoo from the windscreen announced the commencement of a sudden downpour. 'OK,' she said cautiously. They were at the side of a busy road, after all. She could still run, if she had to.

Dylan was frowning and drumming his fingers on the steering wheel. Where should he start? At the beginning. Where else?

'I actually wanted to be a novelist, to start with,' he said. 'I used to write in my spare time, after work. It was all pretty simple then. One man, one laptop, one bedroom. But then I got published and all hell broke loose.'

Nell listened in astonishment, trying to take it all in. He hadn't been pretending to be OutdoorsGuy, he had been pretending not to be a famous author. That was the first point.

The second was that the woman who had rushed in had been his French girlfriend. The third was that he had then ended their relationship. The fourth was that the girlfriend had burned his house down. And destroyed his book. The fifth was that he had spent many months recovering in hospital.

It was all so dramatic that it was hard to believe, but Nell knew it was true. Not just because it had been in the newspapers, either. She could see it in his eyes. They were full of anguish. The pain in them was raw, bleak – and so familiar. Did she not see it in her own mirror?

Her suspicion and doubt gave way to sympathy. He had suffered so much. Small wonder that he had lost faith in relationships. As she had herself.

It was striking how similar their stories were. Different in detail and degree, but in many ways the same. While her life hadn't been in danger, and Joey hadn't been as crazed as Beatrice, they had both, through no fault of their own, found themselves in terrible circumstances.

Although – the dreadful realisation struck – perhaps, in part, at least, what had happened to him *was* her fault? 'If I hadn't thought you were my internet date I'd never have spoken to you and she'd never have found us together, and . . .'

He reached over for her hand, to stop her. His touch was warm and sure. 'Look, Beatrice was insane. It was probably only a matter of time.'

But Nell felt racked with guilt, remembering what she had yelled at him from the bedroom window. 'I thought you ruined my life. But actually, I ruined yours.'

'Stop it,' Dylan said, squeezing her hand gently. 'But now you mention it, just how exactly *did* I ruin yours?'

Nell raised her head, sniffed, took a deep breath and prepared to describe how the disastrous online date had driven her, still more disastrously, into the arms of Joey, the first non-virtual available man she had come across.

Then something occurred to her. 'That pub. It started everything.'

'How do you mean?'

'Meeting you there. Everything that happened to you happened after we met in that pub. And everything that happened to me did, too.'

'O-K.' He looked puzzled. 'But what *did* happen to you?'

Nell hesitated. If what had happened to him was horrible

and dramatic, what had happened to her was ridiculous and pathetic.

But Dylan had told her everything and she must do the same. 'It was like this,' she began.

Dylan listened. He said nothing for a few minutes after she had finished, during which Nell felt a miserable, sinking certainty that all her fears had been justified. He thought she was stupid. He would reject her, just like Joey had.

In fact, Dylan was imagining the lonely girl in the downstairs flat, penning her catalogue copy as all London went on around her. It twisted his heart. Just like himself, slaving over his novel as the waves pounded the cliffs. How similar they had been, he and Nell, and how vulnerable to predatory, careless types like Joey and Beatrice.

'What an idiot,' he said.

'Me, you mean?' Nell spoke resignedly.

Dylan snorted. 'God, no. Him. If I'd been there, I'd have married you instead.'

A sharp excitement jabbed through Nell. Did he mean it? Of course not. He was just being chivalrous. But what a wonderful – and terrifying – thought.

'Still want to get out?' he asked her, a small smile twitching his wide mouth.

She shook her head and he started the engine. The metronome of the indicator struck up, the car nosed out of the lay-by.

They drove silently back to Edenville. Both of them, instinctively, seemed to realise that after such a tremendous mutual unburdening all that remained to be said was nothing.

Life was strange, Nell was thinking. She felt oddly calm. Terrible things had happened. But now both their sorry tales might have a happy ending. Where did they go from here, though?

'I'll be going to the hospital every night.' Dylan broke the silence as they drew up outside Beggar's Roost. 'I could take you if you wanted.'

'Yes, please,' Nell said, in a bright, breathy tone of voice that wasn't the one she intended to use.

'Great,' he said. She got out and he drove away. But just round the corner, where the village gave way to fields, he parked and got out, the sheep scattering in surprise and baa-ing in alarm as Dylan punched the air.

PART THREE

PART THREE

CHAPTER 49

'Just had a rather interesting phone call,' said Jason as, that same evening, Angela swept up to his managerial flap in the Edenville Arms.

'That's a first, then,' said Angela witheringly. Jason recoiled, hurt. That was aggressive, even for her. Whatever was the matter?

As no apology was offered, Jason mentally picked himself up and dusted himself down. Angela was obviously upset about something.

'What can I get for you?' he asked, ushering the Director of Human Resources into Pumps.

'Just an Aperol Spritz,' Angela grumbled.

Jason raised a well-brushed eyebrow. 'Cutting down on the alcohol, are we?'

Angela looked at him angrily but did not reveal that her doctor had advised this precaution. Or that she was going back for more tests. It was none of anyone else's business.

'Aperol Spritz then please, Ryan.' Jason caught the eye of the handsome young barman. As Ryan started to clatter cluelessly about, Jason watched him lovingly. He was a terrible barman, but that wasn't what he had been hired for. Jason wasn't sure he would ever have the courage to admit, even to himself, exactly what Ryan had been hired for. As Ryan's strong, young, festival-braceleted wrist mixed the drink in entirely the wrong proportions, the manager suppressed a frisson of longing.

Angela took the glass and downed it in one. 'I needed that,' she said, slamming the vessel back on the bar. 'Another,' she commanded Ryan, who paled behind his facial hair.

The prospect of sitting through one of Angela's rages, sent Jason's glance longingly towards the optics. 'A double G and T for me, please, Ryan.'

He was rewarded by a thickly lashed and understanding wink. As the drink was handed over, their hands touched. The world spun around Jason for a moment; he felt that he might swoon.

Angela had marched over to a window table and plonked herself down. Jason floated over, still on a cloud.

'Any news on Dan?' he asked, hoping to cheer her up. Being the vengeful type, she must presumably get some satisfaction that the man who had scorned her had been cut down in his prime.

Angela didn't comment. She couldn't bear to think about Dan in the hospital any more than she could bear to think about what she herself had been told within its dread walls. All her fear, worry and anger were funnelled into what had happened outside it: the encounter with Adam Greenleaf and Nell Simpson. If only, Angela thought, she could conclusively get rid of that exasperating woman. Perhaps some particularly horrible new assignment, to some particularly unpleasant department . . .

It was, Jason thought, unusual for Angela to be this silent. He had pressed most of the customary buttons, but with no response. He tried again. He'd been saving the best until last. Angela was sure to welcome this piece of news.

'I heard that Juliet Turner's left Caradoc,' he said. 'Gone to live with her mother, apparently.'

He had expected exclamations and a barrage of excited questions; for a bright, spiteful flame to roar up in Angela's eyes.

But her eyes – much less heavily mascaraed than usual, it seemed – remained expressionless and directed towards the window. The name of Caradoc sent alarm bells ringing through Angela, but none she was prepared to let Jason see. She decided to shut down this line of conversation as, sooner or later, by word or gesture, she might let slip that she knew more than she was willing to say.

'I'm not interested,' she said, to Jason's absolute amazement. Never once, in his whole experience of her, had Angela failed to be interested in a piece of gossip. Let alone one of this magnitude. Something, clearly, was very wrong indeed.

He watched her stand up. 'I'm off,' she announced curtly. As usual, she didn't offer to pay. And while Jason was happy to comp her, the occasional offer would have been appreciated.

'Busy evening?' he asked pleasantly.

'Yes,' Angela said, skewering him with a killer gaze. 'I've got to go and arrange my teabags. Then I'm reorganising my shampoo bottles. Both of which will be a sight more fun than sitting here with you.'

With that she swept out. Jason stared after her, thinking that he had never got the chance to tell her about the phone call. Which had, for all Angela's slurs, been quite interesting.

Someone called Eve from some big publishing firm had rung earlier asking whether they had a writer called Dylan Eliot staying. She had information that he was in the area and was anxious to track him down.

'No,' Jason had told her. They had no one of that name in residence. Eve had been very disappointed, and Jason was

385

concerned about this. He wanted to help her, not least because, at the back of his mind, he cherished the idea of writing a tell-all novel about hotel-keeping. He'd told her he'd keep a lookout.

Nothing looked different, but everything had changed. So Nell thought as she flew up the steps to the weddings office the day after Dylan drove her back from the hospital. She felt a wonderful lightness, as if floating above the ground. The thought of tonight, of seeing him again, made her heart beat tattoos and tight knots twist in her tummy.

She burst in, pink-cheeked with excitement, only to see Julie looking glum behind her console.

'What's the matter?' Nell asked. She wanted everyone to be as happy as she was. Especially Julie, who had helped her so much and was usually so positive. 'Is it Carly and Jed again? Don't tell me, they're not stopping at the candlelit ball; they want a fifty-foot-high effigy of Colin Firth in the garden to burn at the end of the party.'

A flash of humour briefly irradiated Julie's downcast features. 'No, although I'm not ruling it out. Angela's just rung. She wants to move you into another department. As of now.'

A surge of indignation went through Nell. She was enjoying working with Julie; what business was it of Angela's to move her? On the other hand, she felt too happy to cause trouble. She didn't want a row, not today, anyway.

'Which department?'

'Sustainability.'

Nell knew, from her extensive reading about the estate, that Pemberton had installed a system of generating its own heat and electricity. 'You mean the hydro and the heat pumps in the ponds?'

'Partly that,' Julie agreed. 'But the latest initiative, which the

Earl's really proud of, is the Waste Heat Derivative System.' It was obvious from the way Julie spoke that it had capital letters in front of it. 'That's what Angela particularly wants you to concentrate on.'

'And what's that, exactly?' Nell was feeling marginally less keen now. The word 'waste' did not augur well.

'Basically, it takes everything from the visitor toilets – and the ones in the house for that matter – and pumps it all into a huge tank. From which, somehow, don't ask me how, enough heat is generated to keep the radiators everywhere going all winter.'

'Oh. Right.'

Julie looked her in the eye. 'Apparently the smell in Sustainability is horrendous. No one normal can sustain it for more than five minutes.'

Nell swallowed. So, a sewage farm, basically.

Then she smiled. Well, she could cope with that. Right now, she could cope with anything.

At Byron House, Dylan was also facing unpleasant truths. He had just told Anne, the manager, about Dan's indisposition. She was alarmed.

'They say he's holding steady, though,' Dylan assured her. He had received the good news this morning, from Dr Akim. 'He's out of immediate danger.'

'Send him our best, won't you?' Anne said worriedly. 'We love him to bits here, we really do.'

Dylan returned to the greenhouse where he was planting seeds in pots in the hope that they would grow to surprise and delight the residents. He had never actually planted a seed before, so it would be a surprise and delight to him too.

The usual sequence of visitors came past: the old lady wanting a pound, the man in the tracksuit bottoms, various friends and relatives of the inmates, either accompanying them or pushing them round the garden in wheelchairs. Dylan nodded at them all and exchanged cheery words with those that offered them.

He worked absorbedly at his pots, enjoying the routine of repeated movements: filling the little containers with compost, drilling a hole with a pencil and dropping a tiny seed in each. He enjoyed the feeling of starting all these new lives, now his own life seemed finally set on a new, exciting direction.

He could barely wait to see Nell; the hours were crawling past. For all he had slept little, he felt well rested and bright. The sun poured through the greenhouse windows and he felt it passing through his skin and irradiating him inside. He felt filled with a boundless energy.

'Excuse me.' A well-modulated, refined voice interrupted him.

Dylan looked up. The woman looking quizzically back at him was very old, but still handsome and high-cheekboned. Her hair rose elegantly from her forehead in waves of palest lavender. She wore tweed trousers and a white shirt buttoned at the neck. Was she a resident, Dylan wondered. Or a visitor?

'Can I help you?' he asked.

She leaned on the smart, long-handled black suitcase behind her and looked imperiously at Dylan.

'I'm looking for Terminal Two,' she said crisply.

A resident, then. Dylan opened his mouth to say that they were nowhere near the airport but suddenly Dan appeared in his mind, shaking his head.

'I'm afraid I don't know where it is,' Dylan confessed instead. The woman gave an affronted toss of the head.

Anne was hurrying across the lawn. 'Now come on, Sheila love. Let's get you inside.'

'Anne, my dear. How lovely to see you. I was just asking this very nice young man here . . .' Sheila made a gracious gesture at Dylan, 'whether he knew where Terminal Two was. Unfortunately he doesn't. Do you?'

'Just let me take that suitcase for you, love.' Anne smiled at Dylan as she led Sheila away across the lawn. 'New arrival!' she mouthed over her shoulder.

The sustainability department was by no means as bad as Nell had thought, or Julie had warned. This was partly because of the setting.

It was in some former barns on a hillside at the edge of the estate. The views over the countryside were wide and beautiful. Fields rippled away in waves, like a green sea, turning purple towards the horizon. To add to the nautical effect, a brisk west wind was blowing when Nell arrived, filling her lungs with bracing air and sweeping what smell there might have been clean away.

The Sustainability people were another reason to be cheerful. Geoff, the manager, was just as lean, bearded and earnest as might have been expected, but had a winningly charming dog that he brought to work, a golden retriever called Topsy. Sarah, Geoff's assistant, was bouncily enthusiastic, with apple cheeks, dreadlocks and a T-shirt that said 'Compost Mentis'.

Both Sarah and Geoff were obviously passionate about their subject and delighted at the attention – 'usually all anyone wants to write about is the farm shop.' Diligently Nell scribbled down bullet points about economic, social and environmental outcomes.

Yet, all the time, she had a sense of not really being present. Even as Sarah enthused about the Pemberton Estate's desire to positively impact on the here and now (there was a lot of jargon in Sustainability), Nell was aware that her own here and now were on hold. They would only begin after work, when Dylan appeared at the Beggar's Roost gate to drive her to visit George at the hospital.

As it happened, other excitements waited her on her return to the cottage. A note had been pushed through the door announcing that the online beds she had ordered had been delivered. To the Edenville Arms, unfortunately, but Jason was very helpful when Nell called and promised to send them over while she was out. He had even offered to send a handyman along with them to assist in their assembly. But Nell, while grateful, turned the offer down. She had chosen beds that were especially easy to build and planned to erect them herself. It would be the triumphal final touch to her new home.

Now she stood by the gate, waiting for Dylan's car to appear. Her insides were twisted in a screw of apprehension. What if, after all they had said to each other, after all they now knew, he didn't come? Nell's phone rang. She pulled it out with jittery fingers. Was he ringing to cancel?

'Just checking what I need to bring up for the weekend,' Rachel said.

'Uh . . .' said Nell, who had temporarily forgotten even that Rachel was coming. She tried to think. What *did* Rachel need to bring up for the weekend?

'Things to garden in, I'm guessing,' Rachel prompted. 'And have those beds come yet?'

Nell confirmed that they had. 'I'll be putting them up later.'

'That sounds a bit worrying. Are you any good with a screwdriver? I don't want to collapse in the night.'

'Thanks for the vote of confidence.'

'You're welcome. I'll be off then. See you on Friday and, oh,'

Rachel added, as if this were an afterthought, 'keep out of the way of strange men, won't you?'

Nell had a feeling that the last sentence was the whole point of Rachel's call. Her friend was checking up on her. What would Rachel say when she learned of the latest developments? That she was seeing Adam Greenleaf, who Rachel had told her to avoid. And who wasn't really Adam Greenleaf at all, but Dylan Eliot.

It was going to take some explaining. And now was obviously not the moment. A movement caught her eye; Dylan's grubby little car was coming down the road towards her. Except that it looked a lot less grubby now; positively gleaming, in fact. Nell smiled. Had he been to the carwash?

CHAPTER 50

Dylan, seeing the figure he had feared might not be there, could not stop grinning either. He was still smiling when she climbed in, and her heart looped the loop. He was devastatingly attractive in jeans and a check shirt. The ends of his hair curled darkly on his collar and the muscles in his forearms slid and tensed as he drove the vehicle off. The lean edge of his jaw looked shaved; he smelt of pepper and lavender.

Dylan wanted to tell her how absolutely knockout she looked in the black-and-white dress with the tiny flower print. And with her hair drawn back into a ponytail, revealing the shape of her face and cheekbones. He wanted to kiss those full pink lips that looked like a strawberry swimming in cream. But his hands remained fixed on the steering wheel. He had business to discuss first.

'About yesterday.' he began.

Her soaring heart now sank. He *had* had second thoughts. Telling him about Joey had been every bit the mistake she had spent half the night worrying it was (the other half had been spent thinking about what Dylan had told her about Beatrice).

'What about it?' If he wanted to pretend there was nothing

between them, she would let him. Better end it now, before it began, than break her heart later.

'About the things I told you. About me being . . . you know . . . a writer.'

Understanding dawned on Nell. He was telling her that he did not have time for both his work and a relationship. That his art came first. At least he was being honest.

'You mean you can't see me and write at the same time. That's fine.'

She was surprised when he slapped the steering wheel. 'God, no,' Dylan exclaimed, almost veering across the road in his agitation. 'That's the exact opposite of what I mean. I *want* to see you.'

A hot blade of excitement shot through Nell. He wanted to see her!

'But I want you to keep my secret. I don't want anyone else knowing that I'm, you know . . .' Dylan paused, then added fiercely. '*Him*. Dylan Eliot. The *famous writer*. That I *was* him, I mean. Because obviously, I'm not now.'

Nell looked at him. She understood the urge to create a new life, new identity, new job. None better. Had she not done the same thing? But surely at some stage in the future, he might change his mind. She could not be the only person keen to see a follow-up to *All Smiles*. 'But you will write again, don't you think?'

She was unprepared for the heat and the vehemence of his reply.

'Never,' said Dylan. 'Never, ever again. Don't even mention it. That part of my life is over.' His voice was flinty; his face set. 'So you won't tell anyone?'

'No,' she agreed hurriedly.

Panic, Dylan realised, had made him over-emphatic. He

393

hastened to repair the damage. 'I'm sorry. I just get so scared, remembering everything.'

'Hardly surprising,' Nell reassured him. She got scared about remembering everything too.

Entering George's ward with its long rows of beds, Nell could see someone had moved into the bed opposite the old man. Someone asleep, but recognisable nonetheless. Someone with shoulders so broad they extended across the entire width of the pillows, and legs which reached to the very end of the bed. A flash of joyful surprise went through her as she recognised Dan, Dylan's colleague, the one who had helped save George. That meant that Dylan, who had gone in search of the private room his friend had been in yesterday, would be here at any minute. The two of them would be visiting the same ward from now on.

Perhaps, Nell thought, that would make things easier with Rachel. She had tried to avoid Dylan, but medical circumstance had made it impossible.

'He's been moved to a general ward,' Dr Akim was telling Dylan at the same moment. 'He's out of danger.'

'That's great news.'

The doctor gave him a warning look. 'But he's still not very well. He'll be in for some time. That OK with you?'

'Why wouldn't it be?' Dylan was surprised to be asked. What business was it of his?

'Mr Parker is worried that you will have to do all the work on your own. You work together, no?'

Dylan was touched that Dan should, in his parlous state, be thinking of him. 'He shouldn't worry about that,' he said. 'What's wrong with him, anyway? Do you know yet?'

Dr Akim's level, steady gaze held his. 'He's been poisoned.'

Dylan was so shocked his jaw dropped. '*Poisoned?*'

The doctor nodded.

'You mean – the soil?' Dylan pursued. 'Tetanus? Like you said before?'

Dr Akim shook his head. 'Something he ate. It's difficult to say exactly what it was, though.'

Dylan thought of Dan's rat's nest of a house and his fast-food diet.

'Lives alone, does he?' Dr Akim shook his head, tut-tutting. 'What that man needs is the love of a good woman.'

George greeted Nell with a smile. He seemed more than usually lively. 'New chap over there,' he said, nodding at the sleeping Dan. 'Seems very pleasant. He's a gardener as well.'

'Yes, and guess what. He's one of the men who saved your life.'

'Is he really? He never said. I must say thank you when he wakes up. Seems very tired, poor chap.' The bright eyes fixed on her. 'How's the garden? You know, it's very kind of you to water it for me. It's hard work and takes such a long time.'

'It's a pleasure,' said Nell, launching into a description of how the different flowers were doing. She wasn't quite certain about all the names.

'Big white flower, about ten big petals, very flat, like a plate?'

'Clematis.'

'Oh yes. Well, it's going great guns. All up the side of the house. And the walls are absolutely dripping with wisteria. Last night, when I was watering, it smelt wonderful.'

George nodded his big white head. 'Edwina planted that. She loved wisteria.' He put out a hand to Nell. 'You look so very much like her, dear. It's quite uncanny. As you know, we never had any children and that was the great sadness of

Edwina's life. But I'm sure that if we'd had a daughter, she would have looked just like you.'

Nell was touched. 'That's a lovely thing to say.'

George smiled. 'We were lucky in so many ways, Edwina and I. Lucky to survive the war and still have each other. What we had was much more important than what we didn't. I wouldn't have had it any other way.'

As, now, Dylan entered the ward, Nell felt a surge of excitement.

'Here's, um, Adam,' she said to George. She must remember to call him that. Maintain the fiction, as it were. 'He helped you the other day as well.'

Dylan spotted them and approached the bed, smiling.

'Delighted to meet you. And thank you.' The old man extended a wrinkled hand to the younger one. His hazel eyes flicked between Dylan and Nell.

Dylan remained standing as Nell said goodbye to George. He could see that Dan was asleep, so there was no point in him staying any longer.

'Fancy a drink?' Dylan asked as they left the ward. He had spent most of his time by the sleeping Dan's bedside, watching Nell talking to George across the ward. 'It's a lovely evening.'

'Good idea.' She felt glad he had asked. George had not wanted to join them for some reason, which had been awkward.

'Edenville Arms?' he suggested.

They looked at each other. 'Should we?' Nell asked. Their history there so far had been chequered, to say the least.

He smiled at her. 'Definitely.'

CHAPTER 51

Sitting at the back of Pumps, by the window, was Angela Highwater, huddled in confabulation with Jason.

The manager was still reeling. Angela had come in earlier and done something absolutely unprecedented. She had apologised for her rudeness on her last visit. 'A bit of a bad day,' was all she would reveal about the reasons. Jason didn't probe. He was happy to forgive and to move on.

Now, finally, he was telling her about the phone call from the London publishing house.

Within their fringe of mascara – albeit not so thick as usual – Angela's eyes were wide and excited. 'Really? Round here? A celebrity author?' She wasn't a big reader and hadn't heard of Dylan Eliot. The nearest she had recently got to literature was *Murderous Death* at the Chestlock Pavilion Theatre. And the least said about that the better.

'This editor woman thinks he might be,' Jason hissed, flicking one of his frequent glances back towards the bar. Ryan was on duty again and currently struggling with a Pimm's.

Angela looked round to see who might possibly be a disguised writer. No one in Pumps. Apart from herself and Jason there was just a pink-faced man calling over from the bar to his wife. 'Shirley! What's your poison?'

Angela jumped, and her spritz slopped over the table.

'What's the matter?' asked Jason.

'Nothing,' snapped Angela, but then, remembering herself, added 'Sorry, Jase. Another bad day.'

She was having a lot of bad days, Jason thought, smiling to show he accepted the apology. What was wrong with her? Angela was looking worse than he had ever seen her. Her hitherto high degree of personal grooming was just a memory these days. 'Heard anything from the hospital?' he asked.

'Hospital?' Angela looked at him indignantly. What did he know? She had told no one she was ill, nor did she intend to. She was going back for more tests tomorrow and was dreading it.

'I was just wondering whether there was any news about Dan.' Jason wondered why his companion's face was so white.

'No idea.' Angela did her best to sound detached.

Jason sighed. 'I know it sounds selfish, when the poor chap's so ill. But that van of his is still rotting in my car park and it's not doing much for the view.'

A couple now came into the bar; Nell and Adam Greenleaf, Jason recognised. 'I've sent the beds over,' he called.

'What beds?' demanded Angela. She too had spotted the couple and did not like what she saw. 'What's going on?' she demanded of Jason.

He filled her in about the furniture, but refrained from offering his views on any other matter. A romantic at heart, Jason was pleased that things had moved on since Adam and Nell had spent the morning yelling at each other outside the pub front.

That had been unfortunate, but Jason didn't bear them any ill will. A few guests had heard a disturbance, but none had their hearing aids turned up high enough to hear anything specific.

And it was obvious there would be no recurrence of the drama. Even though the thin line between love and hate seemed to have been crossed in this case with amazing speed.

Jason slid a look at Angela. She looked annoyed, as he had expected. But there was something else there: desperation? Perhaps even helplessness. Jason knew, as did everyone on the estate, that Angela had done everything she could to hamper Nell.

But Nell seemed to prevail, even so. The woman had staying power; she was a survivor. A life-saver, literally, and with the knack of getting people on side in a way Angela had never managed. Take Geoff Diggle of Sustainability. He could be an odd sort of stick but Jason had heard he'd actually called Human Resources to enthuse about Nell and congratulate them on employing her.

He watched the couple take their drinks outside. They were talking and laughing as if they had known each other for years and yet there was an excitement about them that seemed entirely new-minted. Look at them, Jason thought indulgently. Whispering sweet nothings. Young love – well, young-ish – was just so touching.

Dylan and Nell were, in fact, discussing more practical considerations.

'I have to do something about Dan's place.' Dylan was frowning at his pint. 'He can't go back to that pigsty. He'll just get whatever lurgy he has all over again.'

Dan's house was the sort of place people put on special suits to clear out. Yet he had to do it, Dylan knew. His boss didn't seem to have anyone else.

And, actually, he didn't really mind. Working at Byron House had given him his first taste of helping other people. It was a sensation he realised he had seriously underrated.

'And I've got George's garden,' Nell said. 'And the key to the house. I guess I'll just have to keep looking after it all until we know what's going on.'

They smiled ruefully at each other. 'We seem to have got ourselves into all sorts of complications,' Dylan remarked. She had the feeling that he meant more than just their caretaking responsibilities.

She sipped her wine. 'Plus, I've got the beds to put up in my own house. I should be going and getting on with it really.'

'I'll help you,' Dylan said immediately. This helping thing, it was addictive.

They walked slowly through the village. The air was warm and smelt richly of grass. The grind of distant baling could still be heard, along with the plaintive cries of sheep.

Bright flowers nodded over the low stone walls of the gardens. The giant red poppies had gone to bed for the evening. Nell admired the brilliant colour, noticed how the crimped edges of the petals were folded into scarlet tricorn hats.

'Wow,' said Dylan as they approached Beggar's Roost. 'You've cleaned it all up. It looks amazing.'

'I can't take all the credit,' Nell admitted. 'I've had a bit of help, you could say.'

'I can see. From some fairies, I'm guessing. Or some superheroes.'

She let them in. Watching his eyes switch from side to side, taking in the details, Nell felt a swell of pride at what she, Rachel and Juno had achieved in such a short space of time.

She'd done a fabulous job, Dylan was thinking. Pieces of vintage furniture which suited the idiosyncratic size and shape of the old building had been mixed up with newer items. She obviously had a good eye.

'It's seriously cool,' he said. 'You've got great style.'

'It wasn't really me. My friend Rachel chose everything.'

'Is she an interior designer?'

Nell laughed. 'She should be. Actually, she works in an insurance office and she's studying in her spare time to be a barrister. She's also a single mother; her daughter's a trainee Miss Marple.'

'They sound terrifying.'

'Oh no, they're amazing.' Nell seized the opportunity to praise her friends. 'I can't wait for you to meet them. They'll . . .'

She was about to say 'love you', but stopped herself. Something was telling her not to rush this, not to assume or predict. Of course Rachel would love Dylan – when she got to know him. It would obviously have to be stage-managed quite carefully.

Dylan was now admiring the glass-fronted bookcase in which Rachel had arranged the works of Dickens. 'Read these, have you?'

'Afraid not. But I'm going to.' Nell had happily imagined herself sitting by the fireside, absorbed in *David Copperfield*. 'Have you?'

He opened the cabinet and took out *Oliver Twist*. 'Dickens was my mentor, so far as it went.' Dylan flicked through the pages. 'He showed me how to write, basically. Comedy alternating with tragedy. Plus lots and lots of description. Spit spot. And there you have it.' He snapped the book shut, and smiled at her.

He was being too modest, Nell thought. There was more to *All Smiles* than a mere exercise in imitation. She thought of the book he had lost and wondered what it had been like. The same? Better?

'What was it called?' she asked hesitantly. 'The book that . . .'

She stopped as he frowned at the floor. She thought he wasn't going to reply, but then he said, '*Charm Itself.*'

'Good title.'

He shrugged. 'My editor came up with it.'

'Editor?'

'Eve,' he said, in a musing tone. 'Eve Graham. She was always very good at titles. She thought of *All Smiles*, too.'

A flash of excitement shot through Nell. This was much more information than she was expecting. Perhaps he was thinking about writing again. Were the juices of creativity flowing once more? And if so, might it have something to do with them meeting each other?

He was looking directly at her now. 'But that's over,' he said. 'I never want to see her again. Or write again.'

'Let's get on with those beds,' she suggested.

CHAPTER 52

DIY had never been Dylan's strong point. Perhaps ironically, given the number of volumes he had sold, he had never even put up a bookshelf. Let alone put a bed together.

'I'm not sure where to start,' Nell said, setting out small packets of screws in plastic bags and doubtfully consulting a piece of paper with the instructions on it. 'I think this is translated from Chinese. "Put piece wood on wooden piece and through hole connect." What does that mean?'

Dylan took the paper. 'I think I might have understood the Chinese better,' he said. 'Put together sides and screw through from other side.'

'I think it's telling us to connect the pieces of wood together with screws,' Nell concluded. 'But I think we know that already.'

Dylan stood confidently above the pile of wood planks and small plastic bags. He was hoping that if he looked down on it masterfully enough, he could get it all to behave.

Nell, more practically, was arranging the wood into a shape vaguely resembling a bedframe. 'I think we need to get the sides together and put the slats across to join them. Then we match up the right screws to the right holes and bingo.'

'Which are the slats, though?' Dylan scratched his head.

'All the pieces of wood look the same.'

His chest was still heaving from the almighty effort of dragging the mattresses up the stairs. They had weighed about a million tons each.

'I think they're these ones, the paler ones.' Nell, on her knees, smiled up at him. It felt delightfully intimate to be assembling flat-packs with Dylan. Such a classic young couple rite of passage; the sort of thing millions of men and women struggled with together every weekend.

'The good news is,' she added, 'that we don't need a screwdriver. Which is just as well, as we don't have one.'

'You mean we can just mind-meld it?' He'd considered various angles, but not the Mr Spock one.

Nell laughed. 'No, we can connect everything together with a two-pence piece. Look!' She waved the instructions, pointing at a little drawing in which a coin was connected with arrows to the groove in the top of the screw.

Dylan knelt beside her and examined the screws in their packets. He didn't wish to advertise quite how utterly clueless he felt; blokes were supposed to be good at DIY. And he'd already heard rather more than he wanted to about someone called Tim and his gang of merry builders who'd cleared the cottage out in the first place. It was hard not to feel that his manhood was in question.

Half an hour later, they had got nowhere. The two-pence approach was useful for getting each screw halfway into the piece of wood it was intended for but it went no further, and the end result was dangerously rickety. It would collapse under a light mattress, Dylan reckoned. Under those mothers they'd dragged upstairs, it had no chance.

'Maybe they weren't two-pences, they were yen,' Nell was ruminating.

'I don't think it matters,' Dylan said. 'Look, I hate to bring up the word "power tools" here . . .'

'That's two words.'

'. . . but do you have any? Or know where you can get some?'

Nell was about to shake her head when a brilliant thought struck her. 'George might have one. Next door. I'm sure he wouldn't mind . . .' Nell scrambled to her feet. 'Let's go and have a look.'

The sky outside had changed from the eggshell blue it had been when they went inside the cottage. They now stood in the Beggar's Roost garden staring at coral rags of sunset spread against a sky of pearly violet.

'It's so lovely,' Nell whispered.

She was ultra-aware of how close Dylan stood in the gathering darkness. Her fingers seemed to be straying towards him of their own accord, pulled like metal to a magnet. She yearned to have his arms about her, as they had been outside the hospital, except properly now, not impulsively or out of pity.

Then she clenched her fists, breaking the circuit. It was too soon. She did not need another involvement, let alone with Dylan. She barely knew him and, as Rachel had pointed out, what she did know was distinctly strange. And Rachel, of course, didn't know the half of it.

Dylan followed Nell as she went down her path, out into the road and back up the other side into the old man's garden. It struck him that he could as easily have climbed over the low dividing wall, just as he could have kissed her, just then. Her face had suddenly seemed so near; he could feel her breath on his cheek, smell her light, herby perfume.

But he had stopped himself. Was he mad? Things between them were going well; there had been, so far this evening, no rows, hysterics or unexpected revelations and that was a first. So why rock the boat? Plain sailing was what was needed now, letting things take their course. Was that the same thing? He wasn't sure; he knew even less about sailing than he did about DIY.

She was unlocking the old chap's door now and Dylan stood a few feet back, respectful. She seemed to appreciate this; turned and smiled. 'I think it's OK if you come in.'

She shut the door and switched the light on. Dylan stared round. It was like stepping back fifty years. Seventy, even. Stone flags. Wooden stairs. Plain white walls.

Nell had disappeared at the end of the passage and he followed. The old chap's kitchen looked like something from a museum: a black-lead stove with a rag rug in front of it; a plain wooden table, much worn and scrubbed; a stool that Tess of the D'Urbervilles could have used to milk her cows from. But clean, Dylan could see; everything was shining and cared for. The evening light glowing through the small, deep-set windows gave the simple, unpretentious room the quality of a painting. Beautiful. He felt the fleeting urge to write his impressions down, then dismissed it. He was here to look for power tools, not gather literary atmosphere.

Nell was looking in various cupboards; they seemed, from where Dylan stood, to be full of plain white plates and large bowls. 'Where would he keep his tools?' she wondered.

'Maybe in there?' Dylan gestured towards a grooved door beside the kitchen sink. It led to a scullery which smelt of damp newspaper and leather; a row of clean boots, he saw, was lined up in the shadows on several open copies of the local freesheet.

Dylan glanced up at the shelves above his head; various boxes were stacked up here. He could see a glimpse of orange flex in one of them. Bingo.

He carried out his prize to Nell. She was no longer in the

kitchen, however. He found her down the passage in the old man's sitting room. It was tiny but cosy, with a small sofa and an armchair opposite a solid fuel stove with clear glass doors. The chair was evidently the old man's; a folded newspaper was on the arm and an empty cup and saucer were on the floor close by.

There was a framed photograph of a couple on the wall; the guy in RAF uniform, Dylan saw. The woman, meanwhile, was a knockout: her skin pearly, her teeth straight and white, her silky pale hair parted in the centre.

'My God,' he blurted, 'she looks just like you.'

Nell decided not to go into how she had been confused for Edwina. 'They were married for sixty years,' she said. 'Can you imagine that? Being in love with the same person all your life?'

Dylan felt, suddenly, that he could, absolutely. And definitely with a woman who looked like this. He looked closer at the airman in the picture. 'He's got a caterpillar badge.'

Nell peered. 'So?'

'It means he's used his parachute.'

'Why?'

Dylan smiled. 'Chrysalis, you see. Opening up into a butterfly.'

Such a romantic image, Nell thought, in such a deadly context. 'How do you know that?' She would be able to surprise George, next time she visited.

He shrugged. 'Kind of thing you pick up if you're a boy, I guess.'

The drill helped, inexpertly applied though it was. A couple of hours later, the three bedframes were up and two of the mattresses on them. Dylan was heaving the last one into place to the sound of Nell, in one of the other bedrooms, ripping the plastic off packets of new sheets.

He went to find her; she was stuffing a pillow into a case. 'Well, that's it,' he said. 'Done.'

She put the pillow down but then looked self-conscious as if not sure what to do. They glanced at each other and Dylan, remembering his hesitation in the garden, took the initiative. It was probably entirely the wrong thing, but he was going to do it anyway. He might not have another chance.

He turned and pushed the door shut; in the same swift movement trapping her in his arms. She arched into him; they clung to each other. Neither was sure who sank to the bed first; perhaps they both sank together.

Dylan's kiss made Nell melt inside; the touch of his tongue almost made her faint. Longing roared inside her. They moved silently, with wonder, gasping softly as pleasure pulsed and built. Nell had once read that the best sex took either three minutes or three hours. She was to discover over the course of the evening that both were true.

Afterwards, between, they lay huddled together. Her face pressed into Dylan's hair, which tasted of salt and smelt of pine. Nell felt that she never wanted to move. It had all been so perfect. She felt a fierce, burning happiness. It was, now, quite dark beyond the windows. But Nell felt that, inside her, a brilliant light had been switched on.

CHAPTER 53

'This salad's amazing,' Rachel said that Friday night, positioning some more beside her pasta.

The salad was George's. He had urged Nell to take whatever she wanted from the vegetable garden. She and Juno had picked the lettuces earlier that evening, after the two Londoners had arrived in their Land Rover.

All five types were in the salad, along with some fresh peas that Juno had podded with enthusiasm. 'This is great!' she had declared, popping open sheath after sheath and delighting in the tightly packed row of little balls within. 'They look like tiny green toes!'

The peas, quickly boiled and tossed while warm in the olive oil and balsamic dressing, were sweet and delicious. Everything was delicious, Nell felt, glancing around from time to time at the kitchen in the candlelight. She loved the way it looked blurred, shadowed – and wonderfully romantic.

She could still sense Dylan's presence. The feeling of him in the cottage was so strong Nell marvelled Rachel hadn't detected it too. Perhaps she was preoccupied; her talk so far had been about her imminent law exams. After that, Nell gathered, there would be interviews at the various chambers she wanted to join as a trainee barrister.

It was unusual for Rachel to share her worries; she was the most self-sufficient person Nell knew. But the competition for places was apparently ruthless and Rachel was obviously nervous that, as a single mother who studied in her spare time, she would have little chance against the sleek twentysomethings who'd been through Oxbridge and had every type of parental support.

'It does look good in here,' Rachel remarked, finally switching out of exam mode.

'I'm still not sure what to do about curtains,' Nell said. The ones in her flat had always looked slightly wrong; the hooks popping out of the track all the time.

'Get some blinds,' Rachel advised, twirling up her spaghetti. 'I'm thinking of getting some in the flat. Thinking of getting the whole place done up, in fact. Now that I've had such success doing up your place.' She grinned at Nell, who gave her a sharp look back.

'I thought you'd just had it painted. You had painters in. That's why I couldn't go back with you last week, remember?'

'Oh yes,' Rachel frowned with mock recollection. 'Silly me.'

Nell looked at her. 'So you *were* telling porky pies.'

'White lying,' Rachel admitted with a cheerful shake of her burgundy curls. 'I knew it was better for you to stay here.'

'And definitely better for us,' Juno now interjected. She had, until this moment, been deep in her latest Agatha Christie, twirling her pasta up with her free hand and reading intently despite her mother's instructions to stop because the candles were bad for her eyes. ('Mu-um! People read with candles for hundreds of years!')

'How's the book going?' Rachel asked.

'Good,' said Juno. 'No one knows who the poisoner is, but I've got a good idea already.'

The word 'poisoner' made Nell's thoughts fly to Dan in the hospital. Dylan had explained the mysterious circumstances of his illness. Now she explained it to the others.

Juno was so electrified that she dropped her fork. 'Poisoned! How exciting!'

'Not for him, the poor thing,' admonished Rachel.

'Can we see him?' Juno begged, eyes wide through the glasses that shone in the candlelight. 'When you next go to see George? I'd like to ask him some questions about who's poisoned him.'

Would that be a good idea? Nell pictured a helpless Dan undergoing a fierce cross-examination by a determined ten-year-old Miss Marple. 'I don't think he knows.'

'Of course he knows!' Juno rebutted this argument with a wave of her pasta-laden fork. 'People always know who's killed them,' she added.

'You mean people are always murdered by someone they know,' Rachel corrected. 'Which, I have to say, is borne out in real life. I've been studying a lot of cases where it's happened.'

Nell could almost physically see her thoughts flying back to her exams, and reached a hand over to press that of her friend.

'You'll be fine,' she said, and meant it. Rachel had steely determination, which she had obviously passed on to her daughter.

On the subject of Dan, Juno was like a dog with a bone. There was no chance, Nell could see, that she was going to pass up the possibility of meeting a real-life poison victim.

'*Please* can we see him? Please? *Please?*'

'Well, he's in the same ward as George,' Nell allowed. 'And so I guess you might be able to. It depends.'

'On what?' demanded the child, keen as ever for specifics.

Whatever job Juno grew up to do, Nell thought, it would certainly be done properly.

'Well, he might be asleep. Or not want to talk. Or,' Nell said, trying to stop a certain note of anticipation entering her tone, 'he might have other visitors.'

Letting Juno see Dan, now she thought of it, would kill two birds with one stone. She could arrange it so Dylan would be visiting Dan, and then Rachel could meet him.

'Other visitors?' Rachel looked at her levelly. *You haven't been seeing him, surely*, that look asked.

Honestly, wait until you meet him. You'll love him, Nell's look answered.

You have some serious explaining to do, said Rachel's deep frown.

Nell glanced at Juno, whose glasses were, once again, directed to her book. *Tell you later*, she silently mouthed.

'Tell her what later?' asked Juno, without looking up.

CHAPTER 54

'I can see him!' Juno hissed jubilantly, as they entered George's ward the next day.

'Yes, in the middle,' Nell murmured back. 'With the white hair and the dark eyebrows.'

Juno turned to her, her expression incredulous. 'Not George!'

'Mr Farley to you,' interjected Rachel, who was a stickler for politeness. 'In a rude world, manners get you further than almost anything else,' Nell had heard her telling her daughter.

'How do you know which one is Dan?' Nell asked, intrigued.

Juno regarded her gravely through her glasses. 'Process of elimination. Dan's a gardener, so he must be the big tanned one whose feet stick right out of the end of the bed.'

'Oh just drop it, will you?' Rachel was irritated. 'Being boring,' she added, 'is almost as bad as being rude.'

Rachel was tired, Nell knew. She was herself. They had been up late the night before. Explaining the latest stage of the Dylan story had been immensely difficult, not least because there were aspects that could not be revealed. His identity as a writer. His real name.

Rachel had not been impressed that Nell had seen him again, despite her warnings. Still less that she had slept with him.

'Jesus, Nell. Do you never learn?' she had wailed.

She had not even been persuaded by Dylan's efforts with a drill.

'He's a man who put up three flat-pack beds,' Nell pleaded. 'With Chinese instructions. Surely that says something for him.'

'Yes. That says is that he must really have wanted to get into your knickers.'

'Can't you give him the benefit of the doubt?'

In the firelight, Rachel's eyes glittered. 'I'm going to be a lawyer. Doubt's not my thing.'

Nell was silent. The cosiness of her sitting room, with its little chairs and dancing firelight, had been the perfect setting for intimate exchange. Rachel had even brought a scented candle, whose expensive orange and cinnamon aroma had eddied deliciously around them as they talked. But all it had scented was their disagreement. It was clear that Rachel's suspicions had only deepened.

'Let's go to bed,' she had suggested at that point. Stalemate had been reached. Rachel would just have to meet Dylan and see for herself what a wonderful person he was. She could not fail to be convinced after that.

With all this riding on it, the visit to George's ward was a terrifying prospect. Rachel said nothing as they drove to the hospital in the Land Rover. Juno, on the other hand, could hardly contain her excitement. She had her notebook in hand, and a pencil. 'I'm going to ask Dan all about his poisoning,' she announced.

'No, you're not,' Rachel said firmly. 'Not only is it an utterly tasteless thing to do, but the last thing the poor man's going to want is to be woken up by some ghoulish child asking him questions about how he almost died.'

'I could start by asking him something else,' Juno suggested.

'Such as how he felt about saving George – Mr Farley, I mean's – life.'

Dan was sitting up and looking cheerfully around him. He saw Nell and waved enthusiastically. 'There, you see!' Juno exclaimed, her grey eyes blazing in triumph behind her glasses. 'He wants us to come and talk to him.'

'You don't know him, so you can't,' Rachel hissed.

'That doesn't matter,' Juno said, tossing her straight, side-parted bob. 'No one knows anyone to start with. You just have to introduce yourself. Besides,' she added to her mother with unarguable logic, '*you* don't know George.'

'Mr Farley to you,' Rachel interrupted.

'You don't know Mr Farley,' Juno went on, 'and nor do I. But Nell's going to introduce us.'

Nell had certainly intended to, but when they arrived at George's bedside it was empty.

An icy flash of shock went through her. Had George been taken to the home already? Or . . . worse?

'Well, he's obviously somewhere around.' The voice was Juno's. Nell stared at her.

'How do you know?'

Juno gestured confidently at the bed. 'Elementary, my dear Watson. All the sheets are still on and his reading glasses are on the bedside table.'

Nell felt a hot wash of relief. 'Miss Marple strikes again,' said Rachel dryly.

'So,' said Juno, sitting down and looking brightly at Nell and her mother. 'What are we going to do now?' She made a great show of twiddling her thumbs. 'How long must we sit here?' she demanded, crossing and uncrossing her arms and legs and sighing. Her parody of childish boredom fooled nobody; both Rachel and Nell had seen her reading without moving for hours.

'I'm going to find out where George is,' Nell announced. 'Just hang on here a minute, can you?'

Quick as a flash, Juno seized her chance. 'Can you introduce me to Dan?' she asked Nell. 'Go on,' she urged. 'I just did a useful bit of deduction, didn't I?'

Nell looked at Rachel for permission. 'Dan's really lovely. And he seems to be up for some visitors.'

Rachel's breast in its burgundy cardigan heaved in a sigh. Nell could read the doubt in her eyes. She knew Dan's romantic history; it had been part of last night's story, although the version she had told Juno had been expurgated.

'That girl,' Rachel groaned. 'If she wants it, she'll get it. Once she makes her mind up, there's no putting her off.'

Nell gave her friend a look. 'I wonder where she gets that from.'

Nell was late, Dylan saw as he entered the ward. She was not there; neither, for that matter, was George. Perhaps the two of them had gone for a walk, or to the patients' day room for a change of scene.

Dan, on the other hand, had company. A petite woman with a vivid little face, bright lipstick and curly hair tinted a purplish red was sitting by his bed with a serious-looking child in spectacles. Who on earth were they? Relatives? Friends? Dan never spoke about either; admittedly, he rarely spoke much about anything.

Dylan had observed that most children who came to the ward immediately got out their smartphones or tablets. Few of them ever conversed with whatever relatives they were ostensibly visiting. This child in glasses, however, seemed to be not only deep in conversation with Dan, but taking notes.

'A box of chocolates!' she was gasping as Dylan arrived. 'That has to be it!'

'What d'yer mean?' Dan was asking, raising himself on one massive elbow.

'Well,' the child explained earnestly, 'it's a sort of classic situation in a murder mystery story. The killer puts the poison in a box of chocolates.'

'What are you talking about?' Dylan sat down. The small red-haired woman gave him a direct, assessing look.

'I'm Rachel,' she said. 'And this is Juno. I'm guessing that you're Adam.'

He nodded, relieved at this evidence that Nell had kept his identity secret. This, presumably, was the scary friend. He wasn't sure he liked the way she was looking him up and down.

'You look familiar,' Rachel said eventually. 'I feel sure I've met you before somewhere.'

'Don't think so.' Dylan dropped his gaze and cursed those extra-big photographs on the *All Smiles* book jackets. At least he had had his beard then.

He could feel her still staring at him, beadily. Small as she was, and tall as he was, she made him feel uncomfortable. He wished Nell would come back, and provide some sort of a buffer. Where was she? He looked around, willing her to appear.

'Nell's gone to find George,' Rachel guessed his thoughts with alarming ease. 'I understand you work with Dan,' she added, throwing a much warmer smile at Dylan's bed-bound colleague. He, at least, seemed to have this terrifying woman's approval.

'He does that,' Dan corroborated warmly. 'Best partner going, 'e is.' Dylan threw him a grateful look.

'And Nell's the best girl going,' Rachel instantly asserted.

'She is,' Dylan agreed hastily.

'And she speaks very well of you.'

'That's nice of her.' He immediately regretted sounding so

flip. It was nerves but it sounded provocative.

Rachel's reaction was to tip her chin back and regard him from under her lashes. 'I hope you're worthy of her.' She sounded profoundly doubtful.

'I hope I am too. I'll try to be, don't worry.'

He spoke in absolute earnestness, but her expression remained sceptical. 'You make sure you do,' she warned. 'If you hurt her, you'll have me to answer to.'

'Hurt her?' Dylan shook his head, smiling in amazement. The prospect was more than unlikely, it was impossible. 'I'd rather die.'

'Let's hope it won't come to that,' was Rachel's dry response. 'There are enough people in hospital here as it is.'

Juno and Dan were still discussing the poison theory.

'So,' the little girl was saying to the enormous gardener, 'he puts his evil mixture in the chocolates . . .'

'That can't 'ave 'appened,' Dan robustly rebutted. 'That's not real life, that sorta thing. It were summat else what made me poorly.'

'It does seem a bit far-fetched, in real life,' the child soberly agreed. 'But you get it a lot in books. And plays. It was in one I saw the other night, in fact. At the Chestlock Theatre. *Murderous Death,* it was called. One of the characters killed another by putting poison in a box of chocolates.'

Dylan had not been listening closely; merely pretending to do so to avoid talking to Rachel. But Juno's words electrified him.

Murderous Death? Wasn't that the title of the play Caradoc Turner had just been in? Juliet Turner's recently returned husband?

He felt his mind flicker and readjust like a railway station announcement board. Had Caradoc discovered what Juliet and Dan had been up to in his absence? Had he decided to get revenge through the means practised in the play?

No. Of course not. No one would do that in real life. Would they?

The child had turned to her mother for corroboration. Dylan listened, expecting to hear Rachel dismiss the idea out of hand. Laugh, even. But her small, clever face seemed thoughtful.

'It's quite far-fetched,' Rachel said eventually. 'But not impossible.'

Dylan could not let this crazy theory go unchallenged. 'But surely,' he said, 'it's only the sort of thing that happens in . . .'

He was about to say 'the fevered imagination of authors' but stopped. Fortunately, at that point, Nell came back into the ward.

'All smiles!' Rachel exclaimed, sending Dylan's heart somersaulting painfully in his chest. But she meant Nell's happy expression as she came down the ward with old George holding on to her arm.

Apart from the lion's roar of the engine, the way home in the Land Rover was a subdued affair. Nell stared disappointedly out through the windscreen.

They had left Chestlock now and were back in the countryside, rattling down lanes fringed with cow parsley and past fields shaggy with summer growth. Tractors were baling hay in the meadows, ploughing neatly spaced lines through the thick, pale grass.

The air flowing in over the diesel fumes was heavy with warm scent. The road ahead baked in the sunshine, then dived into tunnels of shadow beneath heavily leafed summer trees. It was all so very beautiful, Nell thought. If only Rachel would warm to Dylan, she would be completely happy.

Her hopes that her lover and her friend would like each other had come to nothing. Rachel was being diplomatic, but Nell sensed she was underwhelmed. And, just as depressingly, she suspected Dylan didn't like Rachel either.

'Adam's hot,' Rachel had just allowed, 'but he's not quite my type.'

Nell had hoped they could all have supper together at Beggar's Roost, but Dylan had pleaded that he was tired. Nell knew this was an excuse. She had had just as little sleep, and for the same reasons, yet had never in her life felt so awake and alive.

Hang on. What had Rachel just said? Nell yanked herself out of her reverie. 'Say that again?'

Rachel looked at her from the steering wheel. A slight smile played about her piquant face. 'I like his friend better.'

'Dan?' Nell gasped.

Rachel shot her a challenging look. 'Why not? What's wrong with him? I know he's had an affair, but that's over now. He quite clearly regrets it.'

'You covered quite a lot of ground,' Nell remarked, surprised.

'One tends to with Juno around,' Rachel said dryly. 'She asked him whether he thought it was just a moment of madness and whether the poisoning was a crime passionel.'

'He thought that was a flavour of chocolate,' Juno put in, without looking up from her book. Nell had noticed that she had the unnerving ability to read, talk and follow another conversation all at the same time. 'He said there hadn't been one of those but there had been Eton Mess.'

They postponed the subject until after the return to Beggar's Roost. Later, with Juno safely in the bath, Nell handed her friend a glass of wine. 'It's just a bit surprising, you being interested in Dan,' she began.

She had expected Rachel to redden, or laugh and say something dismissive. But instead she found herself meeting her friend's steady gaze.

'Why surprising?' Rachel challenged.

'He might not be quite your type.'

'How do you know what my type is? I don't go for intellectuals, if that's what you're thinking. Or silver foxes with lots of money.'

Nell, who had imagined both these as perfect fits for Rachel, now wondered if her very short friend looked for her physical opposite in a mate. As well as being enormous, Dan had a certain earthy physicality that was probably very attractive to some women. Perhaps Rachel was one of them.

Of all the unpredictable twists events had taken recently, this, Nell thought, was one of the most unexpected. She would just have to trust that, as Dylan insisted, Dan's kind heart really was his most marked characteristic. Dylan was also of the view that while Dan was silent, he was deep. She could only hope, Nell thought.

CHAPTER 55

Dylan's weekend had been dreary. Rachel's presence at Beggar's Roost had discouraged him from visiting. Nor had he seen Nell at the hospital on Sunday. They had decided to postpone meeting until after Rachel had gone home.

The maddening thing was that, when he did go to visit Dan, Rachel was all he could talk about. The two of them seemed to have taken the most immense shine to each other, which only made his own failure to impress her more stark.

Restless, dissatisfied and frustrated, Dylan had, on Saturday night, even found himself driving down into the village and the Edenville Arms. Here he had a shock.

Jason, plonking his pint on to the bar, had smiled and asked him, quite conversationally, if he'd seen any famous authors about.

Fortunately Jason was rummaging in the till, so he missed the colour draining from Dylan's face and the way he gripped the copper bar-top, as if about to fall over.

'What do you mean?' he asked, when his throat started working again.

'Oh, just that someone from a publisher's in London phoned the other day,' Jason replied brightly. 'She was looking for a writer who she'd heard was somewhere round here. Name of

Eliot. Can't remember the name. T. S., was it?'

Dylan had gone cold with horror. Eve was on his tail! But why? He had told her he never wanted to write again. Nor would he, but neither did he want her blowing his cover.

He had built a new life for himself, and Eve, storming in with her powerful personality, might destroy it, and thereby destroy his precious new peace of mind.

Jason's eyes were on him expectantly. He had not, Dylan realised, given an answer. 'No,' he said, rather more loudly than was necessary. 'I haven't seen any authors round here.'

Bad news came thick and fast that weekend. A difficult couple of days with Rachel was crowned by an announcement at the hospital. 'George is leaving us next week,' Jasjit told Nell as she, Rachel and Nell left on Sunday. 'We've found him a nice home. It's called Byron House and it has a lovely garden. If you like, you can go with him when he leaves. Help him settle in.'

This was some comfort, Nell supposed. She wondered if Dylan had heard of the place. He worked in a care home garden some of the time. She would ask him, once the weekend was over.

'So that's it,' Nell said to Rachel. 'It's all over for his own place. His garden.' The thought was dreadful. What would happen to his cottage now? Could he keep it if he wasn't living there?

'Someone will let you know, presumably,' Rachel said. She seemed uninclined to indulge Nell on any point. She had given her a pep talk on Sunday and persuaded her, among other things, that she needed to tackle Angela about her lack of work space. She could not, Rachel pointed out, keep ping-ponging between the different departments of Pemberton for ever.

True, Nell knew. She now had swathes of material, all of which would have to be written up. She needed a place to sit down, and a computer of her own.

On Monday morning, she rang the Director of Human Resources.

Angela, in her office, heard the phone with dread. She had been expecting this call and her heart was booming within her. The results of her tests were due from the hospital; was this them?

She lifted a hand but it shook so badly Angela put it back in her lap. 'Shall I get it?' Gail called from down the corridor.

'No,' barked Angela. No one else must know about this. So many people hated her; they would either feel she deserved to be ill, or they would sympathise. Angela couldn't decide which was worse.

'Hello?' she said hesitantly into the receiver. 'Angela Highwater, Director of Human Resources speaking.'

'Hello, Angela, it's Nell. I need an office,' the other end said firmly.

Angela glared at the wall. The fist not holding the phone clenched so hard her chipped nails drove painfully into her palm. Of all the people in all the world. Angela's fear and fury now roused itself for an outlet.

'We don't have any bloody offices!' she roared.

Nell held on. Her ears were ringing, but she was determined to tough this out. 'But I'm literally working from my kitchen at the moment.'

'And you'll have to carry on doing that!' yelled Angela. 'We don't have an office. OK?'

Gail popped her head in. 'Excuse me, Angela, but actually, we do. There's the one next door here, the big one that's been empty since Ros left . . .'

There was a thump as Angela's shoe hit the door.

Nell rang Julie. Perhaps, for the moment, she could borrow some space in her office.

The capable Weddings Manager sounded unusually distracted. It was not difficult to guess why.

'What's the latest?' Nell asked. 'Jed and Carly still having a candlelit ball?'

The other end groaned. 'It's been a hell of a job sourcing all the candles. They've needed hundreds to fill that massive ballroom. Needless to say, Jed and Carly wanted ones made with authentic methods, to cast an authentic glow.'

'Surely all glows are the same?'

'You'd think so. But I've got to find some historic ones anyway. As well as a food historian.'

'But why?' The American nuptials were clearly spiralling out of control. Julie was now hunting for an expert in eighteenth-century banquets to supervise the serving of the wedding breakfast. 'Carly's insisting on salmagundi, flummery and braised cheeks.'

'Sounds painful.'

'It is, it is,' Julie groaned. 'And even that's not all.'

Jed and Carly, Nell now learned, wanted their guests to dress up in authentic period costume and take on the roles of characters from *Pride and Prejudice*. 'The best man has to be Mr Bingley and the vicar is being asked to be Mr Collins. They haven't asked the rest of us yet to dress up and be servants, but it's only a matter of time.'

Nell grinned. 'Count on me if they do. I love fancy dress.'

'You might regret saying that.'

Never, Nell thought. After all the help with Beggar's Roost, there was nothing she would not do for Julie.

The phone call from the hospital had still not come through by lunchtime and Angela's nerves were stretched to snapping point. While she could not drink alcohol, she felt she might feel better if she could look at it. She headed for the Edenville Arms.

That this was a mistake was obvious as soon as she entered Pumps. Angela felt almost overpowered with the urge to wrench the gin bottle off the bar wall and drink the lot.

'Spritz, is it?' Jason trilled, inadvertently rubbing salt into the wound.

As Angela scowled at him, he fixed on his best professional beam. He had some news for her.

'George Farley's going into a home.'

As he had hoped, Angela brightened slightly. Revenge, finally, on at least one of Ros's enemies. And one of Nell Simpson's friends, more to the point.

Angela hoped that it was one of those dreadful homes where they doped the old people with drugs and beat them. That was the least George Farley deserved.

'I wonder what's going to happen to his house,' Jason mused. 'It belongs to the estate, am I right?'

Angela gave a jerky nod. The Farley cottage was a nice old place, in its way. Hopelessly old-fashioned, of course; he probably hadn't bought a new stick of furniture since 1942. There wasn't even a fitted kitchen.

The Director of Human Resources took another, musing, sip of her spritz. Actually, the fact that the Farley place would be free could be useful. She wanted to move from the penthouse in the converted cotton mill. People had left the development before, saying they'd heard strange noises in the night; children crying and so on.

Angela had always scorned this, claiming to sleep eight undisturbed hours without fail. Recently, however, she hadn't. And last night she had woken to see something actually standing by her bed. It had been there only a second, not long enough to really be sure. But it had been the size and shape of a very small person.

She did not plan to reveal this, however. The official reason for any move would be that it was more convenient to live near Pemberton. Commuting, even the short distance between the village and the local town, was getting tiring. Quite a lot of things were getting tiring, although Angela was trying hard to ignore this.

And so the Farley cottage would be perfect. She would move in, get rid of George's crappy old stuff and drag the place into the twenty-first century. She would install a wet room, a state-of-the-art kitchen and a big plasma screen. Pave over that messy garden to make a patio with outside heaters and a deck.

By the time she left the pub Angela was feeling almost cheerful. It might actually be quite pleasant, to live in the village.

To live, full stop . . .

When would the hospital call to give her the all-clear, damn them?

Lost in these thoughts, Angela did not notice the woman crossing the car park towards her. She had walked straight into her before she realised she was there.

'Sorry!' exclaimed the other, even though, strictly speaking, it had been Angela's fault. Angela did not acknowledge this, however, but looked the woman coldly up and down. She was small and slimly built with a shining cap of short dark hair. She wore a fitted pale blue dress, very plain, but obviously very expensive. Her legs were bare, but perfectly smooth and tanned, and she wore a pair of elegant low-heeled slingbacks. Her impeccable appearance reminded Angela of how much she herself had let things slide recently. But what else was she to do? She hadn't had the energy . . .

'Excuse me,' the woman said, opening a smart bag and taking out a sheet of paper. 'My name's Eve Graham and I work in publishing. I'm trying to track down a writer who used to work for me. I've heard that he's moved up here. Have you seen him?'

Angela remembered Jason saying that a London editor had called the pub, but she knew nothing about any writer and was about to say so in no uncertain terms. But then her angry glance skimmed the photograph on the press release, presumably of the author. Something about it caught her attention. Angela tipped her head to one side and squinted at it. Was that face familiar? 'What did you say his name was?'

'Dylan Eliot,' Eve replied. Her tone was pleasant, but disappointed. This strange, irritated woman had initially looked as if she recognised him, but now, at the mention of his name, that recognition was fading from her face. Angela thrust the sheet roughly back at Eve.

'He might not be calling himself that, though,' Eve suggested hastily. She had intended to be careful about this possibility, as there was a chance that Dylan had made friends who knew about his past and were prepared to cover up if anyone came enquiring.

This woman, however, didn't look furtive at the new suggestion. On the contrary, a crazed light had leapt into her eyes. She grabbed the paper back from Eve and stared again at the picture of the author. 'Yeah, I know him.'

Eve gasped. 'And he lives round here?'

Angela nodded. She felt she had the measure of the situation now.

It was not possible that this Eve woman was really after Adam Greenleaf, or Dickie Eliot or whoever she had said he was, because he had once worked for her. Who would come up here from London just for that? No, it had to be something else, the motive must be sex. They were, or had been, in a relationship of some sort. Angela's little eyes gleamed. Given that Adam, damn him, now seemed to be in a relationship with Nell

428

Simpson, sending this Eve person after him would make things seriously complicated.

'Yes,' she said to Eve. 'He lives round here all right. And I can tell you exactly where.' Using a nearby car bonnet as her desk, she drew a swift, rough map showing the way to Bess's Tower.

'Thanks so much,' beamed Eve. 'I'll head up there now.' She stretched out a hand to shake Angela's. 'I'm so grateful to you . . .' Eve hesitated. 'I'm so sorry. I don't know your name.'

Angela was about to tell her, then she, too, paused. Another cunning thought was forming. Dickie Eliot didn't have the monopoly on pseudonyms. And for her to use this one would properly put the cat among the pigeons. 'Nell,' said Angela, turning away to her car to hide her smile. 'Nell Simpson.'

Since Jason had broken the news about Eve, Dylan had not emerged from Bess's Tower. Going into the village represented too much of a risk. Nell was coming to see him at the tower tonight, after work and taking George to his new care home. She had visited Dan for him on Sunday, along with her fearsome friend.

Being a fugitive in Bess's Tower had its advantages, Dylan thought. He could go on the roof. He was on it now, leaning over the parapet and looking down over the estate.

This being a summer afternoon, Pemberton was at its busiest. A long, unbroken line of cars was snaking slowly to the estate entrance, each one pausing briefly at the little wooden gatehouse to hand over cash for the car park, or flash a membership card.

The car park itself was ablaze with metal. Family groups in pale summer clothes, the old ones going slowly, the younger ones laden down with picnic bags, the children skipping ahead, were moving from their vehicles towards the entrances to the house, garden and the first of the many loos.

Dylan gazed across the park: the bright green grass, the feathery spread of cedars, the fluffy clumps of elms, the dark crouch of yew. And here were the Pemberton gardens, with paths as thin as pencils between rose gardens and rock gardens. The ponds looked no bigger than ten-pence pieces, the statues were dots and the cascade of water was a mere narrow silver thread. The great house from this vantage point looked like a model of a stately home rather than a real place where people lived and worked. He could see the little entrance doors on to the roof leads, the gilded urns between the more prosaic chimney stacks, the balustrades and the statues. He could see behind the great front pediment with the figure of a helmeted goddess on the top.

It was so peaceful, up here, Dylan thought. He felt safe and hidden; no one, least of all Eve, could possibly find him. The very thought was ridiculous. The green glade stretched about him, sunnily empty. The dappled light danced and birdsong swelled in his ears.

Suddenly, he heard a twig snap. And another.

Dylan bent over the parapet. No one down that side. He crossed swiftly to the opposite wall. Another twig cracked.

Someone was coming. Could it be tourists? But they never got this far up. A visitor?

Dylan was about to dive back downstairs, but then a woman emerged from the trees at the far side of the clearing. He saw her pause; saw her eyes travel up to the top of the building.

He ducked down before she could see him, his heart thudding. He had recognised that slim, elegant form. His first instinct was to crouch there out of view until she gave up and went away, but he knew she would not give up. He was going to have to talk to her. Eve had tracked him down.

CHAPTER 56

Byron House had been easy enough to find. The taxi driver who took Nell and George there had heard of it. Nell had braced herself for a stream of criticism, but he had only good things to say.

The home seemed to bear out this positive report. The outside was not beautiful but its modernity included refinements lacking in George's former accommodation. Central heating, for one thing. The radiators were not needed now, in the blaze of midsummer, but they'd obviously be useful in the winter.

'Looks comfortable,' she remarked brightly as she and George looked into the day room. It was full of cheerful red sofas and there was a piano, as well as a telly being watched by a couple of residents. They looked happy, Nell was encouraged to see.

George did not reply. He had said hardly anything since they'd got here. He seemed absent, almost worryingly indifferent.

'Look,' Nell said. 'There's lots going on.' A large board on the wall displayed notices about 'Down Memory Lane' events; also singalongs, ballroom dancing, zumba classes, whist drives and talks on local history. George read them expressionlessly.

'All your favourite food too,' Nell added, drawing the old man's notice to the pinned-on menu whose options included beef stew and dumplings and fish and chips. Still he said nothing.

An elderly lady was playing the piano in the day room. It was filled with light from big French windows through which Nell could see lawns and trees. 'Looks like a nice garden, George. Shall we go outside?'

Even the magic word 'garden' had no effect. George's shoulders lifted and fell in a dispassionate shrug.

Someone now appeared at their side. A short, wizened creature of some eighty years, in a pale blue raincoat, neatly belted, a headscarf carefully knotted over white permed hair. Her wrinkled face was at odds with her eyes; bright and oddly childlike.

'I've got to get my bus,' she said. 'But I haven't got any money.'

'Oh,' said Nell. 'Er . . .'

One of the residents, she guessed, sliding an anxious look at George. Beneath the bushy brows, the hazel eyes revealed little. But Nell felt sure he was about to refuse to stay another second in the place.

The old lady was now staring up into George's face. 'Can you lend me the bus fare, love?'

Oh no. This was all they needed. Nell looked round for help. There seemed to be no one about.

But George's arm, next to hers, was moving. There was a rattle; he was feeling in his pocket. His hand reappeared with a two-pound coin between his thumb and forefinger. He handed it to the old lady, who snatched it and closed her fingers tightly over it. When she looked back at George, the anxiety had gone out of her eyes. 'Thank you,' she said.

George inclined his big, neatly combed white head. But still said nothing. Had he acted out of sympathy? Nell wondered. Resignation? Or just confirmation of his worst fears?

'Hello!' A grey-haired woman in an electric-blue dress was coming across the day room towards them. 'I'm Anne.' She clasped Nell's hand in a reassuringly firm shake. 'I'm the manager.' She extended a hand to George. 'What do you think of Byron House, Mr Farley?'

Nell immediately felt more hopeful. Anne was very friendly and seemed very capable. Any home run by her had to be a good one. Didn't it?

'Shall we take you to your room?' Anne asked, smiling. 'Given you one of the best ones, we have.' She seemed, Nell thought, to have the knack of being friendly without being patronising.

'I'd like to see it,' she said to Anne, as George hadn't replied.

As the three of them moved off, Nell hesitated to take George's arm. It seemed intimate now the old man's mood was so hard to read. This was a different George to the one she knew.

Instead she walked in front, with Anne.

'It takes time to settle in, sometimes,' the manager murmured.

The corridor upstairs had the same warm flowery scent as its counterpart below. Anne, a few paces in front, led them past a series of doors.

'Here we are!' She stopped before a door with the nameplate 'Mr George Farley'. She pushed it open. 'There you go, George. You go in first.'

George, in his turn, looked at Nell, who gave Anne an embarrassed smile and stepped over the threshold.

The room was a good size, impeccably clean and contained a single bed facing a wardrobe which had a small shelving unit next to it, on which a small flat-screen TV rested. Nell was poignantly reminded of the college room she had occupied as a student. That room had been all about the beginning of grown-up life. This was about the end.

'Look, George,' she said cheerfully. 'Plenty of space. You can put your pictures out.'

George's pictures were in his bags downstairs, in the reception area. Nell had packed them as no one as yet had taken his cottage keys off her and there was no one else to do it. She had taken most of the clothes from his bedroom and on the way out had gone into the sitting room and taken the wedding photograph down from the wall where, for so long, it had hung.

Would he want to hang Edwina up here, though? Looking at George's face, Nell rather doubted it.

The room had a large window and Nell crossed to it. A neat garden lay below, mostly lawn, but with seating areas and paths snaking through it. There was a small greenhouse.

Nell turned. 'It really is a lovely garden, George.' Not the tumble of colour and scent that was his own, admittedly. But better than she had expected.

Anne instantly took the cue. 'Are you a gardener?' she exclaimed. 'Yes? We'll keep you busy in that case, George.'

But George did not react. Nor did he go to the window.

'We've got some very nice gardeners,' the manager continued, undaunted. 'I'm sure they'd be happy to let you lend a hand.'

George had now come to the window but had still not said anything. Despair seized Nell. It was clear that George hated this place and it was all a terrible mistake. But how on earth was she going to get him out of it? And where would he go from here?

Her gloomy gaze fell on an elderly woman walking along one of the garden paths. She was elegantly dressed, with a smooth wave of pale, purplish hair rising from the front of her forehead. She walked with a very straight back, pulling a long-handled suitcase. Nell watched her stop a small knot of visitors. 'Excuse me.' Her voice floated up to the window. 'Could you possibly direct me to Terminal Two?'

Nell felt a movement beside her. George was shifting from foot to foot, trying to get a better look. He wasn't quite smiling, but he was looking a lot brighter.

Nell left Byron House feeling cautiously optimistic. She and Anne had taken George down to the garden, where he and the lady in search of Terminal 2 had struck up a conversation about airports. George's stony gaze had seemed less stony after that.

'He'll be all right,' Anne said, accompanying Nell as far as the security doors at the entrance.

There was a bus stop just past the entrance to Byron House. Waiting, Nell took out her phone to check her messages.

Unexpectedly, it rang.

'I need your help after all,' Julie said.

'What with?'

'How do you feel about spending next Wednesday in a corset? Jed and Carly want a cast of thousands.'

As the bus bowled over the bridge into Pemberton's park, Nell looked around at the familiar scene. As always, she was struck by its loveliness. Would she ever get used to it, let alone take it for granted? She thought of Rachel and Juno, stuck in the city. Still, they would be back again in a few weeks' time when Rachel had finished her exams.

Nell now sent her a silent, long-distance message of good luck. Hopefully, once they were over, Rachel's former good humour would return. Finally she would see the point of Dylan.

The land about her swelled gently in the evening sun, each

slope and rise crowned with tall trees. All deliberately placed to provide the perfect setting for the lovely building now coming into view round the bend.

The bus stop was just before the bridge. Nell got off and crossed it. She paused halfway and leaned over the balustrade to look at the silver river. Beneath the stone arches the water rippled and shone, throwing a display of dancing light on the curved underside.

The woods in which Bess's Tower was hidden rose before her. The tree trunks glowed in the sun as she began the climb. Up and up she went, her footsteps quick with anticipation, through the leaf-shadow shimmering and dancing and the golden sunbeams slashing the way.

Dylan lay in the bedroom of Bess's Tower. He had been here since Eve had left, and he was drunk. As soon as she had gone, he had hit the bottle. Or rather two – of red supermarket plonk, drunk not with enjoyment, just deadly determination.

Nell had betrayed him. Nell Simpson, Eve had said, had told her where he lived.

Dylan felt savage with disappointment. Once again he had allowed a woman to deceive him; once again he had trusted and had his trust destroyed. And so he had reached for the wine. His goal had been oblivion, and he had got there.

He had drunk himself to sleep. He had not even made it to the bed but just collapsed on the floor of the bedroom, cheek rammed into the scratchy seagrass. The glass he had been drinking from tipped over and spilled, the dark red liquid spreading and seeping into the straw. The vinegary stink filled his nostrils as he drifted in and out of consciousness.

But sleep – or stupor – had brought him no peace. Dylan had dreamt of Nell; her face, her broad smile, her wide blue eyes. Eyes he had been a fool to trust. Then he had dreamed of the fire, of being caught in the blaze, of the searing wall of heat drying out his eyeballs, crackling his hair. He had half-woken, panting, heart painfully hammering, gasping for breath, crying out, only to register that none of it was real, and the heat on his face was only the sun streaming through the little chamber's latticed window. Then he had subsided once again into unconsciousness.

Nell, meanwhile, was walking up through the woods. She was near the top now and had expected it to be cooler. Instead it was close and still. Dry leaves cracked beneath her feet and a column of flies twisted above her head.

She wondered if a thunderstorm was imminent. It had not rained for some time and it would be useful if it did, particularly for George's garden. The flower beds next door were, despite her dutiful watering, wilted and heat-parched. *Rain!* she urged the sky, looking up at what she could see of it through the canopy of leaves overhead.

Thoughts of his garden lead to thoughts of George in Byron House. Hopefully his first evening was going well. What would happen to his cottage now? Perhaps, Nell thought, she should consult Angela about it. There would be his things to clear out, too. Who would do that?

She was approaching the top of the twisting tarmac track now and Bess's Tower was appearing through the tree trunks. She slowed to admire the decorative front of the building with its pepper-pot towers, lattice windows and the flagpole at the top. Then, putting on a spurt of pure, excited energy, she bounded across the grassy glade to the steps of the tower and up them to the front door.

She tried the handle; it was open. He was in! Within minutes

– seconds – she would be in his arms. 'Dylan?' Nell called, running from room to room downstairs.

Dylan, in the bedroom, was coming slowly back to consciousness. His head felt tight and his fuddled thoughts moved slowly in his brain. Snapshots from earlier in the day glowed and faded: Eve's disappointed face, the sight of her walking away, shoulders hunched, down the track.

Nell was running up the spiral stairs now. 'Dylan?'

Her nose wrinkled; there was a strange vinegary smell in the air. The door of his bedroom was ajar. 'Dylan?'

She pushed it open further, gasping as she saw the body on the floor, the head in a dark pool of red. *'Dylan?* Dylan!'

CHAPTER 57

Jason, in his cubbyhole in the Edenville Arms, was wondering whether it was the weather. The closeness, heat and mugginess that had characterised the day had only intensified as evening approached. His customers were exhibiting behaviour that reflected a pent-up atmosphere suggestive of impending disaster.

To some, it seemed, the disaster had already happened. The publishing woman, Eve, had clearly had an eventful afternoon, and not in a good way either. Jason had seen her drive off earlier looking full of excitement. Only to return an hour later in an obviously very different mood. Her face was a picture of gloom and things did not seem to have improved since. He could see her now at one of the garden tables, talking tersely into her mobile under a sulky yellow sky.

Jason wondered if it had anything to do with Angela and the conversation he had seen the two women have in the car park at lunchtime. But both of them had seemed very pleased and excited then.

Like Eve, Angela had driven off all smiles; so much so that Jason had wondered, with a stab of jealousy, whether Eve had offered her a publishing contract. Although on what subject

Angela could write a book was anyone's guess. He had never even seen her read one.

Jason, on the other hand, had been gathering stories for years about recalcitrant guests and difficult diners. He could have written 'Confessions of a Manager' at a moment's notice.

Perhaps he still could, although he wouldn't mention it now. There was something about Eve's expression, as she approached his flap, that suggested such overtures might not be welcome.

'I won't be staying the night, after all,' the editor said shortly, rummaging in her bag, producing the key to Spigots and laying it on the shining mahogany surface. 'I have to go back to London.'

Her tone, while friendly, did not invite further questions and Jason accordingly did not ask them. Nor did he point out that cancellation without notice obliged the cancellee to pay the rate in full. He wished to keep his publishing hopes alive in some shape or form.

His phone now rang. Jason, half-dreading it would be Angela, was relieved to find, on the other end, Julie from Weddings. Her voice lacked its usual cheeriness, however.

'I've got a complete clusterfuck on my hands,' she told him.

Wincing at this over-graphic description, Jason braced himself for some wedding-related problem. It would be something and nothing, it always was, and to give her her due, Julie could usually see these difficulties for the storm in the teacup they were. It was unlike her to get in a flap, but, given the permanent flaps her client brides were always in, perhaps the occasional lapse was inevitable. He applied himself to helping Julie regain her sense of perspective.

'Don't tell me,' he said gaily. 'Someone's decided they want melon balls instead of prawn cocktail?' He wished to transmit his awareness that Seventies starters were making a comeback.

'If only it were that simple,' Julie sighed. 'But it's not. Tell me, Jason,' she added. 'How do you fancy spending Wednesday in a pair of breeches?'

'I can't,' Jason said, not without regret. The coming week was a busy one. A big bridal party. 'I've got some Americans coming,' he began.

'Tell me about it,' snapped Julie.

Jason had barely replaced the phone when he saw Angela's car turn into the car park. Her expression did not bode well: it looked as angry as the grey-black clouds now massing in the sky. The heavens were clearly about to open.

Jason watched her trudge purposefully across the car park and gathered his courage, such as it was.

'Cheer up, it might never happen!' he exclaimed.

Angela glared at him. 'It has.'

'Julie's been on to you too? Getting you dressed up on Wednesday, for the candlelit ball? All hands on deck, I understand.'

Jason found himself looking at Angela's back as she marched into Pumps. 'Triple gin and tonic,' he heard her bark at Ryan, who immediately started to drop glasses. Jason winced as he heard them hit the stone floor.

He rushed to his protégé's rescue. 'Triple?' Jason enquired, swooping smoothly into the bar, dismissing Ryan and busying himself with the optic. 'Ice and a slice?'

Angela downed it in one and asked for another. Her appearance, Jason thought, was even more unkempt than it had been at lunchtime. Her make-up, especially round her eyes, was smudged. She looked as if she had been crying. But that was obviously impossible. Angela never cried.

'Everything OK?' he asked, concerned.

'Not really.' Angela grabbed the second drink out of his hand. 'I'm not very well. Not very well at all.'

Her voice was so low and bleak he wasn't even sure she had said it. The manager stared at his old sparring partner. 'I'm so sorry,' he said simply.

He felt all his fear and resentment disappear as if it had never been. Quite suddenly he saw before him, not the all-powerful Director of Human Resources, but a vulnerable human being.

'Is there anything I can do?' he asked.

But Angela just shrugged, turned away and started to walk towards the doorway. Then she stopped.

'You can do one thing,' she said in the same low voice. 'You can tell me how Dan Parker is.'

'I think he's getting better,' Jason began, but his voice was drowned in an enormous clap of thunder, followed on the instant by rain which sounded on the pavement and the parked cars outside like the roll of a thousand drums. The view outside became a sheet of hissing grey.

The storm had broken.

At first Nell had thought Dylan was lying dead in a pool of blood. But the red circle surrounding his head had proved to be merely wine. Dylan was drunk.

Not so drunk that he could not recognise her, however. At her gasp of horror he had slightly raised his head and looked through the hair plastered to his yellow, sweating face. She had been shocked to recognise the expression in his red eyes as hate. He had hurled at her a stream of drunken invective, some of it so slurred she could barely understand the words, although the meaning was clear enough. He was accusing her of betraying him, of failing him and abusing his trust.

Slowly she worked it out. Eve, the woman from the publishers, had been at the tower. She had found him. And Nell had helped her.

'But I didn't! I never told her where you lived! I've never met her!' Nell gasped.

'She shhaid you did. She shhhaid Nell Shhimpshhon . . .'

She did not recognise this man raging bitterly on the floor, drooling and dribbling into a stinking stain. This was a different person from the Dylan she knew. A frightening one full of hate and resentment.

In the end, unable to bear any more, Nell had turned and rushed down the stairs. The front door had still been open and she ran out. Ignoring the gently winding path back into the park, she had plunged down between the trees, her feet crashing into dry leaves as the branches tore at her hair and the sharp-thorned brambles caught and clawed her bare legs.

She had got down as far as Edenville church when she realised how hard it was raining. It beat on her uncovered head, funnelling down her neck. The air roared and hissed and the road, normally grey, was a black and shining river. The gargoyles on the church tower spat and gurgled on to the grass below. Nell's hair stuck to her nose and her lips. The cool, hard water from above streamed down her face along with her hot and salty tears.

She did not care about the storm. In as much as she could welcome anything, she welcomed it. The wild, whipped heavens and the lashing rods of water echoed the wildness and anger she felt inside. All her former passionate joy now seemed as vague and indistinct as the village now looked in the rain. Misery poured down on her, soaking every corner of her soul.

She gave herself to it utterly. Two storms now raged within Nell: the horror of the recent scene with Dylan and all the pent-up emotion she had stored since the non-wedding. She realised that, far from absorbing it and continuing with her life, the humiliation she had suffered over Joey's rejection had merely been repressed. It now exploded; part rage, part hurt, part helplessness.

There was a bench just inside the gate of the churchyard. Nell sat on its soaking seat and lifted her streaming face to the streaming heavens. The storm roared and rattled in the trees, masking her howls and weaving them into its cataclysm. She felt like a force of nature; elemental and raving, possessed of a violent power. Or perhaps a violent powerlessness, because everything she was expressing came from sheer frustration.

Slowly, her yells grew less. There was, after all, a physical limit to how long her vocal cords could maintain this volume of noise. Her fists, shining and slippery with water, ached with the force of being beaten against the bench so many times. As the storm raged itself out, the tumult in Nell's heart subsided and she achieved, if not calmness exactly, a relieving numbness.

As the curtain of water receded, the village and the churchyard came back. Dripping on the bench, Nell looked around at the newly revealed gravestones jutting upwards like grey teeth in green and grassy gums.

One arched one in particular caught her eye. Nell pushed herself up from the bench and approached Edwina Farley's grave. She knelt before it, as she had seen George doing on that day, so recent, which now seemed so long ago.

She envied with all her heart the woman buried below, all passion spent, all earthly trials over, dead and numb and blissfully relieved of feeling. Not for Edwina the knowledge that she must drag the burden of this day long into the future and never be able to cast it off. She had been adored all her life. She had never known what it was to be rejected. Edwina and her might have looked the same, Nell reflected, but their romantic fates could not have been more different.

She leaned her forehead, burning despite the rain, against the rough, cool stone. 'Oh Edwina. Help me.'

Eve had driven only a small way out of Edenville when the violence of the weather forced her to stop. Even with her windscreen wipers at full blast she could not see. Rain exploded on the glass and streamed down it. It was like driving underwater.

She pulled into a bus stop and waited for the weather to abate. As the rain drummed relentlessly on the windscreen, she thought about that afternoon, and what Dylan had said to her.

Eve had been expecting resistance. It was pretty obvious that Dylan didn't want to see her, or anyone connected with his old life. He had told her as much when she visited him after the accident, but Eve was not the sort who gave up easily and besides, she had experience of authors. They said one thing at one time and then, a few years down the line, they were saying and doing the opposite.

It wasn't, of course, surprising that Dylan hadn't wanted to write when she'd seen him in hospital. He was recovering from a near miss with death, and that the fire and his writing were connected in his head was obvious. But with any luck, time and distance would persuade Dylan to pick up his pen again.

Certainly, Eve hoped so. She had never met an author with so much untapped potential. *All Smiles*, of course, had caused a sensation, but it was the potential of *Charm Itself* that excited her. Dylan had not let her see even the first chapters, preferring to keep it secret until it reached completion, but from the discussions they'd had about it, she felt it was taking him in a new, unusual direction.

All Smiles had been written with passion and conviction, but his style had been that of a young man. The emotional maturity of what lay ahead was thrilling. If only he could be persuaded to write it!

But if anyone could, she could, Eve reckoned. She had, after all, discovered him. She could remember the moment so well: flicking rapidly through the first few pages of his manuscript while standing up. And then reading more slowly, feeling about her, eyes glued to the page, for a chair and sinking into it. And reading on and on until around her the office had emptied, the lights dimmed, the sky outside had darkened and the moon had risen over the brightly lit city.

It wasn't until it had sunk below the western horizon and the sun started to peep over the eastern one that Eve had finally let the last sheet of paper in her hand slide to join the rest drifting about her feet in a white and choppy sea. Only then had she looked up at the strip lights on the ceiling, rubbing her stiff neck but unaware really of anything except the excitement inside her, the thrill that every editor craves but few ever experience; the absolute, certain knowledge of greatness.

She had reached for the phone, left a message with his agent, Julian had called back within the hour and Dylan was in her office an hour after that, blinking slightly and unshaven but keen and wildly excited.

But now, the risk was that this moment of literary history, that first stage of launching *All Smiles* on an unsuspecting world, was about to become history itself. Because, as Eve knew – none knew better – it was no longer enough, these days, to write one great novel. You needed a follow-up if you weren't simply to ebb in the backwash of the endless cresting waves of new writers. She had to transmit this knowledge to Dylan, who needed to understand it and to act on it. And until recently, she hadn't even known where Dylan was.

Eve had never expected that, after leaving hospital, her star writer would disappear completely. She had imagined he would stay with his parents for a while, then drift back to London eventually. But Dylan had just vanished off the face of the earth.

Even his mother had no idea where he was. He never called, she said, although he did send postcards. 'Postcards from where?' Eve had demanded immediately. What was the postmark? This had been the first clue, non-specific though it was. A Midlands regional post office covered a pretty wide area.

But then a postcard had come showing a place called Edenville and Eve had wondered if that was a clue. On a hunch, she had gone there. The obvious place to enquire was the pub. And then yesterday, outside it, she had met Nell Simpson, who had proved the final link in the chain.

With what excited exhilaration she had headed up the hill to Bess's Tower! Eve had never seriously doubted that Dylan would want to return to writing. It wasn't just the money. Every author had an ego and wanted an audience. Surely Dylan was now missing the adulation that had been part and parcel of his status as leading-edge Young British Novelist?

The track through the woods had seemed like something from a fairy tale; quiet and sun-dappled with glimpses of enchanted glades between the straight trunks of birch and pine. She decided to park the car at the edge of the track and walk the last stretch. The tower itself had taken her breath away. Impatient though she was to see Dylan, Eve had had to stop and admire it. It had struck her as a supremely poetic spot; the perfect place for a writer. Light of heart, full of excited confidence, she had climbed the shallow stone steps and knocked on the door.

She heard the sound of descending footsteps, then the door had opened. Eve had expected Dylan to look surprised, but not horrified.

'What are you doing here?' he had gasped. 'What do you want?'

She had explained her mission and his brows had snapped angrily together. 'I've told you before. I don't want to write. That's over.'

'But . . .' Eve had objected, now as astonished as he was. Dylan couldn't possibly mean it. Could he?

'Look.' The glint in his eye told her the answer. And that his surprise was now sheer fury. 'I've got a new life now.'

'But . . .' Eve put in again, before launching herself into a passionate speech about his talent, his potential and what he could achieve. What he, as a gifted artist, owed the world, and that of letters in particular.

This did not have the effect she had hoped for. Dylan had snarled that he owed the world nothing, especially after what it had done to him. It was a miracle that he was alive and given that he was, he would spend what time remained to him working quietly in his various gardens or being with his new companion. He did not mention her name and Eve did not dare enquire.

She had lost him, she recognised. After all her rekindled hopes and all the lengths she had gone to, she had failed.

'But just tell me one thing,' Dylan called after her as she turned away and began to trudge back in the direction of her car. 'Who told you I was here?'

Eve paused, rummaging for the name. It was hard to find it underneath all the rubble in her mind. Things had been orderly before but Dylan had, one by one, exploded and destroyed all her plans. 'Nell someone,' she said doubtfully, eventually. 'Simpson?'

She had looked up but he had gone. A flash of drained, white face and a pair of staring eyes were all she had seen before he slammed the door.

Now, sitting in her driver's seat and staring at the javelins of rain hurling themselves at her windscreen, Eve felt like crying. It was her own fault. She had refused to accept Dylan's reluctance to return to writing; had thought she could persuade him through her own indomitable will. Throughout her life and career she had crushed other people's preferences beneath the juggernaut of her own. She had been successful in this, had gained a formidable professional reputation. But perhaps there had been a price to pay. She thought of her expensive but empty flat, looked around at her expensive, recently valeted car and down at her designer dress. Had any of this brought her happiness?

Eve drummed her manicured fingers on the steering wheel. The rain was starting to ease now; she could go. But something was preventing her from starting up the car and driving off. Something, she realised, had shifted within her; she needed to identify it, think it through.

As the storm continued to drift away, the answer arrived. She had been thwarted. Never in her life before had she failed to get what she wanted. Things up until now had had the happy predictability of a good novel. Even the search for Dylan, protracted and difficult though it had been, had had about it the air of a detective story whose end would be entirely satisfactory. But it had not ended that way. What now? she wondered.

Then she shook herself. What now was to return to London, her office and her job and make a star out of some other author. There were plenty of them wanting to become stars, after all. One or two of them even deserved to. Why waste her time on one that didn't?

She was buckling her seat belt when a movement caught her eye. Something was out there. A dog which had failed to make it home in time and now decided to take its chances? No, it was a person, Eve saw, surprised. A woman. A very, very wet woman, who had obviously borne the brunt of the weather.

The rain had now completely stopped. All was silent and strangely calm and the air was full of water vapour. Through this ghostly mist Eve watched the figure come closer. It walked in a blundering, imprecise fashion, staggering from side to side of the pavement as if it were drunk.

She could see now that the woman was tall and thin, without a coat, her long arms clutched about her body and wet hair plastered to her cheeks. Something about her, and not just her soaking condition, told Eve that she was in distress. Great distress. The pale face upturned to the raining heavens was clearly that of a woman on the edge.

She opened the car door and yelled to the figure through the mist. 'Are you OK?' It was a silly question; the woman was obviously far from OK. But the underlying message, the offer of help, was meant kindly and the woman seemed to understand this. She turned her head to Eve and staggered over.

'Get in,' Eve commanded. She might not be able to force a recalcitrant author to return to the keyboard but she could make a woman risking pneumonia take shelter from the storm.

The stranger got in the back and Eve turned round to look at her. Her wide-spaced blue eyes were as blank as an automaton's. She sat up straight, her clothes spreading a dark pool of wetness on the buttery beige suede of Eve's pristine back seat. 'Goodness,' Eve said. 'You are in a state.'

The blankness faded from the woman's eyes and she seemed to focus for the first time. She looked about her, at Eve and at the wet seat beneath her.

'What's your name?' Eve said, as her companion seemed incapable of speech.

The woman did not reply immediately. She seemed to be

trying to remember who she was. Was this, Eve wondered, someone who had lost her mind, who extreme trauma had turned mad and stripped of identity?

What was she to do with such a person? Eve ran her eyes up and down the woman, gathering what information she could. Well, if wetly dressed, though by no means expensively. Hair recently cut, if wild and stuck all over her face and shoulders. No obvious bruises. No wedding ring. Very attractive.

Finally, the woman spoke. 'I'm Nell,' she said in a low voice. 'Nell Simpson.'

Eve's jaw dropped. 'That's impossible,' she said. 'You can't be. I've met Nell Simpson already today and she looked completely different from you.'

CHAPTER 58

It wasn't his day for Byron House, but Dylan went anyway. He would tell Dan he was leaving after he had told Anne.

Dan would be OK. If he played his cards right, he was heading for a relationship with Rachel, a woman who seemed to be on course for a well-paid legal future. If it all worked out and they stayed together, Dan would be well looked after.

Byron House was another matter. Depending on the length of Dan's convalescence, they could, Dylan knew, be without help for a significant time if he left.

But he would leave. After what had just happened with Nell there was no possibility that he could stay. Being in the same place was an unbearable prospect. But Anne must be told. He would do her that courtesy, at least.

Dylan drove to Byron House in his battered car. It was still filled with Dan's cracked and rusting gardening equipment. His head still ached but the one benefit of the most nauseatingly painful, drawn-out, synapse-destroying hangover he had ever experienced was that it acted as a buffer between yesterday's events and now.

Angela was not sure at what point she had known for definite what was wrong with her. Certainly, it was before the consultant's assistant had appeared in the waiting area, apologised for the more-than-hour-long delay and asked Angela to follow her into the consultant's office.

Angela had been immersed in one of the oncology waiting area's creased and battered magazines in which various of life's unfortunates sensationally related holiday mishaps, appalling accidents or unimaginably sordid encounters with near relations. She laid it aside calmly and stood up.

She felt she knew what was coming. She felt that she had known even as she had driven into the hospital car park, passed through the sliding entrance doors and keyed her presence into the automatic reception because the queue at the real one was so long. Perhaps this was why, walking down the wide corridors on her way to the clinic, Angela noticed for the first time that the hospital had a chapel. She had paused and looked in. It was a small room with a bright blue carpet and abstract stained glass. A fudge-coloured wooden cross stood on a fudge-coloured wooden table.

The consultant's assistant showed her into the presence of the expert, a tall, tanned silver fox with attractive bags under his eyes. Angela was only dimly aware that once she might have fancied him. The assistant closed the door behind her with theatrical softness and part of Angela wanted to cry out and ask her to stay; nothing bad, after all, could happen in the presence of the cheerful girl with the pearlised make-up. But the other part of her was resigned.

'You're taking the news very well,' the consultant said, after informing Angela about what was required.

She had accepted without comment what was obviously meant to be a compliment. But how else should she take what she had just been told? The news did not seem the sort of news to which one could react hysterically. It seemed too big and important for that. She must concentrate, consult her calendar, enter the dates she was being offered. There was no point in feeling sorry for herself. If her disease could be beaten, she would use every iota of her energy to beat it.

Angela knew, even so, there was a good chance that it could not be beaten. But instead of feeling panicked she was aware of a new clarity.

Things were different, she realised, and she must approach them differently. From being powerful, she was now powerless. She had used and exploited others, sometimes for her own entertainment. Now she must depend on others to save her.

As she walked towards the hospital exit, hugging her frightening new knowledge to herself, Angela mentally listed the restitution she would make. She would be nicer to Gail, take an interest in her family. Did Gail have a family? Angela had no idea.

She would help her colleagues. Dress up in a stupid costume to help Julie with her American wedding. And give the much-abused Nell Simpson an office at last.

Angela's eye was now caught by the huge blue noticeboard on which all the wards were listed. The fact that Dan Parker was in one of them, and largely because of her, weighed heavy on her awakened conscience. She really had to do something about him, too.

Anne, as Dylan had expected, took the news on the chin. 'Well, thanks for letting me know,' she said. 'I appreciate it.'

Her fortitude made Dylan feel far worse than Mrs Palethorpe's fury. He hadn't felt bad about that at all; on the contrary. He stared back at Anne, half-wanting to change his mind and entirely wanting her to say something exonerating to make him feel better. But Anne, he could see from the distracted way she was shuffling papers on her desk, had mentally added the garden to her always-enormous list of challenges and simply moved on.

'Well, goodbye then,' Dylan said, standing up.

'See you,' said Anne, without looking up.

He drifted out, struggling for the sense of certainty that had sent him in there to resign. But he had either lost it or it had disappeared.

Sensing that anything might be possible – including revoking his decision – in this dangerous mood of vacillation, Dylan knew he should get out fast. But sentiment sent him out into the garden for one last look.

He did not see the old couple at first. They were to the side of the French windows, in the small box garden with the model windmill in the centre. When he did notice them, Dylan was amazed to recognise George Farley. He remembered, now, Nell saying he was moving into a home. So it was this one. What a coincidence.

But it was more than that; more than a mere surprise. This living connection with Nell startled and disturbed him. It was a reminder that, much as he wanted to think of her as unreliable and deceptive, Nell had done a great deal that was good. Dylan pushed the thought away and hurried on. The sooner he got out of this place the better.

Especially as George Farley seemed to have spotted him now. The woman had too; the elegant elderly dame who had pulled her suitcase around and been looking for Terminal 2. Sheila, that was it, Dylan remembered.

Sheila did not have her suitcase now, however. Nor was she looking for anything, although her expression, as she looked at Dylan, was distinctly arch.

George Farley was beckoning at Dylan. 'Young man! A word, if you please!'

The old man's voice was frail yet carried unarguable authority.

Wendy Holden

And something more, that almost sounded like anger. Dylan hurried over. Surely word had not got round already that he was about to abandon the garden? George Farley was a gardener; he was sure to take a dim view of such a desertion.

Up close the jutting eyebrows bristled alarmingly and the hazel eyes positively blazed in the big, jowly face. It was hard to imagine that this fiery old man was the same person Dylan had found nearly dead on the lawn and had helped bring back to life.

He gave George a pleasant smile. 'Nice to see you, Mr Far—'

'Never mind all that!' The old man waved an impatient arm. 'What's all this I hear from Nell?'

'Nell?' echoed Dylan, his smile evaporating. Had she been here then?

George Farley, who had been sitting down, now placed both gnarled hands on his walking cane and struggled to his feet. He gasped and rasped with the effort, but still managed to force out the words. 'She says you've gone off and left her!'

Dylan's fingers pushed nervously through his hairline. He felt exposed and resentful. What business was this of George Farley's? 'She deceived me,' he said shortly. 'She told someone I was trying to avoid exactly how to find me.'

The elegant old lady stirred at this, shaking her beautifully coiffed head. 'No, she didn't!' George Farley rasped, his vehemence turning into a spluttering cough.

'Careful, George,' murmured Sheila.

He turned and patted her hand. 'Don't worry, Sheila.' But the tender benevolence had drained out of his face as he turned back to Dylan.

'I'm afraid she did,' Dylan said. 'She deceived me,' he added. That seemed to do it for the old man.

'*You* were the one deceived,' George Farley thundered. 'It

456

was someone else who told that editor woman where you were, someone who said she was Nell but wasn't.'

Dylan held up his hand, confused. 'Wait, wait. Hang on a minute . . .' But the old man's ire flowed out of him like a river of lava. It would not be stopped.

'George!' Sheila said sharply. 'You're getting excited.'

Dylan was getting excited too. His heart was hammering. Someone else had pretended to be Nell? But who? And why? 'That can't be true,' he gasped.

Aided by Sheila, George Farley was settling himself back down into his chair. He was evidently exhausted by the encounter, yet his eyes were as bright as ever.

'Nell came to see me,' he said, enunciating each word clearly. 'She told me everything. Not just about what happened between the two of you. But about her wedding, about your girlfriend.'

'That's none of her business!' Dylan cried, grasping at what seemed to him the one certainty. 'Or yours!' But his insides were shrinking at what this dignified old man must know about his drunkenness, his ravings.

'It is absolutely her business,' George returned. 'And mine too. I care about Nell very much.' He paused before glaring up at Dylan again. 'And believe it or not, young man, I care about you. You saved my life, after all.'

Dylan felt a bitter triumph. Finally, an acknowledgement!

'I want to stop you making a terrible mistake,' George went on, his tone treading a middle line between earnest and angry, as if what was obvious to him should be obvious to everyone. 'Nell loves you. She hasn't done anything wrong. She never would, she's a girl in a million, and you have failed one of life's most important lessons, which is to recognise a good thing when you see it.' He fumbled behind him with his vein-corded hand for Sheila's elegant one. She took it and squeezed it tightly.

The old man lowered his head, seemingly summoning the strength to continue. Then he raised it again. 'Believe me, young man, I know what I'm talking about. Life is precious and we should celebrate what's good about it, not dwell on what is bad.'

Dylan was silenced. He stared at George, feeling the fury in his heart and head die down. Sitting before him here, his white hair ploughed with comb-lines, his old head bent and his old body gasping for breath, was someone who had been through worse than he ever had.

The bright eyes were on him again. 'You've suffered, young man,' George conceded. 'You almost lost your life in a fire.'

Dylan nodded. Yes, he had suffered. 'But you're not the only one. Plenty of young men I knew died in fires,' George said softly, a faraway look in his eyes. 'Lancasters carried a lot of bombs. They could fall and explode when you touched down. Sometimes they exploded when you took off.' He sighed. 'Plenty of young men died that way,' he added, now looking at Dylan. 'Men a lot younger than you.'

Dylan said nothing. What could he say? 'George!' Anne appeared at the French windows. 'Time for your medicine, love.'

The bright eyes blinked and, caught between the past and the present, looked lost for a moment.

'Still here?' Anne called cheerily to Dylan. He muttered his goodbyes and hurried off to the car park. But his sense of vindication, self-righteousness and grudge had gone. Now all that remained were questions, uncomfortable ones he'd never asked himself before.

Just who did he think he was? What was so special about him? It seemed to Dylan that all his problems, which had appeared so large, important and cataclysmic, were actually of his own making. Had it really been necessary to make such a fuss about not writing? To the extent that he tried to disappear off the face of the earth? Something of the worry that his mother must have been through now dawned on him.

Dylan started up the car. Even the fire, while not his direct responsibility, was linked to his actions. It was obvious from the start that Beatrice was mad. He should have avoided her, or ended the relationship. There had been plenty of signs that little good would ever come of it.

He drove away. He had been an idiot. A selfish idiot. And he could accept all that. Try and make up to people, change his ways. But the part of the story that he couldn't believe, that made no sense whatsoever and that for once wasn't linked to his own actions, was George's contention that someone else had pretended to be Nell.

Why would anyone do that?

He drove into the glade before the tower to find a strange car parked there. Shining, new, expensive. For a moment his heart leapt in spite of himself; Eve was one of the many people in line for a handsome apology. But then he saw it bore the number plate ANG 1.

A woman was getting out. Dylan did not recognise her immediately. Then he realised, with a sinking heart, that here was the ghastly, over-made-up personnel woman, the one who'd tried to chat him up, who he'd actually spotted hanging around the tower. It seemed like years ago.

'Can I help you?' he said coolly.

He noticed that her previously manic smile was muted, almost apologetic, as now she walked towards him.

'Yes, you can help me,' she said. 'You can listen to what I have to tell you.'

CHAPTER 59

Angela was taking the bull by the horns. Having bearded Dylan and confessed how she had misled Eve, she had next gone to the local police station and explained about Dan and Caradoc Turner. She was prepared to face whatever the consequences were for herself.

'I know it sounds far-fetched,' she said to the sergeant, who looked more startled than Angela was expecting.

'It does,' he agreed. 'But what's even more far-fetched is that we've had some communication on this subject already. A letter from a little girl in London.'

He went out of the room and came back with a small pink envelope on which was written, in careful blue biro, 'The Unsolved Poisonings Department, The Police Station, Chestlock, Leicestershire'. The sergeant drew out two sheets of paper covered in more careful blue writing. Angela could see the signature 'Juno'.

None of this made sense until Angela visited Dan at the hospital that afternoon and heard for the first time about his new acquaintance with Rachel and her little daughter. It sounded like early days, as they had only just met each other, but Angela could tell that Dan was optimistic that he was on the brink of something special. He looked glowingly happy. Observing this, Angela felt an unusual and strange sensation and realised she was feeling pleased for someone else for the very first time.

Dan was amazed to hear that Juno's poisoning theory was actually a possibility. He told Angela that he'd got so fed up with the child's endless talk about deadly chocolates that he'd told her to write to the police about it. 'I were joking, though,' he finished.

Dan was forgiving about Angela's own part in the drama. He would not, he assured her, press charges, even though the sergeant had explained to Angela that it was Dan's right. He knew about her health problems, Angela guessed, and he didn't want to add to her difficulties. She had tried to sound grateful; sensible of his mercy, but actually a prison sentence was neither here nor there to her.

It was, very possibly, rather more to Caradoc Turner. He had been questioned by the police, Angela had heard, and a trial was pending. The likelihood was that he would be convicted of actual bodily harm and serve a jail sentence.

Angela's guilt on this count, which was considerable, had been alleviated in part by another letter Dan had shown her. It was from Juliet and was very contrite. In it she described her bitter regret that her infidelity had driven her husband to a criminal act. She planned now to dedicate herself to resolving their problems and making the marriage work.

'Which will be easy enough,' Dan remarked, 'because the main problem was that she didn't like sleeping with him. And she won't have to do that now he's banged up.'

Angela had left the hospital feeling, if not relieved or happy, then a certain satisfaction. Whatever the future held, she had at least faced up to her actions. There remained only one of her victims to seek out now: Nell.

*

'You can't come back and stay with me,' Rachel had said firmly. 'I'm up to my eyes in exams and there's no room.'

Nell clenched the fist not holding the phone. 'You don't understand,' she wailed. 'I can't stay at Beggar's Roost. Or anywhere near Pemberton. This is an emergency. It's over! Me and Dylan . . . I mean Adam . . . I mean . . .' She stopped. What did she mean?

'You mean Dylan,' Rachel said wearily. 'Dylan Eliot. The famous writer. You've just explained. That's who he's been all along, apparently. Something else you decided not to tell me.'

'He made me promise!'

'And you didn't think that was weird? Do you do everything men make you promise?'

'Er . . .' Rachel had a way of making what seemed impossible to argue with eminently questionable. She was going to be a brilliant barrister. But just now that didn't help. On the contrary.

'He's . . . oh God, Rach, he was drunk and he shouted at me . . . awful things. Told me to get out—'

'Yes, I know, you've just told me all about it,' Rachel cut in. 'But come on, Nell. What did you expect? I warned you—'

'Oh *don't*!' Nell gasped, anguished. '*Don't* say I told you so!'

'But I did,' Rachel sighed. 'Look, I'm sorry. I can see things are difficult—'

'Difficult! You could say that!' Had not her relationship with Dylan ended in the most appalling way? Why did Rachel not understand the shock of it, her utter devastation? Even George Farley, who was nearly ninety, had had no difficulty grasping the horror of what had happened when she had been to see him that morning. So why not Rachel?

Somewhere, in the back of her mind, Nell knew that she was

462

behaving very badly. But she was incapable of stopping herself. Her outrage and hurt had a momentum far stronger than any brakes that reasonableness could apply. She plunged onwards, quite out of control. Joey had knocked her off course, but Dylan had completely unhinged her.

'I need to get out of here!' she cried, as much to the white-washed walls of Beggar's Roost as to Rachel on the other end. 'Everywhere I look, it's just full of memories . . .' She trailed off.

'Well, I just can't put you up at the moment.'

Nell had assumed that her friend would sympathise and offer her shelter from the emotional storm, as well as actual shelter in the form of her London flat. But all Rachel could talk about was her exams!

'Don't you think you're being a bit selfish?' she asked tightly.

The sound that came from the other end was a shuddering, deep breath, as if Rachel was trying to control some outburst. 'Look, Nell. I've supported you through thick and thin . . .'

She had. There was no doubt about it.

'. . . despite the fact that you didn't tell me the truth about this guy. I told you to keep away from him but you couldn't . . .'

That was true too. Nell was beginning to see her friend's point of view. Rachel, too, had a life, and other priorities than endlessly clearing up after a woman who could never learn from her mistakes. 'I'm sorry,' she said humbly.

'I'm sorry too.' Rachel's tone was softer now. 'But I'm out of action until my exams are done. This is a crucial week for me, Nell. You'll just have to stay up there. Until the weekend, anyway. You can come down after that if you like. Just try and keep busy until then. Weren't you going to help at that wedding?'

Nell had forgotten about Jed and Carly's wedding, as she had forgotten about everything except her own immediate drama. But Rachel was right, tomorrow was the American nuptials. Could any prospect be worse? 'That's the last thing I want to do! A wedding!' Her voice rose, tragically, on the last syllable.

'Oh come on, Nell.' Rachel was sounding irritated again. 'You promised your friend, didn't you? Your nice friend who helped you with your house?'

'Yes, but Julie's hardly going to expect me to turn up, not after what's happened—'

'Julie doesn't know what happened! How could she? The world doesn't revolve around you, or haven't you noticed?'

This was the final straw. 'Rachel,' Nell screamed, 'don't you get it? When I got to the tower and he was lying there, in that red pool, I thought he was . . . *dead*.'

There was a silence, and then Rachel said quietly, 'Yes, but he wasn't dead, was he?'

The phone at the other end cut off. Nell called back immediately but Rachel had switched to answerphone. She left a message and tried again a few minutes later. Still answerphone. She was vastly relieved when, ten minutes or so later, her mobile rang. She snatched it up. 'I'm so sorry!' she howled.

'Sorry about what?' Julie sounded alarmed. 'Don't tell me you can't make it!'

'Er . . .' As Nell hesitated, Rachel's words came back. *You promised your friend, didn't you? Your nice friend who helped you with your house?* If she let Julie down, it would confirm everything Rachel thought about her. And Rachel would be right.

'Of course I'm coming.' Nell heard herself say. 'You helped me with Beggar's Roost, didn't you? One good turn deserves another.'

Julie sounded vastly relieved. 'I thought you were just about to blow me out.'

'Never,' Nell valiantly assured her. 'Just tell me when and where.'

'The wedding's at five, in the Pemberton chapel. And afterwards there's helping out at the dinner and the candlelit ball.'

'But don't I just come for the ball? Surely they don't want us in the chapel? Isn't that the private bit?'

'They do want you there. You're the cast, basically. The extras in the film.'

'Is it really going to be a film?'

'Only in Carly and Jed's heads,' Julie snorted. 'They're the leading actors and you're the cringing retainers, house servants and so on. Carly wants you to murmur admiringly as she comes in to the chapel.'

A gleam of humour suddenly pierced Nell's misery. Was there a funny side to all this?

'Just one thing, though. The costume supplier's run out of empire line dresses. Would you mind wearing breeches instead? And a tricorn hat, at a push?'

'No problem.' Nell felt like a fool; what did it matter if she looked like one too? And, as her own Prince Charming had twice failed to materialise, why not impersonate him herself?

'But on one condition.'

'Anything,' Julie said fervently. 'Just say the word and it's yours.'

'Can you put me up in your spare room?'

Julie sounded surprised. 'Sure. But why? Has something gone wrong in Beggar's Roost?'

Nell breathed in. 'Kind of.'

'You can tell me about it later. If it's fixable, Tim can sort it.'

No, he can't, Nell thought. Tim could no doubt sort most things, but not broken hearts and distracted minds.

'And you're sure it's OK about the breeches?'

'Fine. I've always fantasised about wearing some.'

'A dream come true then.' Julie chuckled. 'And, actually, you're escaping pretty lightly. Bert Blood's in drag, as a shepherdess. It's just the way the costumes pan out. He's having to shave his cleavage.'

At five minutes to five the following day Nell, resplendent in a frayed silk waistcoat, some battered buckled shoes and a pair of grubby, tight satin breeches whose previous wearers she was trying not to think about, joined the forty-plus rest of the cast in the chapel.

Several of the women in long cotton dresses and shawls, their hair in buns, whispering and giggling, she recognised from the farm shop, cafés and main entrance to the house. Many of the men chuckling at each other's buckles, breeches and smocks she had often seen in the gardens, or driving trailers around the estate roads.

Bert Blood looked even more amazing than expected in an embroidered gown, a wig of considerable height and bright pink circles of rouge on his cheeks. He seemed to Nell to be rather enjoying it; certainly he was taking the teasing he was receiving in good part. Perhaps, after the ill-starred stint as a house guide, he had finally found his vocation.

'Can we have a word?'

Nell turned to see a woman in a tall silver wig regarding her nervously. It took her a few seconds to recognise Angela.

'Er . . . sure,' Nell said apprehensively. 'Is this about the office?'

Angela nodded. 'That and a few other things. Let's find somewhere quiet.'

After everything else that had happened, the news that it

was Angela who had impersonated her was almost too much to take in.

'Aren't you furious?' Angela asked, almost timidly. She had expected excoriation, fury, denunciation. Indeed, she was almost looking forward to it; it was what she deserved.

But Nell simply looked sad. She had only part-absorbed the background reasons for Angela's enmity; they seemed trivial. The main point was that Angela had been to Bess's Tower and explained her innocence to Dylan. Now, at least, she could no longer be blamed for Eve's appearance. But the knowledge brought her no satisfaction. She could hardly bring herself to ask what he had said. She did, nonetheless.

Angela explained, in a low, ashamed voice, that Dylan had been devastated. 'He was going straight round to see you.' She raised her head. 'But I'm guessing that he didn't, otherwise I wouldn't have had to tell you any of this.'

Nell shook her head. 'But I haven't been home.' She pictured Dylan arriving at Beggar's Roost, jumping out of the car, striding up the path, rattling at the door. Almost the worst aspect of the whole sorry matter was that the image provoked no emotion within her. It was as if Dylan's outburst in the tower had killed all her feeling for him. There was a faint and distant echo of regret, but nothing more. All the anguish and the passion had dwindled to a deadening, despairing numbness.

'I'm so sorry,' Angela said, reading some of this in Nell's face. She had expected to bring joy with her revelations. Relief. But the other woman's eyes looked flat and dead.

'It doesn't matter,' Nell said dully. It seemed to her that nothing, now, mattered at all. She would go through life, speaking, doing, seeing. But not feeling, so far as she could possibly help it.

That the first thing she must now do was go to a wedding was unfortunate. But it would be a good test of her new resolve. If she could avoid feeling at a wedding, she could avoid it anywhere.

As Bert's house tour had only whisked through the chapel, Nell had a blurred memory of lots of marble and painting. As the wedding began, she was able to examine the room in more detail. It was astonishingly ornate; hardly a surface was uncarved, undecorated or unembellished in some way. The painted ceiling was entirely covered in figures, temples and trees set against blue skies and billowing clouds. The carved marble altar stood in a carved marble apse containing a painting of a Jesus with truly splendid biceps. It was at this that Nell was gazing abstractedly when the chapel organ struck up and the cast stood to attention.

At the back of Nell's mind had been the possibility that Jed might not turn up; this, after all, had been her own experience of bridegrooms. Jed, however, now entered the chapel, his long, large legs tightly encased in a pair of cream breeches and his enormous shoulders looking still huger in a long, dark coat heavy with silver buttons. His expression was fixed and tremulous; he looked as if he were trying not to cry, which seemed both touching and, given Jed's general force of personality, rather surprising.

Mr Bingley was beside Jed, or at least the friend chosen to impersonate him. The fashionable white-framed glasses he sported possibly struck an anachronistic note.

A chorus of dutiful 'Oohs' and 'Aaahs' now greeted Carly as she appeared in her Elizabeth Bennet dress. They were not as forced as Nell had expected; Carly's demanding and dominating character was effectively disguised in a white silk dress of empire line teamed with a white gauze shawl. She actually looked rather angelic, with her honey-coloured hair in satiny ringlets topped with a coronet of orange blossom.

The vicar, dressed as Mr Collins, stepped forward and cleared his throat. 'Dearly beloved . . .'

The wedding breakfast took place in Pemberton's dining room, a formal chamber on a massive scale whose red walls were punctuated with great marble fireplaces and enormous gold-framed paintings of past Earls and Countesses. Huge windows hung with thick brocade curtains framed long, green views over the park, and a coffered ceiling painted white and gold soared over a table that could seat twenty and was doing so. Carly and Jed sat at each end, invisible to each other through the tall forest of silverware and crystal that grew in the centre. It all looked rather impressive. And the joy of the occasion was palpable. Even to Nell; especially to Nell. She did not respond to it, however.

She threw herself into the work instead, of which, fortunately, there was plenty. Her task was to hurry with plates between the dining room and the makeshift kitchen in the nearby sculpture gallery, where the food historian was supervising the negus. This much-discussed menu item, the one that had caused so much trouble, was actually just warm mulled port.

'What's this?' Nell asked, returning to have a plateful of something grey and gluey thrust at her to carry out next.

'Torrington of sheep's trotters!' declared the food historian, a portly bearded gentleman who seemed immersed in the eighteenth century to an alarming degree. 'A great delicacy. Hurry up now, and come back for the flummery.'

Nell hurried up, trying not to look at the sheep's trotters, let alone smell them.

'Service, please!' called the food historian from behind her.

'Can someone come and carry in the bustard fricassee?'

Angela, meanwhile, sat outside on a bench and watched the staff practise the dances for the candlelit ball. There had been a hasty rehearsal that morning, supervised by Julie and run by a rather harassed local dance teacher. Angela, who couldn't waltz at the best of times, let alone in an awkward dress and sloppy shoes, had already decided that her contribution to the ball would be purely decorative and stationary; she would find a pillar, lean against it, and not move. She didn't feel well enough to dance anyway.

As she observed the farm shop manager, in a white Mozart wig, pirouetting with the large young woman who ran the children's farmyard, Angela felt a curious sense of peace. She had settled all her scores now, confessed to everyone she had hurt. She was ready for whatever lay ahead.

CHAPTER 60

Nell knew the Pemberton ballroom well. She and Julie had walked round it together while Julie puzzled how to make Jed and Carly's dream of a candlelit dance come true. The question had remained unresolved during Nell's time in Weddings but it had now, she could see, been most spectacularly answered.

As Nell entered now, behind the wedding party and the cast of servants, she heard a general gasp of awe. By the time she had shuffled in herself, she could see what had elicited it. The great room, which she had only ever previously seen with daylight bouncing off its polished surfaces, was bathed in the soft golden glow of hundreds of candles. Heritage candles, Nell reminded herself with a smile.

Two vast chandeliers, ablaze with flickering flames, hung from a painted ceiling which seemed alive with mythical animals and winged goddesses. There were more candles along the walls, in the silver sconces set at regular intervals in the polished panelling. All were reflected in the bevelled glass of the windows; as darkness gathered in the park outside, the light danced and glittered in the panes.

The effect was as dramatic as it was beautiful, and the

excitement in the room was palpable as the string quartet struck up for the first dance and the crowd stood admiringly back to let Jed and Carly take the floor.

Nell knew from Julie that she had had a considerable struggle making Handel with Care exchange their micro-minis and skyscraper heels for the prevailing eighteenth-century aesthetic. The four string players had complied, up to a point, but had managed to raunch up the Austen look with their cleavages extensively displayed above their buttoned bodices. Their heavily streaked blonde hair, while nominally pulled back into buns, tumbled wantonly round their faces. The cello player had even managed to hitch up her skirts to feature gleaming, tanned, wide-apart legs.

Jed and Carly, whirling around in the centre of the polished floor as everyone clapped, seemed not to notice this lapse in authenticity. Those that did seemed generally appreciative. 'Say,' Nell overhead Carly's father, in character as Mr Bennet, observe. 'Those dames are really something.'

Dylan, in Bess's Tower, was in a rage of regret. He could not sit still for more than a few seconds, but pacing about the small rooms was making him equally agitated. The Japanese toilet had struck up expectantly five times.

Quite apart from the blaze in his own head, it had been a hot day outside. The warmth gathered in the stones of the old tower walls was now releasing itself inside, making the small rooms stuffy. Dylan decided to go out on to the roof. He put his hand on the rope-banister and mounted the winding stairs.

But it was more than fresh air that he was seeking. He knew that real relief would only come when he had apologised to Nell. Acknowledged to her, too, that he was the author of all his problems. Other people were not to blame for the chain of events in which he had become tangled and trapped, and in which he had tangled and trapped her.

That relief did not seem imminent because now another hideous link had been forged. Nell had disappeared. Dylan had searched for her in all the usual places but there had been no sign of her. Not even at Beggar's Roost. Dylan's fear that she had left the area for ever was becoming a horrible possibility. He had left endless messages on the voicemail of her mobile, which he could now do as he had finally bought one of his own. His first call on it had been to reassure his mother. She, at least, had been pleased to hear from him. Touchingly pleased. Far more pleased than he deserved.

What a bloody fool he had been. Pacing about the tower, Dylan clenched his fists. What should he do? What *could* he do?

Leave. Head to pastures new, start all over again. But the pastures would not be new; if he had learned anything, he had learned that. He would just be repeating old behaviour, running away again from another mess of his own making.

He had, at least, apologised to Eve, who had been cool in her acceptance of his hot, blustering speech. 'Well,' she had said at the end, 'if you ever feel like writing again, you know where I am. But you'll have to call me, I won't call you.' It had seemed fair enough to Dylan. Had he been Eve, he wouldn't have taken his call.

Julian had been his usual relaxed self. 'Good to hear from you, dear boy,' he had purred. 'I wonder if you might swing by the office soon. Latvian internet TV want to turn *All Smiles* into a mini-series.'

Dylan assured him that he would, at the first opportunity.

'Jolly good. Oh, and any sign of the Muse?' Julian added, according to his habit of making the most important part of the conversation sound like an afterthought.

'Not really. But I've felt the odd stirring.' Dylan surprised himself, saying this. But quite suddenly, it made sense. Surely the very least he could do, after what he had put everyone through, was to make it up to them by producing a novel?

And one sure-fire, tried-and-tested way to use up all the agitation and misery he felt was to write it all down. He was, generally speaking, useless and stupid, but he was not useless and stupid at that.

'The odd stirring, eh?' But Julian – like Eve – did not press him on this. Perhaps they didn't believe him, Dylan thought. Well, he would show them. But not just now.

Angela was sitting at the very back of the ballroom while the music, dancing, clapping and laughter went on around her. She concentrated her gaze on the clodhopping feet of the various Pemberton personnel now attempting, with mixed success, to remember what the dancing teacher had taught them. Once, of course, she would have derived a spiteful amusement from all this.

It was while staring at the floor that Angela noticed the candle that had fallen there; presumably from one of the wall sconces. It had rolled, unnoticed, under a low stool near to the one on which she sat herself. The flame from the wick was licking, in an exploratory fashion, the varnish on the herringbone parquet floor.

The alarm shrilled. Handel with Care stopped playing immediately, sprang to their feet and lunged for their instrument cases. There were gasps, exclamations and screams among the guests and cast, but almost immediately the firm tones of Julie rang out.

People were not to panic and were to file out calmly from the ballroom and down the stairs into the main hall. From here they would be shown out into the Earl's private garden, where they would await further instruction.

Nell shuffled out with the rest. Having been at the back of the crowd throughout, she was one of the last to leave. Looking apprehensively behind her at the now flaming corner of the ballroom, Nell's eye fell on the figure of Angela Highwater, who seemed to be having problems tying up her shoes. She was sitting, bent, her head over her feet.

'Angela!' Nell shouted. 'Come on!'

Angela continued pretending to fiddle with her shoes. She had decided that she did not want to come on. What was there to come on for?

Dylan stayed, thinking, on the roof of Bess's Tower long after the blazing setting sun gave way to a silver sliver of moon.

It was quite dark now, and he could see, from his vantage point above the building, something gleaming in one of the windows of Pemberton House.

Gleaming, not glowing as the rest of the windows were tonight. It was unusual for the house to look this illuminated. Every single room was lit up. Pemberton looked like a fancy box with lots of holes in and a bulb inside.

Someone was getting married. Dylan had seen, on his return from Beggar's Roost, a couple in a bonnet and top hat arriving at the house in a horse-drawn carriage. He had only vaguely registered the detail; lots of guests got up in costume. They were obviously, now, having a big party. But this light had a different quality to the dull glow elsewhere in the windows. It was flickering and much brighter; it seemed alive. As well as, somehow, familiar.

He realised that it was fire.

The sight made his nerves shrink and the blood shriek round

his veins. Even from this distance it seemed too close.

His instinct was to hurry back downstairs, into the tower where he could no longer see it. But what about the people in the house? Did they realise that part of Pemberton was in flames? The building was enormous and they seemed to be using all of it. One part could easily be on fire while people in the other parts remained oblivious.

Of course people knew, Dylan reassured himself. And anyway, the house was sure to be equipped with extinguishers, alarms and staff drilled in fire procedure.

But what, a niggling inner voice demanded, if they weren't? What if people hadn't realised? At the very least, the lovely rooms would be damaged. There were valuable paintings in there.

And at the most, people's lives might be threatened.

Dylan had to be sure. His memories of being trapped in fire-ravaged rooms were terrifying. He could not bear the thought of anyone else suffering the same.

He rushed down the stairs.

Nell had reached the Earl's garden when she realised that Angela had not followed her after all. She paused and peered back between the shaped box hedges looming in the darkness.

No one had come after her; she was the last of the line following Julie from the increasingly smoke-filled room to fresh air and safety.

'Angela!' she called, down the alley of hedges which led back towards the house. 'Angela!'

There was no answer. Concern gripped Nell. What if Angela had fallen? Knocked herself out? The fire had evidently been spreading rapidly; the curtains in the corner had been alive with flames as the last of them left the room.

A sense of chaos was developing on the lawn. The fire brigade had been called, but so far had not come. The house extinguishers had been used, and the fire had been beaten back. But the extinguishers had now run out and it had taken hold again. People were rushing back and forth in the darkness, carrying buckets produced from somewhere. They were dipping them in the long lake to the side of the house, the one on whose banks Rachel and Juno had first heard about Nell's new job.

How long ago that seemed! It had been a sweet and sunny day, unimaginably different from this infernal night. The flames from the ballroom could now be seen from the outside. They had pierced the windows and were reaching up into the dark blue night sky; real fire beside the gilded flames on the Earl's carved rooftop urns. The hot yellow, red and orange glittered in the long water.

Nell tried to think clearly over her hammering panic. Should she go back? She could hear Julie taking a roll call of those present. If she could not be ticked off the list, her absence would cause trouble.

As for Angela, it might simply be that she had taken a short cut through the hedge. Nell leapt eagerly on this explanation. Angela was probably with the others now, on the darkened lawn, having their presence accounted for as the bucket chain heaved the water towards the fire spitting its smoke and sparks into the sky.

But, an inner voice insisted, a voice which, while quiet, would not be stilled. What if she was still in the house? The fire had obviously now possessed the ballroom and would be starting to eat the rooms and passages beyond. Anyone lying there, unconscious, might wake to find themselves trapped. Or perhaps, overcome by fumes, might not wake at all.

Nell looked around at the others rushing about her. Men

had their shirts off now, their muscles gleaming in the raging light from the house. If she told one of them about Angela, someone else would take responsibility, risk their life to save the missing woman. Why should she?

Nell tried to remind herself of what Angela had recently done. She was a woman to whom she owed nothing, who had gone out of her way to damage her.

On the other hand, the look in Angela's eyes as she had confessed her actions had been those of a sorrowful and suffering creature. It was that expression that Nell remembered now, and which she knew she would remember the rest of her days if she didn't at least check that Angela was safe.

Nell hesitated no longer. She hurried back towards the house.

Dylan arrived before Pemberton to find a big crowd on the mansion's lawn. The front of the house was by now ablaze; great tongues of fire licked from the huge windows. Swags of carved fruit and fluted columns flared into sight, then into shadow. Gilded detail blazed and dimmed.

The sight of it all made Dylan nauseous. Terrifying memories made his flesh, healed as it was, tingle and burn. He held his hand to his face, trying to keep out the fumes, trying not to let his panic overwhelm him.

Silhouetted against the lit smoke, the bewildered Earl paced up and down in front of his ancestral home.

A woman was taking a roll call of sorts. People were shouting back, confirming their presence. Dylan only half-listened to the names being recited, none of them known to him. But then, suddenly, one was.

'Nell Simpson.'

She was here! Somewhere on this lawn, in the dark!

Dylan felt a rush of passionate gratitude. Fate had, after all, decided to grant him an opportunity. A chance to start again. He held his breath, waiting to catch her voice as it responded. Once he knew where she was, he could go to her. He would fall to his knees, beg her to forgive him.

'Nell?' the woman called, her voice high with concern. 'Has anyone seen Nell?'

No one answered. No one had.

'Is she in the house?' Dylan shouted, as the dread possibility gripped him.

'I don't know,' called back the woman. 'But if she's not out here . . .'

Dylan didn't need to hear any more.

'Angela!' Nell yelled. She was making her way up the main staircase, hurrying along with both hands outstretched in front of her. The fire was more advanced even than she had expected. The whole of the great space above the main staircase swirled with smoke; the passage to the ballroom was thick with it; the wall-paintings obscured and the great carved double entrance already collapsed and charred.

'Angela!'

Nell was losing her bearings. It was no longer possible to tell from which direction she had come, and whether she was walking into the fire or away from it. It seemed all around her now, the violent heat. She could feel her face melting and her hair crackling. She reeled backwards, choking.

She had to get out of here. Now, before it was too late. Perhaps it already was. Of Angela there was no sign. Nor could she hear her over the roaring of flames voraciously devouring oxygen. Perhaps Angela was outside after all. Within the ballroom a falling beam brought with it a shower of sparks. Nell cried out, turned away and pushed into the smoke. Was this the right direction?

As a shower of plaster announced the fall of something much bigger, Nell dodged into a door alcove. Her foot struck something. Something soft. She turned, bent, strained to see through the thick grey air.

A body. Angela's body. Her eyes were closed. Nell grabbed her arm and shook. No response. Perhaps she was dead already. Nell bent, yelled in her ear. 'Angela! Angela!' Still nothing.

She glanced down the passage towards the ballroom. Even in the past few seconds the fire had advanced. Its speed was terrifying, as were the gleeful high-pitched screams it made. It was like a live thing, a great, ragged animal, dazzlingly bright. Nell imagined it leaping at her, roaring in triumph, tearing at her clothes, her hair.

'Angela!' Her voice was a scream now. She dragged at the unconscious woman who lay like lead at her feet. Was it worth it, trying to save someone who might well be past saving? Even if she ran now, she might not get out alive herself.

As another piece of burning plaster exploded into sparks behind her, Nell cried out with terror.

She tugged desperately at Angela again but could only move her dead weight a few feet down the corridor. The wall of heat was approaching much quicker; Nell's very eyeballs were hot now, and the smoke was filling her throat. She was gasping for air, trying to breathe. The floor reared up at her, hissing, splitting and buckling, darkening as the varnish burned.

It was like one of his nightmares about Bosun's Whistle, but this time it was real. Walls of leaping flame thundered about him and smoke seized him in its asphyxiating headlock. His face and body were dissolving like wax in the onslaught and his nostrils were filled with the stink of his own burning hair.

It had been horrendous the first time, but this time it was indescribable. Dylan's fear was dislodging his reason. All he could do was to summon up the memory of Nell's face and fight on.

'Nell!' He was shouting her name through the filthy, whirling air. 'Nell!'

He should go back, before the flames he had escaped last time finally claimed him. They would get him this time. They were determined, hell-bent, closing in on him, screaming with glee. No one escaped them twice.

The tears burned in his eyes before he could shed them. Dylan was shaking and whimpering. He was heaving for breath; each lungful a burning pain.

Was that a figure he could see? Something on the floor, up ahead. It looked human. A fallen statue, perhaps.

'Nell!'

Could he hear something? Someone yelling? The lump seemed to be moving; it looked like two lumps, one pulling at another.

'Nell! Oh my God! You're alive!'

CHAPTER 61

Six months later

'They're here!' Nell leapt to the door of Beggar's Roost. As she flung it open, Dylan could see the postman in his Royal Mail shorts staggering up the path, his arms clamped round the first of what would turn out to be six boxes of brochures.

That, however, was not the 'they' Nell meant. Over the postman's hi-vis-gileted shoulder could be seen a broad grin on a brown face. Dan came up the path tightly holding the hand of an equally brown Rachel. Behind them scampered Juno.

'Where d'ya want me to leave this lot?' the postman asked.

'Just inside the door, thanks.'

'Don't know what's in 'ere but they're bloody 'eavy.'

In 'ere was the physical rebranding of the Pemberton Estate. The virtual version had gone up on the website a few days ago and was proving a great success. Nell and her hand-picked, newly appointed team of marketing and design personnel were moving the great stately home and its satellite businesses on to a whole new level. Everyone was delighted, especially the Earl.

Nell had been helped considerably in her recruitment drive by the new Director of Personnel. Gail had replaced Angela Highwater, who was now convalescent after hospital treatment and considering a move to the voluntary sector. Her fire injuries had been minimal and mostly smoke-related, while her long-term condition had now stabilised after a double mastectomy.

Her psychological condition had also healed; Angela's double brush with death had left her feeling lucky to be alive. Those who had recently encountered her, Jason and Nell in particular, could hardly relate the new, happy Angela with the twisted and dark-hearted creature of the past.

'How was Cornwall?' Nell demanded excitedly of Rachel. They had taken a cottage near Zennor for a fortnight of post-hospital recuperation for Dan and to celebrate Rachel's success at scoring the highest marks in her year in the law exams.

Rachel was full of happy detail about fabulous sea views and wonderful local pubs. There had been a place called the Miner's Arms, in a village called Tremadoc. Dylan said nothing, but was both surprised and glad that neither name gave him any shock or alarm. The old painful memories seemed now a faint echo from a long time ago in someone else's life.

Rachel and Dan were grinning at each other. 'They're going to get married,' Juno declared resignedly.

'Juno!' Rachel exclaimed. 'I've never told you anything of the sort!'

'No, but it's obvious. When you're a top detective like me.'

Dylan hid a smile. He agreed with Juno. Her mother and Dan had definitely been looking at each other in a shall-we-tell-them kind of way.

'OK, we're going to get married,' Rachel admitted, directing a look of exasperated amusement at her daughter.

Nell whooped, leapt to her feet and flung wide her arms. Rachel caught her by the wrists and the two of them jumped up and down like a couple of infants. 'And I've found a chambers I want to join in Leicester,' Rachel added, smiling and breathless.

'You'll live up here?' Nell could barely contain her joy.

'At Dan's house?' Dylan was trying to hide his dismay. He, Nell and Rachel had between them cleaned the place up a lot but it nonetheless remained the original sow's ear out of which a silk purse could not be made. It was hard to imagine Rachel in such a setting. Although he could imagine her, quite easily, dealing with the cheeky boys. 'Shagger's Friend, Shagger's Friend,' they had yelled at him during his solo visits. But, small as she was, there had been something about Rachel which silenced them.

Rachel and Dan exchanged glances again. There was clearly something afoot. 'Come on,' Nell urged anxiously.

'Well . . .' Rachel began. She took a deep breath and looked from Nell to Dylan. She opened her mouth to continue when the postman called through the doorway.

'I've finished, love!'

'Thank you!' Nell sang back.

'Now tell!' urged Dylan.

''Ow'd you like us fer yer neighbours?' asked Dan, grinning.

'Neighbours?' Nell frowned. There was only one cottage next door and it belonged to George Farley. Or it had, having since reverted to the estate.

Rachel was waving a key.

Nell's eyes widened. 'You haven't!'

'We went to see the estate office!' Rachel chanted. 'The place was free! So we've rented it. On a year's lease, initially.'

Nell's beaming joy had only the merest shade of regret in it. That George would not be returning to his cottage was sad in one way, but his happiness at moving into the sheltered flat with Sheila was such as to eclipse all negative feelings. Their marriage after a mere month of acquaintance had surprised everyone, but as George had observed, one couldn't hang around at their age.

*

Nell was now closing the door on Dan, Juno and Rachel, who were going next door to examine their new domain.

'Have you heard anything?' she asked, turning back towards Dylan. As ever, she knew what he was thinking. 'No email?'

His smile was wry as he reached for her. 'Not since I last looked, ten minutes ago.'

He was joking, but nervous. For Dylan had started again. From the bottom. With Eve, he was taking nothing for granted. He had sent her three chapters and a synopsis of a proposed new book. Not *Charm Itself* – he genuinely couldn't bear to go back to that – but another, titled similarly but less hubristically *Charmed Life*. He had put everything into it, his own pain included, and felt it was by far the best thing he had ever written. Or would write, if Eve wanted him to.

Eve had received it a week ago and he'd heard nothing. Dylan was starting to worry that, very possibly, he never would. He had not badgered Julian about it, even so. A week was a perfectly reasonable time to wait.

While he was trying not to think about her lack of response, Dylan couldn't help wondering. He was trying not to care, but he did. Desperately, if he were honest. And yet now Eve was the silent and uncommunicative one. The boot was on the other foot. Now, as never before, Dylan knew what most authors had to go through. He might yet know more; the chances seemed strong that, like so many, he was about to taste abject failure.

But so what? he reminded himself. None of it mattered compared to the single, dazzling, brilliant fact that Nell was restored to him. Against all the odds, in the face of a hideous death and only, in the end, because of the split-second timing of the Chestlock fire brigade. As much as a minute later might have been too late. It was that background of catastrophe, Dylan suspected, that had encouraged Nell, after they both came out of hospital, to agree to his suggestion that they should try again. It was a risk, but as risks went, especially the risks they had both faced, it was a mild one. And so far, it had been no risk at all.

Truly, and literally, they had been through the fire together. Even the formerly sceptical Rachel had finally given the union her blessing.

'OK,' she had said. 'So he saved one life. That might have been an accident. But saving two's a definite trend. He's a hero. And so are you. I'm so bloody proud of you, Nell,' Rachel finished, her voice thick with emotion.

Being heroes, Nell had found, mainly meant they both looked different. His long dark hair had been lost in the fire along with her own. Both of them had short crops now, and looked strange to themselves. Secretly, however, they thought the other looked better. Nell's eyes, Dylan felt, appeared huge and elfin while he, Nell thought, had acquired a new maturity. Without all that hair you could see his features properly, the calm and level set of them, the strong jaw, the intelligent intensity of his gaze.

Dylan's occasional remoteness, now he was writing again, appealed to her too. Perhaps more so than the constant attentiveness of Adam, which might eventually have become claustrophobic.

For the time being at least, there was no suggestion of getting married. It was all very well for George and Sheila, with a lifetime's experience behind them and the absolute knowledge of a good thing when they saw it. She and Dylan needed to get to know each other better. But so far – and admittedly she'd been here before, several times – it looked like a good thing.

Dylan was opening up his email and steeling himself for the usual lack of a message from Eve. Seeing that, most unexpectedly, there was one, he steeled himself instead for a terse line of rejection.

Nell had seen his hands stiffen over the keyboard. She had

heard the suppressed gasp, but she knew better than to say anything.

Nonetheless his silence was making her curious. He was standing by the kitchen table, leaning on it with one hand while his other tapped his laptop, frowning at the screen. But whether it was a frown of disappointment or one of concentration she could not tell.

She took a deep breath and crossed her fingers behind her back. 'What does she say?'

Dylan looked at her. His eyes seemed to be focusing from a long way away. A slow smile spread across his face. 'She likes it, Nell. She wants me to write the rest of it.'

Nell gasped in delight. 'You're back in business!'

His eyes were shining. 'And it's so much sweeter the second time around. This time it's for real.' He caught at her hands and whirled her round.

There was a tap on the door. 'Sorry to disturb you two swinging lovers,' came Rachel's voice. 'But we're off now, to see Jason at the Edenville Arms.'

'Give him our love. And Ryan as well.' The manager and his boyfriend had recently come out, to so little surprise that Jason said he was considering going back in again.

'For a drink?' Nell asked. It was only mid-morning, but there was a lot to celebrate. They should all go.

'To organise a certain little party.' Rachel smiled at Dan.

Juno rolled her eyes. 'Soppy. *Ugh.*'

Dan ruffled her hair. 'All your fault, Miss Marple. If you hadn't been so desperate to talk to me about my near-death experience . . .'

Nell clapped her hands. 'You're having your reception at the Arms? Lovely!'

'And our first night,' Rachel grinned.

Nell's mouth dropped open. 'You're not booking . . . ?'

'The honeymoon suite? Of course! Where else?'

Make your world a brighter place. Pick up a Wendy Holden.

'The perfect choice'
Glamour

Simply Divine

Bad Heir Day

Pastures Nouveaux

Fame Fatale

Azur Like It

The Wives of Bath

The School For Husbands

Filthy Rich

Beautiful People

Gallery Girl

Marrying Up

Gifted and Talented

Wild and Free

Honeymoon Suite

All fourteen titles are available now from

REVIEW